PRAISE FO

'I could not put it down! *'Til Death* ....ler
that has you desperate to know what ....
Andy Darcy Theo, author of *The Light that Blinds Us*

'Wickedly entertaining. *'Til Death* is one of the
most exciting debuts I've read in a long time.'
Bill Wood, author of *Let's Split Up*

'Thrilling and addictive in equal measures.
Busayo Matuluko is a major new talent.'
Benjamin Dean, author of *How to Die Famous*

'A stunning thriller. It's got everything: drama,
gossip, secrets . . . absolutely wonderful!'
Kate Weston, author of *Murder on a School Night*

'Gossip, glamour and a gripping mystery that I couldn't put
down. Busayo Matuluko invites you into a Nigerian family
full of heart, secrets and so much drama. I absolutely loved it.'
Kathryn Foxfield, author of *Good Girls Die First*

'Get ready to fall in love! This captivating thriller
transported me into a world of glitz, glamour and heartfelt
drama so dimensional I felt I was one of the guests.
Matuluko is a major talent.'
Jennifer Lynn Alvarez, author of *Lies Like Wildfire*

''Til Death* is a YA thriller that pulls you in, grips you tight,
and doesn't let go. Busayo has arrived with this one. Prepare
for a thrilling ride that is as satisfying as it is unexpected!'
Tomi Oyemakinde, author of *The Changing Man*

'Funny, clever and authentic with so many twists and turns. Busayo has captured the Nigerian culture so brilliantly in her debut. Absolutely loved it!'
Abiola Bello, author of *Love in Winter Wonderland*

'Matuluko spins a vibrant cast of characters through this exciting mystery filled with heart and humour.'
Aleema Omotoni, author of *Everyone's Thinking It*

'An unputdownable YA thriller with the perfect blend of gossip, mystery and danger. Set in the heart of Lagos and beautifully infused with Yoruba culture, *'Til Death* includes the Wedding of the Decade that all readers will crave to attend.'
Anam Iqbal, author of *The Exes*

'I raced through it. Intriguing, exciting and full of mysteries, with characters who felt so real I want to hang out with them.'
Emily Barr, author of *The One Memory of Flora Banks*

'A sharp, witty, immersive debut with a captivating setting and characters you'll love as much as you distrust.'
Rufaro Faith Mazarura, author of *Let the Games Begin*

'Intricately crafted and brilliantly layered, this debut thriller is filled with nail biting suspense, captivating family drama and a meaningful exploration of living with a chronic illness.'
Hayley Dennings, author of *This Ravenous Fate*

'The glamour, complex family dynamics and juicy gossip kept me flipping the pages just as much as the desire to solve the gripping mystery. Busayo Matuluko's debut is one to remember!'
Channelle Desamours, author of *Needy Little Things*

'TIL DEATH

BUSAYO MATULUKO

SIMON & SCHUSTER
London New York Amsterdam/Antwerp
Sydney Toronto New Delhi

First published in Great Britain in 2025 by Simon & Schuster UK Ltd

1 3 5 7 9 10 8 6 4 2

Simon & Schuster UK Ltd
1ˢᵗ Floor, 222 Gray's Inn Road
London WC1X 8HB

www.simonandschuster.co.uk
www.simonandschuster.com.au
www.simonandschuster.co.in

Simon & Schuster Australia, Sydney
Simon & Schuster India, New Delhi

A CIP catalogue record for this book is available from the British Library.

PB ISBN 978-1-3985-3654-8
eBook ISBN 978-1-3985-3698-2
eAudio ISBN 978-1-3985-3697-5

Typeset in UK by Sorrel Packham

Printed and Bound in the UK using
100% Renewable Electricity at CPI Group (UK) Ltd

MIX
Paper | Supporting
responsible forestry
FSC
www.fsc.org   FSC® C171272

To my father, who is sadly no longer with us,
and yet I still feel him all around me.
Your sacrifices and love inspire me to want to do better.
I hope to continue making you proud.
Sun re o, Baba mi.

To Zainab and Kemi, my biggest cheerleaders,
my favourite people.
Thank you for your unwavering support.
I hope I keep you forever.

To sickle cell warriors, those who are still
with us and those who aren't.
Your strength and resilience is admirable.
Your courage in facing every obstacle is inspiring.
I am so glad you were put on this earth.

LAGOS BRIDE POISONED AT THE STAR-STUDDED WEDDING EVENT OF THE YEAR

IT WAS SUPPOSED TO BE THE HAPPIEST DAY OF HER LIFE. UNTIL GUESTS HAD TO PERFORM CPR ON THE BRIDE AND WHISK HER AWAY TO HOSPITAL . . .

Dérinsọ́lá Oyinlola, Lagos bride, established economist, and featured up-and-coming 'It Girl' in our blog post *The Instagram Pages You Should Be Watching in 2024*, was 'poisoned' last Saturday at her traditional wedding. Before things took a sinister turn, guests were calling it 'the event of the year' on their social media pages.

Sources say that Dérin was 'happily dancing' when, suddenly, she started clutching her chest, her eyes rolled back, and she fell to the ground. The bride's cousin had to start CPR on her almost immediately, soon followed by a renowned cardiologist who was luckily in attendance at the wedding. At this time, he has declined to comment.

Guests stood and watched the horrific events until a fire alarm went off, forcing an evacuation. It has been reported that a stampede was closely avoided. Dérin was rushed to the hospital as soon as paramedics arrived. But that might not have been fast enough due to, you guessed it: Lagos traffic.

Naija Gossip Lounge has reported on the chaos and drama that has plagued Dérin's wedding season. Could this be the final – and literal – nail in the coffin for our bride?

Readers, do we think she partied too hard, or is there something, or *someone*, more sinister involved? Comment your thoughts below.

You know gossip doesn't sleep, and neither do I.

xoxo

THREE WEEKS EARLIER

WEDDING SEASON IS IN FULL SWING AS BRIDE DÉRIN OYINLOLA WEDS KAYODE AKINLOLA

Dérinsọ́la Oyinlola – daughter of affluent businesspeople and Sickle Cell activists Olútáyọ̀ and Zainab Oyinlola – has a busy three weeks ahead of her as she counts down to both her traditional and white nuptials, which her *mother* has boasted to be 'the weddings of the decade'.

Dérin has always been one to watch, with her trend-setting outfits and gorgeous soft glam looks. Returning from studying at university in the UK, she has established herself as an economist of the future while jet-setting and influencing on the side. Who says we can't have it all?

More eyes will be on her now as she's set to wed the only son of one of the wealthiest banking dynasties in Nigeria, Kayode Akinlola, at the young age of twenty-two. Kayode plans to be a paediatrician . . . How cute.

Fans of Dérin have given the pair the hashtag #OyinBecomesAkin since their last names both end the same way.

4

It'll be interesting to see if Dérin can top Àdúràtọ́lá's wedding last year, when she captivated the hearts of many Nigerians with her skin-like illusion tulle wedding dress alone. Àdúrà *still* hasn't revealed the designer, but that didn't stop copycats trying to replicate her look. What do they say? Imitation is the best form of flattery . . .

We wonder how similar Dérin's wedding will be to Àdúrà's . . . Or if she can even reach that level of sophistication, seeing as she's hired an amateur wedding planner.

Trust me when I say, I'll have all the latest scoops on this wedding.

You know gossip doesn't sleep, and neither do I.

xoxo

CHAPTER ONE

There is a special type of obsession Nigerian parents have with being early for flights.

It is the reason why Mum insisted we arrived at Heathrow airport *six* hours before our actual flight.

I'm currently nursing a headache, weighed down by fabric wrapped around my body and on my head, because Mum can't pack within airline weight guidelines. All so she'll have enough gifts for her relatives in Nigeria, because heaven forbid she disgrace herself by showing up empty handed.

That's another thing Nigerian parents are obsessed with.

Their image.

One day that will be the thing that kills them. But for now, it's slowly killing me.

We've been stopped by customs at Murtala Muhammed International Airport. I use the word 'stopped' lightly because they were always going to search our luggage. It's tradition whenever you arrive in Lagos, even if you carry only a laptop bag.

This time though, I might have snuck a few too many mystery novels and true-crime books into my brother's luggage, wherever they could fit. It wasn't like he needed the space. He packed as if he's staying at his friend's uni accommodation for a few nights, and not like we're going to be in Lagos for five weeks for our favourite cousin's traditional and white weddings. Besides, he said I could pack my books in his suitcase – he just forgot to specify how many. As the oldest, Babs has always looked out for me, even when I annoy him. He's only two years older but it feels like he's my third parent. Babs is also the only one in the house who takes my love of true crime seriously.

Love is an intense downplay. An unhealthy but extremely rational *obsession* might be more accurate, all thanks to Uncle Damola, my mum's brother and an actual detective, who got me interested in the topic when I was younger. I know they say turning a hobby into a career is the worst thing you can do because it sucks the joy out of it, but I can't ever see that happening for me. I can't wait to start my Criminology degree so I can direct my passion into something useful.

Well, let me correct myself.

Law *with* Criminology.

The Criminology part of my degree, like my desire to study criminal justice and maybe become a private investigator, doesn't exist in my parents' eyes. Dad wants me to go into family law because 'divorce makes money, and money makes the world go round'. Mum has no real preference; she just wants the bragging rights, especially because Babs is in his second year of Medicine. If I become a lawyer and Babs a surgeon like our parents have dreamed, Mum will be practically untouchable amongst the aunties. Although that dream will soon be squashed when she realizes that Babs doesn't want to do surgery and I . . . well. Don't want to do Law.

The fact that I spend my time researching cases, reading books and watching documentaries about murder mysteries, instead of reading 'normal' novels or watching 'nice' shows on Netflix like the rest of my friends, deeply worries Mum. Shakes her spirit even.

That's why I've been struggling since last year to tell my parents that I have no interest whatsoever in studying Law. I promised myself that I would use this summer holiday, before university starts, to *finally* talk to my parents about how there are careers in Criminology. But three weeks have gone by already with zero progress made.

Ever since I was young, when Uncle Damola would babysit and tell us the PG versions of his cases, I've been fixated on solving mysteries. From finding out who stole my friend Reneé's toy water gun before she could show it off during Golden Time in primary school (surprisingly, it was our teacher, who said the toy was 'inappropriate'), to the mysterious broken cup at the back of the kitchen sink rack last month. (That was Dad. He broke it during one of his frequent late-night feasts and tried to hide it.) No matter how hard I try, I can't get into laws and legislation, and that's not an easy thing to tell your parents who have been planning your law career since the first time you won an argument against them. When I added Criminology to my Law degree on my UCAS application, Dad acted like I was committing an offence by putting my efforts into something else. Sometimes I think they believe I just plucked it out of the air, or I used a random number generator to go to page forty-five of a university prospectus and chose Criminology.

Anyways, now my love, or reasonable obsession, is about to get me in trouble at Murtala Muhammed International Airport.

'Aunty, what do you have for us today?' a portly, badly balding security guard asks, grinning widely as he looks through our things. Mum stares him down, not budging in spite of his tricks. His smile drops when he sees her death stare. They clearly don't know that they're messing with not only a native, but a killer negotiator. The guard's tone changes, fear mixing with audacity when he says, 'Ah, but, Madam, you know this bag is heavy. I'm even surprised they let you take it on the plane. And these books. How can we be sure you didn't smuggle anything in them?'

'Do you think security back in London wouldn't have checked? I'm supposed to believe that you can do a better job?' Mum says, her tone becoming increasingly irritated because we've been held up for twenty minutes now. The man eyes our bags once more, rummaging around for God knows what.

'Madam, if you want to pass, you'll have to pay a hundred thousand naira. One hundred and fifty thousand, and I won't even slice the books open,' he says, his voice low.

I want to protest for the safety of my books, but I know as soon as he hears my accent, the price will hike up higher. I settle for a squeak instead.

'*One hundred* thousand?' Mum yells, catching the attention of people around us. She starts cussing the guard out in Yoruba for wasting her time. The man shushes her and I groan inwardly. Big mistake.

'Don't tell me to shush. One hundred thousand, fún kíni? To bring clothes into the country?'

'Ma, please, keep your voice down. Don't be cheap, it's only fifty pound sterling I'm asking for.' He uses his hands to signal that she should lower her tone. I laugh to myself; he clearly doesn't know that he's met his match. Babs isn't paying any attention; he's still half asleep from the journey and has sat himself on a nearby metal chair. He looks like he's a stray, with the amount of clothes layered on him. I cried headache so I got the least of it and only had to wear a bright blue gèlè over my long box braids, and two cardigans tied around my waist. Mum starts to get irate and asks the man to bring his supervisor down.

'Ah.' The man rubs his bald head nervously. 'It doesn't have to be like that . . . You know what, normally I wouldn't do this, but just for you.' He finally closes our bags. 'You can go. It's okay.'

'Better.' Mum kisses her teeth, then we walk off with our

11

luggage. 'Useless man. Babs, let's go,' she tells my brother, then turns to me and says, 'Lara, call your daddy and tell him we'll be waiting by the exit.'

When we get outside, the heat hits me like a baseball bat – you would think I'd be used to it after our biennial trips, but it is always a shock. I immediately have to take the gèlè off of my head before it worsens my headache.

Babs doesn't seem fazed by the heat, probably because he lived in Nigeria longer than I did, and because of this, Babs is completely fluent in Yoruba. Sometimes his Yoruba accent will even slip into his English one.

I'm fluent too, mostly, but my accent has morphed into East London, so Yoruba just doesn't sound as good on my tongue as it does on his, making me self-conscious when I speak it.

'Is there a better sight!' Dad yells out from a black Jeep. I run over and give him a massive hug. He'd only been gone a week, helping everyone prep for the wedding, but the house felt so weird without him. 'How are you? How was the flight?' He hugs the two of us, then kisses Mum. Babs sits in the car straight away without helping us load the bags. It's like the chivalry got sucked out of his body as soon as we landed.

'Fine,' I say, popping open the boot to put in our luggage. 'They tried to shake us down again.'

Mum rolls her eyes at me then makes her way into the passenger seat. 'Is it not your fault? How did you even manage to pack all those books? If I had known Babs had space, I would have packed my material for Uncle Gbenga's sixtieth birthday.'

Dad whispers into my ear, 'It's even good. I've been looking for an excuse not to go to that party.'

This makes me laugh. 'There's traffic on the bridge. Might be a while until we get there,' Dad continues as he puts the last suitcase in the boot then makes his way into the driver's seat. I didn't expect anything less from Lagos. I'm taking this as the perfect opportunity to dive back into my audiobook; I'd just reached the point in the novel where the main character receives a threatening message, forcing her to delete all her research on the case before the killer comes after her next.

We arrive at Uncle Tayo's just before eleven p.m.

Twice on the journey, the traffic was so bad that we turned the engine off, and I had to switch from my audiobook to focusing on the car radio because my ears hurt from having AirPods in since six a.m.

Uncle Tayo's house blows me away every time. His pure white, three-storey mansion topped with a black roof is illuminated with deck lights as we pull into the driveway. Every time we visit, it seems like he's added another extension, which either means he's trying to show off to his friends or Aunty Zai has talked him into adding a cool new, and totally unnecessary, feature to their home. You would never believe it was just him, Aunty Zai, Dérin and Temi, their house help, who live in the mansion.

Last summer, they added a sauna, which they soon realized didn't make any sense because Nigeria is like a sauna itself, so to compensate they added a cold plunge pool over Christmas. Which is fine by me: it's basically like staying in an all-inclusive hotel.

I'm pretty sure that most Nigerian families have an Uncle Tayo. The one whose motto is *chop life, before life chops you*, and actually can afford to do so because he makes good money. The uncle who's the last one left on the dancefloor when everyone else has sat down because their feet hurt. Just good vibes all around. He's my favourite of Dad's brothers, in part because I always leave Lagos five hundred pounds richer.

'My babies!' Uncle Tayo beams as he races out of the house in a navy-blue fur robe and matching slippers as we unload the car. 'Oya, oya, get their bags and put them in their rooms,' he orders Temi, while grabbing Babs and squeezing him into a hug.

Then he makes his way to me. 'Lara! My second daughter!' He rubs my arms fast as if he's trying to warm me up then ushers me into the house. He's ageing well – he's only just getting a beer belly, and his hair has just started to turn salt-and-pepper, thinning lightly at the sides. He almost looks younger than Dad, who has fine lines on his face from thinking too hard. 'How was the flight?'

'Tiring as always.' I roll my eyes exaggeratedly.

'How many kilograms over this time?' he whispers as he looks over at Mum and her obviously ridiculously heavy suitcase, and I signal eight with my fingers so Mum doesn't overhear us. Uncle chuckles. 'Remind me in the morning to give you your money.'

I laugh to myself. Spotting behavioural patterns is something I've mastered to help me get a detective job after university, so it makes me happy when I win bets with my family.

I gasp every time I walk into Uncle Tayo's foyer, which is illuminated by the warm light of the chandelier on the ceiling. Tall windows are set in the pure white walls and stairs with black bannisters circle the room.

'Where's Dérin?' I whisper. The foyer is so silent you can hear a pin drop.

'She's sleeping. Wedding planning has been stressing her out,' Uncle Tayo says and I nod in understanding.

'And Aunty Zai?' Babs asks, and Mum clears her throat.

Everyone in this room knows exactly what that cleared throat is signal for. We all stare at her, Dad more intently than the rest of us, and she puts her hands up in defence. To put it nicely, that cleared throat is code for *What makes you think that woman would stay up to greet us*? If I was to say what Mum actually thinks, I'd need my mouth washed out with soap.

Aunty Zai and Mum have been not-so-quietly feuding since we started coming back to Nigeria more frequently, and Mum overheard her saying that our visits every other year were stopping her from leaving the country and going on holiday like her friends. I don't know why it matters to Aunty Zai, because she works from home and could fly out any time but, hey, things were said and Mum was not happy, to say the least.

Of course, Uncle Tayo brushes off her comment because he's used to her. But Mum has never forgotten, no matter how much everyone tries to pacify her. In all honesty, Aunty Zai is an acquired taste. If you let her snarky comments get to you, you'll never rest, but if you can block them out, you learn a lot from her.

Uncle Tayo chuckles before answering Mum's question about Aunty Zai, 'She's sleeping too. You must all be tired. I've told Temi to leave some food in your rooms, so eat before you go to bed, then rest well. We've got a long three weeks before the weddings.'

We nod, then disperse to our usual rooms. Being the only girl besides Dérin has its perks: I get the biggest room and I've taken full advantage of that, making sure to decorate it my way so no one else will want it. It hasn't changed since our last visit. The white drapes of my canopy bed are immaculate and my LED lights illuminate the walls in pink. Temi has left some meat pies along with a cup of Milo on my dresser. I scoff them down while putting my clothes away. It doesn't take long for the Milo to kick in and make me tired so I crawl into bed, put my audiobook on and, before I know it, I'm out for the night.

CHAPTER TWO

I jolt awake to the sound of screaming.

I'm thrown into full panic mode and grab the nearest thing that I see, an ìgbálẹ that Temi must've left in my room when he was cleaning up. I race downstairs to the kitchen where the noise is coming from.

The screaming has stopped, but I arm myself with the ìgbálẹ like a baseball bat just in case danger still lurks. Then suddenly it dawns on me that I'm in a house with *four* men and none of them have come to check on the situation. That must mean one of two things: either the men are idiots and they've already been taken hostage or hurt, or this can't be as serious as I thought.

When I walk into the black-and-white kitchen, I realize it's the latter. Mum and Aunty Zai are standing in their white nightgowns with a shattered pink ceramic cup on the floor between them. I clutch my chest, begging my heart to slow down. 'I thought there was an emergency.'

Aunty Zai turns around and I shudder a little at the sight of her – she's wearing one of those overnight face masks with a cartoon character printed on it. It looks like it's supposed to be Ursula from *The Little Mermaid*, but after being warped around the features on Aunty Zai's face, it looks more like Venom. Now I know why Mum screamed.

'Were you going to fight the emergency with the broom?' Mum says sarcastically.

I start to respond, but Aunty Zai interrupts me, her arms flailing as she scolds Mum. 'Adélé. Adélé. Adélé. I'm warning you, it's too early to look for my trouble.' I know it pains Mum every time she realizes that she can't talk back because she's five years younger.

'You scared me.' Mum shrugs, her tone emotionless. I finally lower the ìgbálẹ, which has surprisingly come in handy as I'll need it to sweep up the pieces of broken cup.

'Lara, leave it, don't cut yourself. Temi will clean it up.' Aunty crouches down and takes the ìgbálẹ out of my hands, kissing her teeth. When we get up, she pulls me into a tight hug. She smells like amaretto. 'How are you, my love? I can't believe you're still growing. How tall are you now?' Her voice turns from stern back to its usual nasally fusion of a Nigerian and British accent.

'I think I'm about five foot seven,' I say, my voice muffled by her clothes. She lets me go but cups my face with her hands, squishing my cheeks.

'You're getting so beautiful now. You're looking more and more like Dérin . . . you've even grown into your nose.' She

18

coos and Mum kisses her teeth softly in the background. I have to hold in my snicker.

'Thank you.' I crinkle my nose, escaping from her hands. I've spent enough time with Aunty Zai to not pay her any mind when she critiques my appearance. I just keep reminding myself that I only have to deal with it for three weeks out of every fifty-two. Or I did. I wonder how I'll cope this time, when it's five.

Aunty Zai has more Eurocentric features than Mum and me because her mother was a very light-skinned, mixed-race woman. So while Mum and I have wider nose bridges, Aunty Zai has a slim, narrow one. Our fuller lips contrast with her thinner top lip and fuller bottom one. Her light brown skin with yellow undertones stands out against the brown skin with red or pink undertones the rest of us have. But I'll admit she's not entirely wrong.

It's not by chance that I look like Dérin. It's by design.

All my life I've idolized Dérin. She's my oldest female cousin on Dad's side and the only one I truly relate to, despite our four-year age gap. Dérin lives the life I think, or wish, I could've lived if I'd stayed in Nigeria. The daughter of two wealthy families, who spends most of her days vlogging her fabulous life and living it to the fullest, as well as being a newly qualified economist. Dérin has always been popular on social media for her trend-setting outfits and effortless make-up routines. But after her engagement photos went viral, she blew up on Instagram and Twitter, making her more popular and solidifying

19

her as an up-and-coming Naija *It Girl*. She's even started to gain some global traction. It's a jump scare when I'm mindlessly scrolling my social media and see her face because one of her latest looks has gone viral too. The legendary parties she holds every year have also helped her rise to internet stardom.

The last time I measured how similar Dérin and I looked, we had the same chiselled jawline matched with full cheeks, the same full lips with a strong Cupid's bow, and arched brows. Our major differences are our eyes and dimples. Dérin's dimples are deep; just a faint smile from her would make anyone melt. And mine are soft, and only on the right side of my face. Dérin's eyes are upturned like her mum's, while mine are more of an almond shape. Despite that, it's still easy for strangers to mistake us for each other. It fills me with glee every time they do.

We're testaments to the strength of our dads' genes.

Mum snaps me out of my thoughts when she takes a seat at the long white dining table and says, 'Go and wake your uncle, Dad and Babs for breakfast. Tell them I'm making yam and egg. If they don't want yam there's bread.'

I nod but before I leave, I ask, 'What about Dérin?'

Aunty Zai responds, not looking up from her phone, 'She's already in the shower. She'll be down soon. You should get ready as well. After we eat, we're all going for dress fittings.' Her face mask is finally off and she's back to normal, her skin glowing.

After I shower and change, I have some free time so I decide to poke around the house looking at all the new and pointless renovations, while listening to a podcast episode about the Chicago Tylenol murders. An hour in, Mum catches me, in her words, 'aimlessly wandering' and ropes me into helping out with breakfast.

Dérin comes into the kitchen and squeals when she sees us. She's wearing a flowy blue off-the-shoulder ankara jumpsuit with puffy sleeves. Her make-up is soft with neutral colours, emphasizing her warm brown skin. Her lashes are also done, and her goddess braids up in a ponytail which emphasizes the upturn shape of her eyes.

She is perfection, as always.

'Our newest bride in town!' Mum echoes Dérin's squeal, leaving the chopping board to grab her hands and shimmy with her. 'How are you? You're looking slim; don't tell me they're not feeding you here.'

I clear my throat at Mum, signalling that she shouldn't look for Aunty Zai's trouble again.

'No, they're feeding me fine, just wedding stress . . . and other things.' Dérin smiles at Mum.

'All the blogs are talking about you. People at work have been sending me your engagement photos not knowing you're my niece. I love rubbing it in their faces,' Mum gushes. 'But did you offend that Naija Gossip Lounge? That last article – it's like they're out for blood.'

'Ugh, please don't get me started on Naija Gossip Lounge. They went from being my biggest fan to my worst enemy in literal months – it was like I hit one hundred thousand followers on Instagram and they got mad that I wasn't their little star any more. As if *they* hadn't helped with uplifting my platform. And they've got this stupid idea that I'm trying to upstage Àdúràtólá's wedding because we're in the same social circles. The whole of Lagos *loves* her, so I wouldn't dare, but God forbid there be more than one bride in this city. I just hope the blogs will at least leave me alone when the wedding is over. And *thank you, Mummy*, for the quote. Though did you not think "wedding of the decade" was a bit much?' Dérin purses her lips, but Aunty Zai says nothing, and instead just shrugs without a care. Dérin's finally looks in my direction and makes her way over to hug me. 'Lara, you look stunning.'

I try to hide the fact that I'm internally beaming. It's a weird feeling, knowing how proud I want to make her even though I have no reason to.

'Mmm.' Mum sounds displeased, bursting my bubble. 'She's been eating late and skipping meals whenever she's studying. For the past four months. She'll end up as skin and bones and then what will they say about me?'

'I think she looks fine, Aunty.' Dérin nods in approval. I mouth *Thank you*. She grabs a slice of agege bread from the table, tearing and popping it into her mouth as she makes her way over to her mum and kisses her cheek. 'This is why I love having you around, Aunty Adélé. No one cooks the way you do.'

Dérin has the type of voice that could persuade you to give

up your home if she asked nicely – it's not as nasal as her mum's, but rather smooth and sweet. Almost melodious. Her accent is what I'd describe as Lagos girl. It's a weird fusion of western accents, both US and UK, because for some reason it can't decide. While at the same time a Nigerian accent is fighting its way through.

'Where's Babs, Uncle Niyi and Daddy?' she asks.

'The dining room. We've been here for all of one day and I'm already waiting on them hand and foot,' I mutter under my breath. It's the same thing every time we're here. We arrive and they suddenly forget what a dish is. The traditional values my mum upholds in Nigeria would never slide back in London. I'd slap them round the head with the wooden spoon I cook with if they ever tried.

'Dérin, what is she saying? Is she complaining about cutting onions again?'

'No, no! We're just . . . uh . . .' Her eyes bulge as she tries to change the subject, hurrying me out of the kitchen and into the dining room with the serving plates. 'Morning, everybody!'

The dining room mirrors the kitchen in that everything is black and white, the only vibrance coming from the art on the walls. The table seats ten, which normally works perfectly, but with Dad's youngest brother and his girlfriend arriving today, things will soon get cramped.

Uncle Tayo sits at the head of the table, while Dad sits at the opposite end. Dérin and I lay out the plates, greeting everyone as we take our seats. Mum and Aunty Zai follow us to start serving the food to Dad and Uncle Tayo, while the rest of us serve ourselves in silence. I take two slices of agege bread and scoop up some eggs.

'Where's the ring?' Babs asks, breaking the quiet.

Dérin smiles, looking down at her hand. 'I gave it back to Kayode last week. He's going to re-propose at the introduction tomorrow in front of everyone and ask for Daddy's permission again,' Dérin finishes, and Babs fake gags. She slaps his head, smiling lightly, her dimples making an appearance. 'Speaking of the introduction, what time are Uncle Yinka and Aunty Yemi coming? We have the fitting at twelve.'

'They should arrive in about an hour,' Uncle says. I glance at the time on my phone. Ten a.m.

'Won't they be tired from the flight?' Babs asks.

'They were on an early morning flight from Ghana, only two hours. They'll be fine.' Uncle Yinka won't be tired. That man doesn't know how to rest, whether he's working or partying. It's all or nothing with him. You'd think this would give Aunty Yemi a headache trying to juggle his lifestyle, but instead she acts more like a groupie. Uncle Yinka can do no wrong in her eyes. Everyone thinks Uncle Tayo is the fun one until they meet Uncle Yinka. But the difference between Uncle Tayo and Uncle Yinka is discipline.

'Come, is it true that Yemi and Yinka are married now?' Mum directs her question to Uncle Tayo, but Aunty Zai kisses her teeth at the topic and answers her question.

'Yes, o. I saw the pictures only yesterday, floating around

on Yemi's Facebook. Married since last year, but they're just uploading the pictures now. We are nearly in August! He didn't want to tell us that was why he was calling Tayo non-stop. For more money for a better wedding.' She frowns and everyone on the table dives into the topic.

Uncle Yinka is probably our most wishy-washy family member, hardly at family functions because he's so busy bouncing around. He's not had a steady job or settled location for so many years. I'm surprised Aunty Yemi has stuck around for as long as she has and he's somehow convinced her to marry him. Last I'd heard he was in Ghana starting a clothing business. *No one* knows how that's going. He's hidden his success, or imminent failure from us.

Whenever Dad's shouting on the phone we know he's talking to Uncle Yinka. He was always borrowing money from Dad or Uncle Tayo, as if he was trying to preserve his own fortune. That was until his brothers cut him off late last year after Dérin got engaged; Uncle Tayo, who consistently lent him the most, stopped immediately. Dad followed soon after, growing tired of the problem child of the family. I spent one afternoon listening to their three-hour argument on a conference call about how he needs to channel his energy into business ventures that actually work, while pretending to be studying for my last A-level History exam. If I don't do as well on that module, I'll know it's because I sacrificed my grade for gossip.

After that call, Uncle Yinka chose fashion. Which would seem random, except his cousin, my Aunty Kemi, runs a fashion empire in New York. We all thought maybe, just maybe, he had come to his senses and decided to work for her. But instead he chose to go to *Ghana*.

It doesn't make sense, but it's not my sense to make.

'Ehen, Dérin. Have you been able to reach Alika? I don't know how a wedding planner can be unreachable in the lead-up to your wedding?' Aunty Zai says, growing increasingly frustrated. 'I need to make sure she delivers all the material to my church's fellowship. Mummy Láídé and her mouth is too much. She can't embarrass me like this.'

'Mummy Láídé?' Dérin side-eyes her mum. '*Mummy Láídé* that you hate? Just how many people have you invited to this *wedding of the decade*?'

Aunty Zai looks away immediately, putting food in her mouth, then mutters, 'Just tell her to call me.' She swallows, then decides to go into full-on rant mode. 'With the blogs now talking about us, we can't afford for things to start going wrong and for the whole of Lagos to use it as an opportunity to talk rubbish about us. There'll be more than three hundred guests at the traditional wedding alone. That is too many eyes on us and Alika is too relaxed for how big this wedding will be. If it's Ireti calling, she'll answer in two seconds, but me, I'll be sent to voicemail. We can't play any games. Aunty Bisi's son had one mishap at his wedding and the blogs ridiculed her for two months straight. Everybody laughed at her. I felt bad, o.'

'Zainab, you laughed down the phone to me about it too,' Mum chides.

Aunty Zainab looks caught off guard until she says, 'Exactly my point. If we're not careful, both my enemies and my friends will laugh at me.' She claps her hands and rests them on her stomach.

CHAPTER THREE

An hour later, we're back at Murtala Muhammed International Airport to pick up Uncle Yinka.

We all decided to come because where we're going for the fittings isn't far from the airport. It isn't as humid as when we first landed but the hot air is still making me sweat disgustingly.

You can tell from the way me and Babs are dressed that we're not Lagosians. He's wearing the least amount of clothes he owns: black shorts and a white T-shirt with a pair of slides. I don't have the luxury of underdressing and still keeping cool without being stared at so I'm in a chocolate scoop-necked playsuit with thick straps that I have to constantly pull up so my cleavage doesn't show. A curse of being top heavy. I'm getting impatient waiting around in the sun and I'm almost tempted to go back into the air-conditioned car before a guffaw stops me. I recognize the voice.

'Tayo, Niyi!' Uncle Yinka shouts out as he sees his

brothers. I'm surprised he's not holding a grudge after the last time they talked. He drops his suitcase and runs towards Daddy and Uncle Tayo. Uncle Yinka has always been the thinnest brother and the other two practically swallow him entirely with a tight bear hug.

'I've missed you.' His accent makes me pause. It's American, or should I say *fake* American. This man went to Ghana and came back with a bogus American accent.

Dérin has to pinch Babs to stop him from laughing. 'Where's Aunty Yemi?' she asks, swiftly changing the subject.

'Oh, she's coming. She just walks slow now,' Uncle Yinka says, accent catching me off guard again. My eyes narrow as I realize he's only holding *one* suitcase. His suitcase, not his blushing bride's. I don't know how she does it.

Mum and Aunty Zai finally join us, and I hear them whisper in unison, 'Jesus is Lord.' I turn back at them, confused, then I follow their stares.

The words 'oh my God' pour out of me, as Aunty Yemi finally reaches Uncle Yinka . . . with a baby bump. A very large and hard to miss baby bump. A baby bump so big it makes me question how they allowed her on the plane. 'I – So this is why she walks slow,' I say. Even worse, she's dragging along her own suitcase.

I run to take it from her, still in shock. When I get to her side, I glance quickly at everyone's faces, and, God, I wish I had a camera right now. The last time we saw Aunty Yemi she was just as thin as Uncle Yinka, ready to go to Ghana and follow his wayward plans without any care in the world.

They've hardly contacted us since, unless they wanted money and I guess now we know why.

Uncle Tayo and Dad are gawping. Babs has one eyebrow raised. Dérin is smiling nervously, while Mum and Aunty Zai look like they might burst trying to hide their displeasure

Uncle Yinka looks at the family confused, then it finally clicks in his brain that he hasn't told us that his wife is about a thousand months pregnant. He walks towards Aunty Yemi, stands behind her and gives her a light squeeze. 'Surprise!'

'It's twins.' Aunty Yemi smiles wearily. She points to the left side of her stomach and then the right. 'A boy and a girl.' She chuckles lightly. She looks like she's aged a few years. Last time I saw her, you could mistake her for being only a few years older than Babs, and now she looks tired and bothered. Bags are forming under her eyes.

Mum bursts out laughing – an annoying habit of hers in uncomfortable situations. Everyone turns to stare at her. 'Please, let's go to the car before I wet myself. Welcome back to Nigeria.' She laughs again, grabbing Uncle Yinka's suitcase.

When we walk into Aunty Tiwa's parlour, 'Woman' by Rema is blasting. We arrive with only a few minutes to spare because we didn't anticipate the extra space that Aunty Yemi's baby bump would need, so we spent ten minutes shifting seats to fit everyone in comfortably.

Tomorrow is the official introduction between the families of the bride and groom. It was technically supposed to happen six months ago, in January, when they set the wedding date, but Uncle Tayo insisted at the last minute on waiting until our whole family were together this summer. Apparently, this didn't go down well because it meant that Dérin's fiancé, Kayode, had to fly his family in twice because of the cancellation. But as Uncle Tayo is paying for half the wedding, Kayode's parents couldn't really say anything.

From what Dérin has told us about her in-laws, they seem sweet. But after that mishap, our side of the family had to step up and do the heavy lifting with the wedding planning to help with their wasted expenses. Money helps but it's still strange that they basically washed their hands of planning after one inconvenience.

Because Uncle Tayo and Aunty Zai think they're the Posh and Becks of Lagos, we all have two outfit changes for the introduction. In normal families, the introduction is just the immediate and a few of the extended family meeting up in the house. But our family isn't normal. They've hired two catering companies and ordered a gazebo to be set up in the garden. Dérin is their only child so I should have expected them to go to these kinds of lengths. This isn't even our first fitting; we've been doing them online for months in preparation for the biggest event: the traditional wedding in three weeks.

A slim woman with black-rimmed glasses guides the men to the other side of the parlour to get their agbadas fitted with any last adjustments. As they leave, our family tailor, Aunty Tiwa, walks in. She has measuring tapes draped around her neck, pin cushions strapped to her wrists and pencils stuck in her hair, which is tightly wrapped in a bun. Aunty Tiwa is slender, like the mannequins in her store. She's always had a face that sings comfort, and her chubby cheeks make her look younger than she is. Aunty Tiwa isn't a blood relative, but she's been family for as long as I can remember. She and Aunty Zainab are best friends despite the seven-year age gap between them and they gist like teenagers whenever they're together. No topic is left untouched in a Zainab and Tiwa gossip session.

'If it isn't my favourite bride-to-be!' She embraces Dérin in a big hug. 'How are you, my—' She pauses and I already know what she's looking at. 'Yemisi! What is this?'

Everyone eyes Aunty Yemi once more as she says, 'Surprise?'

'Surprise, ke?' Aunty Tiwa looks at Mum and Aunty Zainab.

Mum holds her palms up in the air and Aunty Zai claps the back of her hands together muttering, 'Ah, kò yé mi.'

'Yemi. Ah, ah, you have my number, why didn't you say anything? The last measurements I took, you were a size eight. Now you're looking like size twen—'

'Don't finish that sentence.' Yemi shushes her.

'We're just as surprised as you. Do you have any more fabric to adjust the clothes for her?' Aunty Zai pleads.

'*In one day?*' Aunty Tiwa scrunches up her face. 'Lie, lie. She'll have to wear a bubu for tomorrow, I'll see what I can do for the traditional and the white wedding.'

'Ah, but I'll be mismatched from everyo—' Aunty Yemi

stops talking when she realizes that we're all staring at her like it's her fault. 'A bubu is fine. Please just add some rhinestones or something.'

'Let's just get started so Aunty Tiwa has time to make any final amendments.' Aunty Tiwa takes Dérin into the back to try on her outfits while we try ours on in the cubicles situated around the store.

The theme for tomorrow is dark green and gold. Being part of the bride's family means I get to wear gold rather than green, thank God, because I hate green. Mum changed my dress design at the last minute without telling me and normally I would be mad, but it's paid off positively this time. I initially wanted something a bit more understated since it's not a main event, but the extra designs on the dress tie together beautifully. The outfit is a soft gold. It has one long sleeve, bedazzled with gold and brown shimmery leaves, while my other sleeve is cut into a shoulder strap. The top is heavily beaded with delicate pearls, so it reflects the light, and the skirt has been left mostly plain, with the shimmery leaves sewn throughout. When I come out of the changing room Mum yelps then runs over to me crying out, 'You look so beautiful. I knew I made the right decision not listening to you, this dress makes your cheeks look less chubby.' She squeezes my face.

I half frown when she lets go. At least there was a compliment in there. Mum's outfit follows the same guidelines as mine, but she's got a sweetheart neckline. 'You look beautiful too,' I tell her.

Aunty Yemi is sitting on the sofa looking at us solemnly. I make my way over to her, having to pull up the dress to move around properly. 'When are you due?' I ask in an attempt to cheer her up, then I realize her pregnancy is the thing that's bringing her down.

'In about a month and a half,' she says, voice muffled, biting into a Gala sausage roll she bought from a street vendor when we were in the car.

'And they let you on the plane?' I whisper-shout.

She nods, taking another bite. 'You can fly up until eight months pregnant. Are you excited for law school?'

The dreaded question. I hate the way I've had to train my face *not* to drop whenever it's asked. I hate that I can't tell people how unhappy the thought of law school makes me without alarming them. I can't tell them that the idea of doing Law at uni just reminds me of how miserable and stressful the last two years have been. Studying subjects I don't care about just to make my university application shine. The sick-to-my-stomach feeling I used to get whenever I had a mock exam coming up and knowing how rigorously I'd have to revise because I couldn't, I can't, disappoint the family. Babs is in med school learning how to save lives and Dérin's an economist who just graduated with a first-class degree, and is now marrying a soon-to-be-successful doctor straight out of university. I cannot, will not, be the family disappointment.

'More than excited,' I say, then swiftly move on. 'Have you thought of any na—' Dérin's entrance interrupts my question as my mouth gapes open.

Dérin's àṣọ òkè is a lighter shade of gold than the rest of the family's, and reflects into a green when the light shifts as she walks. Her top is almost off the shoulder, with both cups of her bodice bedazzled with jewels, while the middle is plain, showing off the two tones in the outfit. The skirt has an added slit with jewels around the outline and following a pattern up to her waist. She's cinched in all the right areas. Skirts have the habit of swallowing most people's bodies, but never Dérin's. If anything, they emphasize her figure. She's practically glowing as she walks out with Aunty Tiwa.

Aunty Zai walks out after her, in a dress the same design as Mum's except hers is covered in a thousand green and gold sparkles. I honestly didn't expect anything else.

The room is still. No one speaks as they take in Dérin. Mum's sniffle breaks the silence. 'It feels like yesterday I was carrying you on my back and now you're getting married.' She wipes away her tears.

'You like it?' Dérin replies. 'You don't think it's too much? I don't want Kayode's parents to think I'm showing off. I've really only met them twice and both of those times have been in unfortunate circumstances,' she says, making her way to the floor-length mirror, fluffing her skirt.

'You look stunning, Dérin,' I say. She gives me a warm smile.

'Is no one going to compliment me?' Aunty Zai chimes in. 'See how I shine, the way it glitters when I move. Hey, omalicha nwa, my mother's first-born daughter and most

35

beautiful child.' Then she goes off on a tangent, calling herself a thousand pet names as she admires herself in the mirror.

Mum mutters under her breath, 'She's her mother's only child.' And I have to bite my lip to stop myself giggling.

Aunty Tiwa bursts out laughing. 'Àgbàyà, ignore her. Does anyone have any adjustments they need me to make before tomorrow? Apart from Yemi and the tent I have to make her.'

Aunty Yemi glares at Aunty Tiwa. Mum is the only one to speak. 'Ah, yes. I've been holding my breath for the last ten minutes. I need to be able to eat tomorrow.'

CHAPTER FOUR

Introductions are supposed to be small, and intimate. But this is more like we're planning to feed the five thousand. Outside, the gazebo is beautifully decorated with fake gold flowers and tea lights accenting every table. The tables themselves are draped with white cloths and fake leaves that cascade to the floor. Drinks are set on them along with plates full of small chops: meat pie, puff puff and samosas. In the middle of the gazebo are two white sofas piled with dark-green cushions with gold flourishes.

I'm upstairs getting my make-up done by one of the artists, and my gèlè is being tied by her two assistants. When the artist steps away, I'm shocked at how well my make-up is done. She's gone for a soft neutral glam, tied together with nude lips, and my gèlè matches the material of Dérin's dress, shifting from gold to green in the light.

When Dérin comes into the room, she's practically glowing. Aunty Zai and I *ooh* and *aah* around her, and the photographer starts choreographing shots before the hot weather ruins her make-up. Just as they're finishing up, we hear a commotion from the staircase. Dérin and I rush towards the window that looks out over the drive at the front of the house. We see Kayode and his family approach in their cars, beeping the horn for the gateman to let them in. Three big Land Rovers drive into the compound and passengers start piling out, carrying gifts wrapped in green and gold plus three massive fruit baskets.

Aunty Zai starts yelling when she sees Dérin's wedding planner, Alika, exit one of the cars. Alika is wearing a cream square-neck top which shows off a lot of cleavage, with a matching skirt that clings to her wide hips, and a pair of stilettos. Her hair is slicked back into a long, high ponytail. She's wearing animal print cat-eye sunglasses and has a white headset in her ear.

'Obìnrin yìí yá wèrè. Why is she coming out of the car with them? When I've been calling her all morning, she did not pick up. Now she wants to show her breasts as she arrives. If I catch he—'

'Mummy, please! Take it somewhere else,' Dérin cuts in, irritated.

Aunty Zai continues making snarky comments about Alika as she heads downstairs to join the rest of the family.

Kayode's parents are dressed in dark green. They seem too young to have a twenty-two-year-old son. Kayode's dad almost looks like the Nollywood actor Van Vicker as he steps out of the car. Kayode's mum is tall and curvy, and her àṣọ ẹbí is fitted to her body with a corset, giving her a pear-shaped figure, and she's added gold dangle earrings and a heavy gold necklace. Her arms are adorned with delicate bangles. She wears dark green heels with a bag and jewellery to match. Her rich brown skin is dewy as she takes off her sunglasses; she has fox-like eyes and a determined stare as she looks around.

Kayode gets out of the second car with half his groomsmen, the rest coming out of the other. Dérin makes *psst* sounds at Kayode from the upstairs window; it takes a while but when he sees her, he breaks into the biggest pearly white smile. Like no one else is around, just him and her together, soaking in each other's presence. Kayode is handsome. There is no denying it. His brown skin and chiselled features look extremely smooth, even from up here.

They met during Dérin's second year of university when she ran against him to be president of the Nigerian Society. Their love story can literally be summed up with the academic rivals to lovers trope because they were wickedly competitive when they first met. When Dérin ended up winning the presidency and Kayode became her VP, something must've drastically changed because they fell for each other. In true Dérin fashion, she is one of the few girls to successfully find a perfect husband in the jungle that is university. Just another aspect in Dérin's life where she has done exceptionally well, and my parents will want me to emulate.

The family downstairs keep Kayode outside for an extra

two minutes just to tease him, and Dérin has to shout through the window for them to let him in as they laugh by the door. Tungba music follows Kayode and his family as they dance their way into the house. As the last person starts to disappear, we run to Dérin's room which overlooks the back garden to continue watching. Dérin throws open the window so we can hear. The MC for today is Aunty Zai's Big Mummy – her oldest aunt – acting as the Alága. Her role is essentially the spokesperson overseeing proceedings and also to provide entertainment. She takes a piece of cloth, similar to what Dérin is wearing, and holds it out as she stands at the entrance to the garden.

'You can't enter yet. You know what you have to do,' she says in Yoruba.

Kayode and his groomsmen look confused for a second, until one of them brings out a wad of money from his pocket and places it on the cloth. Big Mummy makes a joke that maybe Kayode should be marrying her instead. Everyone laughs as Big Mummy picks up the money and ushers them out to the garden.

Kayode's dad, Uncle Fola, speaks. He looks similar to his son but when he talks, his jovial manner reminds me of Uncle Yinka. He introduces his wife, Aunty Ireti, and talks about his family's intentions to make Dérin their bride. Aunty Ireti is gorgeous. She has the regal air of an old Nollywood actress. When the microphone is passed to her, her voice is calm as she says, 'Èsé gàn. Thank you to Dérin's family for welcoming us into your lovely home. Peace be on

40

this house. My husband has already said everything for me, but I'll just say my own too. When Kayode said he had found someone he wanted to bring home to us, ah, as a mother I was sceptical. But after meeting Dérin, there is no way I can be. He has brought home a diamond and we can't wait to welcome her into our home.'

Everyone claps, then a spokesperson from Kayode's family starts singing. The song is about how Kayode has not been able to sleep since he laid his eyes on Dérin and never will be able to until she's his. Big Mummy nods as she listens to the song, then makes her way over to Uncle Tayo and Aunty Zai. They fake-whisper to each other, giggling together before Big Mummy clears her throat and pretends to look serious.

'Tayo, I'm ready when you are.' Aunty Zai winks at her husband and he grins, winking back. Uncle Tayo gestures for Kayode and his groomsmen to prostrate themselves on the floor in front of our family. They do so nearly seamlessly.

Uncle Yinka chuckles and says, 'It wasn't perfect. One more time.'

Dérin bangs on the window and shouts, 'I'm dying up here!' which makes everyone's heads turn as they realize she's been watching all this time.

'Ah ìrò, you will not die, in Jesus' name!' Big Mummy yells back towards the house so Dérin can hear.

She finally gets the signal from Uncle Tayo and it's time for Dérin to go down. The live band starts playing their rendition of 'Olo Mi' by Tosin Martins as we walk in, me

41

first with Dérin following behind. Everyone stands up, waiting for Dérin to grace them with her presence. Kayode's grin is broad. You'd think this man was the Cheshire cat. He stands up then gives her the biggest hug, rubbing the middle of her back. He lifts up her veil, taking a first peek before dramatically slapping his hands against his heart. He hesitates then flings the veil off, nearly taking Dérin's head with it as everyone laughs.

'Firstly, I want to thank you all for coming, especially if you have flown in. It truly means the world to us.' Kayode's South London accent comes out, deep and commanding. 'As you've seen, I've attempted to ask permission with a few trials and errors.' He brings out a red box from his trouser pocket and addresses Dérin. 'But I hope after seeing this, it will solidify your decision.'

Kayode gets down on one knee again and there's not a dry eye in the gazebo as he proposes. Dérin nods as fast as a bobblehead toy, and he slides the ginormous rock on her finger. Dérin grabs his face almost ready to kiss him before she remembers where she is. She smiles widely, tears in her eyes, then lets him go.

The rest of the night is a party for the guests. Both my uncles, Dad, plus Kayode's parents and Alika, move inside the house to discuss Dérin's bride price, the list which is made when a man decides to marry a woman and she accepts his proposal. It's up to the bride's family to decide what items go on the list as gifts to be given to the bride on her traditional wedding day. As archaic as it sounds, I've always

42

liked this custom, although in Dérin's case it's basically symbolic since her family can afford any gift they gave her probably two times over.

'Lara!' I jerk my head around. Dérin motions me to come. When I do, she whispers into my ear, 'I made sure that the menu included ayàmàsé and smoked turkey for you.' I smirk and she winks at me.

'God bless you.' I squeeze her cheeks and she fusses, exclaiming that I'll ruin her make-up.

I love ayàmàsé. From the smoked turkey and assorted meat, tender and beautifully seasoned in the stew, to the chunkiness of the peppers and the spice that makes my nose run, it is truly the best dish Nigeria has to offer.

But what I don't love about ayàmàsé is when the meat or – *culprit* in this case – shaki, fights back and splashes stew into my eye. I'm ready to rip my eye out of its socket just to stop the burning but since that's not possible, I run back into the house to find a sink so I can rinse my eye without ruining my make-up. I don't want to drag the make-up artists out of the party just because I don't know how to eat shaki in a civilized way.

The kitchen sink is occupied by the caterers washing up the dishes, so I head to my room. Drenching my eye with water, I manage to reduce the pain from fiery to warm, but any attempt to save my eye make-up is ruined.

As I get downstairs and walk through the hallway, angry, muffled voices from outside the sitting room stop me in my tracks. I hide behind the nearest tall item – a white pillar – and angle one ear towards the noise.

'What kind of nonsense are you playing at? These are Dérin's in-laws! How could you bring that up during discussions of the bride price?' The voice is Dad's and I have a feeling I know who he's talking to.

Alika, Dérin's wedding planner, tries to calm Dad down. 'Uncle, please, they can hea—'

Uncle Yinka interrupts. 'Niyi, Tayo needs to get a grip. He's wasting the money he promised me on this we—'

'Will you shut up!' Dad's voice cuts off Uncle Yinka's, making me even more intrigued. Dad rarely raises his voice so if he's raising it, and *this loud*, something is wrong.

I move my body slowly, poking my head a few inches around the pillar, holding my breath. Dad takes multiple steps towards Uncle Yinka, making him step further and further back, away from the sitting room and closer to the foyer.

'He doesn't owe you anything. *You* need to get a grip, Yinka. You have a baby coming now. *Two* babies. You need to take more responsibility for your actions. Bringing up money that Tayo supposedly owes you, which he *doesn't*, is inappropriate. Look how you're making us seem in front of Dérin's in-laws, like we're a dysfunctional family. Like we're in debt to you, which we know damn well we're not. J-just stay here. We don't need you in the room any more. If you're not careful, we won't need you at the wedding either.'

The voices stop and a door slams. I peek out from my

hiding place. Alika has her head in her hands, not knowing what to do or who to follow. She focuses on Uncle Yinka, who has paced his way into the foyer completely, trying to pacify him. I pause, not wanting to make any sudden movements as he walks around the room. She tries to touch his arm but he snatches it away quickly. 'Sir, please don't be angry. I'm sure Uncle Niyi did not mean it. Weddings just bring out the worst in people an—'

Uncle Yinka kisses his teeth loudly, and mutters, 'They will see.' Then he runs up the stairs and slams the door to his room.

Alika pauses as she watches him, then looks around in disbelief and whispers to herself, 'I didn't think that would cause a rift so easily. What am I supposed to report back?'

Suddenly my eyes aren't burning any more.

CHAPTER FIVE

This is the second time in this house that I've woken up to screaming.

Like I did the first time, I arm myself with the ìgbálẹ̀, but I grab it with less vim this time. The screams sound less like terror and more like excitement.

When I finally get downstairs, I see that it's Dérin screaming. She's jumping up and down with glee in the front doorway. As I get closer, I see that the cause of her joy is her friends, the bridesmaids, walking up the driveway. They're earlier than expected; last I heard they weren't arriving for another three days. I doubt their rooms are prepped for them after yesterday's chaos.

'Rin!' The first girl drops her suitcase and runs to Dérin with open arms, before squeezing her tight. I recognize Amaka immediately from Dérin's graduation. Dérin always describes her friend as having a butt big enough to store water for a small island. I used to think she was exaggerating, but the way my eyes popped out when I first met Amaka I realized she was right.

Amaka was Dérin's first friend at university. Dérin talked about Amaka to me whenever we were on the phone; they had been inseparable from their first day as freshers to third year. Dérin cried for two days when she had to move back to Nigeria and leave her, as if Amaka wasn't grown and rich enough to come and visit.

Amaka is plus-sized wearing a sage sundress with tiny straps and white Converse with brown stains, probably from the mud and sand on the way here. She has long goddess braids flowing all the way down her back.

'Oh my God, did you forget I put my things in your suitcase, Amaka? You can't just drop it like that, they're fragile.' Another girl follows behind Amaka, grabbing the suitcase from the floor as she walks through the door and plops numerous pieces of luggage in front of me. She's vaguely familiar, dressed more casually in a matching pastel-pink velour tracksuit and white Air Force trainers. She's slim at the top and heavier at the bottom, dark-skinned with lips slicked in gloss. Her lace frontal wig is freshly laid and still in rollers from the flight. She looks like a Black Elle Woods.

'Could you take these to our room? And when you're done, get me some water? It's so hot outside.' She has an unplaceable accent, almost like a blend of Irish and English.

I turn around to see who she's talking to. When I face her again, she stares at me with a puzzled look which I mirror. 'You're talking to *me*?'

'Are you not the housegirl?'

My mouth falls open. I look down at myself to see how I could be mistaken for the help, then I remember the 'weapon' I'm carrying. The broom, plus my bonnet, must have given her the wrong idea.

Before I can open my mouth, Amaka speaks, breaking away. 'Seni, if you don't respect yourself. That's Dérin's cousin.' Her accent is an East London one, like mine.

Dérin snickers and pulls my bonnet off, letting my braids loose. 'The bonnet swallows her features,' she says and they all open their mouths in realization while I roll my eyes. Amaka grabs me for a hug, squeezing me tight.

'You know I'm a hugger.' She squeals again and honestly, it's too early for it.

'Amaka, you know I'm not,' I say through the few air pockets I have. Amaka apologizes and lets go with a wide smile on her face.

'You look so different from graduation day, Lara. You're glowing, somehow. I can't put my finger on it.' She ponders.

'I think we know why.' My eyes settle on the witch who mistook me for a housegirl, Seni, as she smirks. 'She's grown into her nose.'

I ought to yank her hair out.

But thankfully, almost like she's read my mind, Amaka does it for me. The wig barely budges. 'Seni, keep quiet. Don't make me get out your pictures from Year Ten,' she warns her, and I'm glad Amaka has my back.

My head turns as someone approaches me from behind.

'Aunty Zai-Zai!' The girls squeal as they see her.

'My darlings! You're early?' she says, hugging them one by one. 'How was your flight?'

I'm more than over the reunion, so I decide it's time to take my ìgbálẹ̀ back to my room.

'Um, so are you not going to take my luggage?' Seni says before I leave. I give her a look that says, *What do you think?* Then scoff as I head back up the stairs.

The last thing I hear is Amaka and Dérin playfully kissing their teeth and the sounds of luggage being dragged further into the house.

When I come back downstairs, I'm greeted by the smell of breakfast which makes me pause mid-scene in the other audiobook I've started this trip. Like Poirot, the protagonist has gathered all her suspects to reveal who she thinks is behind the camp murders. I inhale deeply: fried plantain, fresh agege bread, sausages and egg sauce are laid on the dining table. Babs is scooping chopped fruit into bowls.

Dérin's friends come out of the kitchen laughing, carrying plates and cutlery, and Mum and Aunty Zai follow them.

'Oh, Lara? Welcome to the world. How was your hibernation?' Mum asks as she sees me. A person can't even sleep in after a long and stressful day without getting shade. I subtly roll my eyes so Mum can't see, a trick that I've perfected over the years, then take a seat at the table. Uncle Yinka and Uncle Tayo are already sitting down. It's a tight squeeze now that the girls are here but we make it work somehow. After Amaka and Dérin lay the table, everyone starts eating. I don't join in the small talk until I've eaten to the point of satisfaction.

When I finally refocus, I notice Uncle Yinka's stiffness whenever a part of his body almost touches Uncle Tayo's. After the dispute between Dad and Uncle Yinka, it was hard to think about anything else for the rest of the party. I'd attempted to have fun and dance, and stuff my face with the small chops, but my mind kept going back to their angry exchange. Dad is too empathetic for his own good. He takes other people's burdens on his shoulders and he's much more tolerant than Uncle Tayo, so if Dad was *that* mad, Uncle Yinka must've behaved badly in the room with Kayode's parents. I can't imagine how mad Uncle Tayo must have been.

I narrow my eyes, biting my fork as I replay yesterday's scene trying to detect clues as to why Dad got so angry. It's not like Uncle Yinka hasn't embarrassed his brothers or acted greedily before.

Dad doesn't look angry this morning, though. Mum is basically feeding him his eggs and rubbing his bald head any moment she can. They look like lovesick puppies.

Last night, you wouldn't have known he'd argued with Uncle Yinka, from the way they rejoined the party so naturally. Uncle Yinka spent the night getting drunk and dancing with Aunty Yemi, passing around glasses of Courvoisier for the guests, making sure everyone was having a good time. Uncle Tayo and Dad also behaved normally, while Mum and Aunty Zai got into another of their rows. It was strange, as if my mind had made up the whole angry encounter.

I doubt Dérin even knows what went on. She's also like Dad in that she takes the stress of the world onto her shoulders. Any inkling that something wasn't running smoothly yesterday, and she would've fixated on it. She's ridiculously superstitious too; to her, almost everything is a sign.

'There's enough food on the table, you don't have to chew the cutlery,' Babs says, snapping me out of my thoughts. I sneer at him, and he mirrors my expression.

'Hey. Your room is next to Mum and Dad's. Did you hear anything last night?' I whisper.

'Nothing you want to know about,' he says, picking up a piece of agege bread from his plate.

'What? Ew, gross, not *that*. Like them arguing about something or someo—'

I'm interrupted as Mum asks the girls why they've arrived so early when they weren't due for another three days. Amaka explains that they planned to arrive yesterday to surprise Dérin at the introduction, but Seni forgot her passport, so they missed their flight.

I try to steer Babs back to our conversation. '*Yesterday*, Uncle Yinka and Dad got into an argument.'

'When are they not arguing? If they weren't related, Uncle Yinka would not exist in our lives.'

'That's exactly why I need you to keep an ear out for m—' I'm interrupted again, by Dérin speaking.

51

'It's actually better that you guys are here earlier. I was worried Aunty Tiwa wouldn't be able to cope with adjusting your measurements so soon before the traditional.'

'I'll even call her today and see if she can fit us in. The earlier the better,' Aunty Zai says, then gets up from the table and starts clearing plates. Amaka stops her and I quickly put my AirPods in, then look down, pretending I can't hear anything so I don't have to help with cleaning up.

'Dérin, let them clean and you come to my room. I need to ask you about some things,' Uncle Tayo says and my attention switches to him. I look at Uncle Yinka and notice how his jaw clenches. Dérin nods and then walks out of the dining room with Uncle Tayo. He looks mournful and rubs her back as they leave. I need to find a way to listen in on that conversation.

'Lara, carry that bowl into the kitchen for me.' Babs uses his chin to point to the black bowl that previously held the plantain.

'I would love to, but that oil from the food has just run through me.' I laugh weakly as his expression hardens. 'I'll be back in two secs, just need to use the *toilet*.' I whisper the last word in an attempt to make it seem urgent.

I run out of the room before he can continue, darting up the stairs as quietly as I can, careful so the flap of my slippers against the floor doesn't draw any attention. I creep into Babs' room, which is next door to Uncle Tayo's, and place my ear against the wall. I can hear muffled voices but they're too faint to make out words. I look around for a cup that I can place against the wall. Thankfully there's one in Babs' bathroom. I dash the toothbrush out of it, wincing as it clashes against the sink, then tiptoe back to the wall.

In my novels, the amateur sleuths make it seem like cups give you super hearing. Either it's a lie or these walls are thick as hell. All the cup has done is increase the muffled sound from completely incomprehensible to you can make out most of the words if you stay very, very still.

'I thought they were okay with it?' Dérin asks. From what I can make out, she sounds confused.

'They were, or so I thought. I think Kayode is the one who offered, they didn't seem up for paying for anything. Your uncle even caused a fuss when he heard about it, but for his own selfish reasons. That man. If he tries to talk to you about money, Dérin, change the subject quickly.' Uncle Tayo kisses his teeth.

'So, you'll have to pay for both days by yourself, or just the traditional?'

'Everything. The traditional, the rehearsal, the white wedding, everything.'

There's silence now.

'I don't mind having a small white wedding. Half the guests are Mummy's anyw—' Dérin says, but Uncle Tayo butts in, telling her there's no way he'll let her downsize her wedding. They go round in circles, but the conclusion is that Kayode's family don't want to contribute anything to the wedding. But why?

I've been gone long enough to use the toilet twice, but I've got all the information I need, so I stand up away from the wall. I put Babs' cup back in his bathroom and make my way out, gently closing the heavy brown bedroom door. I turn around and immediately bump into someone.

'Oh m—' Seni rubs her chest as she moves away from me. She narrows her eyes. 'I thought you needed to go to the toilet.'

I purse my lips. 'Well, I just came out of a bedroom. Which has a toilet . . . so?' I give her a look that says *you can work out the rest.*

She raises her hand and her ridiculously long acrylics point from me to the other side of the hallway. 'But your room is over there, no?'

'My toilet hasn't been flushing since yesterday.' I shrug.

She narrows her eyes further, then starts to walk off, saying, 'Don't worry, we've cleaned already.'

I nod, getting ready to walk downstairs anyway, when a door further down the corridor opens and Dérin comes out.

'Oh, Lara, hi.' The glimpse of worry on her face switches to a smile as I turn around. She brushes her palm across my arm then walks past me.

I look up as I realize I've been caught. Seni is staring at me from across the hallway, her head laid on her palms and elbows resting on the bannister. She has one eyebrow raised and a slight smirk on her face.

'I'm not going to tell,' she says, standing up straight again. 'But you shouldn't be prying into business that doesn't

concern you. If it did, it wouldn't be behind closed doors.'
She finally walks off to her room.

I should've yanked her hair when I had the chance.

CHAPTER SIX

We're all packed into the car, ready to get measured one last time before the traditional wedding. The whole design process has been through phone calls, pictures of styles sent on WhatsApp and the occasional FaceTime check-up. Even though we're nervous to see the dresses, you'd never be able to tell from the buzz in the car. Mum and Aunty Zai have called a short truce after their argument last night and have decided that old-school afrobeats is the most appropriate introduction to Nigeria for Amaka and Seni.

Dérin and Seni are singing their hearts out to P-Square songs as if P-Square wrote the songs for them and them alone. We scream for another thirty minutes, all the way through Lagos traffic, finally getting to our destination with the most immaculate energy. When we arrive at Aunty Tiwa's shop, the songs switch to new-school afrobeats with Burna Boy blasting from the speakers inside the parlour.

As we enter, Aunty Tiwa is singing at the top of her lungs

in the style of a gospel choir, while hand-stitching gems onto a dress. Mum playfully pats Aunty Tiwa on the back, scaring her and causing the girls to snicker. Aunty Tiwa clutches her chest then accidentally pricks it with the needle she's holding.

'Adélé, you people need to start announcing yourselves,' she says when she catches her breath.

'Please, why would we? So we can risk missing this?' Mum says, laughing and elbowing Aunty Zai. Her laughter dies down when she realizes Aunty Zai is straight-faced, which makes the rest of the girls laugh. 'Ahem, the girls have come early.' She signals to them as they stand next to Dérin.

Aunty Tiwa puts down the clothes she's holding and makes her way over to them.

'Is Ireti coming?' she asks.

'No, she has a business meeting, so she won't be able to make it,' Dérin says. I notice her disappointment as she looks at the floor.

Aunty Tiwa ushers us into the dressing rooms to try on our outfits. Amaka and I went for a similar hourglass silhouette style with either an embroidered bodice or embroidered skirt. While the queen of Sheba, Seni, has decided she wants to try upstaging the bride. I swear she's got more jewels on her one outfit than Dérin has on all three of hers combined. *Plus*, extra embroidery on her gèlè. She's just lucky that Dérin encouraged us all to go crazy with our designs because, if I were the bride, I would've torn her clothes in two for the audacity.

Since Dérin's dresses have already been adjusted, she's

decided to give us a few sneak peeks of her traditional outfits. She comes out looking regal in coral and revels in the compliments she receives from us all. Dérin blushes then comes to sit down as Mum, Aunty Tiwa and Aunty Zai go and inspect the other bridesmaids' dresses.

Dérin waits for them to be out of earshot before redirecting the conversation. 'I have something to tell you all. It's about Kayode.' My ears prick up like meerkats peeking out of a hole. I have a feeling that I know what she's about to disclose, but I've been itching for the full details since her and Uncle's talk this morning. I was almost going to give in and ask her myself.

'Ah, do we need to beat him up already?' Amaka says, getting ready to stand up but Dérin grabs her hands to pull her back down.

'No, ah, ah. You know he would never do anything that would resort to a straight beating,' she says, and Amaka makes an upside-down smile in agreement. 'It's something Daddy told me this morning, about his family.'

I'm listening attentively when I see Seni, who's sitting opposite me, quirk an eyebrow at me. I break the eye contact quickly.

'You know how we planned to split the costs between both families because it was important to all of us,' she starts, 'and it's a ridiculous amount of money to expect one family to pay. No matter how well off. Well, when they spoke about the bride price yesterday, Kayode's parents said they don't want to pay for anything. According to Daddy, they said it's traditional for the bride's family to pay, so they shouldn't have to.'

Would you look at that, the cup on the wall trick works every time.

An accidental, exaggerated 'Oh, no *way*' slips out of me and everyone turns in my direction. 'Sorry,' I whisper. Seni's gaze has not left my face.

'Do you think Kayode knows about this?' Amaka asks.

Dérin shakes her head. 'Kayode wasn't there when they discussed it, we were still outside celebrating. It's just weird because they seemed to be okay with paying in the beginning, so I have no idea what's changed. Or maybe they were faking it because Kayode asked them to split the costs in front of me. You know Yoruba people love to save face. I don't even want to bring it up with Kayode in case he starts something with his parents over the matter.'

'Do they seem snobby? Or like traditionalists?' Seni asks, finally taking her gaze off me. Dérin shakes her head and then pauses as if she's unsure.

'Maybe Aunty Ireti?' says Dérin. 'She's so sweet but you can tell she's more reserved than Uncle Fola who was a party boy when he was younger. When Kayode and I were dating in my first few months back from uni, she visited a lot and made a care package for me at their house if I ever stayed over. She treats me like the daughter she wanted . . . and now has. It's just weird because when we got engaged, they talked about how they were so excited to splurge on the wedding because Kayode is their only child, like I am to my parents, so they wanted to do it *big*. But if they've changed their minds it feels icky because it means all this time that Daddy has been putting down payments on everything, expecting to be paid back, they've just been, I don't know, quiet? Expecting him to uphold tradition? I genuinely have no clue. I told you guys about them wanting Kayode and me to sign a prenup right?'

The girls nod while I'm left in the dark. A prenup did not come up in the conversation I overheard earlier. It's the sensible thing to do considering they're both from affluent families who will need to protect their assets, but it's surprising.

Maybe Kayode and Dérin are protecting themselves and their families' fortunes just in case the relationship won't last? Twenty-two is young to be getting married, that's a recurring comment in all the blog posts. Naija Gossip Lounge, in particular, is eager to find out the 'real reason' they're getting married. As if love isn't enough.

Dérin twists her mouth like she's not sure if she should say her next words. 'Daddy thinks I should sign it after the disagreement yesterday. He also thinks they're not paying because Uncle Fola is turning fifty this year and wants to save all his money for that,' she half mumbles. 'But you didn't hear that from me.'

That's new information too. I wonder if Uncle Tayo thinks they're the type to do that, be selfish like that. I haven't seen that they are, but I've only met them once, at the introduction. Have they shown Uncle Tayo any indication they would hide their money? Splurge it on themselves rather than Kayode? I wonder what their relationship with Kayode is like, if they're as close as Dérin is to her parents?

'That's dumb, because Kayode is their only son,' says Amaka. 'Why would they not want to spend money on him? Maybe, as things were being paid for, they realized they couldn't afford both weddings so they're hiding behind tradition? Or maybe they saw how big the introduction was and decided their funds couldn't match,' Amaka suggests, ending with a laugh. 'I thought introductions were supposed to be small, Rin. Why was I getting FOMO through Instagram?'

Dérin laughs too and goes into more details about the introduction, while I zone out of the conversation. I know there's more to the story, and it's not just my nosiness making me think that; something about Dad's argument with Uncle Yinka was weird.

My attention is snapped back to the present when Amaka nudges me. 'You're coming with us too. We're going clubbing tonight.' She turns back to Dérin. 'Call Kayode, tell him to bring his finest groomsmen. Wait, you're eighteen, right?' she finishes, looking at me.

'*Freshly,*' I deadpan. Then we hear people starting to pour into the shop.

'Guess we don't need to call him, he's arrived just in time,' Amaka says, alerting us. Kayode, a few of his *very handsome* groomsmen and Babs are here. Kayode hands a bouquet of white roses to Dérin, then hugs her, his hands going to the small of her back. Then he makes his way along the rest of the party, hugging each of us. Everyone embraces but I notice from the corner of my eye that when Seni and Kayode hug, she stiffens and his jaw clenches ever so slightly. My eyebrows quirk up involuntarily, and I peek around the shoulder of the groomsman I'm holding to get a better look.

'You're not supposed to see me in my dress. It's bad luck,' Dérin says as Kayode basically runs back over to her. She playfully shoves him.

'It's only bad luck if it's the white wedding dress,' he says and kisses her neck. She squeals and it's cute or whatever, but I'm more intrigued by the interaction between him and Seni. They looked like they both wanted to be anywhere but here, together.

Dérin takes Kayode and the other groomsmen over to where all the aunties are so they can do their own fitting for their traditional wear. As the men start to exit the room, their chatter leaves with them and I hear Amaka say to Seni in a harsh but hushed tone, 'If you can't handle it then why did you come? Did you expect to not see him at all? Because if you didn't, I'd love to live in that empty space up there, that's supposed to be a brain.'

My face pales from second-hand embarrassment, but it's so hard not to smile. I love being in the right place at the right time, especially when it answers questions I have . . . In this case, do Seni and Kayode have a history?

'That face is always a bad sign,' Babs says, blocking my way. I look up at him in annoyance.

'*My face?* How dare you?' I say with fake upset, then lower my voice. 'Anyways, did you just hear Seni and Amaka's conversation? Intense, right?'

'Yeah, it was, and it's none of your business.'

'How can it not be my business when they didn't really bother to keep it a secret?'

'Lara, your love for gist is something you need to give up to God.' Babs looks at me like I need an intervention.

'God knows my heart. Now, do you have any clue what they're talking about? Because earlier when Seni was hugging Ka—' I don't finish my sentence before Babs gives me the most delicious information.

'They're probably talking about Kayode.'

I pretend to look confused as if I'm not already two steps ahead. 'Why would they be talking about Kayo—'

'Ladies, ladies!' a voice booms, turning all our heads towards a young handsome guy gripping a bottle of Clase Azul, white teeth blinding the entire parlour. His muscly arms and toned body are highlighted by his black True Religion T-shirt and dark-blue jeans. He has low-cut sponge twists and a skin fade.

'Joseph?' Amaka says, her tone confused.

'Joseph?' I say, also confused but speaking more quietly because the only Joseph I know, that we *all know*, does not look like that.

'How did you get here? *Why* are you here and who brings Clase Azul to a fitting?' Amaka continues and my eyes dart back and forth as I watch the interaction. Babs and I start to edge closer. He may not be as nosy as me, but he enjoys the drama just as much.

'Amaka, what kind of questions are these? We ain't seen each other in ages! Give me a hug, give me a hug,' Joseph says pulling Amaka in, his voice extremely deep but smooth. He doesn't sound the slightest bit offended by Amaka's interrogation, almost like he was expecting it. 'You know you're in *my* aunt's parlour, right?' He pauses for it to sink in then says, 'the Clase Azul is to liven the lot. I'm sure you've seen the bozos Kayo has chosen as groomsmen. Anyways, it's good to see you too. What did I miss?'

Seni doesn't look as shocked to see him as the rest of us. 'If it isn't the devil incarnate himself.' Her voice drips with amusement as she eyes him up and down then breaks into a smirk. I'm officially confused by this entire interaction. 'How are you here?'

'Kayo didn't tell you? I'm his favourite groomsman. Chosen by Aunty Zai and Aunty Tiwa themselves. Landed yesterday, just in time to,' he sniffs the air, 'stir some shit up.' He gives a wicked grin.

A laugh comes from the back of the room then is followed by the faint sound of something smashing on the floor. Joseph's gaze leaves ours and then lands on the person's. He smiles, wide and sincere. Our group's heads turn to see Dérin standing there, the white roses on the floor next to her along with a shattered vase.

'You guys are supposed to be getting married, and you still can't tell him that you hate white roses, huh?' Joseph says, and I almost choke. Talk about applying the pressure! He walks towards Dérin and gives her a hug. He holds her tight, but she doesn't hug him back, going almost limp out of shock.

'W-what are you doing here?' Dérin says, like the air has been knocked out of her. Her eyes grow wide as they look at Joseph. 'I told you to come in two weeks! Not today! How did you even know where we were?' She laughs nervously.

'Why would I not be here for the wedding festivities? I landed last night – unfortunately after the introduction – so that I wouldn't miss a *thing*.' Joseph lets go of Dérin and then eyeballs the rest of us. 'Why does everyone look like they've seen a ghost?' he says, then turns to Amaka. 'Boo,' he whispers and she squeaks.

He starts towards the dressing rooms and then stops. 'Lara? I ain't seen you in time! You look different.' I frown. Who *is* this guy? He puts his hand out for me to shake and I nod, not knowing what else to do, 'Joseph, or apparently the devil incarnate.' He smiles quickly then approaches Seni and says to her, 'Walk with me.' She's reluctant at first then does as he says.

I whisper, 'Wait, no, is that Joseph as in, Joseph, Joseph? As in—'

'Dérin's ex, Joseph.' Amaka gulps.

After initially being forced out to the club, truthfully a night of dancing and drinking was just what we needed. Ending it with a suya vendor, five minutes away from the club, was exactly what our imminent hangovers crave. I've been picking at Kayode and Dérin's meat for the past two minutes, patiently waiting for mine to finish cooking on the barbecue.

We're all standing around, discussing the night's events, laughing and cracking jokes. The typical after motive debrief that I can't wait to do more of once I start university. Somehow, despite the awkwardness created by Joseph earlier, everyone seems to have warmed up to his presence. The last time I saw Joseph he was a scrawny teenager, attached to Dérin's hip and barely a passing thought to anyone. I'd completely forgotten how close Aunty Zai and his mum were before she died and Aunty Tiwa took him in.

Now, Joseph is this big presence. He's grown and has this annoying type of charm that makes him easy to listen to. You find yourself mad at what he's saying and then two seconds later he's already fixed it with the right words.

'You want onion?' the vendor asks and I nod as he stacks it up for me on folded newspaper, dropping a toothpick next to it. Babs makes his way over to me with Amaka. His toothpick appears out of nowhere as he grabs some of my food.

I elbow him away, picking at the meat and watching the scene around me, until I suddenly remember Amaka's conversation with Seni a few hours ago. 'Were you okay earlier? I overheard you and Seni arguing about something in the parlour.' I try to sound innocent, though I don't really care about the witch's feelings.

Amaka kisses her teeth. 'Ugh, don't mind her. I'll tell you

66

properly later. I don't want to ruin a good night thinking about her attitude.'

Babs chimes in, 'What did Kayode say when he saw her? I can't lie, even I was confused that she was a bridesmaid.'

My eyes narrow as Amaka is about to speak, but I interrupt needing clarification first. 'Babàníyì, have you actively been keeping information from me? What does that mean?' I ask with a frown.

'Seni was Kayode's girlfriend . . . before Dérin.'

A COLLEGE DEGREE IS JUST AN ACCESSORY FOR RICH KIDS, RIGHT?

Well, it looks like festivities for Dérin Oyinlola's wedding are about to kick off. Dérin's best friends, Seni Akhalu-Sanusi, pictured in the pastel pink Juicy Couture tracksuit (just because Juicy is back in, doesn't mean we have to wear it), and Amaka Ibuaka, pictured in the sage sundress. My lack of commentary on the latter should be enough to show my opinion on that outfit.

Dérin took her bridesmaids and Kayode's groomsmen for a night out on the town, several cameras spotting them afterwards gisting at a local suya vendor.

So nice of the rich to act like they're relatable.

What intrigued me more, was Joseph Lawal's presence. Tech whiz and son of late Lagos philanthropist Moníló̩lá Lawal and multi-billion real estate investor Kehinde Lawal.

There are whispers that Joseph and Dérin used to date, so one wonders how she went from dashingly handsome Joseph to, well, Kayode. Maybe money made the change easier to bear.

And what must one think, having your ex celebrate

68

your intended nuptials with your future husband. Is Dérin having her cake and eating it too?

You know gossip doesn't sleep, and neither do I.

xoxo

CHAPTER SEVEN

'Everything is so *loud*,' Amaka says as she walks into Dérin's room wearing chunky brown sunglasses. 'I never knew how deafening doors could be until this morning, when everybody, *everybody*, slammed one.' She collapses onto Dérin's bed, her pistachio-green satin nightdress and matching robe flailing everywhere.

I too, found everything extremely loud this morning which is how I ended up crawling to Dérin's room. Of course, perfect as ever, she woke up looking graceful, as if she didn't even have a sip of alcohol last night.

Dérin's room is the cosiest in the house, even nicer than mine, because it doesn't follow the same hollow black-and-white theme Aunty Zai has for the rest of the house. It's splashed with greens, blues and pinks. Her bed is huge too, a Californian king bed, so we can sleep on it together and never feel like we're cramped. Even though she has LED lights around the room, she mostly illuminates it with the lightbulbs from her vanity. It's my favourite place to spend time because she has a comfy director's chair that makes me feel like I'm on a movie set. It's also where she films her 'get ready with me' videos that have made her famous.

'Kayode, I'll call you back,' she whispers lightly into the phone. I roll my eyes. She didn't end her call when I walked in here twenty minutes ago, so I had to try and sleep through every lovesick giggle.

'Did Kayode say anything about Seni?' Amaka asks, propping herself up on the bed. My ears perk up. I really need to see someone about my addiction to gossip, but when a topic is as juicy as this, you can't blame me for being so invested.

'He didn't mention anything to me. Why, did something happen?'

'If it did, I was too drunk to tell,' Amaka says, lying through her teeth.

I frown at Amaka but quickly change my expression to one I hope looks perfectly casual. Evidently not perfect enough, though, as Dérin squints at me then shouts, 'You know something!'

How could she tell? Is my poker face that bad?

'You've been in my bed for the past twenty minutes, laying like a dead fish and you had information?' Dérin says, shoving me hard. My face gets swallowed by the thousands of pillows.

'I don't think it's even anything.' My voice is muffled until

I lift myself out of the cushion fortress. 'I saw, or heard, *Amaka* and Seni arguing about her not wanting to see Kayode. Seni didn't confirm or deny but her face said it all,' I huff, as I finally prop myself back up, then shove Dérin into the pillows on her side. 'You, yourself, why didn't you tell me they used to date? And you, Amaka, you're here lying.' I mimic her voice, '"I was too drunk to tell." My *back foot*.'

'Amaka!' Dérin yells, pulling herself up from the pillows. 'You can *lie*. Just sitting here withholding information.'

Dérin leaps up from her bed and grabs a bundle of leaves held together with twine, and a lighter. When she sparks it, smoke emits and it smells woody. 'They dated before I knew Kayode properly, some time after freshers' in first year and Seni never brought him around us. She would always go and see him, she hardly spoke about him. But our uni had a lot of Nigerian students, so the name Kayode didn't even register with me. I mean, there was talk of many Kayodes amongst the girls, but I only met *my* Kayode at the end of first year when I ran for president of the Nigerian Society, and at that point he and Seni had 'broken up'. Kayo and I started dating at the beginning of second year, and he didn't even know I knew Seni. Not until he took me to the gala at the beginning of third year. That night was *so* awkward, but my and Seni's friendship wasn't gonna end over some guy she'd briefly dated. Kayo doesn't think it's a big deal. I mean you know first year, *especially* freshers', doesn't count. Plus, it ended abruptly.'

'Ugh, not sage! See this is why I didn't tell you. You

72

overreact. But of course he doesn't think it's a big deal. He's a guy.'

Dérin starts waving the sage around the room, and her voice turns panicky. 'When we did get together and everyone found out who was who, it was never a problem at uni because Kayode was always at his medical placement studying or working. *I* barely saw him in third year. And after uni it wasn't a problem because Seni and Kayode were never in the same room unless they needed to be. Seni was *fine*. Shit only started being weird after Kayode proposed. Maybe she didn't think we'd actually stay together. I was . . . on and off with Joseph before I took Kayode seriously.'

'The question is, do we bring it up now, or address it when it becomes a problem?' Amaka asks. 'Because you know it'll be annoying having to force you all to play nice over the next few weeks.'

'Not when, *if*. Positive vibes only. Ẹ jọ́ọ́,' Dérin pleads, waving the sage faster.

'That's not your only problem. Have you figured out who's sending you those notes? You haven't said anything since the last time you told me about them and I know you're keeping things secret, Rin'

I lift my head from my lap. 'What notes?' I ask. Dérin gives Amaka an annoyed look.

'I—' she starts, but there's a brief knock on the door and then it opens. We see Seni standing there, looking like a child come to tell their parent that they've thrown up. Her face is slack. She has a pink nightdress on, with a matching robe

73

that has feathers all over plus a matching sleep mask, and her hair is in rollers. I wonder how she had time to do that considering we came home in the early morning.

'Why is everything so loud?' Seni says, making her way over to the bed. It's loud because Mum and Aunty Zai are playing music in the kitchen while cooking. They also went out last night but, clearly they didn't party as hard if they felt like they could continue this morning. 'Why are you burning sage?' she asks.

Dérin immediately changes the topic. 'Did everyone have fun last night with their respective groomsmen?' she squeals. 'Amaka, you seemed to be having a lot of fun with David.' Amaka's eyes roll.

'All I did was help a white man find his rhythm.' She lies down then immediately gets back up when she remembers something. 'Also! Did you guys see the Naija Gossip Lounge post? That candid made us look so good, I'm about to make that my WhatsApp DP.' Amaka smiles mischievously. 'Catty, though. Personally, I wouldn't have that tracksuit comment if I was you, Seni.' Amaka teases Seni, as if Naija Gossip Lounge didn't insult her too. Seni threatens to throw a pillow at her when there's another knock on the door.

I pull myself out of the thick sheets. Temi, the houseboy, comes in with a bouquet of light pink roses. The girls all gush over it, while I'm fixated on how bright the light coming through the doorway is. Temi puts the bouquet on Dérin's lap. I squint at his face, spotting his tense jaw as he heads back out of the room.

'What does the card say?' Seni enquires. Dérin looks for it, and as she reads it her face pales. 'What? Why is your face like that?' Seni asks.

Dérin's breath hitches. 'It's from Joseph. It says: *Clearly I'm the only one who knows what flowers you actually like. Call me when you're free. J.*'

The room goes silent as we all take in the cheekiness of the message.

'It's time to talk about the elephant in the room,' Seni says and Dérin sighs.

'You guys didn't end on the best of terms. What is he doing here? Why did Aunty Zai make him a groomsman?' Amaka fires off questions.

'He's Aunty Tiwa's nephew! Our mums were best friends and we've known him for years. My parents are so attached to him,' Dérin snaps. 'How was I not supposed to invite him?'

'By *not* inviting him,' Seni says firmly. 'How did he worm his way into being a groomsman?'

'I'm supposed to tell my mum no?'

'*Yes*, Dérin. You say you already have a set list of people and you don't want to have Joseph in the wedding party. You people-please way too much,' Amaka says.

'They're the ones paying for the wedding. Besides, I didn't even know until it was too late, that's why I asked him to come in two weeks. Not now. If he has to be a groomsman, I don't want him here for pre-celebrations. I want him to come for the wedding, play his role, and leave. My soul threatened to leap out of my body when I saw him at the parlour.

75

I thought he'd maybe be silent out of respect for what me and Kayode have, but now I know he has no respect,' Dérin says and Seni clears her throat, looking at her with an eyebrow quirked. Dérin's head tilts in confusion. She doesn't say anything for a second, then waves the sage around the room more frantically than ever. 'I feel like I need more sage or something.'

'Seriously, though, with a card like that, how is this wedding going to go smoothly?' Amaka asks and Dérin shoots daggers at her.

'The wedding will go down smoothly, don't speak that into existence. I'll fix it.'

The music stops downstairs and Mum shouts, 'Food is ready, o. Or I should come and serve you upstairs?' She's so dramatic it pains me. We all clamber out of bed and the others head downstairs like zombies while I stay behind to use Dérin's bathroom.

I pee, holding my head in my palms as I realize a headache is forming, and fast. After washing my hands, I search for paracetamol in Dérin's bathroom cabinet. Grabbing the last two tablets, I throw the sachet into her nearly empty bin and, as I do, two torn up pieces of paper catch my eye. I see flecks of what looks like printed words. I crouch down to pick the pieces up, holding them together at the tear. I gasp as I read what's in front of me.

YOU'VE IGNORED ME FOR TOO LONG.
NOW I'M GOING TO DO THINGS MY WAY.

I quickly shove the pieces of paper into my pocket, check myself in the mirror one last time and leave Dérin's bathroom.

The heat isn't helping the headache I've been nursing all morning. Dérin, Seni and Amaka didn't warn me how bad my first hangover would be. They've all managed to recover and go food shopping with Aunty Zai, Uncle Tayo, Mum, Dad and Babs for the summer party. I'm the only one in the house and to be honest, I could do with the alone time. I've spent most of my day resting with an ice pack on my forehead; and in the few hours I'm awake, I'm either listening to a new podcast about the psychology of what makes a criminal a criminal or thinking about Dérin's note.

My head has hardly drifted from it all day. This note is threatening, and ominous . . . and *weird*. It clearly isn't the first note because it states that Dérin has been ignoring them. Whoever 'them' is. Amaka seemed concerned when she mentioned the notes this morning, and now I can see why. This has been going on for a while. But the question is, exactly how long? Dérin is the type to hold things in, so she wouldn't have told Amaka the first time she received a note. And she wouldn't have told her parents because they would've had someone watching her door twenty-four-seven by now. They wouldn't take this kind of thing lightly. But she *did* tell Amaka. Which means the writer must have been persistent and threatening enough for her to finally say something. I look at the note again.

NOW I'M GOING TO DO THINGS MY WAY.

What does that even mean? And who could it be from?

I think of people we know. All the true crime podcasts, documentaries and books I devour always say the same thing: suspects are usually someone close to the victim. And if this person is threatening to ruin the wedding, then it's someone with a reason as to why they don't want it to go ahead.

The first person that comes to mind is Joseph. He's the main red flag because he doesn't strike me as someone who takes no for an answer, so threatening to do things *his way* seems very him. I mean he already is, by showing up at Aunty Tiwa's parlour uninvited and inserting himself into the celebrations two weeks earlier than he was supposed to. Not to mention shamelessly sending Dérin flowers and criticizing Kayode's gifts to her any chance he gets. The white roses made Kayode look bad in front of her friends. Surely it's only a matter of time before he says something worse in front of the wrong group. If he's brazen enough, maybe even in front of her parents or in-laws?

I don't know when Dérin received this note. What if it showed up just after Joseph arrived in Lagos? Is he threatening to go grander? Is he going to progress from sending gifts to public confessions of love, or worse?

And for what? To win Dérin back? Or, in his own words, 'stir some shit up'?

Seni? Maybe. She hasn't actually shown her possible

distaste for the wedding, but she can't be happy about it. If Seni has been threatening Dérin anonymously, it would make sense for her to come back to Lagos, not for the wedding, but to 'do things' her way. Maybe she's hidden her unhappiness about Kayode and Dérin's relationship for the past three years? She's been acting pretty normal since she arrived. Slightly off since seeing Kayode, but that makes sense, as he is her ex. I wonder if yesterday was the first time Seni has openly shown her feelings about the whole situation. I wonder if they've all even seen each other since they left uni? Or did the distance – Dérin back in Lagos, Kayode at medical school and Seni at uni doing her master's – make it easier to bear? Even though she's technically had *three* years to come to terms with everything, some people do suppress painful facts, and maybe Seni is one of them? I wonder if it's become real now that she's flown three thousand miles to Nigeria for the wedding and is forced to confront the truth? If she's behind the notes, I wonder if she's reached her breaking point and this is the result?

Or, though this is doubtful, there's the possibility that she's a better person than me and is still happy to be a bridesmaid for Dérin, despite her and Kayode's history. Maybe she's putting their friendship before him and sucking it up. I wouldn't want to be in her position. I wouldn't be happy if my best friend asked me to be a bridesmaid at her wedding to my ex, no matter how close we are. If she was a normal human being, I'd feel sorry for her. But she's a witch so I can't give her grace or put all this past her.

No one else comes to mind as I lie in bed and glance over at the whiteboard on my wall. Last time I was here, I had just finished my GCSEs and wanted to get a head start on A-level preparation, so I asked Uncle Tayo to install a study board in my room. He went the extra mile and installed a massive whiteboard which could double up as a screen, with a projector. Since I've been here, I've only used it to watch TV, but now I can finally put it to good true-crime use. I open the desk drawer to grab some of the stationery left over from the last time I was here, and tape the two pieces of the note together, then stick it on the board. In a far corner, I write down the initials of my two suspects – only their initials, to maintain anonymity, just in case anyone comes into in my room – then I write down what makes them suspects. I'm going to solve the mystery of who has been writing these notes to Dérin, and more importantly, why.

I guess this is the start of my investigation board.

CHAPTER EIGHT

'Lara!' Mum shouts my name from the bottom of the stairs, as I lie in bed listening to my podcast while researching *notes as an intimidation method* on my laptop.

I can hear everyone lugging shopping bags into the foyer and I groan. One of the perks of not going to the supermarket was that I wouldn't have to help carry the shopping. Mum calls me a second time, and I heave myself out of bed. It's dark outside my window. Gosh, how long were they shopping? And how long have I been in my own little true-crime research bubble? I open my door just as Mum and Dad make it to the top of the stairs. They go into their bedroom and I follow close behind.

'Your aunty wants to talk to you,' Mum says, brandishing the phone.

I resist the urge to glare at her. *Which one?* I mouth.

She doesn't answer and instead shoves the phone at me. 'H-hello?' I say, taking it.

An annoyingly familiar voice bellows down the phone. 'Our lawyer-to-be! How are you, my dear?' Once again I resist the urge to glare at Mum. Aunty Bimbola has been checking up on me every two weeks since Mum told her I signed up for law school. She's a family lawyer, in the same sector that Dad wants me to go into. Yet he refuses to acknowledge that Aunty Bimbola is always stressed out, has a terrible work-life balance and is constantly emotional from work seeping into her home life and marriage. But it's okay because she works for one of the top law firms in the country.

'Hi, Aunty,' I say wearily, then I go through the standard answers I always give when forced on a call. 'I'm fine, thank you. They're fine too. School is good, I'm surviving. No, results aren't out yet. Yes, I am excited to start soon. Amen. Amen. Amen. Thank you, Aunty. Love you too. Thank you again. Byeee. Bye, bye, bye.' Then I hand back the phone to Mum, trying to hide my annoyance.

Mum shouts for Babs, before deciding to leave the room to go and find him. But it's *me* that had to come to her.

'Daddy,' I say. He's scrolling on his phone, reading glasses on, most likely catching up with the news. I take a deep breath and say, 'About family law . . . What if— what if I didn't want to go into it at all?'

He looks up at me and is still.

It feels like he's been staring at me for hours when he says, 'I know what the issue is', and I feel like my throat is closing up. 'You want to go into criminal law, like in those books and shows you like.' I open my mouth to clarify that

I don't want to do Law *at all* but he continues, 'Lara, I've told you; those jobs are not easy. Look at Uncle Damola, he had to reduce his hours because it was starting to get to him. The TV glamorizes all that. You will be dealing with a lot. And then when it comes down to you defending someone guilty or persecuting someone innocent, will you be able to handle that? Stick to family, corporate or even entertainment if you really want something light. You won't enjoy criminal. I know you better than you know yourself.' He finishes and I'm left speechless. It takes me a few seconds to find my voice before I can reply.

'I don't think that's true, because the point I'm trying to make is, I won't enjoy Law . . . at all.' It's the first time I've said these words out loud to him.

His face hardens and I'm scared of what he will say next. 'What do you mean by that? Your applications are already in. You can't change them now.'

I can feel myself getting emotional and I have no idea why. 'The thing is, I can. On results day. It's called clearing, if things don't work out but they obviously wi—'

'Lara, change it to what? Why would you want to change a plan you have worked so hard for? You're almost at the end and now you're thinking of using clearing for what, exactly? You got three unconditional offers, and you turned them down for two conditionals. Was that your plan all along? To change? Under the disguise that they are better universities?'

'No, I—' My cheeks go hot because he's right, but I didn't expect him to get there so fast.

Dad starts to shout. 'Why are you fighting success? You have everything set up for you, people to help you, Aunty Bimbo being one of them.'

I'm fighting back tears. 'Why do you think if I changed careers, I wouldn't be successful? I'm still me, I'm sti—'

There's a knock on the door as it slowly swings open, followed by Dérin's voice saying, 'Lara?' Dad's eyes settle on her. I turn my head, hoping I've composed my expression. I nod to Dérin and her eyes lock onto mine. 'Can I speak to Lara for a minute, Uncle?' she says, grabbing my hand and pulling me towards the door. Once we're in the hallway, she rubs my forearm. 'What just happened? I could hear raised voices.'

'I'm fine. Don't worry,' I say, sniffling. 'How was shopping? Did you get everything you needed?' I don't know why I'm so emotional about the whole thing, but just the look on Dad's face was enough to make me cry.

'We did.' Dérin watches me, worry etched on her face. She grabs my hand and takes me downstairs to the kitchen. The house is so quiet. Everybody else is in their rooms, fatigue finally taking over. Dérin stares at me again and there's so much sympathy in her eyes, it makes me uncomfortable. She must notice because she attempts to smile and says, 'Have you eaten? Do you want indomie?'

I look at her like a puppy that's just been scolded. Dérin moves fast and asks, 'Is beef okay?' as she takes the pre-cooked meat out of the microwave and I nod rapidly. When I try to help her out by grabbing a small scotch bonnet, a knife and a chopping board she says, 'It's okay, Lara, I offered.'

I brush her off. 'No, I want to,' I reply as I dice the chilli into fine pieces. At home I use hot pepper powder, but something about using fresh chillis when Dérin makes indomie tastes ten times better.

The kettle clicks and Dérin pours the water into the pot plus three packets of noodles: one and a half for her, and one and a half for me. One is never enough, but two is always too much. It's a weird type of science. As the noodles boil, she takes a seat next to me and nudges my arm.

'What were you and Uncle talking about earlier?' I figure there's no better person to discuss this with than her.

'Uni.' She nods as if that explains everything.

'I can tell you've been stressed about it. Every time I called, you were studying. I think you'll be a great lawyer, Lara. There's nothing to worry about,' she says as she grabs the chopping board from me and puts the chilli and the beef into a pan. The air soon fills with a mouth-watering peppery smell. She pours the beef flavour sachets, plus a few other seasonings, into the pan, then drains the noodles, leaving a little water in the pot to stir-fry them with.

'I don't want to be a lawyer,' I confess. 'I want to study Criminology and Forensics. I haven't fully figured it out, but I want to help solve mysteries. Not necessarily for the police, maybe by myself as a private investigator or a criminal profiler. I think I could be really good at it if I was given the chance.'

Dérin doesn't say anything while she finishes cooking,

leaving me alone with my thoughts. Have I said something stupid? Maybe she agrees with Dad.

It's hard to explain that I can't see myself living the life he's projected onto me since I can remember. The past three academic years I have studied so hard, nearly breaking myself to get offers from the best law schools in the UK. Doing extracurricular activities that will make me desirable and improve my university personal statement. Sacrificing parties and hanging out with my friends to spend time studying because I was so worried about my future.

Exams came and went, and I don't doubt for a second that I have achieved top grades, but all that work made me realize: I've had enough. I've been through too much, done too much, for a dream that is Dad's, not mine. This summer hanging out with my friends, and now here in Nigeria with my brother, Dérin and her friends, actually enjoying myself, I realize I've missed out on so much. I don't want to dedicate my life to something I don't care about, no matter how disappointed Dad will be.

Dérin separates the noodles, putting half in a bowl and leaving the other half in the pot. Then she drops a fork in front of me along with the pot of noodles. I wonder if that's what makes Dérin's indomie taste so good: eating it straight from the dish she cooked in.

'Are you mad at me too?' I ask. 'You're not eating out of the pot with me.'

'I can't eat out of the pot, it'll rain on my wedding day.' I roll my eyes at her superstitions. 'Will the unis let you change courses or will you have to take a gap year?'

'The two that have accepted me let you change. I made sure of that before I applied.' I smile sheepishly, twirling my fork around the noodles and shoving them in my mouth.

'Then do it. Change courses. Don't let Uncle and Aunty decide your future for you. You'll end up regretting it when you're stuck doing something you hate four years down the line. I wouldn't worry too much, Lara. It was probably just the shock of him hearing it. You know how they've been bragging about you since your GCSEs.'

'What? Please. All they ever do is brag about *you*.' I put on a mock-proud voice. 'Look at Dérin and how much she's accomplished, she does so well, she's achieved so much. Oh, Dérin has landed an internship with J.P. Morgan. She's going to be earning so much by the time she graduates. You know Dérin already had years of work experience by the time she was eighteen; why don't you intern with Aunty Bimbo in the summer?'

Dérin stares at me, chews slowly, then gets up and collects her phone from the counter before sitting back down. She opens WhatsApp and brings up the messages between her and Dad, scrolling through them for me to read, then she does the same with her conversations with Mum. There are pictures of me in my room studying: one with me fast asleep with my books all around me, and another few with me in the zone not even noticing my photo being taken.

'Firstly, please do not ever put me on a pedestal. I am so far from perfect,' she says and I scoff. She gives me a stern look to show she's not joking, then hands me her phone. 'Under this picture your mum said: *Look at my Lara. She works so hard; she's barely eaten today. Warn her for me.* Then this one from your dad: *My princess, fast asleep from running her brain all day.*'

My eyes well up with tears.

'They've been sending me these updates since you started sixth form. You know how Nigerian parents are with their image, it will kill them one day. *Lawyer* looks better on paper than *Private Investigator* or *Criminal Profiler*. But trust me, Lara, sit them down and give them time to really process it. I think you'll be shocked at how supportive they are,' she says, taking another forkful of noodles from her bowl. 'Well, your mum . . . okay, she may need some time. She's been preparing her bragging rights speech since you guys were young.' She giggles which makes me laugh.

'I think we'll have to take her to the hospital when she finds out Babs doesn't want to be a surgeon.'

'If I haven't told you lately, I'm really proud of you, Lara. So, so proud of you.' She brings me in for a hug, and this time I really do start crying. 'I'd trust you to solve any case,' she whispers in my ear. I smile widely into her hair.

We break apart and continue eating, her last sentence still in my mind. 'Dérin, why didn't you tell me about the notes?' I ask. She pauses, fork in mid-air.

'Did you latch onto that thing Amaka said in the bedroom?' Her jaw tenses. 'It doesn't matter, they're nothing anyways.'

'Dérin, they're not nothing. I found a note in your bin.

The person is threatening you. How long has this been going on for?'

She scans my face, as if she's wondering if she should tell me anything or avoid talking about it, until she says, 'The notes? Three months. The messages, six months.'

'*Messages? Six months?* Someone's been threatening you since the beginning of the year and you haven't said a word to anybody apart from Amaka? What the hell? Do you not think these threats could be real?'

'I've had six months of hurtful insults and fake stories ever since our engagement photo went crazy all over Instagram in January. A lot of the new followers were incredibly kind, while others are so . . . People on the internet are really weird. It's mainly one Instagram account that's doing the most. I've blocked them multiple times, but they keep coming back. It's a lot of nonsense, like, I'm not pretty enough for Kayode. I'm not good enough. There are better people for him. That we're too young to get married. Marrying Kayode will ruin me because, apparently, they can't decide who's the victim. That Kayode is in other girls' DMs and they have the evidence to prove it, but when I ask for the proof it's crickets. I know it's all false anyways, because unless Kayode has a burner account, I have all his passwords. I just think that stupid Naija Gossip Lounge has made people brave enough to speak to me anyhow. It's the notes that worry me. They started off light, like the Instagram messages, but now they've become more threatening.'

'Why haven't you told anyone? This is not normal.

In fact, it's very abnormal. It's terrifying! I'm surprised you of all people haven't fasted and prayed for two weeks already.'

'I'm scared of the consequences. I'm getting more and more notes. I used to just get them at home, but now they've started to find me when I'm out. I don't know where this person is or what they can actually do, but so far the threats have been empty.

'I'm surprised I've been able to hide it this long, but I don't want to worry Mummy and Daddy, or put them at risk. I don't know what this person is capable of. I'm not sure how they got our address, but I guess I've always lived in this house. Then there are the yearly parties, and sometimes strangers gatecrash. The island is big but the island is small . . .'

'The notes. Do they all say the same thing? To stop the wedding?'

'Basically, yeah.'

'Do you think they could be coming from Joseph?' I ask.

'Joseph? No, he's harmless.'

'He's not entirely harmless. The note I found declared that they were going to *do things their own way*, which Joseph seems to be doing by showing up in places he's not welcome and delivering unwanted gifts. Honestly, if anything happened to you, he is giving the police so much evidence by playing the stalker ex-boyfriend.'

Dérin looks at me like I'm exaggerating. But I read a *lot* of criminal case studies. Globally, sixty-two per cent of all women killed by men die at the hands of their current or former partner. If anything happened to Dérin, Joseph and Kayode would have to be the first suspects.

'I need to see all the notes. You must've kept some others?'

'That was the only one I threw away out of anger, and you have that now. I've kept the rest. Especially the sinister ones.' Dérin gets up and brings out a ceramic jar from underneath the sink. 'The only time my parents enter the kitchen is when you guys are here. They don't cook so they don't snoop around in here, the way Mum does everywhere else. I have more hidden in my room.' She takes the lid off the jar and hands me a few crumpled pieces of paper.

They start off simple, reiterating what Dérin said: that she should leave Kayode, she doesn't deserve him, she would be better off cancelling the wedding because Kayode is already messaging other girls.

Dérin hands me two more notes, and my eyes grow wider as I read. These are much angrier. These also have letters underlined sporadically.

IF YOU WANT TO KEEP LIVING A FAIRY TALE, DROP THE WEDDI**NG PLA**N**NING NOW.**

IS IT S**HAME OR LUCK THAT YOU'RE PRETTY? EITHER WAY I'LL PLAY NICE, FOR NOW. CALL OFF THE WEDDING AND THINGS C**O**ULD BE SO EASY.**

'Woah. I don't even feel like I can finish my food.' I shudder. These are way worse than what I imagined. 'Dérin, These *cannot* be taken lightly! They're threatening to harm you.'

'You're having the same reaction I have whenever I receive one, but then nothing happens. It's like whoever's sending them just gets a kick out of seeing me on edge.'

'Where and when did you get these two?' I ask, trying to keep the panic out of my voice.

'The fairy-tale one was delivered to the house some time at the end of April. Then the one about playing nice was when I was out at dinner with Kayode when he came to visit in the middle of May. While Kayode was in the bathroom, a waiter gave me a drink with a note and said it was from an anonymous customer.'

'This is . . . I mean who would know your routine?'

'Apart from everyone that lives in this house? Kayode. Amaka and Seni too because I call them often, but they don't live in Nigeria so . . . My work friends maybe? Alika, my wedding planner? I don't know, my routine hasn't changed much over the years.'

Seni landed in Lagos with Amaka. That means she would've needed someone else here in Nigeria to follow Dérin around for three months to send the notes. Seems like a lot of effort when she could just speak to Dérin as a friend about the wedding, emotionally manipulate her and plant seeds of doubt in her head about Kayode if she wanted to deter her from marrying him. Joseph said he arrived in

Lagos two days ago, so he would've had to have someone follow Dérin around, too.

'At Aunty Tiwa's parlour Joseph said he landed in Lagos the day before. But that was still earlier than you asked him to be here for the wedding. Is it possible he was lying? Could he have been in Nigeria all along?'

'Joseph visits Nigeria often, but I lost touch with him after our break-ups so I wouldn't know his movements,' Dérin says.

'Break-ups?' I ask.

'Joseph and I have broken up so many times over the years. He never used to take them seriously. But he had no choice after the last time because I had actually met someone else.'

It's a lot of effort to hire someone, in another country, no less, to send these notes, and not be caught. What if this is just an anonymous weirdo? Who's jealous of the life Dérin portrays on her Instagram and believes what all the blogs, especially that bitter Naija Gossip Lounge, write? Jealous enough to make it their hobby to creep Dérin out so that she cancels her wedding?

Alika is the odd one out in Dérin's list of people. We don't know anything about her, apart from the fact that she's the wedding planner, so would need to know the ins and outs of Dérin's schedule in order to do her job. She's new to our lives, which isn't necessarily bad, but, in this case, isn't good either.

But a wedding planner planning to destroy the wedding? That's a bit mad, even for me.

'If someone cared enough to ruin your wedding, it

93

wouldn't be hard for them to learn your daily routine. It's all documented on your Instagram. From now on, if you're going to post your usual videos for socials, or where you are for a brand, or anything, post it when you've left the location. That way they're one step behind you at the very least. I want to help you with this, Dérin. Do you trust me to find out who it is, and if I can, to put a stop to things?'

'I can't exactly say no now, can I?' She smiles unconvincingly. It's like she's only now realizing how much this has been weighing on her.

Noises start up around the house and the kitchen door creaks open. Amaka is standing in the doorway with a smile on her face. 'I smelled indomie.'

CHAPTER NINE

'I need chairs over there,' I shout at everyone, one hand on my hip.

It's the next morning, and Alika is standing beside me. 'Plus, the tables need to be set up at the front and back of the room, and I need decorations, people, *lots* of decorations. Remember it's a bachelor-and-bachelorette party first and an end-of-summer party second. I need everyone with strong lungs on balloon duty, because *someone* had just one job and still managed to fail at it.' I stare at Babs. 'The quicker we do this, the quicker we can go and eat.' I mumble the last part, because as I watch their sullen faces, I realise it is eight a.m. and I'm already barking orders at them. Even I would be annoyed at me.

'Everything Lara just said!' Alika co-signs. I've been watching her every move like a hawk. At present, I don't think she could be behind the notes. Mostly because her skills as a wedding planner are appalling and I don't see how

95

she could stay under the radar as a stalker for so long if this is how she conducts herself, but I'm not writing her off.

Today is the bachelor-and-bachelorette-end-of-summer party. It comes as no surprise that Dérin holds *the* best parties, and her end-of-summer party in particular is legendary. *Everyone* is invited. The daughters and sons of wealthy Nigerians, musicians, actresses, socialites. The party trends on blogs for an entire week, it's that big a deal. And this year, with the wedding fast approaching, Dérin has decided to make it also a joint bachelor-and-bachelorette party.

In Dérin's absence, Alika and I have taken charge of making sure everything is running smoothly. Right now, Dérin is getting her wig installed, then her and Uncle Tayo will buy some last-minute drinks for the party. Dad's gone with them too. Thank God, because I do not have the brain capacity to continue our argument right now.

I gathered everyone downstairs as soon as it was appropriate. No one's eaten or even bathed because of how tired they were from yesterday's shenanigans; us with our late-night indomie and the adults who had another night of partying. Frankly, they are all a little smelly but that is beside the point. We have a mission to fulfil.

'Why are you all still looking at me? Move, move, move!' Everyone finally scatters and picks up the pace. I stand around keeping a watchful eye.

'And what will *you* be doing?' Mum says, from behind, startling me. I hesitate, looking at her, wondering if Dad has told her about our conversation yesterday.

'I will be . . .' I drift off, slowly sliding away from her. 'Uh, hello?' I pull out my phone and answer a fake call, scurrying to the other side of the room. I have a feeling that Mum doesn't know about my discussion – if you can call it that – with Dad, because she is incredibly vocal about the tiniest of things. I would've been shaken out of my sleep by the shouting if she knew.

It's one p.m. now and Dérin will most likely be back around three. The plan is that the make-up artists can work on me and the girls while Dérin gets dressed. Then she'll get her make-up done, and we'll all be ready! It's a win, win, win. No stress on Dérin, no stress for me and no confrontations with my parents.

'Is there anything I can do to help you, Alika?' I ask her.

She turns around with a confused look on her face. 'Uh, me? No, I think I'm okay.'

I nod but don't want to leave yet. Now could be the perfect time to ask her a couple of questions without looking suspicious. 'How long have you been a wedding planner?'

She looks at me like she's hesitant to say. 'Truthfully, this is my second wedding.'

'Woah, really? Dérin must've been impressed by you,' I say with fake excitement in my voice. 'Can I see pictures from your first one?'

Alika whips out her phone. 'Actually, Dérin did—'

The doorbell rings, startling everyone in the room. Mum leaves and moments later, she reappears with Aunty Ireti. 'Dérin!' she cries, spreading out her arms towards me.

She's holding a bag and the bangles on her arms shake as she moves.

'Oh, that's not—' Alika says, but stops with a snicker. 'This is Lara. Dérin is out getting her hair done at Rayo's Palace,' Alika says in Aunty Ireti's direction, her tone surprisingly informal.

Aunty Ireti nods, giving a half-smile, then pauses. 'It is freaky how similar you and Dérin look. Kayode did say you looked *scarily* alike, but I'm seeing it more closely now than at the introduction. I'll have to be careful.'

'It is freaky. We blame our fathers' strong genes. I will take that hug, though, if it's still on offer,' I say and she smiles, embracing me.

'I've come to help with the decorations for tonight since I couldn't make the fitting the other day. Don't worry, me, your mum and Zainab won't stay long at the party. I've heard how embarrassing Zainab can be from Adélé. We'll leave early so that you youngers can have fun.'

I roll my eyes at Mum.

'Adélé, ah, ah,' Aunty Zainab exclaims in Mum's direction. 'Is she my in-law or yours?' Aunty Ireti and I laugh.

'I saw lots of pictures from the fitting, you all looked beautiful.' Aunty Ireti rubs a hand over my fresh braids. 'How are preparations for the wedding? Dérin must be getting more and more excited?'

'She *is*.' Minus, you know, the threats. 'Thank you for coming to help, Aunty Ireti. You didn't have to, but you have perfect timing. We've just started.'

Aunty Ireti smiles at me, then looks at Alika and her smile falters a little. 'Alika.' Alika looks up from her phone. She shifts a little as if she's scared. 'You were supposed to pick up Dérin's dress for tonight.' Aunty Ireti shakes the bag she is holding in front of Alika's face. 'Lolade had to call *me* to come and collect it. How does it look to people if I've hired you and I'm doing your job? You want word to get out and spoil my image, abi?'

Damn.

'Oh my God. It slipped my mind, I'm so sorry,' Alika says. I try to keep my expression neutral as I watch their interaction.

'If you can't handle this simple task, how will you handle the others? Go and put it in Dérin's room.' Alika immediately runs over, grabs the bag then leaves. Aunty Ireti raises an eyebrow and looks at Aunty Zai.

Aunty Zai claps her hands together then shrugs. 'She should be more on top of things. Dérin is already under stress.'

'I'm telling you, my sister,' Aunty Ireti agrees. Mum grimaces from behind them as she watches. I look at her with an expression that says, *be nice*. She responds by twisting her lip. Aunty Zai and Aunty Ireti leave for the kitchen as they talk about caterers; Mum follows close behind.

Minutes pass and Alika still hasn't come back downstairs. I walk out into the foyer to see if she's there, but it's empty. I jog upstairs to Dérin's room; it doesn't take this long to literally dump a dress and leave. As I approach, I see that the door is slightly ajar. I crack it a little wider, and my mouth falls open as I see Alika standing in front of the full-length mirror, holding Dérin's dress up against her body, folding it into her figure so it looks like she's wearing it, as she admires her reflection. Alika brings out her phone and starts taking pictures of herself. Then I see her start to unzip the dress; her eyes almost glazed over like she's lost in this moment. There's no way I can stand here and watch her put on Dérin's dress.

A few seconds after I knock she calls, 'Come in!'

I enter, and she's holding the dress as if she's just about to hang it by Dérin's wardrobe.

'Hey,' I say, and there's an awkward pause, 'I was looking for you. Wanted to check that everything is okay? You've been up here for a minute. Plus, we never finished our conversation. I wanted to see the pictures of the other wedding you've done.'

'Oh yeah.' She brightens then brings out her phone from her pocket. Her fingers move fast, like she has something to hide. She's swipes far up her photo album so I can't even see the pictures she took with Dérin's dress.

Alika reaches the photos she's looking for and starts describing everything she did in detail. I'm half listening to her and half seeing if she'll swipe to something weird on her phone. The pictures from her last wedding are nice, but it's much smaller than what Dérin has planned. Like Aunty Ireti said, I wonder how she's going to cope when it comes to the traditional *and* white weddings. I wonder why Dérin decided to go with her if she has so little experience.

As Alika keeps swiping, my attention is drawn to the flood of Instagram notifications she's getting. They all say that someone has liked her comment. There's also a thumbnail picture of Dérin and Kayode's official engagement photo. This must be from the @bellanaijaweddings Instagram account. Dérin gave them an exclusive on her and Kayode's love story. Alika swipes them away so fast I can't keep up.

'Ahh, that is so beautiful. Could I take a picture and show Dérin?'

'I could just send it to he— Oh, okay,' she says as she sees me whipping out my phone and taking pictures of her screen. I don't really care about what she's showing me, nor do I know what I'm looking at, but the burst of activity has intrigued me.

'Thank you so much. Let me know if you need anything!' I say, guiding her out of Dérin's room before she has any time to think about what just happened. My eyes are glued to my phone as flick through the photos and walk down the stairs. I come to an abrupt stop when I accidentally bump into Uncle Yinka.

'Sorry, Uncle, I was distracted.' He has a sketchy look on his face. I coach mine to stay blank. 'We've barely talked since you've been here.' I'm sure my eyes twinkle as I realize I can kill two birds with one stone. I take him to the nearest chair in the living room. 'Are you excited to be a dad?'

'Ah, of course.' He sits down, crossing his legs. The sketchy look is slowly disappearing but his fake American accent is more than present. 'I feel like I was born to be one. I mean, I practically raised Dérin.' My nose turns up because I know that is absolutely untrue. If anyone had a hand in raising Dérin it was Dad before he left Nigeria. I decide to ignore Uncle's claim.

'Have you picked out any names?'

'Yemi wants to be in charge of that and I don't blame her. Carrying twins is not easy; I'll just co-sign where needed.'

The conversation sort of fizzles out when I realize that I don't really know what else to ask him, without bringing up the obvious question about his fight with Dad a few days ago.

'Um, how has Ghana been? Were you able to make a lot of money?' As I finish, I realize that was probably the least subtle way to ask about his financial situation. Surprise and confusion flash across Uncle Yinka's face as he looks at me.

'Ghana wasn't bad. I love the way of life, but unfortunately my business wasn't that successful there.' He leans back, pondering. 'I think I might move back to Nigeria. Try and convince your uncle to let me work for him again. He will need help with making some money with all he's spending on this wedding. Too much, way, way too much just on three days of celebrations.'

As he finishes his sentence, Aunty Yemi waddles into the room. I stand up to help her walk to the nearest chair. Uncle Yinka stays seated.

She must've heard our conversation because she adds, 'Your business wasn't successful because you didn't try. You wasted the inheritance Mama left for you all and you haven't let anybody forget it, as if it wasn't *your* fault. We are not moving back here unless you can come up with a proper plan. One that doesn't involve begging your older brothers for money. Ah, ah, when will you learn?' Aunty Yemi continues to give him an earful while he pretends not to listen. It feels awkward that I'm still in the room. 'If you thought he wasn't going to spend a lot on Dérin's wedding, orí ẹ kò pé, you're mad. His only daughter, his only *child*, and you think he has time for you, tuh. You lack so much critical thinking.'

This is the first time I've heard Aunty Yemi speak to Uncle Yinka this way and I'm almost . . . proud. Before they left, she was compliant in his shenanigans, all but egging him on, so for her to change so drastically now that they're back, she must be really fed up with his attitude.

'Mama left you five *million* naira. That's more than most people will ever touch in their life and *you wasted it*. Tayo was smart and used his inheritance and the connections Mama already made for you all before she died to start his business. Brother Niyi moved his family over to the UK and he works hard despite having to start again from the beginning. You? What did you do? You spent it partying and drinking.'

Apparently, they've forgotten I'm in the room.

'What is five million? When Tayo got fifteen, Niyi ten? Does it make sense? They owe me the difference. *Wo*, whether Tayo likes it or not, I will be collecting that money from him. You're even talking now but when I was spending the money you weren't complaining.' At this last sentence

Aunty Yemi all but lunges at him, throwing out insults.

This is not like her at all, but I don't blame her. My uncle's addiction to money is like nothing I've ever seen; Aunty Yemi must've heard this speech over and over and she's now reached her breaking point.

My eyes dart back and forth as they go at it with each other. I know exactly what money they're talking about. It's the money Dad put into our savings account when we settled properly in the UK. Converted to pound sterling, it's not as much as it sounds, but it's way more than most people have and will give me the best start in life once I finish university. To hear that Uncle Yinka spent it all on partying is insane. If Dad received just over sixty thousand pounds all those years ago, that means Uncle Yinka has wasted the thirty thousand pounds he inherited.

'Please, why are we arguing? I already told you about Moses and if that doesn't work, I will find a way. You can trust me, na,' Uncle Yinka says with a finality in his voice.

My ears perk up. Who is Moses and how is he going to help with Uncle's money problem?

'Trust *who*? Moses that doesn't know his left and right, talk less of arranging any nonsense mon—'

Mum walks into the room and looks at Uncle Yinka, then Aunty Yemisi and finally me. 'Oh, I didn't know we were having a family meeting. Ẹ kú ìpàdé o,' she says sarcastically, putting her hands on her hips, eyes darting between me and Uncle Yinka. 'When you are ready to help us again, please come and honour us with your presence. Yemi?'

'Ma?' She looks around.

'How far?' Mum asks and Aunty Yemi nods wearily, as if the preceding conversation has drained her. 'When you are ready to eat, let me know. I'll make you some food. In fact, ogbeni, iwọ nko? You won't make her something to eat?' Mum says, making Uncle Yinka rise and walk quickly towards the kitchen. She eyes his every move.

Who *is* Moses? I'm racking my brain for if I've met or heard of him. Is he involved with the notes? A pawn Uncle Yinka is using to get Dérin to call off the wedding so the money isn't spent on her and flows back to him?

As I'm thinking, Mum's eyes land on me again. I get up as fast as my legs allow and make my way back to the room where everyone is decorating.

My phone buzzes with a message, which reminds me what I was doing before Uncle Yinka. I continue going through the photos of Alika's phone, zooming in to see the comment she posted, but I can only make out the beginning.

Rumour has it that this bride has chosen me-

I'm going to assume the rest says *as her wedding planner*. I go onto the @bellanaijaweddings Instagram page, find the post on Dérin and Kayode's wedding story and immediately see Alika's comment. People obviously love it because it's got the most likes. Lots of the other comments are positive too. They all gush about the attractiveness of Dérin and Kayode. They boast about how they can feel the love from the screen.

And then there's one account that spews the opposite.

**Sources say, the bride had to propose to the
groom for the wedding to happen.**

This is the first negative comment. It's from an account named @ajebotashamer. Someone else has responded with question marks, but there's no answer.

I click on Dérin and Kayode's wedding hashtag, #OyinBecomesAkin and scroll through the posts. @ajebotashamer has left a nasty comment, either unnecessary negativity or weird rumours, under every picture.

This must be the account that Dérin said was sending her hateful messages.

Most of the comments are easily debunkable. However, some of them, just a few, are enough to make me twitch. If I was a random person, I could easily believe the rumours and unknowingly help spread them.

**Kayode's daddy's bank is no longer the richest in Nigeria.
A family like that are only after Dérin for her parents'
money. It must've been his plan all along.**

**Someone's ex is still in the picture. Remember, if you kiss,
I tell. It'll take more than lip gloss to keep me quiet.**

That last one is extremely close to home. The comment was written the day after we went clubbing. Dérin definitely didn't post about that on her Instagram. The only one who did was Naija Gossip Lounge: in their article they said there were whispers that Joseph and Dérin were exes. Maybe these are the whispers.

I wonder who could be feeding them this gossip. The more I find out, the more it becomes clear it could be someone we know. Or, is the culprit a random person who was in the club at the same time as us? Before, I thought I needed to look out for people closer to home, but maybe anyone could be doing this.

The notes show that someone knows Dérin's movements. Were they stalking her that night too?

Most people see a wedding photo, maybe take inspiration for what they would like for their own wedding and then move on to the next picture on their feed. What would be the point of exposing Dérin's supposed secrets to a bunch of strangers? Are they spreading rumours for Naija Gossip Lounge to inevitably make into stories, or are they getting their information from a reliable source?

The other question is, why?

@ajebotashamer's profile gives me nothing: no pictures, no bio. Nothing to work a lead on. I google them, but all that comes up is their comments I've already seen. One of the websites I saved from a podcast episode on how to collect evidence has finally come in handy; it compiles all the public comments from an Instagram account into a PDF file for easy viewing. I click on my bookmarks, select the website and type @ajebotashamer into the search bar. A PDF soon appears: all the comments are listed and next to each one is the date it was posted and the hashtag #OyinBecomesAkin.

@ajebotashamer has *only* commented on posts about Dérin and Kayode.

This is targeted malice.

Ajẹbọ́tá is Yoruba for a wealthy person from a privileged background. So, an ajẹbọ́tá 'shamer'? It's clear that this account is fuelled by jealousy. Dérin is an ajẹbọ́tá, yes, but she's humble about her wealth . . . mostly. She documents it, sharing her lifestyle with her followers but not flaunting it. *They* don't think so, though.

I scroll through the pictures of Alika's phone again. One of the notifications is different: it's an alert that Dérin has posted on her story. I head over to Dérin's Instagram and view it. It's the classic video you take of yourself when you're in a hairdresser's chair in the salon. I let out a groan, and call her instantly.

'Please tell me you're not still in the salon right now.'

'I've just left. Why?'

'*Dérin*, seriously. You posted a video of you in the hairdresser's chair almost thirty minutes ago. Any psycho could've found you in the salon by now.'

'I didn't post the address, though,' Dérin says. I can hear traffic in the background.

'In the corner of the video I can see a bright yellow sign with the name of the salon. Imagine what someone who is out to get you could do with that tiny snippet. I mean it when I say, only post when you are gone. *If* you have to post.'

'Okay, okay. I'm sorry, it's force of habit. I've gotta g—'

'Wait, before you do, the account that keeps sending you hate, is the username @ajebotashamer?'

'Yeah, that's the latest one.'

'Latest?'

'There's been loads. Every time I report them, Instagram takes the page down but they always come back like a week or two later. They must be using fake email addresses. It's not always the same username, but it's always the same messages.'

'Don't report this account, I'm going to keep an eye on it. If you have any screenshots of the private messages you've received, send them to me.'

Moments later, a bank of the messages, almost forty screenshots, flashes up on my phone. They're from numerous Instagram accounts, but they all have the same tone. I'm almost certain that it's one person sending them. And they're as threatening as the notes. They get angrier the more Dérin ignores them.

I type the earliest account name that messaged Dérin six months ago into the website that collects Instagram comments. Over half of the comments are about Dérin and Kayode, but there's something else. Five months before they started attacking Dérin, their earlier comments were directed at another couple, Bámidélé and Àdúràtólá. The comments are equally jealous and hateful, but not as malicious as the ones sent to Dérin. They go from:

Such a beautiful bride, it's a shame she had plastic surgery to look that way.

to:

Wishing the couple the happiest marriage. If it lasts . . .

I recognize Àdúràtọ́lá's name – it was mentioned in Naija Gossip Lounge's blog post that started the countdown to Dérin's wedding, and Dérin said they're both in the same social circle. Could Naija Gossip Lounge and @ajebotashamer be linked? As 'unbiased' and 'harmless' and 'just for entertainment' as the blog tries to be, they often do come across as bitter. The break between the comments makes me wonder if this person is purposefully targeting wealthy brides.

I manage to track down Àdúràtọ́lá's Instagram page and send her a screenshot of the now-deactivated account, one of the DMs it sent her and one of the DMs @ajebotashamer has recently sent Dérin, with this message:

> I'm so sorry to contact you like this. Would you be able to tell me anything about this Instagram page that was sending you hate last year about your wedding? The same thing is happening to my cousin right now and I want to get as much information as I can to send it to the police.

Let's hope this comes back with something.

We've got an hour until the party officially starts, and it's been hectic. Despite the official wedding planner being present, I've somehow become the self-appointed party planner today. Lord knows what Alika is actually doing. How she is three years older than me and this is her actual job, I have no idea. I'm the last to get ready because the caterers arrived late which meant that the food was set up late. Dérin was also delayed because she decided to change her eyeshadow look halfway through getting her make-up done, and I had to wrangle Aunty Zai and Mum's slots with the make-up artists due to their last-minute addition to the party.

The theme for tonight is glitz and glam so I'm wearing a black embellished corset over a matching pair of palazzo trousers. I look at myself in the mirror, making sure my hair is okay; I've pulled it into a ponytail, with two loose pieces framing my face. I zhush it around, loosening the ponytail in places before grabbing my bag and making my way upstairs. Aunty Zai is on the landing with Amaka and Seni, wearing a silver blazer dress which is tightened around her waist. Her boobs are held up by tape and I'm wondering whose party she thinks this is?

I'm just glad to see they're all ready. Amaka was having the worst time trying to get her outfit on. She bent down and her bum, the size of a small island, split the seam of her dress so she had to raid Aunty Zai's wardrobe for a replacement outfit. Thankfully, she managed to find a blue cowl neck dress embellished in matching beads. I'm slightly side-eyeing Aunty Zai for having a dress that short in her closet, but hey, I'm just here to round the cavalry.

Seni had no problems, unsurprisingly. The better she looks, the harder it's getting to dislike her; she's annoyingly well put-together. She's wearing a cream long-sleeve crop top and a matching figure-hugging skirt, beaded with pearls that shimmer as she walks. Her hair is up and has curled front pieces framing her face and draping over her bun.

Amaka looks at me as I walk in their direction and gasps. 'You look beautiful,' she says with a smile. Seni compliments me too and I successfully withhold my side-eye.

'Thank you, girls. Thank you. The make-up artist really tried,' Aunty Zai says, taking the compliments for herself. I laugh to myself and allow it because she does look gorgeous. I scoot them downstairs then head off to find Mum. When I walk into her room she's wearing a slinky gold dress and putting on gold drop-down earrings. Babs is with her, fixing his tie; he's wearing an all-black suit and a white shirt.

'Ah, ọkọ mi. You look gorgeous. But why aren't you wearing earrings?' she says as I walk in.

'I was on my way to steal a pair. Where's Daddy?' I say, looking around for him.

'We sent him out to get more ice for the drinks.' I nod, thankful that she still seems to have no idea Dad and I argued, so I make my way over to her jewellery box to rummage through it. I settle for the same pair as Mum's, but silver, and pick a matching silver chain. I also steal a few of her rings; nothing too flashy but something to decorate my hands.

'Your aunty is an àgbàyà; she wants to be involved in everything Dérin does. I even overheard her planning to renew her own marriage vows next year.' She kisses her teeth. 'We'll stay at the party for an hour or so, then we'll be going out again. We won't embarrass you.' She elbows me playfully.

'Please, Aunty Zainab isn't here for any of you guys' wahala tonight. She's taped her boobs up so high, plastic surgeons are asking who's her doctor.'

'La-ra!' Mum drags out the syllables of my name. 'Who taught you how to gossip like this?'

'You did,' Babs and I say at the same time. She looks at us in fake shock.

'Besides,' I continue, 'you need to be nicer to Aunty Zainab. You guys are like the worst frenemies. You cannot have held a grudge for so long just because she once said she wanted to go on holiday instead of staying here when we visit.' My tone is teasing, but really I'm dying to know the real reason they're so on and off with each other.

She laughs then studies both our faces. 'I think you're both old enough to know the family drama now.' A small smirk creeps over my face.

'Lara, at least *try* and hide your smile,' Babs says and I scoff.

'I'm not mad at Zainab for saying she'd rather be out of the country. Please, I know the woman is shallow. I've known

113

that for twenty-four years, since I started dating your dad. I've held a grudge because that comment she made wasn't about flying out of the country. She was speaking about how she was ready to leave the country *and* your uncle, if not for the fact that we flew in that summer to help fix their marriage. She didn't want us meddling in her business. As if I would willingly waste thousands of pounds on a trip if it wasn't necessary. She was incredibly ungrateful for our efforts. Not to mention unwelcoming. How can you be inhospitable with such a big house, with fancy gadgets? The gadgets do the talking for you.'

My heart sinks. 'They were going to break up?' This is not what I was expecting to hear. I thought it was going to be a funny story of Mum being petty so I could tease her about it.

'They did everything but sign the divorce papers.'

Oh. Wow.

'But they're okay now, right?'

'They're fine.' She waves me away. 'Zainab has lived a very cushioned life. She flees when there's stress because she's never had any before, and she has a sharp tongue. I don't hate her. I just love giving her a tough time. I think I'm going to love giving Ireti a tough time too. They're cut from the same cloth, both striving for fake perfection. Anyways, are you two having fun? Hopefully the trip is helping you forget about results day, Lara.'

It *was* until Dad and I had that ridiculous argument when he accused me of running away from success by choosing another career.

I make a small smile and nod, trying not to give her an insight into my mind. 'It's fun being back. We should come more often.'

'Who's paying for the flight? Me or you?'

'Daddy,' I say with a sweet smile, and Mum and Babs both roll their eyes.

CHAPTER TEN

As expected, Black people never know how to keep time.

It's ten minutes past eight when we get a call from Dérin, who is waiting alone in her room, ready to make a grand entrance downstairs, telling us that the groomsmen are stuck in Lagos traffic. How hard would it have been for them to leave early? All they've got to do is put on a shirt and trousers. Shirt. Trousers. I give up.

The whole family, plus Aunty Ireti and Alika wait by the door, welcoming guests as they pile in, ushering them into the games room where things are set up. Every guest has kept to the theme, looking more glitz and glam as they arrive.

'Lara! Could you come up here a second!' Dérin shouts from the top of the stairs. When I get to her room, apart from noticing that everything is scattered around, her dress immediately catches my eye – mostly because I'm seeing it styled and because it looks *so* much better on her than it did on Alika earlier. It's stunning, with puffy tulle sleeves and plunged at the front, revealing her cleavage. It's like a subtle wedding gown with sparkles covering the fabric.

Her braids have been taken down so her natural hair is tucked into a jet-black wig, with old Hollywood curls. She has gems stuck all over it, and a little veil covered in sparkles resting on her shoulders. If this is what she looks like at her bachelorette, I can't imagine what she's going to look like at her wedding.

'I was just about to go downstairs when I saw this on my dresser. Do you have any idea how it got there? I've been in the spare room getting my make-up done for the past hour,' she says, voice shaking, as she puts on her earrings.

I approach her dresser and see the item in question. 'It's a box of cupcakes? With wedding rings on them and a black-and-white picture of you and Kayode. They look so cute; can I have one?' I say, fingers itching to pick one up.

'Don't touch them!' Dérin hisses. 'Just read the note on the side.'

I move slowly, following her instructions. *'We're so glad you made us a part of your day,'* I read aloud. *'Thank you for being a valuable customer always. Love, Rayo's Palace.* I don't get it. What's wrong with this note?'

'I called Rayo to say thank you. He said he never sent them.' I drop the note instantly. 'He said he normally would send cupcakes on a special day, but because he's my wedding hairstylist he planned to send them on my actual wedding day, not tonight. Which is why I'm asking, where did those come from?'

I groan. 'I told you not to post where you were. Did @ajebotashamer view your story today?' Dérin points to her phone, signalling for me to check. I go straight into her Instagram and scroll through who has viewed her story. With tonight being the bachelor-and-bachelorette as well as the end-of-summer party, there are even more people watching. But luck is on our side because it doesn't take too much searching to find the account; the algorithm must know Dérin goes to their page often.

Whoever is running the hateful Instagram account must've sent the cupcakes. Rayo is Dérin's regular hairdresser, but he also gained a lot of clients after Dérin started tagging him in her Instagram posts. His social media accounts are full of clients thanking him for the cupcakes they receive as a thank you for their custom. He *always* sends them because his brother, Rotimi, is *the* patisserie chef for the rich and famous here in Lagos and it's good business for both of them. Everyone's wondering if Rotimi will bake Dérin's wedding cake.

'I think we can assume it's from them.' I remove one of the cupcakes from the box, careful not to touch any of the icing. 'Text Rayo and say that you're going to post these on Instagram as if they're from him. The missing cupcake will make @ajebotashamer think you've already eaten one, so maybe they'll pop up and claim them as their own. It would be another way to show you that they can get to you anywhere, any time. Post it before you come downstairs but a few minutes after I've left you. It'll give me a chance to . . .

118

test some theories. I'm also gonna ask Temi if he knows who delivered them.'

I run downstairs, careful to not trip in my heels as I reach the foyer. The aunties and Mum are in the party, but Alika is still standing by the front door. Seeing her reminds me that she also knew that Dérin was at Rayo's Palace today. Could the cupcakes be from her?

My phone chimes a moment later with the notification I've been waiting for: Dérin's post. But Alika's phone doesn't. She holds it tightly, but it doesn't make a sound. It must be on silent.

I start up a conversation, seeing if I can catch her out in a lie. 'Did you see the cupcakes that Dérin got today?' I say, holding up my phone to show her the story Dérin has just posted.

'Mmm, from Rayo? He's so sweet.' Her voice is trance-like. 'I saw someone take them up to her room while she was in make-up.' She doesn't stutter. 'I've heard he uses the most expensive baker in Lagos. Reserved for the illusive.'

'You mean exclusive?'

She doesn't blink and instead says, 'Isn't that what I said?' Her head tilts ever-so slightly, like she's daring me to question her further. She's watching me with the same zombie-like gaze as when she was trying on Dérin's dress.

'I'm dying to have one. I think we'll have to pass them out halfway through the evening.'

'Yeah, just shoot me a reminder.' She smiles, turning her head back towards the door. My eye twitches. If she knew they were poisoned, she would've suggested that we don't give them to guests, right? Is that supposed to make me believe they're harmless? Or is she just trying to throw me off the scent?

There's something there . . . I'm not sure what, but there's something.

The doorbell rings moments later and Alika goes to answer it. Kayode's groomsmen and friends pile in. Joseph is the last to enter, peeking his head around the door with a devious smirk on his face. He's dressed in a white suit with black accents. I must keep an extra-close eye on him to see if he slips Dérin a note tonight. Alika may be acting weird right now, but I can't focus all my efforts on her. Aunty Tiwa walks behind Joseph slowly, her dress not giving her much room to move. I jog over and give her a hug.

'Aunty!' She embraces me back. 'I have a question to ask you, do you know when Joseph arrived in Nigeria?'

She smiles at me, confused. 'Why don't you ask him?'

I wave my hand at her playfully. 'You know he never tells the truth.' She snickers at that.

'The day before you did your fittings for the traditional wedding.'

'Really? I was hoping he was lying this time.' I deflate and she pokes my head jokingly, not understanding what I mean.

Aunty Zai comes out of the games room and shouts while doing a little shimmy, 'Is that my son-in-law?'

'Yes, Aunty!' Joseph says cheekily and Aunty Tiwa glares daggers at him.

'Move, jare.' Aunty Zainab laughs, shoving him out of the way. I look at Aunty Ireti, who isn't clued up on this 'inside joke'. She looks at Joseph with an intrigued frown. I watch her until she tears her eyes away from Joseph and settles on Kayode. Her frown relaxes a bit when she sees the stern look on his face.

Kayode doesn't look at Aunty Ireti. Instead, he focuses on Aunty Zai as he walks towards her, forcing his face to turn into a smile. Before he reaches her, he shouts 'Èmi ni yẹn!' in reply then pulls her into a big hug, lifting her up in the air. 'Where's my bride?' he calls out.

Dérin's voice faintly replies from the first floor: 'I'm here!'

Ugh, they're so gross. But they're so cute, I could shed a tear.

It takes five minutes for everyone to settle, after which we finally give the DJ the signal that we're going to collect Dérin from upstairs.

As Amaka and I leave the room, Seni starts marshalling everyone into teams for the games. Amaka and I don't get far as Dérin is already making her way down the stairs, dress bunched up in her hands.

'So, you people forgot about me, abi?' she says, and a laugh escapes me. She's so annoyingly eager to get married.

'How are we supposed to have a bachelorette party without the bachelorette?' Amaka asks and Dérin rolls her eyes playfully.

'Anything?' Dérin says meaningfully in my direction.

'*Something*, but I can't be certain.' My mouth twists and

she nods at me. Amaka glances back and forth between us, not understanding what we're talking about.

'Does he look good?' Dérin asks, and we both nod. She squeals, clapping her hands together, her diamond ring glistening. We knock on the games-room door, and Seni opens it. Kayode is standing there, ready to walk into the centre with Dérin. He lets out a small gasp when he sees her and pushes past me to get to her.

'Hey!' I give him a playful shove.

The DJ starts playing 'Askamaya' by Teni then announces into the microphone, 'Ladies and gentlemen, allow me to introduce the future Mr and Mrs Akinlola! Make some noise for the bride!' As the happy couple dance in to the music, everyone's phones are out filming them.

When they've finished and the songs continue, everyone comes to greet Dérin and compliment her outfit. Dérin looks around at the room, slightly tearing up at all the love she's receiving. Thankfully, it looks like she's no longer worrying about the cupcakes.

After we've finished taking pictures with everyone, the DJ announces that it's time to split into the pre-arranged teams. Amaka, Seni and I group together and Kayode follows us. Looks like he's stuck with Seni tonight. Meanwhile, Dérin is paired with Babs and Joseph. Some kind of emotion flashes across her face when she realizes. I give her a soft look that lets her know that everything will be fine.

Kayode calls over to Dérin's team. 'If you lot think you're going to win, you're mistaken. Lara is a cheater,' he says, putting me in a headlock. I pinch his arm, forcing him to release me, and everyone laughs.

Then I hear Seni mutter 'cheaters never prosper' loudly, causing Joseph to choke on his drink, and a strange expression crosses Kayode's face. It takes all my willpower to not react. What does that even mean? Dérin and Amaka both confirmed that Seni and Kayode dated during first year of uni and that Kayode and Dérin started dating at the beginning of second year, so who is being dishonest and who is the cheater? Seni's attitude these past few days has been pissing me off. She goes from being okay to being shady as hell. Why come to the wedding if you aren't over your feelings?

'Let the games begin!' the DJ announces.

CHAPTER ELEVEN

Wow, I never knew how great it felt to win until this moment. What feels even better is when your whole team is just as determined as you to win. We're all going out for blood.

The game we're playing is like Simon Says. The cups are laid on the floor in a line, one cup per two teammates. The DJ's supposed to name an action for us to do before we can grab the cup. The person who grabs the cup first wins a point for their team. Mum and the aunties take part in this one; for most of the games they've been in the corner gisting, eating and showing off on Facebook Live. I've had to politely tell Mum to get out of the way more times than I can count.

I'm up against Dérin now. We get into position, hands by our sides, and lock eyes. She smiles, then all of a sudden her face twitches like she's in pain.

'Are you okay?' I whisper, trying not to draw any attention. She takes a moment to answer, almost as if she's waiting for the pain to pass.

'My back's hurting a bit.' She winces, stretching herself out. 'I'll be fine, don't worry. I think it was the way I was sitting in the salon.' I nod in response, not wanting to prod but keeping a watchful eye.

'When you go back up to change, I'll get you some ibuprof—'

'Are you all ready?' the DJ's voice interrupts. 'When I say a body part, you put both your hands on it. When I say cup, you grab the cup as fast as you can. Do you understand the rules?' he says and we all nod.

'Head . . . hips . . . shoulders . . . feet . . . head . . . cup!' he shouts and I move as fast as I can to grab it. I succeed and do a little victory dance. 'Point goes to Kayode's team.'

'Ah, ah, now. Some of us are getting older; how can you say feet, then head, then expect me to be fast enough to bend back down to the floor?' Aunty Zai says and everyone laughs. It's not her age – the dress stretched across her boobs is just so tight it's preventing her from bending down.

Joseph creeps up behind me, nudging my arm lightly while holding a plate filled to the brim with jollof and fried rice, two portions of peppered fish, one portion of peppered smoked turkey, and beef. 'You play dirty. I could use someone like you on my team.'

'What team would that be? And are you planning on leaving any food for everyone else?'

He gives me a fake sneer. 'I was planning on sharing with Dérin.'

'With *one* fork?'

'Not like we haven't shared more than saliva before.' He shrugs.

'When did you become so . . . I'm just gonna say it. Shameless? Desperate? A borderline àgbàyà.'

Our heads turn as the DJ congratulates our team. Amaka hands out everyone's prize medals, while Dérin heads upstairs to get changed into her more 'casual' outfit.

'What is shameless about trying to get the love of your life back? In romance novels it'd be seen as noble,' he says, nonchalantly scooping up a spoon of rice.

'This isn't a romance novel, Joseph. This is Dérin's wedding. The time for you to back off is now, more than ever. She's getting married to Kayode and she's happy with Kayode. Why can't you see that?'

'Kayode is her second choice; he only became an option because I wanted kids and Dérin didn't. Now that she does, it's time for her to see that I'm right here. She's always been happier with me. You can see it. I can see it. Everyone can, and it's time she does too.'

I frown. 'That doesn't make any sense. Dérin has *always* wanted kids. Maybe it's time you realize that it was an *I don't want to have kids* and the *'with you'* was silent.' Joseph's face grows angrier, then I say, 'If you'll excuse me. I need to go and get her some painkillers.'

'She's in pain?' he asks, face softening.

'That doesn't mean you can come upstairs! Stay here and stop being everywhere you're not supposed to.' I head upstairs to find ibuprofen in my room, then make my way

126

to Dérin's. I knock but no one answers.

'Dérin?' I say, opening the door slightly. When I poke my head through, she's on her bed, squeezing her eyes shut tight. 'Are you okay?' I race inside. 'Is your back still hurting?'

It takes Dérin a moment to respond. When she finally does, her speech is strained. 'I'm mostly fine. It just keeps coming in waves, almost like stabbing at the top and middle of my back.'

'Here's the ibuprofen,' I say, passing her the sachet and then a glass of water from her bedside table.

'I think I might need something stronger if I'm going to make it through the night. Could you open the top drawer of my bedside table and grab me the white sachet with purple writing, please?' I follow her instructions. There are a lot of medications in there. I finally see the one she's asked for. It's codeine.

'Why do you have codeine? Isn't it addictive?' I ask. Dérin pops out two pills from the new sachet then swallows them with water.

'I had a slipped disc last year, so I was prescribed some because the pain was *bad*. Haven't taken a pill since I recovered a few months ago, but today I feel like I need it.' She readjusts herself. 'Have you eaten?'

'I'm worried about you. We can call the party off.'

'We can't cancel. I'm not going to let a little pain ruin my fun.' She starts pushing me off the bed, forcing me to stand up. 'Go and eat. I'm going to get changed anyways. Just make sure there's some food left over.'

I take my leave reluctantly and head back down to the party, walking into something reminiscent of whale sounds to the rhythm of afrobeats. Aunty Zai has fully taken over the DJ's microphone and is singing her rendition of 'Buga' by Kizz Daniel and Tekno. I do a deep, deep sigh.

This song has a literal chokehold on aunties worldwide. Everyone's faces are a mix of shock, laughter and embarrassment. Except for Aunty Ireti and Mum who are waving around napkins to the beat of the music, while Amaka performs the song's dance in the middle of the room. I am so embarrassed that I don't know whether I should be bringing out my phone to film this or putting a stop to it. Aunty Zai's voice wavers as she attempts to join in with Amaka's dance moves.

The music comes to an end, and I think they're going to show us some mercy, until Aunty Zai requests another song. Okay, it's time to wrap this horror show up. I walk over as calmly as I can and stand in the middle of their mischief corner. Laughter ceases as they see my expression.

'You had one job, and that was get this lot out before nine-thirty.' I direct my speech to Babs and he snickers.

'Mum has me on Facebook Live duty. I got carried away making sure I got the whole thing.'

I roll my eyes then lower my tone. 'Make sure you send me a copy of that.' Babs nods with a grin before an arm pulls me away.

'Lara, mi, let us have fun. When am I going to party like this again?' Aunty Zai says, her shoulder now resting against me. I can smell alcohol on her breath and it's all making sense now.

'You're going out tonight . . . to meet your husbands . . . at the lounge.'

'Ah, true, true, true. Ladies, we should go,' she says, hurrying Mum and Aunty Ireti. Aunty Zai kisses my cheek, then Mum too. Aunty Ireti squeezes my arm, smiling at me before they head out.

I plop down on the nearest sofa, but I can't stop thinking about Dérin. Deciding to check on her again, I make my way to her room. As I reach the top of the stairs, I see Seni walking out of her own room. I wave, and as soon as she sees me, her face morphs into a guilty expression. Two seconds later, Kayode walks out of Seni's room too, closing the door behind him.

My own expression turns from confusion to shock, until a deep laugh pours out of my mouth. I clap my hands together as I frown at the sight in front of me.

'You two must be having me on.' Before I know it, I've taken off my heel and have it raised in the air as I hobble quickly towards them. Seni tries to back into her room, but Kayode is in the way and there's nowhere for her to go.

'At her bachelorette party? At *your* bachelor party?' I point my heel between them. 'How insane and unserious can the both of you be?' I whisper-shout. 'Dérin is literally up here getting changed and *you two* are coming out of the same room together? A room that she let *you* stay in.' My heel is pointing back at Seni.

'What do we have here?' a familiar voice says from behind us. I turn my head and see Joseph, a smirk on his face as he climbs to the top of the stairs. He brings out his phone and takes a picture of the scene, his grin widening.

A flash of anger crosses Kayode's face. 'Why are you everywhere you don't need to be?' he demands.

'Man can't even use the toilet without being interrogated? I think that question needs to be directed back at you guys,' Joseph replies.

Kayode opens his mouth to speak, then closes it almost like he's scared to say what he wants to. 'I— I was tired of things being awkward between me and Seni. I asked if we could talk because we're going to be seeing each other more as the wedding approaches.'

'So, you decided that her *bedroom* was the best place?' My eyebrows skyrocket.

'In hindsight, that was very, very stupid,' he says and I give him a *you think?* look. 'I would've done it downstairs, but Aunty Zai had started singing karaoke and we couldn't hear each other over the racket. Lara, I promise you, I wouldn't do that to your cousin. I love her with everything in me.'

'The kitchen? The living room? Even the fucking gym, Kayode. And you,' I point at Seni, 'nothing to say? You don't want to clear your name?'

'I mean, I was going to until you came charging at me with a stiletto,' she whisper-shouts. 'We were just talking. I didn't even want to, trust me. Nothing happened.'

'Lara?' Dérin shouts from her room. All our heads turn

towards Dérin's door. I rush Seni, Kayode and Joseph into Seni's room, staying in the hallway myself. 'Lara, is that you?' Dérin calls out again, and I panic. I flail my arms around, attempting to calm myself down before answering.

Dérin sticks her head around her door. 'Lar— Oh, it is you! Why didn't you answer?'

'Sorry, I was on the phone! Coming.' I move quickly, sneaking a glance at Seni's door before following Dérin into her room. 'Did @ajebotashamer comment on your post about the cupcakes?' I ask, trying to come across as normal as possible.

She shakes her head. 'They've viewed it, though,' she says, signalling for me to zip up her dress.

'Have you ever had any suspicions about Alika?'

'No, not really. Did you see or hear something?'

'Nothing concrete. Just . . . Why did you choose her for the wedding? She's only planned one wedding previous to yours.'

'Mummy recommended her. Alika's last wedding was nicely done for a novice and she offered a discounted price because we were taking a chance on her.'

'Did that not seem weird to you?'

'No. We're already spending a lot on the wedding and planners are expensive. It was a godsend.'

I furrow my brow. Alika is borderline unqualified, with nothing going for her except a recommendation and the offer of a discount. Still, Dérin chooses to hire her for the most important day of her life.

Interesting.

CHAPTER TWELVE

It's two a.m. and this is the most insanely packed party I've ever been to.

Dérin is feeling better, or possibly she's just getting better at hiding the pain. She's the life of the party; you'd never know the discomfort she was in a few hours ago.

My eyes haven't left Joseph, because it's incredibly suspicious – and annoying – that he was upstairs in the first place. To deliver a note, check on the cupcakes or see Dérin? Seni has been keeping her distance but that hasn't stopped me shooting sly daggers at her and Kayode whenever Dérin's not looking. I don't *not* believe that they were just talking.

What's really getting to me is how easy it would've been for whoever is stalking and tormenting Dérin to ruin her night in an instant. If there is something harmful in those cupcakes and she unknowingly ate them, thinking they were a gesture of goodwill, tonight could've been over before it began. This is sick and twisted. Far past a bitter person wanting to expose fake secrets on the internet.

My mind is still racing as Alika comes up behind me. 'You okay?' she asks.

I nod, not about to bare my soul to a stranger. I look around the room, taking it all in. 'You must make a lot of money planning weddings.'

She smiles coyly. 'Not yet. There's not many people in the luxury wedding business that are willing to take on a newbie. But maybe with this one, if I get the job done right, then people will want to book me and there'll be a big paycheque coming my way. Excuse me, I'm going to go and introduce myself to one of the Ojoras.' She gives me a handful of her business cards. 'If you happen to talk to anyone important tonight.' She nods at me and then moves on. I watch her walk out of the room, then spot Joseph. He's arguing with Temi; he looks angry, his voice is raised and he's jabbing his finger into Temi's chest. My expression hardens. I'm getting annoyed as I walk over to them both.

'What is going on? Why are you speaking to him like that?' I hiss at Joseph. He motions for me to look at his white shirt.

'He dropped a fucking cupcake on me. One with Dérin and Kayode's faces on it, as if that's what I needed tonight,' Joseph sneers. Temi excuses himself to find a rag for Joseph to clean himself with.

'Y-your tie . . .' My eyes bulge. Joseph's once-black tie is turning orange as the cupcake icing sinks in. As if it's been wiped with bleach. Oh my God.

'What the fuck is in these?' Joseph moans, but I'm not listening. I scan the room, looking to see if anyone else has a cupcake. Almost everyone by the drinks table is holding one. The acid in my stomach rises to my throat as I watch people's lips touch the icing. The icing that was potent enough to *bleach* Joseph's tie. I'm paralysed. What do I do? Do I go around whacking cupcakes out of people's hands? That would cause a scene. Or do I let this play out? No. I can't do that. Shit. I need to move fast. Now. I run over to the drinks table, grabbing the bowl that was once filled with ice and carry it over to everyone holding a cupcake.

'I'm sorry, you can't eat that. It's been in the sun.' I swipe the cupcake from the nearest bystander's hands, plunging it into the bowl. I rush around, grabbing every single cupcake I can see. 'This has been in the sun. Yes. The sun, sorry. You can't eat that. So sorry! There'll be other treats. Sorry, sorry. I promise the cookies are better. The sun – sorry. I— Babs!'

Oh my God.

'Babs!' I slap the cupcake out of his hand. Amaka, standing next to him, protests, but I shout to silence her. 'How many of those have you eaten?'

Babs says, 'This would've been my seco—'

'What! Since when? How do you feel?'

'Since . . . three minutes ago? I feel fine. Why did you slap it out of my hand?' He's getting annoyed.

'You're sure you're okay?' I ask slowly and he nods, confusion in his eyes.

'Why are you looking at me like that?'

134

'Where did these come from?' I ignore his question, panic rising within me, as I watch him closely.

'I don't know. All I did was eat one.'

For fuck's sake.

These parties are always the talk of the town. If the cupcakes contained something that made the guests ill, it'll definitely make the blogs. Dérin is already a hot topic for them to gossip about and she hasn't even done anything bad. Giving the guests food poisoning, or worse, would make Naija Gossip Lounge spontaneously combust with glee at the opportunity to ride the Dérin hate-train even more. News like this would make guests reluctant to attend Dérin and Kayode's actual wedding. And by Lagos standards, that is the worst. Image really is everything.

Suddenly, there's a panic as people start to run out of the pool room. I can hear splashing, getting louder and louder. Babs, Amaka and I all run to see what's happening. As we enter, there's a woman at the side of the pool vomiting violently while another holds her hair back. Guests rapidly exit the pool, disgusted and fearful that they'll catch whatever this woman has.

'Oh my God. I hate people who can't handle their alcohol.' I grimace, averting my eyes from the scene.

'Oh yeah, like you're a pro,' Amaka teases. 'That's Amina Olawale. She doesn't drink. Her whole brand is the "my body is a temple" spiel. People love her for it. Did you say those cupcakes had been left out in the sun? 'Cause I saw her holding two earlier.'

Fuck.

Babs slowly turns to me. 'I can't lie, my stomach feels weird.'

'*Babs?*'

'I think I feel fine,' he says, then squirms and carries on, 'Yeah, I don't feel fine. My stomach hurts. A lot.'

'Babs! What do you feel?'

'Woozy,' he almost whispers. 'Queasy. Hot and then cold.'

I say the first thing I think of. 'You need to throw up.'

'No . . . I don't think I'm there yet—'

'No, seriously.' I pause, unsure if I should tell him the full story. I trust Babs the most out of everyone, but telling him the truth right now could interfere with my investigations. 'I didn't want to say earlier because you seemed fine and I couldn't mention it in front of the guests, but Dérin got those cupcakes from somewhere that should be on an episode of *Kitchen Nightmares*. I had to lie to guests that they were bad because they were left out in the sun all day. If you don't make yourself throw up and get them out of your system, you're most likely going to get food poisoning.'

'There are tablets for food pois—'

'Babs!'

'All right.' Babs rolls his eyes, then follows me out into the hallway to the downstairs toilet.

Guilt floods my body. I should've binned the cupcakes as soon as we got suspicious of them. Sounds of full-body retching follow us down the corridor. The noise makes me shudder. I run into the kitchen with the bowl of cupcakes in my hand, take one out, put it in the back of the fridge, and throw the rest in the bin. I make a mental note to remind myself to move the saved cupcake to the mini fridge in my room later. When I exit the kitchen, Babs walks out of the bathroom at the same time.

'I still feel weird, like my heart is thudding,' he says, rubbing the back of his neck.

'Let's get you some water.' We walk back into the games room and find Amaka and Seni.

The music halts, and the DJ passes a microphone to Dérin. The dancefloor disperses feedback as she starts to speak.

'Woah, that was loud, sorry about that, guys. Hello! We just wanted to thank you all for coming to celebrate tonight, we can't even begin to tell you how much it means. Your dedication to us as a couple is so heartwarming.' The crowd cheers. 'And to those who turned up for my end-of-summer party, it's a bit earlier this year but you still came to celebrate and I love you for that. Here's to breaking the internet again!' Dérin ends and lifts her glass up in the air; everyone cheers, whoops and claps.

Phone notifications start to chime around the room. They ring from the pool room and there are even faint sounds from the foyer. Dérin and Kayode look around the room in confusion as the guests focus on their phones. It seems that everyone who lives in the house has been left out of the loop.

'I'm sorry. I didn't get a notification. Could I see?' I say to the person next to me. They hand me their phone. The headline reads:

BREAKING NEWS

HEATSTROKE OR POISON?

I told you I'd have the latest scoop.

Sources say that cupcakes were swatted out of party-goers' hands at Dérin Oyinlola's bachelor-and-bachelorette-end-of-summer party, which is still ongoing.

Maybe not after this drops.

The reason for the forced removal of the sweet treats: 'They were left out in the sun for too long and no longer good for consumption.'

But moments later, a guest was seen vomiting up those same black-and-white cupcakes. All over the pool room, actually. Image attached. Apologies in advance, Amina. I do like you, I swear.

I might not be a scientist, but I thought food poisoning doesn't happen instantly? Am I wrong or were the cupcakes just really that bad? Or is something more sinister at play?

You be the judge. Or I guess, some of Dérin's guests, if they stay, will, as the night goes on.

Cheers to breaking the internet 🥂

You know gossip doesn't sleep, and neither do I.

xoxo

Whispers start to travel around the room. Everyone shuffles uncomfortably, looking like they don't know if they should stay or leave. Some people grab their bags and immediately start heading out. Dérin looks at me intently to clue her in. I'm stuck in my step and I feel my body start to flush with heat. All I can do is mouth, *I'm sorry*.

Dérin's eyes dart around wildly, not understanding me. She whispers for Alika, who's stood frozen in the corner of the room, her phone glued to her hand as she stares at the screen. She snaps out of it then runs to Dérin and shows her. Dérin's eyes widen as she reads the article. She keeps gasping. Kayode reads the article over her shoulder. His forehead creases as he mouths, *Poison?*

Amaka whispers in my direction, 'Why didn't we get the notifications too?'

'We have international numbers. I've heard that for breaking news topics Naija Gossip Lounge has a mass texting feature – they can reach everyone in the country with a Nigerian phone number at the same time. I thought that was unrealistic, but apparently not. They really make sure what happens in Lagos, doesn't stay in Lagos. In her speech, Dérin said, *Here's to breaking the internet.* Naija Gossip Lounge used practically the exact same words in their article. I think they're here. Or definitely were.'

We all look around the room as if we'd be able to spot them.

Why would Naija Gossip Lounge say *poison*? The damage that will do to Dérin's wedding is irreversible. Guests will think irrationally and erratically as soon as they see that word. *Especially* because there's photographic evidence of Amina vomiting. With her reputation and her position among the Lagos socialites, any attempts to save the party are probably doomed. Moments go by and more and more people digest the article. I hear shuffling around the room, and whispers grow into full-blown chatter. Amina emerges from the pool room, stares at Dérin and Kayode, then cuts her eyes at them and storms out. A few more people start to follow her.

Kayode takes the mic from Dérin in an attempt to bring back the crowd. 'Hi, guys. Listen, I'm sure everyone here has been a victim of Naija Gossip Lounge's B.S., so let's focus back on having an amazing night.' Scattered applause skips around the room then the music restarts.

It takes a *long* while to get everyone's attention back on the party. Almost an hour and a half of awkwardness persists as the guests discuss the article. Every conversation is a mix of Nigerian, British and even American accents saying variations of 'thank God I didn't grab one,' and 'this is why I don't eat outside food. You really never know.'

We're not going to live this down so close to the wedding. I've been restlessly tapping my feet, my back is tense and I have a headache so bad I might even need some of Dérin's private stash of codeine. After Kayode's announcement, she stormed upstairs and when Kayode and I tried to follow, she stopped us, saying she wanted to be alone. I'm worried she's freaking herself out into one of her superstitious spirals. I feel so guilty *I* could throw up.

Kayode and the girls continue to mingle with the remaining guests while Babs and I keep to one corner. He's been taking it easy since his vomiting episode. Babs is not a complainer so I'm scared he could be in more pain than he's letting on.

The one positive thing to come out of this is that we know for certain that the cupcakes contained something harmful. And the only saving grace is that Dérin didn't eat any of them.

As I watch the party dwindle, I notice that both Joseph and Alika are nowhere to be seen. I decide to grab some ibuprofen and then look for them. Either of them could've been behind the poisoned cupcakes. Just because Joseph's tie got bleached, doesn't mean he's innocent. 'I'm gonna go to the toilet.' I get up.

I walk upstairs for what feels like the thousandth time tonight, scrolling through the wedding hashtag to see if I can find any new comments from @ajebotashamer. They'd definitely relish Dérin's new misfortune. I turn to walk to my room when I almost collide with someone. I drop my phone and Temi picks it up. He looks like he's just come from Dérin's room.

'Sorry, Lara. I didn't see you there,' he says hastily, handing my phone back to me, then quickly starts to make his way to his room on the second floor.

'Uh, that's okay,' I say, disoriented. 'Oh, wait! Temi, the cupcakes in Dérin's room. Did you bring them down?'

He nods sheepishly.

'Who asked you to bring them out?'

'Aunty Zainab, before she left with the rest of the aunties.'

Aunty Zai? What? I wasn't expecting that.

When I don't say anything else, he continues walking upstairs. Aunty Zai can't have known anything about them being dangerous. Poor, unsuspecting Aunty Zai, thinking they were a cute gift from Dérin's hairdresser.

I spend about twenty minutes in my ensuite bathroom, psyching myself up to force my way into Dérin's room because she can't be alone wallowing the entire night. I start to walk along the corridor when I hear voices coming from the foyer. Peering down over the bannister, I see Joseph and Dérin talking. I immediately wonder if he's telling her about Kayode and Seni's earlier private encounter. Dérin doesn't need to know about that, especially with the latest party catastrophe.

Dérin looks stony at first, but the more Joseph talks, the more her face relaxes. I can't make out what they're saying over the music. Her eyes continue to soften, then they're closing. My eyes bulge as I watch them step closer to one another. They get even closer and then it's *extremely* close. In the darkness it looks like Dérin leans in, their lips almost touching until she seems to realize what she's doing and backs away. She shakes her head, opening up a healthy and necessary distance from him and attempts to walk back into the party, until voices burst into the house.

'*Poison?*' Aunty Zai shouts as she enters. Dérin is a few

143

steps away from Joseph so things don't look as bad as they did mere seconds ago, but her head swivels from left to right as if she's worried that them being alone together seems compromising. Aunty Zai continues, 'In my household? Poison!' The rest of the adults shuffle in, their night ruined by the blog.

I start to walk down the stairs and the sounds of my heels hitting the floor tiles alert everyone to my presence. Both Joseph and Dérin turn their heads to me. I try to give them a neutral stare, but I'm sure my face lets them know what I just saw.

'Aunty, there are still guests in the house,' I say, trying to calm her down.

'Poison, Lara!' Her eyes are huge and her emotions are out of control. 'To make matters worse, that demonic Naija Gossip Lounge found out and sent its evil blog post to everyone in the country. My phone has been ringing, ringing, ringing. I don't even know what to say. What am I supposed to say? Why would that stupid blog accuse us of poisoning the guests? With the wedding so close? How were the cupcakes left in the sun? I put them in Dérin's room! What nonsense are they talking about?' Aunty Zai angrily flings her bag on the floor.

Dérin looks at me once more as we now both know how the cupcakes made their way upstairs. Then she walks over to her mum to calm her down.

'It's as if that stupid blog has it out for the wedding. They've been vicious with their news since that first countdown article. Even the way they're speaking about Kayode, I don't like it. They need to be stopped!' Aunty Ireti is raging too.

Mum looks at Aunty Ireti and Aunty Zai as if she can't relate to their problems. She attempts to fix her face by staring elsewhere, her eyes eventually landing on Joseph. 'What happened to your tie, Joseph? Why does it look like it's been bleached?'

Joseph startles, his blending into the background now disturbed. He opens his mouth to speak and I pre-emptively wince at the possibility of him confirming that the cupcakes *were* laced with something. The last thing we want is Aunty Zai and Uncle Tayo freaking out about there being a *real* threat made tonight.

Dérin butts in, not giving him a chance to speak. 'He spilled food on himself and the dummy wiped his black tie with bleach. I had to help him wash it off.' She saves herself with the excuse.

'Your aunty is the most sought-after tailor in Lagos and you still don't know not to do that?' Mum tuts, then playfully knocks Joseph on the head.

'So, what are we going to do?' Aunty Ireti asks the room.

No one says anything for a moment until Aunty Zai makes a displeased sound and says 'What do you mean, *what are we going to do?* We continue as normal.'

CHAPTER THIRTEEN

How we've all managed to get down here for breakfast, or brunch, rather, is beyond me. The party ended just before four a.m. and that was only because Seni slowly started kicking people out – and thank God she did. Everyone at the table looks dishevelled. I'm pretty sure Amaka and Aunty Zai slept with their make-up on. Aunty Tiwa stayed the night after helping us clean up, sleeping in one of the guest bedrooms. The only person missing from the table is Dérin, so I head up the stairs to get her. I assume she's having a lie-in after last night's drama, but she still needs to eat something. Plus, this is the perfect opportunity to ask her what the hell she was thinking when she nearly kissed Joseph in the foyer last night.

There's no noise coming from her room, so I knock. She shouts for me to come in. Her voice sounds muffled and when I walk in she's not on her bed. I almost enter her bathroom to check if she's there until I see a white sock poking out from beneath the other side of her bed. I walk quickly around to that side, and see her sprawled out on the floor.

'Thank God you're here,' she says, breaking down into tears. 'I can't move. I've been calling out for the past ten minutes, but this house is too big, no one heard me.' She grows frustrated, still crying. I rush over to her side.

'What do you mean you can't move?' I ask, panic increasing.

'My back . . . the pain.' She's full-on crying now. 'It's never been this bad. It's never been this bad, Lara.' She shakes her head slowly as she talks.

I feel like I could cry with her. I tell her to stay there, then realize what an idiotic thing that was to say. I run out into the hallway and call out for Mum. She doesn't respond so I rush down the stairs and into the dining room.

'Why are you running around like the house is on fire?' Mum says when she sees me.

'It's Dérin. She can't move,' I say, and everyone's faces fall. They drop their cutlery and speed out of the room, me along with them. Aunty Zai enters Dérin's room first and panics the most.

'Dérin, what's wrong?' Her voice rises with worry as she sees the tears on Dérin's face. She immediately moves into drill sergeant mode. She orders the men to move Dérin back to her bed and lie her on her front as gently as possible, emphasis on *gently*. Mum is instructed to go downstairs and get a hot-water bottle. I'm told to go to the medicine cabinet in Aunty Zai's room and find Deep Heat and Voltaren, and

147

when I get back Seni is instructed to speak to Dérin to distract her from the pain as Aunty Zai massages the spicy-smelling cream into Dérin's back. Babs is on the phone to Kayode, and Uncle Tayo is on the phone to the family doctor.

When Mum comes back upstairs, she places the hot-water bottle on the bed, and she's also brought a glass of water. Aunty Zai opens Dérin's bedside drawer, gets the familiar codeine sachet and pops two pills into her hand. She helps Dérin to move onto her back, sitting her up with pillows propped behind her and places the hot-water bottle where the pain is focused. As she passes the glass of water to Dérin, Dérin's hand seizes up as if it's too heavy. Aunty Zai swiftly grabs the glass before it falls. Aunty Zai looks shocked but she quickly smooths over her expression, trying not to panic. She holds the glass near Dérin's face, pops two pills into her mouth, then helps her drink.

'Pèlé, ọmọ mi. Kayode and the doctor will soon be here,' Aunty Zai says. Dérin smiles wearily then breaks down in tears again, covering her face. Everyone in the room is silent: faces full of shock, confusion and sympathy.

'I'm sorry. I didn't mean to scare you all,' she sniffles.

Ten minutes pass and Kayode arrives. We hear the doorbell ring and then rapid footsteps up the stairs. He rushes into Dérin's room. Dérin breaks down again when she sees him. Kayode greets everyone in the room and then climbs into bed with Dérin, moving her gently onto her chest. She cries onto him, and this time a tear runs down my cheek too. I swipe it away, not wanting to draw attention to myself. The doctor arrives soon after; a short, slim, dark-skinned man with grey hair. Aunty Zai dismisses everyone except Uncle Tayo and Kayode from the room.

We all walk downstairs, almost in a trance. The food is stone cold by the time we get back to the dining room, but no one really has an appetite any more. We all sit at the table, waiting for the doctor to leave Dérin's room, the image of Dérin in agony replaying in our heads.

Twenty minutes later, a door opens upstairs and we all stand up in anticipation. Uncle Tayo, Aunty Zai and the doctor all join us in the dining room.

'She's going to be fine,' he says. 'I've provided her with medication and the wedding should be able to go ahead. She's at the worst stage now but it will hopefully get easier as she goes on. I will check in often, but all you can do is keep her distracted.' Relief washes over all of us.

'What was wrong with her?' Amaka asks, voice almost a whisper.

The doctor looks at Aunty Zai and she shakes her head. He looks back at us and says, 'I can't break patient confidentiality, I'm sorry,' then takes his leave. Aunty Zai sees him out.

'Thank you all for helping. Dérin will be fine. Girls, you can sit with her but everyone else just continue as you were. She's strong,' Uncle Tayo says.

I feel kind of lost, not knowing where to go. I head into the kitchen to warm up my food so I can try to eat something before going back upstairs to see Dérin. I'm on my last bite when I start to feel sick so I scrape my remaining food into the bin, then put my plate in the dishwasher. Mum walks in as I'm about to leave and asks me if I'm okay. I nod, trying to hide a tear that threatens to fall. She realizes, then pulls me in for a hug.

'It must have been scary seeing her like that. It's okay,' she says and wipes my eyes. 'Dérin will be okay.'

I just don't know how true that is.

There is so much going on. Dérin has a stalker threatening to cause chaos and ruin the wedding. Joseph seems set on getting Dérin back no matter what. Alika, the worst wedding planner in the history of wedding planners, is acting very strange, and I don't trust her as far as I can throw her. Naija Gossip Lounge is hellbent on destroying Dérin's character and finishing off the wedding in the process. Then there's Kayode and Seni acting like tortured forbidden lovers.

Is Dad right? That I wouldn't be able to handle being a detective. Not because it's not as glamorous as it's portrayed on TV, but because I wouldn't be able to cope with keeping so many secrets and switching my emotions off. I feel like I'm drowning in all this information. I need to talk things through, pinpoint what everything means. If I don't get to the bottom of this soon, it could all end in disaster, and I need to stop that from happening.

I take a deep breath and head back upstairs to Dérin's room. The girls and Kayode are watching a movie with her.

'Can I speak to Dérin alone, please?' Kayode's face drops – he must think I'm going to tell her about his and Seni's encounter yesterday. I give him a slight nod to reassure him

150

that I won't, then he tells her that he's going to get her some food. The girls follow him.

'What's wrong?' Dérin asks, looking at me like she's trying to figure out what's on my mind.

'I saved one of the cupcakes from the party. I'm going to find a lab that can test it. That way, when we find the person responsible, we have evidence of probable harm, maybe even worse dependent on the substance the lab finds. The cupcake icing bleached Joseph's tie. That was the real reason it was orange,' I say and I watch her jaw clench. 'I think I managed to take back a majority of the cupcakes from the guests, but I wasn't there when they were handed out. More people could fall ill in the next few days. I need you to be prepared for that possibility. I need you to be prepared for the blog posts, the comments and the whispers. I need you to be prepared for if people message you and say they're not coming to the wedding. Nod if you understand.' Dérin is stunned into silence, but nods slowly. 'We can't procrastinate on the notes any more, we need to act. Do you have the rest of them?'

'They're in the left-side compartment of my vanity. In a gold box. But, Lar—'

She doesn't get to complete her sentence before two notes are in my hand and I'm making my way out of the door.

YOU WERE SO EASY TO FIND, DÉRIN.
YOU SHOULD BE MORE CAREFUL.

AREN'T YOU LUCKY THAT YOUR HAIRDRESSER DIDN'T LEAVE ANY SCISSO<u>R</u>S LYING A<u>R</u>OUND? I'LL HAVE TO TR<u>Y</u> HARDER NEXT TIME.

What are we dealing with?

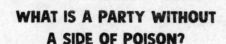

WHAT IS A PARTY WITHOUT
A SIDE OF POISON?

The information has not stopped rolling in about Dérin Oyinlola's bachelor-and-bachelorette-end-of-summer party. The bride promised to break the internet, and that she did. The hashtag for this star-studded event? #CupcakeGate.

Some partygoers are saying that the cupcakes they ate put them in hospital. One even needed to have her stomach pumped. But that report was from our resident party girl, Tolani, who needs hers pumped every three months, so who knows how reliable that story is.

Rumour has it that the cupcakes in question were from the highly praised patisserie chef, Rotimi, brother of celebrity hairstylist and Dérin's personal hairdresser, Rayo.

The pair *were* a sought out duo before #CupcakeGate. We wonder if this incident will dampen business for both brothers.

We have on good authority that Rotimi was hired as Dérin's wedding cake designer. I guess we can now officially rule him out. We'll be intrigued to see who else is in the running for the much-coveted position. And what about Rayo? Will he remain Dérin's hairdresser for her special day, or will he blacklist her?

Should Dérin be charged for the victims' hospital fees? It's not like it'd make a dent in her fortune . . . Kayode's maybe.

You know gossip doesn't sleep, and neither do I.

xoxo

CHAPTER FOURTEEN

'Get dressed, we're going for a drive,' I say to Babs, picking up a shirt from the floor and throwing it at him, then searching his drawers for trousers.

I can feel Babs' stare on the side of my head. I'm sure he's annoyed that I've interrupted his solitude, but time is critical. 'What last-minute plans has Dérin got for us now? I want to chill today; my stomach is still rough from the party.'

'I'm sorry about your stomach,' I say, pulling out some grey cargos.

'It's not like you caused it,' he says, walking into his bathroom to change.

Babs comes out dressed and again asks where we're going. I motion for him to follow me before grabbing the cupcake out of the mini fridge in my room and walking downstairs. I head to the kitchen and Mum and Dad are there. Their conversation halts as I open the door. They look like they're discussing something serious. I freeze, hoping it's not about

155

me or uni because I can't do that right now. I attempt to leave slowly, but then I remember I should probably tell them I'm going out.

'Babs and I are going to the cinema,' I say, poking my head around the door. Mum's head turns fully towards me, her lips pursed. Dad also looks like he wants to say something, but he's as stubborn as I am and so won't. I must be the one to make the first move, as if the argument was my fault.

'Who's taking you?' Mum asks.

'Temi, if he's free. If not Babs and I will take an okada.'

'Lie, lie,' Mum says.

'A bus?' I pout.

'Never. If you get kidnapped, it's me they will now blame,' she says and I groan. 'Temi takes you or you don't go.'

I sigh, trying to ease my frustration. 'I'm going to ask him,' I mutter and excuse myself quickly. I find Temi at the front of the compound. He's on the phone and the conversation looks tense as his hand rests on his head. I wait for him to finish, but when he moves his hand from his head he sees me and quickly says bye to the person on the phone. I shake my head and mouth *Continue* but it's too late as he runs over to me.

'I'm really sorry. Babs and I need a ride to this address if you're free?' I show him my phone, and his head tilts.

'Of course, but it's over an hour away. By the time we get there it'll be nearly two p.m. Traffic might be bad on our way back.'

'That's okay.' I grab Babs' arm forcefully. 'Gives us more than enough time to bond.'

As Temi predicted, the journey takes a while. We spend most of the car ride listening to music, sightseeing through the window and catching up about things.

'Dad and I got into it the other day about uni. I told him I didn't want to study Law,' I say, facing Babs.

'I'm guessing things aren't good if you're only just telling me now.' He looks at me with concern. 'You can't take anything Dad says personally, Lara. It probably came as a shock because in their eyes, you've never shown an interest in any other subject.'

'You don't even know what he said. He accused me of running away from being successful . . . like I couldn't be successful at anything else but law.' I tut. 'And that isn't true. I've always shown an interest in criminology. I basically eat, sleep and breathe it. I'm always annoying you guys about it too, so how can you say I've not?'

'Lara, you talk about criminal *cases*. But to the untrained, and often uninterested, minds of our parents it sounds like you're always talking about law. It sounds like your interests lie in the aftermath, not the before. You're constantly going on about "how can he only get twenty-five years, instead of a whole-life sentence". Or "because of this case they had to create this law so that there was a standard procedure in place". I don't even know any of the words that have just come out of my mouth just now, but it sounds like lawyer talk. Obviously Dad would be shocked if you said you want to swap courses.'

I'd never thought of it that way. A little groan escapes my lips.

'Relax, you'll be fine. But *thank you* for taking the first blow.' He rubs his hand over the top of my braids. 'Next time you're going to disappoint them, let me know so I can piggyback on your news. Your whole new career path trumps me not wanting to do surgery.'

I start to open my mouth to fight back, but Temi speaks. 'We're here.' I duck my head to take a better look. The green building has a blue-and-white signboard on it reading *Idowu Lab Testing Centre.*

'Why are we at a lab?' Babs asks.

'How do I put this . . . I don't think we're related, and its only taken me eighteen years to be able to raise the funds to discover the truth.' I sigh, holding my hand out with fake sympathy. He slaps it away and kisses his teeth then gets out of the car. I laugh to myself and exit too. 'Temi, did you want to stretch your legs and come with us?' I ask as I walk past the driver's seat.

He shakes his head. 'Labs freak me out. You never know what they're harbouring. I'll stay in the car, thank you.'

'Why does he get a choice?' Babs asks, but I pull him along, ignoring his protests.

I stop him just before going inside. 'The reason your stomach hurts is because there was something in the cupcakes.'

'Yeah, funny.' He scoffs.

'I'm serious. Whatever was on the icing bleached Joseph's

tie. I need to find out what was in them.' Babs scans my face as if he's trying to work out if I'm being for real. My expression doesn't shift as I give him an intense stare.

'Lara, you swear you're not making things up?' Lines appear on his forehead.

What is it with the men in this family not believing me? My jaw tightens. 'Ask your stomach.' I swing the lab door open, no longer caring if Babs follows me inside or not.

The reception area feels like a GP back home; the interior has leather sofas in the waiting area and a water dispenser in the corner. There are two doors, one that says *Staffroom* and the other which says *Toilet*. A chemical smell hangs in the air. The window separating us from the lab has a sign that says *Ring for attention*. I ring the bell and wait patiently. Babs finally decides to walk into the room behind me.

Moments later, a lanky man appears at the window. He's so tall, it almost looks like it hurts him to not look anyone at eye level. He bends slightly as he opens the window to talk to us.

'How can I help you?' His voice breaks like he's just started puberty.

'I'd like to test this cupcake, please. For any substances other than normal ingredients. Poisons and harmful chemicals included . . . if that's how it works.' I give him a simple smile. He looks at me confused. Then amusement creeps across his face.

'Been watching too much Nollywood?' He grabs the ziplock bag containing the cupcake from me.

'Something like that,' I say. 'How much would it cost?'

'Eighty-one thousand naira,' he says and I have to do the maths in my head. About forty pounds. Not bad.

'How much if you can get the results to me in less than three days?'

He scoffs. 'Impossible. It'll take four days to do thorough testing.'

'How much for that?'

'Double,' he says and my eyes narrow.

'You're lying,' I say. 'Your eye twitched when you said that. Don't let the accent fool you: my mother and father are very stubborn people. I *will* negotiate with you for hours until you bring the cost down.'

'Ugh, please, she's not lying. For your sake and mine, what is the real price?' Babs groans from behind me. The man pauses like he's thinking about it, but I know he's going to concede any minute.

'One hundred and twenty thousand naira,' he says. 'Last, last.' He tries to keep his eye still, but I know he's still lying. I don't have hours to spend arguing with him. Time is ticking.

I roll my eyes and then agree with a nod. 'Card?' I put my hand out for Babs to give me his.

'*My* card?' he protests. 'Where's yours?'

'Why would I pay for this? You're older than me,' I deadpan. 'It's only sixty pounds. Don't be cheap.' Babs kisses his teeth and then slaps his card in my hand. 'Thank you.' I type his PIN into the card reader and he asks how I know it, but that's none of his business. The lanky man hands me a form to fill out with my contact details and the promise to have the results in four days. 'Lovely doing business with the both of you.' I turn to smile to Babs, then usher him out of the room.

We walk outside to find Temi still in the car and on the phone. He finishes his call and unlocks the doors for both of us to get in.

'Was there a toilet inside?' he asks as we get in. 'I'm desperate and it's a long drive back.'

'Yeah, you'll see it as soon as you go in.'

'Back soon,' he says, walking into the building.

God, I hope those cupcakes come back with something, and something big.

CHAPTER FIFTEEN

I've spent today isolating myself from everyone.

Temi was right – the Lagos traffic was bad, so we got home late last night after our trip to the lab. I decided to have an early night. And I've stayed in my room ever since.

Thankfully – well, not thankfully – because of Dérin's injury, the house has been eerily quiet. Uncle Tayo let Kayode stay over at Dérin's request because he's an important part of her recovery. The only time he's left the house is to get some more clothes and other essentials. Otherwise, he's been here to relieve Aunty Zai of caring duties. It's like the incidents with Joseph and Seni never happened.

I've checked on Dérin periodically through texts. She keeps insisting I come to her room to watch movies with her and the girls, but I've brushed her off, using the excuse that I need to rest after a hectic few days. A half-truth. Mum and Dad haven't bothered me much either. Dad and I still haven't spoken, and Mum sends me messages through

Babs, who brings meals to my room.

For the past twenty-four hours, I've been combing through my favourite mystery audiobooks and online files, and binge-watching multiple episodes of the TV shows I love to work out how to formulate a cohesive bank of secrets.

The only good thing about studying my butt off for the past two years is that I know my brain, and I know how it processes information. I need to see everything mapped out. Once I see it, I'll know where to start and what to do with the information. Even if it's just to get it all out of me because it's driving me crazy, to put it lightly. The other benefit of becoming a hermit is that I've been able to focus on my investigation board and update it with my new findings.

I've put most of it in code or added the initials of new suspects, and barely highlighted anything so it looks like revision. Only the most inquisitive and nosy minds would bother to sit down and read it. Even then, only Uncle Damola would understand it.

I've talked myself around in circles multiple times. As much as it's about the *why*, it's also about the *how*. If I can figure out how this person is able to dance around us so easily and go undetected, it will make finding them easier.

I study my research on the investigation board. The people most able to fly under the radar, and who also have a clear motive, are Joseph, Seni and Uncle Yinka. Joseph and Seni both have their history with the bride and groom. But they weren't in the country when the notes first started, which means they would've had to hire someone to help them.

Joseph has an agenda, that much is clear; he's very loud about wanting to win Dérin back. Loud enough to send her threatening notes and create a fake Instagram page to sow seeds of doubt in the public's mind? In Dérin's mind? Potentially.

Seni may want to win Kayode back – it's clear they have unfinished business. Or maybe she's so bitter she just wants to break him and Dérin up and humiliate them in the process.

New to the list of suspects is Uncle Yinka, who couldn't be discreet even if he tried, but also has secrets of his own. They may not be causing problems now, but something tells me they will later, especially after his argument with Aunty Yemi about Moses, whoever that is, and his threat that Uncle Tayo will 'see'. I don't know if he has the brains to be the faceless stalker but his greed, especially for Uncle Tayo's money, makes him extremely questionable. But like Seni and Joseph, he was abroad when the notes began. So, even if he's smarter than he seems, he too would've had to hire someone to deliver the notes.

All these scenarios involve a separate person. Someone tasked with actually passing the notes to Dérin.

Alika's name keeps flashing up in my mind, so I add her initials to the investigation board. She doesn't have a clear motive, but I feel there's more to her than meets the eye.

Her choice of words when we spoke about Rayo's cupcakes was weird. *Really* weird. The 'illusive'. She didn't correct herself even when I pointed it out.

'Illusive' means based on an illusion. When something is

illusive, it's not real. The way Alika said it made it seem like she didn't believe . . . well, Dérin. @ajebotashamer seems set on debunking the idea that Kayode and Dérin are a perfect couple. Could Alika be behind the account *and* the notes? Alika started working with Dérin around the same time the messages started. It wouldn't be hard for any of my suspects to enquire who Dérin's wedding planner was and bribe them into doing their dirty work. Alika herself said she's not making that much money from wedding planning right now.

But would she want to ruin her career before it's even really begun?

I open the Instagram DM I sent to Àdúràtọ́lá, the bride @ajebotashamer was sending hate comments to last year. She hasn't replied. I don't blame her for not checking her DMs; I'm honestly surprised she still has them open. If someone had been flooding mine with horrible messages, I'd stay off Instagram. I just wish she would, because that might make it easier for me to find a few missing pieces.

If Instagram is my only hook right now, I have to be strategic with it. I log out of my account, then type @ajebotashamer in the username section and click 'forgot password'. It takes me to the page that asks me if I have trouble logging in. I click 'next' and a message pops up.

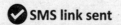 **SMS link sent**

We've sent an SMS message to 234 * *** **61
with a link to get back into your account.**

The number behind the account is Nigerian. Finally a lead I can work on.

I scroll through my call log:

Alika: +234 763 342 6874
Joseph: Nigerian Number: +234 006 341 9902
Seni: Nigerian Number: +234 891 222 1704
Uncle Yinka: +234 040 573 0419

None of their numbers match.

It dawns on me that I've potentially alerted @ajebotashamer to the fact that I'm trying to get into their account. But maybe that will frighten them rather than fuel their malice. I want them to be scared that I'm close to discovering who they are.

My eyes land on Alika's business card stuck on my investigation board. I hadn't noticed that it included her full name. I type *Alika Amenze* into Google.

pinterest.co.uk
https://www.pinterest.co.uk > alikaamenze

Alika Amenze (AlikaAmenze) – Profile – Pinterest

TikTok
https://www.tiktok.com > Discover

Alika Amenze | TikTok Search

AlikaAmenze

1.2K+ followers

Wedding Planner Goddess (@tildeathdoyoupart)

International Wedding Planner in Lagos, London and beyond

as seen on @bellanaijaweddings, @weddingdigestnaija and

@naijagossiplounge

In order to show you the most relevant results, we have omitted
some entries very similar to those already displayed.

If you like, you can repeat the search with
the omitted results included.

I repeat the search but nothing different comes up. I can't believe that's it? Her whole life is on three social media accounts? There are no personal Facebook profiles, which is understandable because she's basically Dérin's age. Her Instagram page doesn't even have any tagged photos.

I type in the name of her wedding planning business next:

TilDeathDoYouPart

The same results come up: TikTok, Pinterest and Instagram accounts, this time focusing on her business. All with similar unremarkable results. There's one blog article with a minor mention in a photo caption from what I'm assuming was

Alika's first solo wedding. Literally just:

Wedding planner: TilDeathDoYouPart

I look up from my laptop to the notes Dérin has been receiving. There are five now stuck on the investigation board, all as ominous and sinister as each other. I've been staring at them almost non-stop between all my research.

What's baffling me is the underlined letters. There's no consistent pattern. They're sporadic. At the same time, at least one letter in every note is underlined.

AREN'T YOU LUCKY THAT YOUR HAIRDRESSER DIDN'T LEAVE ANY SCISSORS LYING AROUND? I'LL HAVE TO TRY HARDER NEXT TIME.

IS IT SHAME OR LUCK THAT YOU'RE PRETTY? EITHER WAY I'LL PLAY NICE, FOR NOW. CALL OFF THE WEDDING AND THINGS COULD BE SO EASY.

YOU'VE IGNORED ME FOR TOO LONG. NOW I'M GOING TO DO THINGS MY WAY.

IF YOU WANT TO KEEP LIVING A FAIRY TALE, DROP THE WEDDING PLANNING NOW.

YOU WERE SO EASY TO FIND, DÉRIN.
YOU SHOULD BE MORE CAREFUL.

The letters make up: RRYSOTOINNI

I've spent hours trying to unscramble them, but I can't make any sense of them.

I write out the letters on my investigation board, spacing them out so they're clearer.

R R Y S O T O I N N I

· I put the letters through a word unscrambler website multiple times, and it gives me actual whole words:

NONSTORY

SORORITY

NOTIONS

But even those don't use all the underlined letters, so it can't be right. I split them in half and put them into the unscrambler again and still nothing pops out. Google brings up no results, and, instead, suggests I've made a spelling mistake.

I need another pair of eyes on this. But right now I'm fried and I need to wake up for the blood drive in twelve hours' time.

Investigations will have to wait.

CHAPTER SIXTEEN

The most important thing (the *only* thing, God willing) for me to do today is to hydrate enough to give blood.

Every year, Uncle Tayo organizes a blood drive at a hired-out centre and donates equipment to hospitals in poorer areas to help treat people living with sickle cell, in the family's name. I'm involved for the first time this year because I'm finally old enough to donate. Sickle cell is a disease of the blood where the red blood cells have an abnormal crescent shape, which means they carry less oxygen around the body. Nigeria is the sickle cell capital of the world, with the highest number of sickle cell carriers. Unfortunately, it carries a lot of stigma here. Despite it being an inherited disease people don't want to be associated with it, whether they carry it, or live with it.

Sickle cell can be managed through blood exchanges or transfusions, as well as medication, but the problem is that not enough people in Nigeria donate blood, which often leaves a lot of people living with sickle cell at a disadvantage. It always fills my heart with pride whenever Uncle Tayo hosts his blood drive because he makes it his mission to debunk stigma and help those who need it the most. He's been a huge advocate since his mother, our grandmother, told him the story about her brother passing away at an early age from what they now know was sickle cell. His mother didn't grow up with money, but married into it, and so, with her new-found financial power made it her mission to spread awareness. We don't have enough Black donors in the UK either which again puts people with sickle cell at a higher disadvantage when needing blood transfusions or exchanges.

I put on my white low-top Converses to pair with my white ribbed bodycon dress. I've done my make-up lightly, so I line my lips with brown liner and put on a clear lip gloss, grab my bag, then head downstairs.

'She's alive!' Uncle Tayo says as I walk to the car. I go over to greet him and he hugs me, kissing my head. 'How was your day off?'

'Fine,' I say sweetly and make my way over to Kayode's car. I get in the back seat, next to Amaka and Seni, and browse my phone until Dérin finally eases herself into the front passenger seat. She's wearing dungarees over a light blue top and her wig is blown out, curved into her face. Once she's in, she turns around to face us, smile as wide as ever. 'Is everyone ready to give blood?'

'Um, *yayyy*,' Amaka and Seni say, excitement missing

from their tones. The early morning start has obviously killed their vibe.

'Oh, come on. There'll be a DJ and refreshments. Even gifts to take home. It'll be a lot of fun,' she says, singing the words as if she's coaxing children to open their mouths for spoonfuls of food.

Kayode gets in a minute later and waves to us in the car mirror, then he and Dérin talk as we follow Uncle Tayo to the venue. The journey isn't long, about fifteen minutes, but it's enough for me to get into the new mystery audiobook I'm currently listening to; we're just about to find out who put the dry ice in the secret tunnel and killed one of the students at the school.

When we get to the blood drive, Kayode's family are already sitting in the waiting area. We pile in to join them just before the pastor, who usually blesses the blood drive, starts to speak. This year's sermon is about infidelity and adultery. I make sure to clear my throat several times so that certain people make sure to listen hard and well. Kayode gets the hint, giving me side-eye. Dérin also shuffles in her seat whenever I fake-cough.

The pastor's story is about a father whose child was born with sickle cell disease, despite him having the genotype AA and his wife having the genotype AS. As this is not genetically possible, when his child tested positive for the disease, he knew that his wife had been unfaithful and she had to confess. The pastor links this story seamlessly to the importance of testing your genotype before you marry someone in order to prevent the spread of sickle cell, or at the very least, to help those who have the disease. Uncle Tayo then joins the pastor to talk about the importance of donating blood.

'The mortality rate of children with sickle cell is too high for us to sit back and watch. Ethnically matched blood is important because their bodies will not reject the blood that *we* are able to provide. How can you be content with the medical treatment that most of us have observed here in the country? How can you be a truly selfless being – as Pastor preaches – if you are allowing this to continue, knowing that you can help? At the cost of what? An hour to two of your day? If the government isn't going to do anything about it, we need to take matters into our own hands and start donating blood to help those who need it the most. It has to start with us.'

When he finishes, everyone claps then the pastor leads a prayer over everyone and for the success of the blood drive. Before we know it, it's time to donate. The hall is split into three parts: pre-screening where everyone fills out questionnaires to see if they're eligible, the actual donation side filled with healthcare practitioners, and the recovery corner, where aunties will be handing out containers of food and boxes of juice to replenish people. We all fill out our pre-screening forms and drink the bottle of water given to us before donating.

I finish my form and hand it to a nurse who checks it then ushers me off to get my blood drawn. She puts a tight cuff around the top of my arm and cleans my skin, then inserts the needle. She gives me a stress ball and tells me to squeeze periodically.

Amaka and Seni are on either side of me. Seni looks like she's about to throw up at the sight of the needle, while Amaka looks weirdly relaxed. I close my eyes, waiting for the ten minutes to be over as my arm starts to feel tingly. When I open my eyes I notice Dérin standing across the hall: she isn't donating.

Amaka must notice at the same time because she shouts, loud enough for everyone to hear, 'Rin!'

Dérin walks over to us, embarrassed. 'Was that really necessary?'

'Why are you not giving blood?' Amaka asks. 'I thought I saw you doing a form.'

'She can't give blood,' Seni says matter-of-factly, which makes Amaka and me lean forward, before being told by the nurse to lie back down. We're both silent, waiting for Seni to continue.

When she doesn't, our heads turn back to Dérin, who looks caught off guard. 'She's right, I can't. I didn't pass my pre-screening.'

'Oh. What question made you fail?' Amaka asks, then does a big gasp, and whisper-shouts, 'Are you pregnant?' Her smile is disturbingly wide.

My eyebrows skyrocket. 'You're pregnant?' I whisper.

'I am not pregnant.' Dérin rolls her eyes. 'I got my ears pierced three months ago, and the form says you have to wait four months before you can give blood if you've had any recent body piercings or tattoos.'

'A baby would've been better,' Amaka says, then lies back down.

Dérin scoffs, then Aunty Zai calls her over and she excuses herself. I look at Seni, confused. I knew Dérin had got her ears pierced but I didn't make that connection. Also, Seni wasn't near Dérin when she filled out her form. Now that I think about it, I'm not entirely sure Dérin *did* fill out her form. She was mostly holding the iPad and watching Kayode answer his questionnaire.

'How did you know she couldn't give blood?' I ask.

Seni straightens in her chair, almost like she's avoiding the question. 'I knew about her new piercing, and I'm a regular blood donor so I've memorized the rules by now.'

'Oh . . . I'm surprised you're not used to the needles, then,' I say.

'I'm needle-phobic, but I don't want that to stop me from donating to people that need it. My sister has sickle cell so I help when I can.' She squirms then smiles. I smile back.

It's funny how I can go from thinking she's Lucifer's right-hand woman to thinking she's a decent person. The nurse removes the needle, sticks a plaster on my arm, does her final checks and tells me I'm good to go. I get up from the chair, wiggling my numb fingers as I walk over to the refreshments area where Kayode and Babs are drinking juice. Seni and Amaka follow a few minutes after. The hall is full, much fuller than the one at the drive I attended two

175

years ago. Uncle Tayo has put in a lot of positive work over the years and it's so nice to see the fruits of his labour come to life. Dérin comes over with a beaming smile. It's the brightest I've seen her since her back injury.

Two minutes later, Joseph makes his entrance, sunglasses on and car keys in hand.

'Party people.' He nods at us, taking his glasses off. Everyone half smiles when they see him, except for Kayode who looks like he's trying not to scowl.

'Why aren't you donating?' Amaka asks.

'Vampires can't give blood. They take it.' Seni scoffs, then grabs a bag of plantain crisps from the table. Joseph chuckles to himself, stops and then chuckles again as if this is all so funny to him. There's something about his face that is annoyingly charming but also so punchable.

'Passed my pre-screening, but my iron's low.' He shrugs in Amaka's direction, then directs his attention to Dérin. 'I need to talk to you, though.'

Kayode says, 'Hell no,' at the same time as I say, 'Absolutely not.'

Joseph chuckles again like we've told a joke. I don't want to provoke him because I know exactly what kind of ammo he's got.

'I could talk to *you* – actually?' He gives a devious half-smile, half-frown in Kayode's direction. 'Got a lot I could talk to you about.'

'Joseph,' Dérin warns him. Nobody else knows what he could have to say, but I unfortunately do.

'The fuck's that supposed to mean?' Kayode starts to get irate, standing up from his seat. 'I'm tired of seeing you everywhere. You add nothing to the wedding and you cause issues wherever you appear. When is it going to become clear to you that she chose me and not you?'

'Ah, shut up, you whiny little rich boy. If we weren't in public, I'd put you in your place.' Joseph's gun fingers come out and Amaka has to stand up and pull his arm down.

'Grace and decorum, please! Like you said, *we're* in public.' She grits her teeth. 'I'm tired of playing peacemaker because I'm the only one who had the brains to date outside of our friendship group.'

'Ouch?' Seni butts in.

'You shut up.' She points at Seni then continues speaking to Joseph and Kayode. 'Can you and Kayode stop refusing to use the braincells God gave you? How long have you guys had to *fix* this situation, and you still haven't?'

Joseph ignores her and continues to Kayode, 'That's your fucking issue, you know. You treat her like she's some prize you've won. You don't even realize the gem you have in front of you.'

'*How would you know?*' Dérin erupts, getting out of her seat. 'Stop making assumptions about my relationship!'

'Okay, let's go.' Amaka pulls Joseph away as more people turn to stare. Even our parents start to look.

Seni says through a forced grin, 'Smile, we're on *Candid Camera*.' She darts her eyes towards someone at a nearby table who is not so discreetly filming us.

THE GIRL IS MINE

Well, well, well.

We guess those whispers were right about the love triangle between Joseph Lawal, Kayode Akinlola and Dérin Oyinlola. The men were seen fighting over our blushing bride at the Oyinlolas' annual sickle cell blood drive. Heated swearwords were exchanged between them, and if you listen closely, you can hear a tiny violin playing in the background.

The plot thickens and thickens.

Will we ever make it down the aisle in one piece? Or will we be attending the wedding of Dérin and someone else in the near future?

Video attached.

You know gossip doesn't sleep, and neither do I.

xoxo

CHAPTER SEVENTEEN

Four days have passed since I asked the lab to test the cupcake, which means the results should arrive at any moment. I'm anxiously waiting by my phone. The last two days have been packed with tedious wedding prep, that, fortunately, haven't involved the majority of the family, so we've been using it as much-needed relaxation time. But tonight, Dérin has arranged a rehearsal dinner.

I'm sitting at the dining-room table reading my latest murder mystery novel and checking my phone practically every ten seconds for news from the lab, when Aunty Zai sits next to me and pulls me into a hug. I fight the urge to escape her grasp.

'When will we start prepping for your wedding, Lara?' she says as she pats my hair then she squeezes my cheeks.

'I need prospects for that, Aunty,' I try to say, but it comes out muffled. She lets go of me seconds later.

'I've always wanted another girl to spoil, so make sure

to start looking for a husband when you get to uni. And promise me, when the time comes, you'll both look up your genotypes before going any further.'

I stare back in shock.

'*Further?*'

'Haba, do you think I live under a rock? I'm not your mother,' she tuts.

I want to move the conversation swiftly on before it ends up becoming a lecture on the birds and the bees. 'Speaking of weddings, Aunty. What made you recommend Alika to Dérin? She's . . . kind of use—'

'Useless, abi?' Aunty Zai kisses her teeth. 'Me and her have argued the entire planning process. Because she came recommended from Ireti she spends all her time helping her out as if *I'm* not the mother of the bride.'

'Aunty Ireti?'

'Ireti recommended her. Alika did one of her relatives' weddings nicely and she needed more weddings in her portfolio. I shouldn't have let my Dérin's be a second trial run.'

That is interesting; and makes things extra confusing. Maybe Alika is more credible than she seems, if Aunty Ireti recommended her? It still doesn't change the fact that she was a literal ghost before her previous wedding.

'At Dérin's party, cupcakes were given to the guests. Temi said that you told him to hand them out. Why?'

'From Rayo? Dérin doesn't have a sweet tooth. They would've gone to waste. Now I'm realizing they should have. I'm so pissed off with that stupid Naija Gossip Lounge for insinuating nonsense. Why are you asking me these questions?'

'Just confused, sorry. Dérin didn't know where they came from, so she got worried.'

'Ah, ah. Temi answered the door and I was with him when he got the package so I put them in her room. Why would Dérin be worried? She needs to relax, she's going to ruin her health.' Aunty Zai sighs.

It's now just two hours until the rehearsal dinner and everyone is running around like headless chickens. It's freaking me the fuck out.

I leave my room and go to Amaka's to see how she's getting along.

She's not.

Amaka is still carving out her eyebrows. 'Oh, hello! Here to help?' She smiles. My face goes from shock to slack. 'I'll take that as a no.' She frowns, walking around the room towards the wardrobe.

'I— I'll be back. Let me just make sure everyone else is somewhat ready.' I shake my head, walking out of the room.

Seni's room is at the end of the hall, so I go to hers before going to Dérin's. Walking by the door reminds me of her and Kayode emerging from it during the party, but I shake off the memory and knock. Seconds later, she shouts for me to come in. She's basically ready apart from taking her rollers out, and putting on lipstick and shoes. Today's wig is chocolate brown with blond highlights.

'How many wigs do you own?' I ask, squinting. 'I feel like I've got to take notes.'

'I've lost count, honestly.' Her voice is muffled as she lines her lips. 'What's up?'

'Would you mind helping Amaka with her make-up? She is very, very behind.' I deflate.

'Sure, give me two seconds,' she says, and I clasp my hands in prayer, thanking her.

Then I take my leave, making my way over to Dérin's room. She's on the bed, glass of water in hand and head tilted back, popping pills into her mouth. My eyebrows knit in concern. 'Are you okay? Is your back acting up?' As I make my way over to sit on her bed, she gulps more water then looks at me. Her eyes light up.

'You look *gorgeous.*'

I fake blush. I'm wearing a pair of black leather trousers with a pale-yellow crop top that has thin, wispy straps, and I've done my make-up with a light smoky eye, brown lipliner and nude lip gloss combo. I kiss her on the cheek to say thank you.

'My back isn't hurting, it's just my regular medication. Vitamins and stuff.'

I mouth *Oh.* Then get back to the task at hand.

'Of all people, I thought *you* at least would be ready.' I clap my hands loudly, which startles her. 'Why do you only have your clothes on? *Why* isn't your make-up done?'

Her lips flatten into a line. 'I just want to sleep.' We both stare at each other, then burst into laughter.

'This was your idea,' I say, wiping a tear from my eye.

'I know, but in hindsight . . . I just, I want to sleep.' She grimaces. 'It's been non-stop the past two weeks and I'm tired. I don't want to socialize any more; I want to *nap* for like three weeks after this is done. Will you do my make-up?' She clasps her hands, begging. 'Please?' I roll my eyes and nod, getting up to grab her foundation and concealer from her vanity. 'Could you do it while I lie down?'

'Absolutely not,' I say, as I follow Dérin to her vanity and start on her eyeshadow. Five minutes later, I hear a phone vibrate. My head snaps around so fast I almost give myself whiplash. I crawl onto Dérin's bed to grab my phone. The screen reads *No Caller ID*.

My eyes grow wide. It's the lab. 'Hello?' I answer. 'This is she. Yes, I can confirm that I asked for the testing of a cupcake.'

The woman on the other end is impatient when she speaks to me. 'We've tested the sample you provided and we have not found anything unusual, suspicious, poisonous or harmful to the human body.'

'*Nothing*? That's not possible. People got sick from them. Do you need more time to run tests?'

'Madam, I can assure you we did a very thorough test. We spent more time on your sample than we would have liked to, or usually would, on a fast-track order. Our findings are correct and final. A full report has been sent to the email address you provided. Have a nice da—'

'Wait, sorry! I hear what you're saying, but I need you to understand that I saw the *icing* bleach a person's tie. At the very least, your results didn't come back with traces of bleach? Chlorine? Even hand sanitizer?'

The woman on the phone stays silent, but I can hear typing in the background. 'I've just found the report on the system. I'll read it out for you.' I put the phone on loudspeaker so Dérin can hear too. 'Butter, eggs, caster sugar, sodium bicarbonate – which is baking powder – salt, flour, milk, vanilla essence, icing sugar and cream cheese. That is all. I'm sorry.'

'Okay. Thank you.' There's defeat in my voice. The woman on the phone tells me to have a nice day then cuts the call. I turn to Dérin. 'There's no way that's right. There is *no way*. Amina immediately threw up, Babs felt queasy and forced himself to vomit, more people have said the cupcakes made them ill, and some were even hospitalized. Joseph's tie was *bleached for God sakes!*'

It's shocking. It's brilliant. It's infuriating. I am livid. I have nothing that shows probable harm to Dérin. I have no strong evidence apart from the notes, which could easily be disputed because this crazy stalker hasn't acted on them. Nothing physically dangerous has actually happened to Dérin, even though her reputation is in ruins.

'Well, this is great. So, what was that? Mind games? How would they know which cupcake I'd go for? Did they just hope that I would eat them all and not wake up? I don't get it. I don't get any of it.' Dérin starts to cry and her voice

184

breaks. 'Rotimi has refused to do my wedding cake because of the bad press he's received after the Najia Gossip Lounge blog post, so now I have no wedding cake designer. And I just about have a hairstylist because Rayo is equally upset. I have to put all my energy into finding a new wedding cake designer because Alika needs to focus *her* energy on making sure the guest list is airtight. And to make matters worse, I got another one.'

'Another what?' I ask, scared for the answer.

She cries through hiccups. I try to calm her down, bringing her in for a hug and rubbing her back. Nothing works for a while. This breakdown is the culmination of all the emotions from the party, the blog posts, the fights with Joseph and Kayode. She needs to cry it out. I would cry too if it wasn't the counterproductive thing to do right now.

She sniffs as she finally speaks. 'I got another note ... and a "present". My dress for tonight came back from the dry cleaners ripped all over. Like a knife or scissors had slashed through it repeatedly. I didn't even post about tonight or the dress; how would they know?'

She pulls a note from under her pillow.

YOU CAN'T PLAY CAT AND MOUSE IF THE MOUSE STOPS LEAVING THE HOUSE, SO I THOUGHT I'D COME TO YOU.
DINNER DRESS TODAY. WEDDING DRESS TOMORROW.

'Oh, Dérin,' I say, squeezing her arm sympathetically before studying the note again. The letters *A*, *V*, *H* and *E* are underlined this time.

HAVE? I remind myself to add the note to my investigation board.

'I will find out who is doing this to you. I promise.'

If it's the last thing I do.

I manage to finish Dérin's make-up in thirty minutes.

As soon as we are all downstairs, the doorbell rings. As Aunty Zai approaches the front door, she looks at us and dramatically braces us all, practising a wide smile before turning around and opening it.

There's a burst of greetings as Kayode's family walk in. Uncle Fola greets Aunty Zai before walking over to Uncle Tayo, Dad and Uncle Yinka, who are dapping each other up. Aunty Zai squeals at the door as Aunty Ireti comes in, her arms wide in greeting. She hugs Aunty Zai first, then Aunty Yemi, then moves to Amaka and Seni. This is the first time I've seen Seni and Aunty Ireti interact. There's a stiffness to their hug that makes me wonder if Kayode introduced her to his mum when they were dating and now things are awkward. Aunty Ireti embraces me then moves to Dérin, squeezing her tight. She rubs her hand over Dérin's hair.

'Is everything okay, dear? Your eyes are red,' she says, concern in her voice. Kayode approaches Dérin and holds her face to look at her properly.

'You're going to ruin my make-up,' she teases Kayode,

pulling his hands off her cheeks. 'I'm fine. Seriously, just wedding stress.'

'Alika is supposed to be taking that burden away from you?' Aunty Ireti says, but she phrases it like a question. 'What can we delegate to her?'

Dérin pauses as if she's thinking about the best thing to pawn off to Alika. 'I need a new wedding cake designer. That would be the biggest help.'

'Consider it done,' Aunty Ireti says, bringing out her phone to text Alika.

Moments later, Aunty Tiwa and Joseph walk into the house. I eye him as we exchange hellos. 'Anything devious planned for tonight?' He gives me a wide grin.

'Nothing you need to know about. Bring it in.' He pulls me in for a hug.

I smile as I say into his ear, 'I know about the kiss.' He pulls away from me immediately and starts to speak but I interrupt, 'And the notes too.' I'm still not certain he's the culprit, but gauging his reaction doesn't hurt.

His expression starts changing but I'm distracted by Amaka grabbing my arm to walk me to my seat. She's been uninterested in all things Joseph since the blood drive. I can't imagine how many awkward moments like that she must've witnessed, being in their friendship group.

Tonight's menu consists of gourmet versions of meals Dérin and Kayode have had on their travels as a couple. The thought of a sit-down dinner as a host is hellish: you have to make sure conversation is constantly flowing so that no one feels awkward, while hoping that the food is actually edible.

The caterers start taking away our plates and replacing them with our second course out of six. They give a little synopsis of the meal, telling us about how Kayode asked Dérin to be his girlfriend properly when they snuck away for a few hours on a holiday with their friends in Morocco.

'Dérin, when do you plan to move to the UK?' Aunty Tiwa asks. 'Kayo, you're supposed to start your Foundation Year One as a junior doctor at the end of August, right?'

'Yeah. Foundation year training normally starts at the beginning of August but I'm starting at the end of the month because of the wedding,' Kayode answers.

Then Dérin continues, 'My contract at work ends in December so I'll have to stay here until then. It's hybrid so I'll be able to travel to the UK some weeks, but for the meantime Kayode will be holding the fort and getting the house ready for me when I move back for good in the new year.'

'Bold of you to trust him enough to get the house ready. Men don't have an eye for decorating.' Aunty Tiwa chuckles to herself.

'I've already warned him, he can't buy anything without my consent over FaceTime.' She smiles and the table laughs, Kayode shaking his head.

'Is your back okay now?' Aunty Ireti asks, and Dérin nods. Aunty Ireti continues, 'Kayode was prepared to stay the entire week. He came home talking about how excited he was to live with you.' She laughs, and the table *awws* while Dérin blushes and Kayode hides his face.

'It's like they want me to barf this food back up,' Amaka says to me and I snicker.

Conversations travel around the table as we land back on the main subject: the traditional wedding.

'I've already told him that no one is playing "Last Last" at the wedding on Saturday,' Dérin says, staring playfully at Kayode. 'No groom of mine is going to be happily singing his heart out about his relationship being over.'

Kayode interjects, 'Lara, the song is timeless. Come on, convince her.'

'The song is not timeless. It's over-played.' Amaka rolls her eyes.

'Maybe we compromise and get the DJ to play the instrumental,' I say and everyone laughs.

Dérin reiterates. 'No, no, no. Not at my wedding. It's like a bad omen. We might as well call the whole thing off if that plays.' She fake shudders.

'You know, Ireti, you said it before, but seeing it now so closely is really fun. Lara looks a lot like Dérin,' Uncle Fola says, smiling softly. 'They even have the same mannerisms.'

Out of the corner of my eye, I catch Aunty Ireti staring between us.

Aunty Zai chimes in, boasting in her nasal voice, 'Lara is like my second daughter. When they were younger we used to joke that I gave birth to her.'

Mum clears her throat and I give her a watchful eye. 'That

was all me, my sister. It's their daddy's genes that don't allow ours to put up a fight.'

'It's good that they got our genes. We all know what your Uncle Gbenga looks like.' Dad giggles and Mum's jaw drops, eventually breaking into a laugh, then the entire table joins in. 'Truly, they look like Mama. Their grandmother. I think Lara looks the most like her, to be honest.' He beams.

Joseph opens his mouth to speak but is halted by Uncle Fola grinning at his phone and rising from his seat. 'Dérin, we wanted to do this after dinner, but it's arrived early. There's something for you outside.'

Dérin looks around the table, but we're just as clueless as she is. I look to Babs for some insight, but he frowns in confusion. The only people grinning are Uncle Fola and Kayode.

Uncle Fola leaves the table, then Kayode, and they're soon followed by everyone else. We all walk out of the dining room and into the foyer. Kayode pulls Dérin to his side, then puts his hand over her eyes. Uncle Fola opens the front door, and we all gasp.

'What? What is it?' Dérin squeals, bouncing up and down. Kayode counts down from three then removes his hand from Dérin's eyes, and she gasps. 'A Rolls-Royce?' Dérin squeals.

I look around. Everyone who lives or is staying in this house is showing a mixture of shock and . . . somewhat delight because we're all thinking the same thing. Meanwhile everyone who *doesn't* live here grins like Cheshire cats. Seni and Amaka are trying not to look confused.

'It's the Ghost. I remember you saying you wanted the one with the stars on the roof. I got you a personalized licence plate too.' Kayode pulls out the keys and Dérin takes them from him in disbelief.

She starts making her way to the car until a voice stops her.

'Okay. I'll bite. Since we are all thinking it,' Uncle Yinka says, his deep chuckle almost sinister. 'Why would you choose to buy Dérin a Rolls-Royce, instead of using that money to help pay for the wedding?'

CHAPTER EIGHTEEN

Chaos ensues. Quite literally.

'Yinka!' all the adults of our household shout. Aunty Yemi insults him: 'Kò sí nkan ní ọpọlọ ẹ.' It's true, there can't have been anything in his brain when he said that.

'What does he mean, "help pay" for the wedding?' Kayode asks, looking around at everyone. No one answers, and Uncle Fola and Aunty Ireti look like they're crawling back into their skin. 'Dérin? What does he mean? We agreed that we'd be splitting everything?'

Dérin's mouth opens then closes, and her eyes dart to her dad. Kayode tracks her gaze and faces Uncle Tayo, his eyebrows sky high. Uncle Tayo looks at him then at Kayode's parents, but no one says anything.

'At the introduction your parents said that they wouldn't be paying for the wedding. It's not a big deal, it was just a shock because of previous agreements,' Uncle Tayo enlightens everyone.

'At the introduction?' Kayode's voice rises. 'That was nearly two weeks ago! How long were you going to keep this from me?' He directs his words to his parents. They don't move an inch.

'Ẹ j ọ, please, let's come inside. We can talk about this over dinner,' Aunty Zai says and tries to usher everyone into the house. Half of us get indoors, but it's clear that Kayode isn't moving. Neither are his parents or Dérin.

He searches his parents' faces, then continues, 'Is this because of—'

'Kayode. Don't,' Aunty Ireti shushes him.

What was he going to say that needed to be so urgently silenced?

'Uncle, did they at least give you a reason?' he continues. 'Because I can't see why my parents would deliberately go behind my back and deny you paymen—'

'They said it after they asked for a prenup,' Uncle Yinka butts in, and all the adults groan again. Aunty Yemi hits him on the head, making him yelp.

'A prenup?' Kayode is stunned. 'Who agreed to that? When were you going to tell me? Uncle, Aunty, please know that from the start I have always thought the amount of money we're spending on the wedding is ridiculous to ask one family to pay and I have never requested a prenup from Dérin. I can't understand why my parents would be so rud—'

'Kayode, that is enough! We brought you up better than that,' Uncle Fola says sternly. 'It's tradition for the bride's family to pay for the wedding. We will continue to support you and Dérin after you get married, hence the car, but we also have other things to think about.' He bows his head, almost like he's ashamed. I wonder if that rumour about Uncle Fola's business tanking is true? Or maybe they would prefer to spend their money on his fiftieth birthday? Aunty Ireti's eyes are focused on Dérin's face, her expression unreadable.

'When have we ever been ones for tradition?' Kayode flails his arms up and down. 'I've been saving since I met Dérin because I've known for that long that I wanted her to be mine.' Joseph scoffs lightly, but I'm the only one who reacts with a disgusted look. Kayode continues, 'That's only some of the money we're using for the wedding. Half of everything we've planned has been *your* ideas that *you* agreed to pay for! Or have you got any other kids you've neglected to tell me about that you'd prefer to spend your money on?'

'*Kayode!*' Uncle Fola exclaims, shocked.

'Dad, does this make me look like a reliable person in front of my in-laws?'

'God, you can be so reckless. Not only with your actions, but with your mouth too,' Aunty Ireti snaps. 'As if this whole thing is about you only. Have you thought about how this looks for us? How we feel? How *I* feel about this whole thing?'

'Feel about *what*, Mum? I'm not taking the money out of your pockets to spend it on bullshit.'

Aunty Ireti is stunned into silence.

'Is it your *mother* you're speaking to like that?' Uncle Fola's expression grows wild.

Kayode's expression falters, immediately realizing his mistake. He starts, 'No—' but is interrupted by Aunty Zai.

'You know what, i-it's okay. Kayode, please, the money you have, use it for the house and for your and Dérin's life together. We'll handle the wedding, everyone please just come inside,' Aunty Zai begs. Dérin finally moves, tears pooling in her eyes. She places a hand on Kayode's shoulder, but he stays still, staring at Aunty Ireti and Uncle Fola.

'I don't think we can revive dinner,' Aunty Ireti says, avoiding eye contact. 'Or rather, I don't want to. I think we should just go; I can't even look at Kayode right now.'

'Ah, no. We can't let the night end like this. E ma binu. I apologize on behalf of Yinka and Kayode,' Aunty Zai says, rubbing her hands together and pleading, but Aunty Ireti doesn't budge.

'Nah, Aunty, don't apologize. That's fine by me,' Kayode says with finality. He strides away from his parents and disappears inside.

Aunty Ireti looks at him in shock, mouth slightly open. Then she grabs her husband in a surge of anger. Uncle Fola tries to nod at everyone, but Aunty Ireti pulls and pulls at him until they reach their car. Her expression hardens as she mutters to him and I catch her words: 'I told you this would happen.'

'Ònírànú.'

'Ajé ni yẹ.'

We go back to the table, hoping maybe we can continue to

make conversation over dinner or even pretend as if nothing happened. But no. As soon as we sit down insults start flying.

All the aunties and uncles cuss Uncle Yinka. It's more than deserved. They've gotten up from their seats and surrounded him as if he's their prey.

'Èwùrẹ́ òṣì. I'm even insulting goats by comparing you to one.'

'Ìkà ni. Ìkà. Look at his head, shaped like a bowling pin.'

I can't tell who's going in the hardest. It's mesmerizing to watch; it almost makes me wish I had a bag of popcorn.

'Let me ask you something: why is everyone angry at me?' Uncle Yinka complains. 'Kayode, did I not do you a favour? That's how they would've kept it all from you. It's even good Dérin is signing a prenup. At least my money won't be wasted if things go wrong.' His hands are thrashing around in protest. Kayode looks at him but doesn't say anything. He's holding on to Dérin, whose eyes are red. Seni, Amaka and I are watching the spectacle unfold from our seats. Joseph stands behind his, evidently not wanting to eat any more, Babs, the pillar of silence, taking it all in.

'*Your money?* You're sick. Classless man!' Aunty Zai shouts.

'It wasn't your place to say anything,' Uncle Tayo asserts.

'We were *all* thinking it. A *car*? Come on, now. Brother mi, you know you've been spending too much money on this wedding anyways. I did you a favour,' Uncle Yinka says, dumbfounded.

'When will you stop telling me how to spend my money? As if I would take financial advice from you. As if I would reduce my budget for my only daughter, my only child. You simply said something because of your own selfish attempt to borrow more money. You're a disgrace. Wo.' Uncle Tayo licks his index finger and swipes the ground then stands back up. 'For as long as Dérin lives you are never touching my money ever again. Lie, lie. You must suffer. Any money I even think about giving you is going straight to Yemisi. Forty-two years old and you still can't manage your own money. When will you learn? Àgbàyà oshi, old for *nothing.*' Uncle Tayo kisses his teeth and then walks out, cursing under his breath.

Aunty Zai kisses her teeth too, then follows her husband. Then Mum, Dad and Aunty Tiwa leave. Aunty Yemisi is left, frowning at Uncle Yinka as her hand rests on her belly. 'See how you've just disgraced yourself. I refuse to go down with you.' She makes a *tsk* sound then waddles out.

Uncle Yinka looks around at the rest of us, no emotion on his face. Then he scrapes his chair back from the table, gets up and strides out of the room as if he's done nothing wrong.

Everyone is silent until Babs breaks the tension, looking at Kayode. 'Well . . . welcome to the family.'

'Lara, can I borrow you for a minute?' Joseph says. He gives everyone a sickly-sweet smile then moves towards me, ushering me out of the room quickly. 'Just arranging a few surprises.'

'It's not a surprise if you tell every—' Amaka says but the door closes before she finishes.

'What did you see?' he asks, crossing his arms. It takes

me a second to figure out he's not talking about this evening's events.

'Sorry, what was not clear about the fact that I said I *saw* you kiss Dérin at the party?'

'I didn't kiss Dérin; *she tried to kiss me,*' he hisses and I roll my eyes so hard they start to hurt. 'No, deep it. Really deep it. I want Dérin back, so if we kissed, why would I keep that to myself? I would sing like a fucking bird. Replay it in your head. Who leaned in?' He puts one hand on my shoulder and I shrug him off.

Am I being gaslit or is he telling the truth? I look away from him, trying to replay the scene and believe my memories.

'You're seeing it, aren't y—' he starts.

'Shut up.'

'I'd be ready to whistle-blow the whole thing. I'm actually innocent in this situation, for once.' He shrugs then crosses his arms again.

'I don't think that's how you use *whistle-blow.*' I scowl at him. 'But if you're ready to do that, why have you kept it in for so long? So you can continue sending Dérin threatening notes?' I stare him down, trying to see if he wavers when I mention the notes.

'What are you talking about? What notes?' His eyebrows furrow. 'Just tryna scare me into confessing something that's got nothing to do with me, so you can go running to Dérin and fumble the bag for me.' He's read me so easily it makes me uncomfortable in my skin. 'Back to your other question, though. What good would telling anyone do? All I want is

Dérin. I need something that will make her truly believe that *I'm* better for her. The photo I took of Seni and Kayode is good, but it's not incriminating. But give me time and she'll call off the wedding. I know it.' He gives me a playful smile.

'I'd love to live in that head of yours for an hour. Truly. Must be an endless loop of cuckoo sounds,' I say, trying to sound unfazed.

His face drops. 'Witty. I hope you'll come to our wedding,' he says, starting to walk away from me before I blurt out:

'Does Dérin's happiness mean nothing to you?'

He turns back to look at me, his eyes scanning my face. 'Why do none of you seem to get that she'll be happier with me? She's only with Kayode because of a technicality, and she needs to understand that.' Then he turns around and heads back to the dining room.

How can wanting kids be a technicality? I follow him but as soon as I get into the room, there's a loud knock on the front door.

Everyone looks at each other, confused. We're not expecting anyone, especially at nine p.m.

Dérin goes to open the front door and we all file into the hall after her. In the doorway stands a man holding a red giftbox. She takes it then turns to smile at Kayode. 'Babe? A car wasn't enough? What else did you get me?' Kayode looks puzzled. He doesn't say anything. Dérin mirrors him as she starts to open the giftbox. 'This isn't from you . . . ? Is it from you?' Her voice grows frustrated and she glances at Joseph.

But Joseph looks just as perplexed as Kayode.

Dérin turns pale as she looks at me. Her head whips back to the deliveryman who is walking quickly to his car. She drops the box and runs after him. 'Who sent you?' she screeches, but the man keeps walking. She screams and screams, 'Who sent you, who did the delivery come from? Please just tell me, who sent you?' But the man continues and gets into his car, not flinching one bit as Dérin's screams become more and more uncontrollable. She starts banging on his window, then tries to open his door. His tyres screech as he drives out of the compound, leaving Dérin a puddle of mess on the concrete.

All the adults and Temi come rushing down the stairs. They see the giftbox on the floor, they see Dérin outside and they all bombard us with the same question: 'What is going on?'

None of us have an answer. I don't know what to say, but I have a feeling that whatever is in that box is from the same person sending Dérin all of those sinister notes.

Aunty Zai and Mum beg Dérin to come inside, not understanding why she's distraught and sobbing uncontrollably. Amaka and Kayode try to explain as best as they can, but they don't know the true reason either. None of them know why this gift has sent Dérin over the edge. None of them know what lies in that box.

'Don't open it! Please don't open it!' Dérin wails as she sees Uncle Tayo pick up the box.

Uncle Tayo is so worried he accidentally snaps at Dérin. 'Wait, now! You are scaring me. How can we know what's going on if we don't look?' Uncle Tayo opens the box cautiously. 'It's just an envelope.' He shrugs his shoulders. Mine and Dérin's breath hitches at the same time.

Uncle drops the box and opens the envelope. It looks like a photo, blown up to the size of an A4 piece of paper. His face falls and his jaw clenches as he studies the image. 'Get out of my house,' he snarls in Kayode and Joseph's direction.

'Me?' Joseph croaks.

'Him,' Uncle Tayo says, rushing towards Kayode. 'Get out! *Out!* How dare you!'

'Daddy, what's going on?' Dérin sobs. Uncle Tayo passes the photo to Dérin. Her, Mum's and Aunty Zai's faces scrunch up as they try to figure out what they're looking at. 'Is this— Is this you coming out of Seni's room?' Dérin asks and my eyebrows shoot up. 'On the day of the party?' The colour drains from Kayode's and Seni's faces.

Then, sounds none of us were expecting ring across the compound. We all look at each other. The last time something like this happened, at the party, Naija Gossip Lounge dropped the breaking news article. After that incident we decided to all switch to a Nigerian phone number so we wouldn't miss out again. So we could be more prepared. And now . . .

No one moves, all of us struck by the same thought: what if this picture is now on the internet? Amaka breaks first, her hands trembling as she takes her phone out of her back pocket. She looks at the screen and then her eyes shut and a sob escapes her.

No. No. No. No.

'UN-BREAK MY HEART' OR 'UP OUT MY FACE'? WHICH DO WE THINK DÉRIN WILL BE SINGING TONIGHT?

Everyone has secrets they hope no one will ever discover. But, they've never met me.

The plot is thicker than yam porridge at this point. An anonymous source sent in a picture of the groom, Kayode Akinlola, and Dérin's best friend and bridesmaid, Seni Akhalu-Sanusi, coming out of a room *together*, on the night of the bachelor-and-bachelorette-end-of-summer party.

What were they doing? Well, the looks on their faces and their close proximity to each other don't leave much to the imagination.

We all thought Dérin was the most sought-after beauty of the moment, but it looks like Seni is here to take her place. The battle of the Queen Bees will be fun. It's a shame the prize is still Kayode. But who knows, maybe Seni can win over Joseph too?

How will this wedding ever go on? And as for the song choice? I think Dérin should pick 'Un-Break My Heart'. Can't go wrong with a little Toni Braxton . . .

Picture attached.

You know gossip doesn't sleep, and neither do I.

xoxo

All of a sudden there's the sound of liquid splattering on the ground. Dérin has run to the nearest plant pot and is vomitting the contents of her stomach.

'What the hell did you do?' I spit at Joseph. 'Are you that hell bent on ruining this wedding?' I grow angrier the more I speak, taking off my slippers and throwing them at him.

'*I didn't do this,*' Joseph objects.

'You're the one who took the picture! You're the one who's been sending Dérin gifts non-stop. Messing with her head. The constant games. The notes. When are you going to get it into your head? *No one wants you here.*' I step closer and closer to him until our faces are less than an inch apart.

'Are you skunked? Have you forgotten our earlier conversation? Do you think I want to see Dérin like this?'

'What the fuck is wrong with you?' Kayode tackles Joseph to the ground, nearly taking me down too. Kayode's about to punch Joseph when Temi and Babs run over and pull the pair apart. Amaka is stunned into silence, watching the entire scene.

'It's not what it looks like *at all*, Dérin,' Seni says, but Dérin ignores her.

She looks up at me. 'Lara, you're in this picture too.' I whip around, not knowing what to say. She erupts into a sob. 'I can't do this any more. It's not worth the stress. I don't want to see any of you, get out of my house. *Especially you.*' She glares at Seni. 'The wedding is off.' She runs into the house and up the stairs.

'*Hey!*' Uncle Yinka exclaims with joy. Everyone stares at him in disgust.

'You heard her. All of you get out,' Uncle Tayo orders.

'Haba, we can't kick Seni out,' Mum says.

'And why not?' Aunty Zai scrunches up her face. 'Look at the pain they've caused Dérin.'

'Zainab, be reasonable. Where will she stay? Who does she have in Lagos?'

'And is that my problem? After what we've just witnessed? After what all of Lagos, all of Nigeria, has now just witnessed? You think I will keep them in my house? You can pretend you're a saint, Adélé, but me, I'm not. Seni should have thought about that before entering the room with Kayode, so she can *get out*. She'll be better in Kayode's parents' house, clearly,' Aunty Zai says and storms upstairs with Uncle Tayo and Aunty Tiwa.

'This is too much,' I hear someone mutter under their breath and, when I look up, I'm surprised to see Temi shaking his head. He grabs the plant pot Dérin threw up in then disappears in the direction of the downstairs toilet. Uncle Yinka leaves almost straight after like he's trying to hide his glee. Such a sick and twisted man. Aunty Yemi waits a while before following him, as if she wants nothing to do with his wickedness.

Babs, Joseph, Kayode and I are left with Seni, Amaka and my parents.

'Seni, you'll stay in Amaka's room tonight,' Mum instructs. 'Don't come out until anyone tells you to. Everyone in this house becomes so unreasonable when they're angry. No emotional regulation at all.' She kisses her teeth.

'Adélé,' Dad says firmly.

'Leave me, is it not true?' Mum retorts. 'Can you both explain this photo?' Mum asks Seni and Kayode and they both nod. 'Better. Give her time to cool off. Kayode, you should go, but keep your phone on. As for you, Joseph . . . What did you do again?'

'I didn't send the gift to the house or the picture to the blog. I swear to God.'

'You are literally the only person who has that picture,' I snap.

Joseph charges towards the photo lying on the ground and snatches it up. He stares at it like it's a foreign object. 'This isn't even the photo I took.' He whips out his phone and then shows the picture on his screen compared to the one in his hand. 'The angle in the printed photo is head on. Lara in front of me. This wasn't fucking me.'

'Language,' Mum says.

Joseph is right. The printed photo is a different angle to the photo he took on his phone of the events of that night. Everyone stares at each other as they all realize Joseph is telling the truth. They have no idea just what that revelation means.

Bile threatens to come up from my stomach. I grab the photo from Joseph, pick up the giftbox lying on the ground and rummage through the confetti, looking for what I know is in there. I find it in no time, and open it discreetly.

**A REMINDER THAT ALL YOUR SECRETS
ARE MINE.
CALL OFF THE WEDDING.
YOU HAVE THREE DAYS.**

Well, it looks like they finally got their way.

CHAPTER NINETEEN

I've been up all night unable to sleep. I can't stop thinking about the evening's events.

I feel bad for Dérin. I feel bad for Kayode. Some part of me even feels sorry for Seni and Joseph. I don't blame Dérin for calling it off, but I can't believe the wedding is over before it's even happened. The photograph was the straw that broke the camel's back.

The image of the deliveryman is stuck in my head. No remorse or guilt when he saw Dérin screaming and crying. That type of callousness isn't taught; it can only be bought. I wonder how much it must've cost to be so heartless. To watch a girl break down in front of you, guttural screams coming out of her. For him to just drive away like that . . . I just know we're dealing with a truly evil person.

But that's not the only thing that's been keeping me up. I've been racking my brain, unable to figure it out until now. I've been staring at my investigation board, waiting for it to click. Then it finally did.

This latest note. It doesn't have any letters underlined.

What does that mean?

Was it a one-off, spur of the moment, from someone filled with so much rage that they forgot their method of madness? Or did someone else send it?

What could Dérin have done to provoke something so spiteful? She's stopped posting wedding updates on her social media, and the only time she's left the house is for necessary errands. I mean, apart from the party, which annoyingly hasn't stopped trending because of #CupcakeGate, Dérin has stayed low key.

The note was to show dominance over Dérin. I examine the photo on my investigation board. Whoever took it had to be by the stairs, looking up at us. How did I not see them? How could I have been so careless to have that outburst in the corridor when we were entertaining hundreds of guests downstairs?

Sending it to Naija Gossip Lounge was an unnecessary evil. It was a humiliation tactic, a final nail in the coffin to stop Dérin walking down the aisle with Kayode.

Another thought surfaces in my whirling mind. What if it was Naija Gossip Lounge who took the photo? They were also at the party undetected – we saw that with #CupcakeGate.

Naija Gossip Lounge wouldn't want to get Dérin and Kayode's wedding called off, though, surely? The drama is their blog's biggest hit at the moment; there would be very little for them to gossip about if the wedding was cancelled.

But, maybe this is all a game to them. They don't care about the consequences, just so long as they remain popular.

I can't shake the feeling that the lack of an underlined letter means something.

I switch my pink LED lights to white, fully awake now.

I stare at my investigation board and study all the notes closely. There are six with underlined letters, one note without. I need to try to understand what the underlined letters mean. I add the letters *A*, *V*, *H* and *E* from the note Dérin received with her ripped-up dress to the others I scribbled down a few days ago. They stare back at me:

R R Y S O T O I N N I A V H E

I move the notes that have more than one letter underlined to the right-hand side of the board:

AREN'T YOU LUCKY THAT YOUR HAIRDRESSER DIDN'T LEAVE ANY SCISSO<u>R</u>S LYING A<u>R</u>OUND? I'LL HAVE TO TR<u>Y</u> HARDER NEXT TIME.

IS IT <u>S</u>HAME OR LUCK THAT YOU'RE PRETTY? EITHER WAY I'LL PLAY NICE, FOR NOW. CALL OFF THE WEDDING AND THINGS C<u>O</u>ULD BE SO EASY.

IF YOU WANT TO KEEP LIVING A FAIRY TALE, DROP THE WEDD<u>I</u>NG PLA<u>N</u>NING NOW.

**YOU'VE IGNORED ME FOR T<u>O</u>O LONG.
NOW I'M GOING T<u>O</u> DO THINGS MY WAY.**

**YOU CAN'T PLAY C<u>A</u>T AND MOUSE IF THE
MOUSE STOPS LEA<u>V</u>ING THE <u>H</u>OUSE,
SO I THOUGHT I'D COM<u>E</u> TO YOU.
DINNER DRESS TODAY. WEDDING
DRESS TOMORROW.**

I move the note with a single underlined letter to the left:

**YOU WERE SO EASY TO F<u>I</u>ND, DÉRIN.
YOU SHOULD BE MORE CAREFUL.**

I know the first note Dérin received was:

**IF YOU WANT TO KEEP LIVING A FAIRY TALE,
DROP THE WEDD<u>I</u>NG PLA<u>NN</u>ING NOW.**

The underlined letters in this note spell *INN*. But when I look closer, only one *N* is underlined perfectly, while the second is underlined only halfway. I strain my eyes, looking at what it's trying to show, but have no clue. I grab a whiteboard pen out of my desk drawer and trace the shape of the two underlined *N*'s. I do it over and over again and come up with the same result: *M*. It's a wonky *M*, but it's an *M*.

IM? That doesn't spell anything.

I'M?

I stare at the investigation board again, looking for underlined letters which spell a word that could sensibly come after 'I'm'. It's a random method but it's all I've got right now.

**IS IT <u>S</u>HAME OR LUCK THAT YOU'RE PRETTY?
EITHER WAY I'LL PLAY NICE, FOR NOW.
CALL OFF THE WEDDING AND
THINGS C<u>O</u>ULD BE SO EASY.**

SO.

It's like a game of hangman. 'I'm so.' They're so what? Devious, evil?

I *think* I've cracked these two notes, so I start a new section on the far right of the investigation board, placing them there. I write the underlined letters out as words next to them. I feel good knowing I could be on the right track. But with only guesswork and no solid timeline, it's unclear in what order the notes arrived. I can't wake Dérin to ask her, not now in the dead hours of the morning, and especially not after last night. I'm not even sure she wants to see me after finding out what I kept from her about Kayode and Seni. I would hate for her to think I did it to hurt her feelings rather than protect them.

There's one person I know who would both be up at this hour and willing to help me find an answer. I dial Uncle Damola's number. He answers in two rings, his face filling my screen.

'Lara! How are you, love?'

'I'm sorry if I woke you up. I need your help with something.'

'Do I look like I've only just woken up?' He smiles then shows me his surroundings. The sun is rising above the dewy roads and the greenery on the path by his house. I never thought I would miss London, but suddenly I do.

'Oh, good, you're on your way to work. I need your detective brain.'

He flips the camera back onto himself. 'Why, what's wrong?'

It takes me about twenty minutes to explain everything. His only response is . . .

'Wow.'

'I know. It's a lot. I've think I've managed to decipher the underlined letters in two of the notes. They read *I'm so*. That means the letters spell something. I think there's a hidden message in the notes. It's staring me in the face, but I can't find it. I don't even know if it's finished.'

I watch Uncle Damola nodding as he says, 'So how are you going to decipher it?'

Uncle Damola's question stuns me a bit. His belief in me means so much, but I don't want to disappoint him. Because the truth is . . . 'Honestly, Uncle, I don't know. I'm a bit stuck.'

'No, you're not, Lara. Think about it.'

I stop pacing around the room and stand opposite my investigation board, analysing my findings. He patiently waits for things to click. 'I think . . . that I need a timeline of the notes and then I can go from there. I might already have a couple of words, so finding out if there's a message based on the order the notes were sent would help.'

Uncle Damola stays quiet for a beat, then says, 'You know what that means.' I do, and I don't want him to say it. 'The only person who can solve that for you is Dérin. Unless anyone else knows she's getting the notes?'

Amaka. She first mentioned them nearly three weeks ago.

'I just don't want to upset Dérin any more than she already is. She looked so betrayed when she saw the photo last night.'

'I know, but it's better to do the harm now than let whoever is writing these notes do it for you or something worse. You're close, Lara. Keep at it.' He smiles from the screen.

'Thank you, Uncle.'

'Ah, ah, ah, before you go – where are your parents in all this? I know Lagos police can be useless, but Zainab would have done something. I'm even surprised Adélé hasn't called me about it.' I don't say anything, and I guess that's enough because he continues, 'Lara, don't tell me you're doing this by yourself?' I stay quiet, pursing my lips as he persists, '*La-ra!*' He drags out my name just like Mum does. 'I'm being serious when I say do not keep this to yourself. This is sounds dangerous. It's not a small thing that you can solve alone. You need help, you need resources.'

'I will get help. I just need enough . . . evidence,' I groan.

'The notes are enough evidence.' He gives me a stern look. 'Don't be a hero.'

I want to roll my eyes, but I know his intentions are good.

If I get too close to the truth, God knows what the person could do to me, let alone Dérin. I need to be strategic. I nod at his face on the screen. 'I won't be.'

'Ei, with this wedding now being cancelled, I hope I can get a refund for my flight.'

I roll my eyes playfully. 'Talk to you later, Uncle.'

The call has reaffirmed why Uncle Damola is my favourite uncle; he's Mum's brother but nothing like her at all. He's the reason I believe I could have a successful career being a private investigator or a criminal profiler, because he managed to do it despite the odds being against him. He's the hardest worker I know, and truly one of the reasons why I fell in love with solving mysteries.

I hope I make him proud.

I wake up almost four hours later after nearly frying my brain trying to make a timeline of the notes. As much as I want to solve it myself, it's just not possible without Dérin's help.

I don't think I'll tell her about the hidden message until I know what it means. Better to be safe than sorry, in case it's something even more sinister than what she's suffered so far. Not like it could be more evil than shredding her dress and hand-delivering an incriminating picture of her best friend and fiancé together, let alone trying to poison her with cupcakes.

I brush my teeth then make my way downstairs and into the dining room. No one is around. I walk into the kitchen, but it's only Temi there. He doesn't hear me because he's got earphones in.

He's growing increasingly angry as he shouts down the phone, 'Be reasonable, na. I, I . . .' He stutters repeatedly as if the person won't let him get a word in. 'I, I . . . See, we didn't agree to this. It's too much. I . . . it's too much.' The voice in his earphone shouts, loud enough that I can hear it. Temi tries to say something, but then stops abruptly; the person on the phone must have cut the call. He kisses his teeth loudly, running a hand down his face. He turns around and startles when he sees me.

'I'm so sorry. Didn't mean to eavesdrop, just looking for everyone.'

He breathes in deeply. 'My family back home are starting to be difficult with their requests. Because I'm in the city and they're in Ayetoro . . . That's a town if you didn't know.'

'I kno—' I start to say, but Temi continues talking like it's a relief to get it all out. 'I'm expected to fund everything, and the pressure is increasing, it's getting to me.' He sighs. 'Sorry, it's not your problem.'

'No—'

'Aunty Zainab and Dérin have been at church since seven a.m. Your mum and dad are upstairs. They're not hungry.'

'Oh . . . is Seni still in the house?'

'Yes. In Amaka's room. Aunty Zainab went to Seni's room to see if Seni was actually gone, so she really can't be seen in the house until Dérin is back.'

I nod and thank him, taking my leave and walking

straight upstairs to Amaka's room. I knock but don't bother to wait for an answer.

I wish I had. Amaka is on the bed rubbing Seni's back as she sobs into a wad of tissues. They both look up, surprised, like I've intruded on an intimate moment, and to be fair I have. I pause in the doorway, taking in the scene, before joining Amaka on the bed. I put a comforting hand on Seni's shoulder because, while I'm here for a reason, I don't have any reason to be heartless.

'I just can't believe she was ready to kick me out, as if I'm not equally a victim of the article. How am I gonna show my face here again when the whole of Lagos thinks I'm a groom-thieving harlot?' Seni heaves a sob.

There's my reason. She doesn't care about Dérin or her feelings, or about the wedding being cancelled. She's crying because she was nearly kicked out yesterday and her image is tarnished. *Typical.* The comforting circles I'm rubbing on her back soon turn lifeless. Amaka looks at me, eyes crinkled, as if she's trying to understand why I'm here. I avoid looking at her until Seni's tears start to dry up.

'There, there.' The words slip out as I pet her. Seni looks back at me, annoyed, and shrugs me off her. Deservedly so, I didn't mean for it to sound so condescending.

'Is Rin back from church yet?' Amaka says, moving the conversation along. I shake my head and Amaka continues, 'She's gonna be there the whole day, knowing her.' She tuts. 'She broke a mirror once at uni and doused us both in holy water. I can't think of how bad this will be.'

'We should call her back to the house once we've spoken to Joseph and Kayode. Have you guys heard from them?' I ask.

'Kayode texted me earlier, asked if Dérin went to church. He knows her inside out,' Amaka says. I look at her then nod slowly, trying to pick the best time to say my next words.

'I'm really sorry to take you away from Seni, but I urgently need you, Amaka,' I say in a serious tone. They both stare at me.

'*Now?*' Seni scoffs with exaggerated surprise. '*I'm crying.*'

'I thought you'd stopped,' I mutter under my breath. Amaka pinches her nose as if she's trying not to a laugh. She rubs Seni's shoulder and tells her she'll be back soon. I walk Amaka over to my room. Her eyes immediately jump to my investigation board.

'*What* is this? Is this what you get up to when you disappear? What am I even looking at?'

'I need you to take a look at these,' I say, walking over to the notes. 'What do you know about them?' I ask quickly.

'I only know that they started about three months ago. She laughed when she told me about one of them, but I didn't find it funny because the note was *really* weird. Then every time I would bring it up, she would change the subject.'

'I just need you to identify which note you remember Dérin reading to you,' I say. Amaka's expression grows more and more shocked as she reads through them all.

'How could she have kept these a secret? We need to go to the police! Especially after last night. We can't treat these as jokes any more.'

'Amaka. I promise you we will, but there's something I need to figure out first.' I beg her to stay focused.

She scans my face, looking first angry, then sad and tearful, and finally defeated. 'Only this one.'

AREN'T YOU LUCKY THAT YOUR HAIRDRESSER DIDN'T LEAVE ANY SCISSORS LYING AROUND? I'LL HAVE TO TRY HARDER NEXT TIME

R R Y.

'When did you guys have this conversation? Like, what month?' I ask her.

'Uh, it was around the end of May? Yeah, definitely end of May because I'd just finished exams. She said something about not wanting to bother me with them while I was studying.'

If the first note came in April:

IF YOU WANT TO KEEP LIVING A FAIRY TALE, DROP THE WEDDING PLANNING NOW.

And the second followed in the middle of May:

IS IT SHAME OR LUCK THAT YOU'RE PRETTY? EITHER WAY I'LL PLAY NICE, FOR NOW. CALL OFF THE WEDDING AND THINGS COULD BE SO EASY.

Then this note that Amaka knows about should follow straight after. That would mean the message so far is . . .

'I'M SORRY'?

I'm. Sorry.

What. The. *Fuck?*

CHAPTER TWENTY

Dérin comes home from church an hour later. She doesn't make eye contact when she joins me in the living room.

Temi comes in a few moments later, bringing her a glass of water. She accepts it and slumps down into the sofa, her eyes hollow as she stares at the TV.

I open my mouth to speak but she cuts me off. 'Don't say anything. I'm too tired to argue and my back is hurting.'

'Have you told the doctor?' Concern washes over me. But Dérin continues to ignore me, focusing on the TV. 'Kayode has been waiting for you to call him back,' I whisper. She immediately cuts a look at me.

'Why on earth would I want to speak to Kayode after last night? Can we be for real, Lara? I don't want him anywhere near me.' As Dérin says that, the living-room door creaks open. Seni walks in meekly. Dérin's voice immediately becomes laced with disgust. 'What are you doing here? I thought I told you that I didn't want to see you ever again?'

Seni stands in front of her, then gets on her knees, forcing Dérin to meet her eyes. 'Dérin – Dérin, look at me! You've got it all wrong.'

'So I wasn't looking at you coming out of your room with my fiancé at my *bachelorette* party?'

Seni frowns because that's exactly what we all saw, both in the picture and in real life. 'We weren't doing anything wrong, Dérin, I promise you. It looked much worse than it seemed – to all of you. I—'

'Ugh, save it, Seni! I can't even look at you. You've been bitter the entire wedding period. Do you think I haven't noticed? Don't you think I'm tired of excusing your behaviour in front of other people? When you found out about the engagement you asked me if I was *sure* in front of all the girls. I had to laugh it off and say, "She's kidding!" Even worse, when you suggested I cancel the second introduction after the drama with cancelling the first one, *right in front of my parents.*' Dérin rubs her hands over her face, then massages her temples. 'Did you think people didn't hear all your catty comments at the bachelorette party? I'm surprised it's not all over fucking Naija Gossip Lounge, too. The amount of times I had to say, "Oh, Seni's just tired." Or, "She just has a resting bitch face, it's nothing personal." Or, "Stomach problems, she's *not used to the food* here." Over and over and over again.'

Woah. This is much more loaded than I thought it would be. How much has Dérin been keeping in? How many months' worth of tension and anger is coming out now?

'I'm tired of seeing you *trying* to be happy when something good happens with me and Kayo. The snarky comments under your breath that you think no one can hear, the side glances and the jealous looks you hardly bother to hide. Hell, even my dad's seen them. At least Joseph is more open with his dislike.' Dérin scoffs then crosses her arms. 'If you never wanted to be here, why did you come? Why did you say yes to being my bridesmaid? And *why* would you take my fiancé, your ex, to a room *alone with you* during my bachelorette party?'

Part of me can't help thinking that this outburst is well-earned. What Dérin is saying about the snarky comments, side glances and jealous looks is true. From what she's described, they didn't just begin during the wedding period; they've been going on since she started her relationship with Kayode. It must be exhausting to constantly have to excuse bad behaviour just because of a friendship. But another part of me thinks this is . . . mean? As wrong as Seni is in this situation, it's annoying that she's getting all Dérin's venom when Kayode is equally at fault and not there to take the blows.

Seni has spent all morning crying her eyes out, and she doesn't seem like the straight-to-apology type of person, so I would hope that would mean something to Dérin.

Seni scoffs, then takes a moment to compose herself. 'I'm going to let your comments slide because I can see that you're in pain. Have you taken your meds this morning?'

Dérin softens for a second and then hardens again.

'Is there a point in me explaining myself? It doesn't seem like you're going to believe me.' Seni sighs and then mutters something under her breath. 'I'm sorry, Dérin. I didn't realize I'd been causing you so much hurt while trying to work through mine. I didn't mean to have you make excuses for me. But what irritates me is how you constantly fail to remember that you were practically my sister at uni and as much as you like to act like you didn't know Kayode, *you did*, and still dated him. No matter how unserious the relationship between me and him was, the very mention of the name should've been enough for you to double check who he was, and *you didn't*. I still can't believe you did that to me. I chose to be a bridesmaid anyway because I loved you, Dérin. I loved you so much.'

Interesting choice of words.

Seni's voice quivers, but she clears her throat. 'Half the time I didn't even know I was doing those things. I am sorry if I've been indirectly ruining your wedding experience, truly. I am happy for you and Kayode. I'm not angry at you and I never have been. I'm angry at Kayode. All the comments, the looks, they're all for him. But even if you don't forgive me for that, I'm telling you now: I did not do anything with Kayode in that room. As bad as it looks. I was in there with him for less than five minutes, if even that.'

'Then what *were* you doing?' Dérin asks. 'Why do you look so startled in the picture?'

'You're telling me if someone caught you coming out of a room with Joseph, your ex, you wouldn't be startled?'

224

At that comment I choke on my saliva. They both turn to me, looking annoyed.

'Go and get some water, you look a mess,' Dérin says, and I head for the kitchen. I don't even bother to get a glass, but put my mouth under the tap, take a big gulp, then start to run back into the living room. As I do, the doorbell goes. I debate whether I should let Temi get it, but the ringing becomes frantic and I immediately know who it is.

I walk quickly to the front door and Kayode bursts in.

'Where is she?' he says, out of breath like he's been running.

'She's in the living room. Why is the gate still open—'

'I ran up the street and told the gateman to park my car for me. Is she still mad?' For a doctor, Kayode is not the smartest cookie. He swings open the living-room door, not a care in the world, startling both Seni and Dérin, who are . . . hugging?

'Uh, what's going on?' He gulps, confusion all over his face.

I'm also puzzled as I look at the pair. Not even two minutes ago the situation between Dérin and Seni was uncomfortably tense, and now it's like nothing has happened.

'I was just telling Dérin about why we were in the room together . . . She knows about the surprise. We were caught red handed.'

'She does?' Kayode says, trying to hide how baffled he is, but failing.

'Yes, she knows all about the surprise wedding videos that we've been working on. Just you and I,' Seni says and I squint in surprise. I look at Kayode to see if I can catch anything. There's a slight flicker on his face. He doesn't look totally fazed, but that's *not* the look of someone who's fully in the loop with the story being told.

Seni's claim can't be true . . . Can it? How convenient that it only involves her and Kayode. The perfect alibi for whatever they were doing in her room.

Kayode sighs with relief and I'm even more confused. 'Thank God. Dérin, baby,' he says, kneeling in front of her. She rolls her eyes then gives a small smile.

'You're both idiots,' she says, then pulls Kayode off from the ground. 'You could've easily said something yesterday.'

'Do you know what you're like when you're angry?' Kayode says and she laughs, pulling Seni and Kayode into a hug with her. I'm sure I hear her say quietly, 'I love you.'

What the fuck? All that anger she had for Seni . . . Where was it for Kayode? He deserved it too. She didn't even ask to hear his version of events. He didn't even have to give an excuse, just back up an obviously fake story. I refuse to believe Dérin is this dense.

'That's it?' I accidentally blurt out, and everyone turns to me. What I want to say is *surely* that can't be it. There's no way that can be it, because, Dérin, *that* photo arrived yesterday with *another* note threatening to expose all your secrets. You screamed, you cried, you *threw up*. You hysterically called off your wedding and now . . . all of a sudden, a half-assed excuse and an apology is going to make it better? What the fuck? You are not that naïve.

226

But instead, I fake a sigh of relief. 'So the wedding is back on?'

Everyone looks at Dérin and she nods.

'I'm going to tell the family the good news.' Seni beams, squeezing Dérin's hand before heading out of the room.

I follow her. 'Hey,' I whisper-shout. I grab her arm when she doesn't stop walking. 'I know your story about the surprise wedding videos isn't true. How did you get Kayode to agree to that? Do you even *have* any videos?'

'Get the hell off me.' She pushes my hand off of her arm. 'You know nothing. Now stay out of it before things start to get worse.' She doesn't even bother to look at me as she speaks.

'What do you mean you *loved* Dérin? Why did you use the past tense?' I whisper-scream, but she just keeps walking upstairs. Her demeanour switches from pissed to calm as she enters Amaka's room.

And then she's gone.

After Dérin, Kayode and Seni have made up, I feel like I don't know what to do with myself any more. I'm still in disbelief at how quickly Dérin accepted their story. Did she not want to see the video Kayode and Seni had supposedly been making in the room? Did she not wonder why myself and Joseph were in the picture too? Does she not want any more answers?

The note said Dérin had three days to cancel the wedding. What happens now that it's back on?

The whole family has gone back into wedding buzz mode as if the cancellation never happened. The traditional wedding is in two days, and I'm stuck in this weird limbo knowing that if I don't intervene, something crazy is going to occur.

I need to speak to Dérin alone but she keeps being whisked off to different places. She also seems reluctant to talk to me, whether because she knows she'll have to confront the reality that the notes and the impending danger they pose are *very* real, or because she's still angry with me for not telling her about what I saw with Seni and Kayode. Or even because she knows that I'll question her about why she didn't stick it on Kayode the same way she did to Seni and, even worse, why she believed them so easily without asking for a shred of evidence.

After lunch, the doorbell goes as I'm midway up the stairs. I turn around to see if anyone is coming to answer, but when they don't I jog down and answer it myself. Aunty Ireti is at the door, wearing jeans and a white top but with a black veil over her head.

'D— Lara! How are you, love?' She smiles as she sees me. 'Is Dérin around? I wanted to speak to her.'

I pretend not to notice the name slip as I say, 'I think she's upstairs in her room. I'll call her down to the living room. Do you want anything to drink, Aunty?'

'Erm, a bottle of water would be fine. Thank you, sweetie.' I nod and then lead her to the living room. We startle as we see Temi in there sweeping. 'Eku ise,' Aunty Ireti says to him. 'I can leave if that's better—'

'Me, I don't mind,' Temi says and I grab a bottle of water from the kitchen then run up the stairs to get Dérin from her room. Her face hardens when she sees me. Aunty Zai is with her and looks at me sympathetically.

'What do you need, Lara?' she asks, and I tell them that Aunty Ireti is downstairs.

Dérin groans. 'This is the first time she's spoken to me since the article dropped. I'm fucked.' We all head downstairs to the living room. When I open the door, it looks like we've interrupted a conversation between Aunty Ireti and Temi. Aunty Ireti's expression is stony and clearly she's mid-sentence while Temi looks down on her.

Dérin breaks the sudden silence, looking between the two of them. 'Is everything okay?'

'It's nothing. He just accidentally swept something onto my shoes.' She scrunches her face so her nose crinkles then gets up to hug Dérin. For the first time, Dérin doesn't hug back. 'I wanted to check on you after what happened yesterday.'

Dérin deflates. 'I've contacted our lawyers for a cease-and-desist letter, as well as a retraction and request to remove it from every outlet. I'm not going to let Naija Gossip Lounge think it can ruin my marriage before it's even begun. Kayode and Seni have both assured me that nothing happened in the room, but the picture looks awful. I'm *so* sorry for the embarrassment.'

Aunty Ireti doesn't say anything, her lips pursed as she looks at Dérin.

'Let me talk to Dérin alone, please,' Aunty Ireti says. Aunty Zai nods and we both head towards the door. When we're outside, Aunty Zai and I both look at each other, trying to gauge something unspoken. Then, as if we're reading each other's minds, we both put our ears to the door.

At first, it's muffled, then we both hear Aunty Ireti's voice break through. 'Are you sure you want to go through with this wedding?'

Our eyes widen. 'Why would she ask her that? We just got back to normal!' Aunty Zai whispers to me and I frown, not sure what to tell her.

Aunty Ireti then says, 'I wouldn't blame you if you no longer trust him.' She sighs and then tuts. 'I don't know what that boy was thinking. Since he's been with you, he doesn't talk about anyone else, so I don't know why he would do that. Who could have taken the picture?'

'I'm not sure, Aunty. Things are okay now, though. Kayode and Seni have explained why they were in the room together.'

'Well, why *were* they?' Aunty Ireti asks.

'They've been filming videos for me before each wedding event. It was supposed to be a surprise that Kayode was going to share on the white wedding day, but unfortunately, it's now ruined.' Dérin's voice trails off as she finishes.

'Do you believe that?' Aunty Ireti asks, and there's a silence. I hope that means Dérin is nodding because, if not, her silence tells me that she knows things aren't right, but she refuses to confront that reality. She needs to know the truth about what happened between Kayode and Seni. It's clear she loves Kayode, but the notes are getting more threatening, more dangerous. Maybe cancelling the wedding is for the best, for her safety.

'Dérin, I came here to discuss the argument we had about the money. I would understand if that did not give you much faith in us as your in-laws. Truthfully, like the blogs have been saying and the rumours circulating, we're going through a rough patch, financially, and Fola doesn't want to admit it. I'm trying to look out for him before things get bad, but he doesn't help himself – for example, the car. Fola hasn't told your parents, or Kayode, which is why things were even more embarrassing at the rehearsal dinner. I tried to save face, but, well, we saw how that backfired.' I look at Aunty Zai to see if this is true and her sad expression confirms it. 'We're not going to be able to give you the wedding of your dreams, and if you want an out, we can give you one. I don't know when things will get better.'

'Eh?' Aunty Zai asks. She moves her ear away from the door as if she's ready to storm into the room. I hold her back.

Dérin protests profusely. 'No, never! The wedding really doesn't matter. I'd be happy to downsize, if not for the fact that I'm my mother's only child.' Dérin gives a light laugh, which isn't returned. 'It's just one bump in the road; we'll all be fine. I can return the car if you want me to.'

Aunty Ireti tuts lightly. 'I couldn't ask you to do that. Like you said, it's just one bump in the road.'

There's silence again, then we hear footsteps coming

231

towards us. Aunty Zai and I leap away from the door and she launches into a fake conversation. 'I need to make sure the caterer has the final number of guests attending.'

'That's so true. Don't forget about the takeaway containers as well,' I say, nodding along like a bobblehead. Aunty Ireti opens the door midway through my sentence, not giving any indication that she suspects we've been eavesdropping.

'I better be going so Fola isn't worried. I just stopped off on my way back from church.' That explains why she's wearing the veil.

Dérin sees her out of the house. Aunty Zai and I hold back, watching the two of them hug in the doorway.

'She's a better person than me, sha. If we were broke, the stars would fall before I let Tayo buy a car worth two mortgages to save face,' Aunty Zai says and then walks away.

CHAPTER TWENTY-ONE

It's the next evening and my mind is still on Seni and Kayode, and the notes.

To bury an apology in the notes is audacious. What would someone, who has set out to cause chaos for Dérin's wedding, be remorseful about? I still need to speak to Dérin to get a full timeline for the rest of the notes. I need her to help me help her. No matter how angry she is at me. I leave my room, grabbing the notes, opening her bedroom door without knocking. She looks at me, frowning. She says into her phone, 'Joseph, I'll call you back.'

'Joseph? What the—' I start.

Dérin cuts me off. 'Why are you here?'

I feel a surge of anger. 'I'm here for *this*!' I say, throwing the notes at her as she sits on her bed. She flinches as they land. 'The mystery I've been trying to solve for the last three weeks. Trying to make sure your wedding goes smoothly, that nothing awful happens to you, and *you* are on the phone to *Joseph*. Dérin, I am so . . . I don't know what to do with you. Do you even want to marry Kayode? You made the most massive fuss about him and Seni coming out of a room together, but here you are making evening phone calls to your ex-boyfriend, who you nearly *kissed* on your bachelorett—'

'So you did see that? Were you watching us?' Dérin's voice breaks a little, but I'm too upset to care. I erupt.

'Does that *matter*?! You seem to have forgiven everybody except me. Why?'

'Because you're the only one who owes me your loyalty!' Dérin erupts. 'Forget what Seni said about our bond being sisterly, *you* are my sister . . . and you saw my fiancé and his ex-girlfriend come out of a room together and kept it from me. You kept it from me for so long! Why didn't you tell me?'

'I didn't want to hurt you! The reason I do all of this, have been doing all of this, is because I want to make sure, at the end of the day, you're okay. That you can have the wedding of your dreams and marry the man you love. God, Dérin. I have hated the two of them since I saw them come out of that room. Forgiving them, without even a smidgen of evidence to back up their story, is the most stupid thing I've ever seen you do.'

'Oh, please. I'm cutting Seni off the minute the wedding is over,' she says and I'm immediately taken aback.

'What do you mean?'

'I don't trust her any more. How could I when she's clearly been plotting to steal Kayode from me? Maybe when she sees us going down the aisle together, she'll finally get the hint. I just don't have anyone to replace her as a bridesmaid before the white wedding.'

'Dérin, are you hearing how you sound right now? She's still a person. She's also not the only one to blame, Kayode is at fault too. How are you going to punish him? You know what, I . . . I'm not even going to entertain this. I hope you come to your senses by the time the night ends because that is . . . wow . . . I'm only here to find out the timeline of when you received these.'

She picks up the notes and ruffles through them quickly, as if they mean nothing, then places them back down on her bed in a specific order. 'Here,' she says.

**IF YOU WANT TO KEEP LIVING A FAIRY TALE,
DROP THE WEDDING PLANNING NOW.**

**IS IT SHAME OR LUCK THAT YOU'RE PRETTY?
EITHER WAY I'LL PLAY NICE, FOR NOW.
CALL OFF THE WEDDING AND
THINGS COULD BE SO EASY.**

**AREN'T YOU LUCKY THAT YOUR HAIRDRESSER
DIDN'T LEAVE ANY SCISSORS LYING AROUND?
I'LL HAVE TO TRY HARDER NEXT TIME.**

**YOU WERE SO EASY TO FIND, DÉRIN.
YOU SHOULD BE MORE CAREFUL.**

**YOU'VE IGNORED ME FOR T͟OO LONG.
NOW I'M GOING T͟O DO THINGS MY WAY.**

**YOU CAN'T PLAY C͟AT AND MOUSE IF
THE MOUSE STOPS LEA͟VING THE H͟OUSE,
SO I THOUGHT I'D COM͟E TO YOU.
DINNER DRESS TODAY. WEDDING
DRESS TOMORROW.**

I sit down on her bed and study the order of the notes, piecing the message together. I take out my phone and start to type. Once I've finished, I look at Dérin. 'While working on this, I noticed that the notes have letters that are underlined. I believe that these letters make up a secret message. Follow the underlined letters in the order you've just laid out.'

I watch Dérin's face as she traces each letter, but she frowns like she doesn't understand what she's looking at.

I place my phone on the bed, screen up, with the secret message typed out. I say it out loud: *'I'm sorry I to have . . .'*

'That's gibberish.' Dérin does an unamused pout and I feel sheepish.

'Dérin, look. They're clearly trying to say they're sorry they have to . . .' I pause. My stomach drops. Oh my God. 'Dérin, I think there are two people behind the notes. One person is organizing them and someone else is making sure they reach you.'

'Two people, Lara? That's a bit far-fetched.' Dérin looks at

236

me like I've lost it, but my gut is telling me I'm right.

'Dérin, think about it. Why would someone send you these evil notes, that clearly show they know how to form a correct sentence, and then include a secret message that's gibberish? Why would someone send you these malicious notes and purposefully cause you hurt and pain, to then apologize? That doesn't make sense. The person making sure the notes reach you, maybe *they're* underlining the letters. Maybe they have no idea what each note will say. They just want to leave their message, in whatever way they can. That would explain the mistakes.'

Dérin sits quietly, taking it all in.

'There was another note, hidden under confetti in the giftbox that the photo was delivered in. It doesn't have any letters underlined.' I take it out and put it on the bed:

A REMINDER THAT ALL YOUR
SECRETS ARE MINE.
CALL OFF THE WEDDING.
YOU HAVE THREE DAYS.

I watch Dérin closely.

'Don't you think it was weird that you *finally* saw the person that delivered it?'

'What do you mean?'

'This is the first note that was directly handed to you. This note was much sloppier than the rest. I think the person organizing the notes got angry, as if something happened that evening that made them snap, and this was their way of showing it. I also think that's why there aren't any letters underlined. The second person didn't know a note would arrive, or if they did, they didn't have a chance to include their message.'

Dérin sighs. 'Well, they got their chance later.' She pulls out another note from her bedside table. 'I hid this one. It came the morning after I cancelled the wedding.'

I WOULD LOVE TO REENACT LAST NIGHT.
I HEARD YOUR TEARS WERE OSCAR-WORTHY.
REMEMBER WHAT I SAID: ALL YOUR
SECRETS ARE MINE. NEAR KISSES
WITH YOUR EX COUNT, TOO.
THE NEXT NOTE WILL BE IN BLOOD.
I TOLD YOU NOT TO MESS WITH ME.

DO. THIS.

I type the rest of the underlined letters into my phone:
I'M SORRY I HAVE TO DO THIS.

Dérin and I stare at the screen. 'Did you see the messenger?' I ask and she shakes her head.

'How can they be sorry when they're doing all this? Shredding my dress, sending me the photo, the poisoned cupcakes, *stalking me*?'

'I don't know. But, Dérin, what if they're trying to help you? What if they're trying to warn you? Maybe we should listen to them?'

Dérin interrupts me. 'Are you telling me I shouldn't marry Kayode?'

'No . . . I . . . Is that all you heard me say? I mean, do you really want to marry Kayode? With Joseph somehow still having a hold on y—'

'Joseph does not have a hold on me!' she snaps.

'Dérin, you nearly kissed him,' I say, sounding defeated. 'Every time he's around your eyes still find him, and he clearly still wants you back. Why did you guys break up anyways?'

'My eyes find him because he's set out to ruin the wedding. I didn't nearly kiss him, he nearly kissed me. And the reason why we broke up is *none of your business*.'

I love Dérin, but I know what I saw. As much as I think that Joseph *is* the devil incarnate, he didn't try to kiss her, she tried to kiss him. If Kayode ever found out, he'd be crushed. And this latest note threatens to expose that truth.

'Dérin, the quicker you forgive me, the quicker we'll get somewhere. I am sorry I didn't tell you. You deserved better but, in that moment, I thought I was protecting you. If anything like that happens again, you will be the first person I tell. I promise. But . . . do you really want to marry Kayode?'

She sighs then scans my face, as if she's looking for the answer there. 'I do. I really do.'

'Okay. Listen, I'm going to do some more digging to find out who's sending the notes. I have a few hunches, but nothing concrete. In the meantime, I need you to keep your wits about you. Your traditional wedding is tomorrow and we don't want any more drama before then. Can you do that for me?' I ask, and she nods. I start to walk out of her room, but she calls me back. She runs to pull me into a hug and then whispers the words, 'I'm sorry.'

It's the night before the traditional wedding, but I spend God knows how many hours in front of my investigation board. Working out the secret message in the notes means I'm doing something right, but it hasn't brought me any closer to discovering *who* is behind them.

I look at the section I've labelled *SUSPECTS* and stare at my scribbles. Uncle Yinka is driven by money, but what would he gain from destroying the wedding? Uncle Tayo has made it very clear that even if he loses all his money because the wedding doesn't go ahead, he will *never* help Uncle Yinka financially again. And then there's Moses, who Uncle Yinka claimed will 'help' him with his money problems. Is Uncle Yinka employing this Moses to stalk Dérin and deliver the notes? No one knows who Moses is or what he looks like. Was it him who delivered the photo of Seni and Kayode? Or is Moses innocent in all this, forced by Uncle Yinka to do his evil bidding, and he's trying to tell us that in his secret message?

Joseph and Seni both want the wedding called off, but I'm struggling to work out if they've fully thought through what will happen if they succeed. If Aunty Ireti is right about Kayode being head over heels for Dérin, Seni wouldn't gain anything, apart from sadistic satisfaction that Kayode and Dérin didn't get married. But, in Seni's own words, she couldn't believe Dérin would 'do that to her'. This could really be just about revenge.

Joseph *could* get Dérin back, but at what cost? She will be broken if this wedding doesn't go ahead, and, despite some of her behaviour, she is deeply in love with Kayode. A love like that would not be easy to get over. What would be the point of Joseph working to wreck Dérin? To sweep up a broken person and nurture her back into someone who would love him again. But even then, would the love be real?

And then there's Alika. But her motive isn't one hundred per cent clear.

There is nothing in *her* past that suggests she's a malicious and jealous person, but then there is literally *nothing* in her past, that I can find. She's untraceable until a year ago, which I find hard to believe because of how active she is on her Instagram now. In the weeks since I arrived in Lagos and started following her Instagram account, she's been posting multiple times a day. Alika is the only one out of all the suspects who has physically been around Dérin since the notes started. She's never given any indication that she knows about them, but she does fit the timeline perfectly. I just wish I had more evidence to question her with.

CHAPTER TWENTY-TWO

The day of the traditional wedding has arrived and, no surprise, everything is chaos. We've only been awake for four hours and I want to tap out already.

The make-up artist signals that she's ready for Dérin and I run up to her room. When I arrive, she's taking her medication again. She jumps a little when she sees me.

'Is your back still hurting?' I ask as she hurriedly puts the medicine away.

'It's more a precaution. They need me for hair and make-up?' she asks and I nod.

When we reach the living room, I'm impressed that none of the white sofas have been stained by brown foundation. We sit in the chair to start the glamming-up process, when, ten minutes later, I hear a voice from behind me. I open one eye and smile.

'My favourite detective-to-be.' Uncle Damola's bald head is shining, and he beams as he sees the two of us.

'You both look gorgeous.'

'Don't let her daddy hear that she wants to be a detective,' Dérin says, one eye closed and the other fixed on us, then sticks her tongue out playfully.

'Don't mind him. That old man,' he says then comes to give me a kiss on the cheek. He's holding a giftbox which he lifts towards Dérin and says, 'For you. I'll place it in your room later.' Dérin flinches for just a second and then smiles, as if she's realizing who the gift is from. Uncle Damola studies her, and then looks at me. I shake my head 'no' slightly. His face hardens, but he respects my wishes, changing the subject. 'Lara, you still haven't managed to convince your father yet?'

Dérin scoffs, 'She hasn't even tried.'

I stare at her with one eye and ask her make-up artist if they've got any glue they can use to seal her mouth. 'I tried to tell him, and he's shunned me ever since. How am I supposed to reason with someone like that?'

'Ah, but it's results day soon, Lara.' Uncle Damola checks the date on his phone. 'In three weeks.'

'Yeah, and I've got three weeks to tell him again,' I mumble.

Uncle laughs. 'Babs still hasn't told him he doesn't want to do surgery, has he?' he asks, and I say nope, popping the 'p'. 'You children, you won't kill us. I'm just glad Remi seems like he's still interested in med school.' He smiles as he references my gifted cousin back in London. It's a blessing and curse to be born into such a brilliant family. 'I'll talk to your father after the wedding,' Uncle Damola adds.

243

'Oh, why else did you think you were here?' I say and they both laugh. But Uncle Damola stops abruptly, and he looks at me. He *keeps* looking at me. For a detective, he's so indiscreet. I mouth an exaggerated *No*. But he continues staring at me, with the same look that toddlers get before they do a bad deed after you've begged them to be good.

He claps loudly, scaring Dérin's make-up artist so that her hand jolts from Dérin's eyelid. 'So, what are we doing about the notes?' The make-up artist tries to blend away the eyeshadow that's made its way onto Dérin's cheek, but Dérin moves her hand away.

'*You told him*?' Dérin whisper-yells, getting out of her seat. I hesitate, then nod. '*Why*?'

'I needed some help with a few . . . theories,' I mumble. I wait for her to let rip at me, but she stands pondering, then after a few more heated moments finally takes a seat. She sighs deeply. 'Maybe a professional will finally get things done.'

Ouch? What that supposed to mean? Does she think I've been playing games this entire time? Does she know the efforts I've gone to with my investigation? The sleepless nights, constant thoughts, my investigation board?

'Have you received any more notes? Have you *told* anybody?' Uncle Damola asks.

Dérin starts going through her phone. 'The last note told me the next one would be in blood.' She has a vacant look on her face.

Uncle Damola cocks his head in disbelief. 'Well, thank

God I called for extra security today. Your dad thought it was rash, but it's clear now, you still haven't told them about this.'

'Did you tell them?' I ask.

'I should've!' He crosses his arms. 'This is dangerous. They're threatening your life, and you need to take them at their word before they act on the threats. The last time I was here you had a bad dream and flew yourself to Portugal for a pilgrimage. Why aren't you taking this seriously? What's going on with you?' Uncle Damola is asking all the right questions.

'What am I supposed to go to the police with? It's all speculation. Murders happen every day and they don't get solved. Do you think they're going to care about my little notes? This isn't the UK.' Dérin's eyes are still closed, but her voice wavers.

Dérin's phone trills and I almost throw up, thinking it's another breaking news article from Naija Gossip Lounge. She looks at it and says, 'Speak of the devil and they shall appear. @ajebotashamer has just DM'd me. *Today will be a day full of surprises. I hope you love every one of them.*'

'I'm going to make calls to triple the security. Let an uninvited guest even *dare* try to get in.' Uncle Damola looks at me and says, 'Be wary of all your suspects today.'

Thirty minutes and a thousand pictures later, us bridesmaids are ready to make our way to the venue. A hired driver is already waiting outside Dérin's brand-new Rolls-Royce, looking smart in a navy-blue suit with a white shirt. He nods at us as we approach the car, then opens the door for Dérin to get in the front seat. The rest of us climb into the back. For all the trouble the car caused, it seems like it might've been worth it. I can now tick cruising in a Rolls-Royce off my bucket list.

We're fifteen minutes into the journey when Dérin points out to the driver, 'Oh, you missed the turn back there.' The driver apologizes and Dérin goes back to looking at her phone, but the driver doesn't make a U-turn.

We continue driving down the straight road.

'I said, you missed the turn,' Dérin says again, this time louder. He gives no sign that he's heard her. The car starts to shake on the potholes. There's an eery silence among us, as we all think the same thing. The driver finally stares at each of us in the rearview mirror. The look in his eye makes me want to shrink into my skin.

'Sorry, girls. We're going to have to make a detour.'

CHAPTER TWENTY-THREE

The atmosphere in the car is extremely tense as we continue to drive. Everyone employs a different tactic to plead with or threaten the driver.

Seni goes into lawyer mode: 'The law in Nigeria dictates that you'll be sentenced to a minimum of thirty years in prison for kidnapping. Do you really think any judge would be sane to let you see daylight again? Let us out of this car!'

Amaka is cussing him out, kicking his chair and trying to hit him from the back seat. 'One hard blow and I could knock this car off the road, but I know you'd rather get out of here alive. Let us go!'

Dérin meanwhile has burst into tears: 'I'm supposed to be getting traditionally married today. I haven't lived, I've just about been loved, this cannot be how my life ends. Please! Please!'

I watch everyone and rack my brain for de-escalation techniques. What Dérin is doing is good; her crying appeals to the driver's sympathetic side, if he has one, hopefully enough to make him question his plan. Whatever that is. But Seni and Amaka are only making him angrier. I can see his growing frustration, which we need to diffuse. I have to disconnect from the situation, as if I'm not in my own body. I absorb true crime techniques every day, I've just got to apply them.

The best tactic to de-escalate a situation is to work through the behavioural change stairway model: active listening, empathy, rapport, influence and, hopefully, behavioural change.

But this won't work if everyone is shouting over each other, provoking the driver and making him mad.

'Everyone quiet!' I shout, and the girls are shocked into silence. 'All talking at once isn't going to help anything.'

Dérin stifles a whimper, tears shining in her eyes. I stretch my hand out to her in the front seat. The driver doesn't seem violent, which is good, but it's scary seeing Dérin so close to him.

Active listening.

'What do you want from us?' I ask him, keeping my voice level. He doesn't respond for a few moments and the car continues to shake as we drive down the potholed road.

Then he starts talking.

'All you people know how to do is flaunt your wealth.' He meets my eyes in the rearview mirror. 'You never care for anyone but yourself, hmm? No mind for how everyone else in the country is suffering. All you know is flashy party, expensive cars, expensive trips. Do you even give back?'

'We do. Wherever and whenever we can,' Dérin interrupts, and I squeeze her shoulder to signal for her to stop.

Empathy.

I continue, 'It must be hard for you to navigat—'

'Spare me, omo ajẹbọ́tá. Don't act like you know. You're all from the diaspora, you know *nothing*. All of you just come here during, what is it you call it? Detty December,' he mocks then continues, 'to spend your money, and act as if you know the place, while the rest of us spend the entire year just trying to get by. "Naija is the best place in the world", blah, blah, blah. It's bullshit. Fake. Soon as you leave to better your lives, you forget us at home. All you wan do is better yourself.'

Ajẹbọ́tá . . . @ajebotashamer . . . Could it . . . Is it . . . Is he the person trolling Dérin on Instagram?

'I see,' I say, trying to bring us back to empathy. A good way to indicate that you're listening is to paraphrase everything the person has said back to them to show that you understand why their feelings have resulted in their actions. Then emotional labelling, giving their feelings a name, is important. It lets them know you get what they feel. So, I say, low and slow: 'You sound hurt. Like you're at your breaking point. Life hasn't been fair to you?' I phrase it as a question, so he feels compelled to answer.

'It hasn't.' He looks at me in the rearview mirror, his eyes soften a tiny bit and I realize I've got him where I want him.

Rapport.

'Can I ask your name?' I say, hoping that I don't trigger him. 'I just want to talk.'

'Mos—' he starts to say, then quickly stops himself and responds coldly, 'Solomon.' It means nothing to the girls, but it sounds like he was going to say Moses.

Moses.

Lightbulbs flash in my head and I have to fight to keep my face still. My cheeks flush and I start to get hot as I connect the dots. This is Uncle Yinka's Moses. It has to be. I'd be squirming in my seat if I wasn't between Amaka and Seni.

Influence.

I clear my throat to prevent it from wobbling. 'What can we do to help? To ease the hurt that you're feeling. If we offered you money, would that make things better?' I say, testing the waters.

'Lara . . .?' Seni whispers and I shake my head to shut her up. But, the more I think about it, the more I realize she's right. Screw the negotiation techniques, this man deserves no sympathy from me. Uncle Yinka has probably told him not to get violent, otherwise he would've already threatened us by now. This isn't a hostage situation; this is blackmail. Just like someone has been threatening Dérin. Uncle Yinka? He said he would get the money from Uncle Tayo one way or another, and he clearly meant it. I can't believe he would stoop so low, and with his nieces too. He could've just stolen the car in the night, and it would've been fine, but no. He needed to make a 'threat' against our lives; to make us feel powerless and too scared to want to file a police report. To make it feel like this was a matter of life or death, and on Dérin's wedding day too? What a spineless and undeserving man.

'At the end of the day, money is what makes the world go round,' says the driver now. 'It's not the end to my problems, but it will help, sha.'

'It was never about the country, and that bullshit patriotic speech, then, was it? You wanted money all along?' Amaka's voice rises. 'Let us out of the fucking car, and alive, if you want to see a dime.'

'Amaka . . .' Seni and I wince, trying to settle her down.

'You can have the car,' Dérin says. 'I won't even report it stolen. It's brand new and I'm sure if you sold it whole, or e-even for parts, you'd get a lot of money. Just please. Please.'

Solomon sneers. 'And I'm supposed to believe that.'

'You can believe it and you will, it's not like we'd be able to offer you anything better. We are literally on our way to a wedding. No purses or chequebooks in sight. Stop the games and let us out. You'll go free, we won't say or do anything, and you'll end up much, *much* richer,' I say, growing increasingly mad.

The atmosphere in the car is tense for a moment; no one says anything until Solomon's phone rings. He picks it up and stares at the screen. I try to see the caller ID, but I can't. Then Solomon kisses his teeth like he's snapping out of a trance and turns the steering wheel to stop the car at the side of a dusty back road that none of us recognize.

'Get out,' he orders. No one wastes a moment scrambling out

of the car. I hear Dérin and Seni burst into tears. I stay back.

'I hope the money was worth it, delivering all those evil notes and sending all those hateful messages,' I spit.

He looks at me in the rearview mirror confused and then scowls, 'What are you talking about? Get out of the car, jare.'

I stare back at him, trying to gauge what could trigger a reaction. He doesn't budge, still scowling at me.

'Tell Uncle Yinka I said hi,' I say, before exiting.

His head swivels around as I slam the door. He watches me through the window for a moment before deciding to zoom off. Something tells me Uncle Yinka won't be seeing any of the money he gets from selling the car.

I walk over to Dérin and Seni and pull them into a hug, rubbing their backs. 'My phone is nearly dead and Babs took my charger. Can I use one of yours to call Mum and ask if she can send someone to pick us up?' I say as I break away. Seni unlocks her phone and hands it to me. I dial in Mum's number. She picks up after three rings.

'Hello?' She sounds confused.

'Hello, Mummy, it's me.'

'Lara, where are you?' Her voice turns panicky, and she starts whispering and rustling around as if she's trying to signal for people to come closer to the phone. 'You were supposed to be here fifteen minutes ago.'

'The car got stolen, we're in some random street. I think we're still in Lekki Phase One because we haven't reached the bridge yet. I'll send you our live location on WhatsApp.'

'Jésù ṣàánú fún wa! Niyi! Niyi!' Mum exclaims down the

phone, before calling for Dad. She explains what I've just said to those around her and everyone lets out a resounding '*Ah!*'

Aunty Zai takes the phone from Mum. 'Are you all okay? Is *Dérin* okay?' I look up at Dérin. Amaka is wiping her face while trying not to smudge her make-up.

'We're all fine. He wasn't violent; he wanted money and we gave him the car instead so we could leave.'

'O-okay. Find somewhere safe to wait then send your mummy the address, we'll come and pick you up. Quickly, Lara, please.'

I nod to myself then cut the phone. 'They're sending a car now. I'm just gonna text Mum the address . . .' I say, my voice trailing off as I see Kayode's name in Seni's call log. Yesterday at eleven p.m., while we were all supposed to be sleeping.

'You okay?' Amaka asks.

'Y-yeah, sorry, I was just looking for WhatsApp. I'm so used to my phone.' I laugh wearily, exiting Seni's call log and texting Mum instead. I pass the phone back to Seni, pretending I haven't seen anything even though I'm suddenly blind with rage.

'How did you know what to do in the car?' Seni asks.

'I just remembered a study from a true crime book about de-escalation tactics. You're supposed to listen to and hear them out enough to get to a level where they're disarmed and then you can influence them in your favour.'

'You saved our lives,' Dérin says, pulling me in for a hug. My tense body relaxes as I put my arms around her. I want to tell her that after the driver slipped up with his name, it was obvious he wasn't going to hurt us, but what would be the point? Uncle Yinka will get the karma he deserves after today.

I'll make sure of that.

A car comes for us soon after and we arrive at the venue forty minutes later, the traffic clearing up on Lekki-Ikoyi bridge some time later. Everyone is outside waiting for us. Dérin and Kayode's pictures are displayed on stands as you walk up to the venue, there is a red carpet and photographers wait with cameras around their necks for guests to arrive.

Dérin runs out of the car into her dad's arms and bursts into tears.

'Dérin, it's okay. It's okay. Má ṣòkùn. You're not hurt, are you?' Uncle Tayo asks, wiping her tears.

'No. Lara saved us. She talked him out of whatever he was planning, but we had to give him the car so that he would let us go.' Everyone turns towards me, completely shocked, apart from Uncle Damola and Uncle Tayo. Uncle Damola puts his fist up slightly in the air to signal well done. Uncle Tayo mouths *Thank you* at me, while rubbing Dérin's back.

I look around to see if Uncle Yinka is anywhere in sight. He's over by the door, practically hiding behind it. Aunty Yemisi stands in front of him, holding her bump and watching us with concern. She and their future babies don't deserve a man like him in their lives.

Aunty Zai goes over to Dérin and hugs her tight, then

escorts everyone inside so we can get things started. She lets us know that the make-up artists have set up in the dressing room just in case we need to touch up our faces, then instructs Alika to tell the DJ that Dérin is here and the wedding will begin soon.

Mum comes into the dressing room with us and grabs towels to wipe the dust from our clothes and shoes, then sprays us with perfume. We've already been delayed by nearly two hours. About ten minutes later, Aunty Tiwa comes in to see how we're doing.

She and Mum fill us in on everything that's happened in our absence. 'Kayode is okay,' Mum says. 'He was going to come and pick you up, but we had already sent a car and we didn't want to risk losing another person.'

'The delay in your arrival worked in our favour anyways,' Aunty Tiwa says. 'For some reason, the decorators had left our side of the hall undone. We had to wrap the chairs and finish the room ourselves, with Temi and Joseph's help.'

Dérin pauses the make-up artist who's setting her under-eyes. 'Why wasn't our side of the hall decorated?'

'I don't know, it was odd. They kept saying they had only been instructed to do the other side. That's all they were booked to do. They said that they thought it was unusual, but because no one had changed the instructions, they'd booked to do another event in the afternoon so had to leave,' Aunty Tiwa continues. Dérin and I stare at her dumbfounded.

'Why didn't Alika say anything?' I ask. It's literally her job to fix these things.

'She'd been arguing with them for a while and it seemed like she was getting nowhere. Once Joseph offered to help set up, we were fine. Are you guys all good with Joseph now? I've been sensing some tension, and the articles haven't helped,' Aunty Tiwa asks, looking at all of us. None of us know how to answer.

Aunty Yemi pops her head round the door. 'Are we ready to start?'

CHAPTER TWENTY-FOUR

From downstairs, we hear a microphone sound on as the DJ asks everyone to take their seats. Dérin's head turns towards the sound, and the make-up artist has to move her back into position.

'Why are her eyes watering?' Amaka says. 'Dérin. What's wrong?'

'I'm getting married now. And there's no longer enough time to do a first look with Kayode,' Dérin says, fanning her eyes so the tears don't fall.

'Aww . . . Suck it up right now. You've had your make-up done twice today, and I don't think dear Claire here wants to do it a third time,' Seni says, eyebrows raised. 'Let's get you ready and then we can go out and watch. The first look will be even better now 'cause it'll be around all the people you love.'

'Exactly,' Amaka says.

'Speaking of people you love, it looks like I've come at

the right time.' A familiar, annoying voice interrupts our conversation.

'I thought the devil only appeared when you spoke about him,' Amaka sneers.

'You lot are gonna have to stop calling me the devil, before it sticks. I'm here to give Dérin something,' Joseph says, as he walks in wearing a light pink agbada and matching fila, holding a massive bouquet of flowers. He smirks at Dérin as her eyes widen. 'Don't look so surprised. You know what that first card said.'

'What are you doing here? It's bad luck,' Dérin hisses.

'Last I checked, it was only bad luck for the groom. But you know, I'm more than happy to replace him.' The room goes silent. Joseph gives Dérin an amused smile. I want to gag. 'Ladies, do you mind if I ask you to clear the room?'

No one moves.

'Dérin, I don't thi—' I start to speak, but she puts her hand up to stop me. I ignore her and continue, 'I'm serious, I really don't think you sho—'

'It's okay, just stay nearby.' There's defeat and annoyance in her voice.

I look around to gauge everyone else's reactions, because even though they don't know what I know, this is still a stupid decision. A very stupid decision to let your ex, who you nearly kissed at your bachelorette party, come and visit you in your dressing room, on the day of your traditional wedding, before you're about to marry your fiancé and the love of your life. Nobody seems surprised, as if they've witnessed Dérin's weak spot for Joseph many times before. I, however, can't believe it. We all shuffle out of the room awkwardly.

'If you think I'm not eavesdropping . . .' Amaka tuts, pressing her ear to the door.

'Do you hear anything at all?' Seni asks.

'Nothing. I hope this doesn't mean they're kissing,' Amaka says and I choke on my saliva. God, I need to stop doing that.

'Why did they break up if they keep pulling back to each other? I don't get it. Why would she be so stupid?' I say, my true thoughts sounding harsh.

'Joseph and Dérin were long distance for basically all of secondary school,' Amaka explains. 'Joseph studied in the UK, and Dérin in Nigeria. When Dérin moved to the UK for sixth form, things were great, then the problems started because Joseph wanted to take a gap year to do an apprenticeship in Nigeria. Dérin was angry and hurt because they'd had two years of bliss together and that was supposed to continue because she was moving to London for uni. But it was like Joseph wanted things to regress by going back to long distance.' Amaka sounds exasperated. 'There was a whole argument about Joseph being selfish and only thinking of himself. That went on until Dérin did her first year at uni in London, while Joseph stayed in Nigeria for his apprenticeship. But when Dérin came home for the holidays, she was always ridiculously happy. Nigeria was common ground and she could finally spend quality time with Joseph. Their parents even wanted them together . . . Until Kayode.

Dérin meeting Kayode was the thing that finally broke them up. Broke the arguments, the on-and-off toxic cycle. All of it. But for some weird reason, both her and Joseph act like they never got the chance to process that their relationship was over. I guess it's a hard habit to kick when you've been doing it for a decade. It's like uni can be split into the Joseph Years and the Kayode Years.'

'If Joseph was the obvious choice, how did Kayode end up in the picture?'

Seni shrugs and sighs, arms crossed. 'She saw a future with him. She fell in love with him. Joseph was still in the picture at the beginning of Dérin and Kayode's relationship, but she eventually cut ties with him. We thought for good.'

Is that what Seni meant by calling Dérin a cheater? That there was an overlap between Joseph and Kayode?

'Why would Joseph fix up *now*? When he knows that Dérin's getting married. Why would he only put effort into her when it's basically too late? I . . . I can't even imagine how Kayode feels. Is he just supposed to take this, knowing that Joseph will always be around? That there will always be this annoying person waiting for him to fuck up so he can swoop in and take Dérin back.'

I don't say it out loud, but I'm also considering how Seni must feel. Seeing Joseph have such a hold on Dérin while she's marrying Kayode, someone she obviously has complicated feelings for.

'During this entire holiday, Joseph has spoken to you the most,' I point out to Seni. 'What has he been saying?'

Her arms unfold. 'He's bee—'

The door swings open, Amaka nearly trips over and Joseph leaves the room, flowers no longer in hand. He looks frustrated as he jogs down the stairs and out of eyeline. We all walk back into the room. Dérin is sitting on the edge of the sofa, staring at the floor. When she looks up her face is unreadable, but then she smiles at us.

'Shall we go look at the hall? It's beautiful.'

We all shuffle uncomfortably, heading out of the room one by one and making our way into the viewing room. An advantage of this venue is that it has a balcony with one-way windows opposite the dressing room, overlooking the entire hall. There are seats lined up in a row for us.

We gasp as we fully take in the hall. It's massive, filled almost to the brim with gold chairs arranged around round white tables, one half designed with blue sashes and the other half with purple. The centrepieces are a mixture of white camellias, accented with pink and blue baby's breath, tall candles in cases and palm leaves. At the front of the hall is the head table, decorated the same, but with two thrones in the middle, one with the letter *D* embroidered on it, the other with the letter *K*.

The live band starts playing 'Beru Ba Monuro' by Yinka Ayefele, the cue for Dérin's bridesmaids to get downstairs and dance into the room with the family.

Aunty Zai and Uncle Tayo are standing in the hall entrance, and we can see them looking around for us. I leave Dérin with a bag of plantain chips and an energy drink, making sure she takes a sip and a few bites before I follow the girls downstairs. She fusses for me to go, but knowing Dérin, she'll forget to eat all day.

As I get to the entrance, the live band starts singing and Aunty Zai takes centre stage, dancing hard and praising God, with Uncle Tayo trying to keep up with her. Her outfit sparkles and shimmers under the lights. Uncle Tayo's agbada is mostly gold, and his awotele is intricately designed with raised patterns that also glimmer in the light.

Tonight, our side of the family is wearing gold while Kayode's are in silver. They went back and forth for a while until it was decided that it would make more sense for the bride's family to wear gold, to signify 'how precious Dérin is'. Truthfully, Aunty Zai wouldn't have it any other way. The àṣọ ẹbí colours are not only an identifier, helping guests know which side of the family each member belongs to, but it's also an important sign of unity.

Mum and Dad dance in behind them, with Uncle Yinka and Aunty Yemi following. Then it's us, Dérin's bridesmaids, with the rest of the extended family. We keep getting held up by Aunty Zai who stops to dance with her arms up and butt out. As the song dies down, the immediate family dances over to the long white sofas, while the rest of the extended family take their seats on Dérin's side of the hall.

Big Mummy, our Alága ìjokòó, introduces the families and invites everyone to pray for them, as the bridesmaids make their way back up to Dérin, leaving Amaka below for her maid of honour duties.

Dérin beams at us when we reach her. 'You all looked so cute!'

Our heads turn as the live band begins drumming. Big Mummy starts singing songs of praise. Kayode's parents, Aunty Ireti and Uncle Fola, are at the beginning of their family's trail dance. Aunty Ireti, dressed in a silver off-the-shoulder iro and buba, smiles as she dances, the wedding plaque in her hand. But there's one problem. The handpiece draped over her shoulder is gold. Not silver. *Bright* gold. It clashes with Uncle Fola's fila which is silver like his agbada.

'Why is she wearing gold?' Seni whispers. No one on Kayode's side of the family is supposed to wear gold. The dress code is silver for them and gold for Dérin's family.

'Maybe . . . she's signifying the two families joining together?' I respond sceptically.

'But why would she not warn Aunty Zai—' Seni starts.

Dérin interrupts her. 'I allowed it.'

Her hands are clasped tightly as she watches Kayode's parents dance in. She turns around to us. 'They came up with the idea a week ago; it's supposed to be a surprise for everyone. Symbolizing them marrying into the family. I didn't tell Mum because she'd go overboard with things,' she finishes, then turns back around to watch them dance in.

Seni and I stare at each other in uncertainty, but try to look happy as we take our seats by the balcony. Dérin's explanation isn't convincing, and neither was her tone. She was just as surprised as the rest of us.

I look over to where our family is sitting, the front middle of the hall, all in a row. Everyone is turned to watch Aunty Ireti and Uncle Fola dance in. Aunty Zai is smiling hard in an obvious attempt to hide her confusion. Mum fails as she's clearly whispering to Uncle Damola about it. Amaka looks up at the mirrors, where we are watching from the one-way windows, and even though she can't see us, she's making it clear that she's not sure what's going on either.

The music quietens as Kayode's family gets closer to ours. The majority of Kayode's extended family goes to sit down on their side of the hall, while Uncle Fola, Aunty Ireti, and a few other important family members kneel down in front of Aunty Zai and Uncle Tayo.

'Ẹ jẹ́ ká gbàdúrà,' Big Mummy says, instructing both families to pray. She takes the gold plaque from Aunty Ireti and holds it up. 'Daddy, Mummy, on this plaque is the proposal letter that the Akinlola family have brought to you in the name of Jesus. Ẹ̀gbé mi dìdé, Zainab.' Aunty Zainab stands up as Big Mummy gives her the plaque. She then passes it to Amaka to read out the declaration. The plaque is a letter of intent to the bride's parents, symbolic of a proposal, and is presented to her family. Normally I'd be reading it aloud as a younger member of the bride's family, but Amaka and I are sharing duties as co-maids of honour.

Amaka reads, 'From the family of Mr and Mrs Akinlola to the family of Mr and Mrs Oyinlola. I am directed by the entire family to give you warm greetings in the name of our God. We are seeking your permission to formalize the love and courtship, between our beloved Son, Olukayode and your precious Daughter, Oluwase . . . Oluwashindara Dérinṣọlá.' Amaka clears her throat in an attempt to hide a stutter when she says Dérin's name. 'We have learned from him and from keen observation that she possesses amazing qualities that anyone would be proud of. She combines brains and beauty that are rare to find, and we cannot wait to welcome her into the family.' Amaka finishes then looks up at us with a weary smile on her face.

'Ẹ se, my dear,' Big Mummy says, taking the plaque from her. Amaka sits down, but she bounces her knee like she's worried about something. She whispers in Mum's ear then races towards one of the doors. Within two minutes she's upstairs with us.

'Lara, can I borrow you for a second? Your mum needs you.'

'Yeah, sure,' I say, stepping out into the corridor. Amaka's face drops; she covers her mouth with her hand then makes a gesture that shows she's trying not to scream. 'What's wrong? You're scaring me,' I say, moving her away from the doors so Dérin can't hear us, panic rising inside me.

'Dérin's name is not the name on the proposal letter I just read out.'

'It's okay, Dérin is her middle name. You didn—'

'No, I know that! Of course I know that, that's not why I stuttered. It is not Dérin's name on the plaque. I had to manually correct myself as I was reading otherwise I would have ruined everything before it started. Lara, I'm freaking

265

out. What am I supposed to do? Is it a mistake? Do I say anything? Do I n—'

'Amaka, please, you're rambling. Whose name is on that plaque?' I ask firmly.

'Seni's,' she whispers and my eyes widen.

CHAPTER TWENTY-FIVE

'Why the fuck would Seni's name be on that plaque?' I say, trying to keep my voice, and my rage, down.

'I don't know. I . . . I had to physically stop myself from shouting,' Amaka says, pacing up and down the corridor.

Too much is going on today: the attempted kidnapping, Joseph and Dérin, Aunty Ireti wearing gold, and now the plaque?

'Do you think Seni knows?' I ask.

'I mean, I don't think so. The way Kayode's parents brought it in, it seems they didn't know either. After I read it out loud, one of the aunties took it from me. I was so spaced out I didn't even see which one.'

'It was Big Mummy, which is good. That's our side of the family so we just need to find it and hide it before anyone el—' As I finish my sentence, Big Mummy's voice interrupts, asking the crowd if they're ready for the groom. Amaka and I look at each other, silently agreeing to retrieve the plaque before anyone else can see it. We both head back to the balcony.

Big Mummy speaks into the microphone after Kayode and all his groomsmen have made their big entrance into the hall. 'Now that is how you do an entrance!' The crowd roars, and Dérin whistles loudly. Kayode and all his groomsmen laugh and dap each other up. 'Olukayode. I need you to specify again for the crowd, who did you come for?'

'Dérinsọlá, ma,' Kayode says as the microphone is passed to him.

'Good. Some men will go to the house of their in-laws, and they will forget the name they came for,' Big Mummy says. Upon hearing that, Amaka goes into a coughing fit. Seni starts patting her back, but Amaka doesn't stop.

'Are you okay? Do you need water? Let's go get you some water,' I say with fake concern, grabbing her hand and taking her downstairs.

'You have to admit what Big Mummy just said was a strange coincidence,' Amaka says in a hoarse voice.

'*Everything* is strange today. Let's just find the plaque; by the time we do, it'll probably be Dérin's turn to dance in. We should use that kitchen door so that we don't disturb things and hopefully no one will see us,' I say pointing to the white door swinging inwards and outwards as kitchen staff walk through.

'We're going to smell like food,' Amaka whines.

'The whole hall will smell like food at some point.' I tut, and drag her in.

'Ah, sister mi. Ṣé o wa alright?' one of the caterers says

as she sees us walk in. She's sitting next to a massive pot of amala, beating out the lumps. On the other side of her, a girl in a pink apron is working on Dérin's cake. I gasp, distracted, because this is the first time any of us have seen it. She's got cake decorating tools set out all around her. She pours a bottle of sugar syrup over the top tier, and then uses a cake scraper to perfect the edges.

'Everything is fine, ma. We just need to get to our side of the hall; we're not supposed to be down yet,' Amaka answers, bringing me back to focus. The caterer nods and signals the way out.

We thank her and follow the path which leads us to the back row of tables on our side of the hall. The hall looks even bigger and prettier as we walk into it. The pink lights have now changed to a pale blue so that everyone can see better.

Big Mummy's voice blasts through the microphone. 'No more laughing; serious time, suck in all the bellies. Oya left, right: hands up.' Kayode and his groomsmen follow her instructions. She then commands them to march to the left and to the right, which makes it look like they're doing the Candy dance while the drums play in the background. This is the perfect distraction needed to look for the plaque.

'Where did you last see it?' I whisper to Amaka, holding my dress up so I can walk more easily.

'I think it was on the table behind us, by the white sofas. At the front of the hall. How are we going to get there without being noticed?' Amaka whispers back.

Big Mummy booms into the microphone, 'So, this is how

we're going to do it. When I say in the name of the Father, you raise your hands up. Of the Son, you go down like this.' Big Mummy spreads out her arms and bends halfway over, instructing the boys on how to ask permission. 'Then of the Holy Spirit – you all dobale. Okay?'

'Now is our chance. All eyes will be on Kayode,' I say, walking towards the front table with Amaka on my tail, dodging around other tables filled with guests.

'In the name of the Father,' Big Mummy starts as we reach the front of the hall.

'Do you see it?'

'And of the Son.'

'I can't find it anywhere,' Amaka whisper-panics.

'And of the Holy Spirit,' Big Mummy says and all the groomsmen dobale.

'Here!' I say, moving a bottle of Moët out of the way, stretching my hand forward to try and reach the plaque.

'Lara, what are you doing?' Aunty Yemisi's head turns towards me, her face twisted in confusion. There's no time to loiter before someone takes the plaque from me and sees what it says.

'One of the photographers wants to take a picture of it. We'll be back in two minutes,' Amaka says, pulling me as soon as I grab the plaque. It's heavier than expected and I nearly drop it. We run out through the hall and back into the kitchen.

I catch my breath and then skim-read the plaque out loud. 'We are seeking your permission to formalize the love and courtship, between our beloved Son, Olukayode and your precious . . . Dérinṣọlá. I . . . I'm confused. This says Dérin's name on it.' I look up at Amaka.

'What? N-no it doesn't. It says Seni's.' Her forehead wrinkles, as she comes over to look at it.

'I . . . Wh-who switched the plaques?'

CHAPTER TWENTY-SIX

'Amaka, you're sure you didn't just say the wrong name?'

'Why would I say the wrong name? Dérin is my best friend; I wouldn't stutter and fuck up her wedding on purpose. It's being filmed!'

I ponder for a minute, wondering what to do, but I'm drawing blanks. I believe Amaka, but whatever's going on is weird. There's no way Seni could've switched the plaques herself because she's been upstairs all this time. Joseph has been with the groomsmen for their entrance so it couldn't have been him. Uncle Yinka has been sitting at our table since the celebrations started, very obviously preoccupied with something on his phone.

My mind whizzes back to earlier in the day when Dérin received the latest Instagram message from @ajebotashamer. What did it say again? *Today will be a day full of surprises. I hope you love every one of them.*

'Your room is next to Seni's. Did you know she

called Kayode last night?'

'She what?' Amaka spits out.

'You didn't hear her on the phone, last night, at eleven?'

'No! I knew how *insanely* busy today would be, so I got an early night. I wanted to be prepared. Which, looking at the situation we currently find ourselves in, was clearly impossible.'

I nod and we both leave the kitchen and make our way upstairs, taking the plaque with us. We'll return it later when it's less suspicious.

'If we have the original, that means someone else must have the fake one. We need to find out who. If the wrong person gets hold of the fake plaq—'

'Did you guys forget that we have a view of the entire hall?' Seni interrupts me as Amaka and I reach the top of the stairs. She's standing in the corridor by the door of the viewing room. 'Not a bottle of water in sight. And yet, oh, look,' Seni's face brightens with fake surprise, 'the plaque!' She crosses her arms, glaring at us like we've done something sneaky.

'Where's Dérin?' Amaka asks, ignoring her comment.

'In the bathroom. We have to be down in five minutes. Now, why do you have the plaque?'

'It was chipped. I noticed when I was reading it,' Amaka says, lying through her teeth. 'Knowing Dérin, she'll think it's a bad omen so we've decided to hide it until we can fix it later.'

Seni's face softens. I hide the plaque underneath a bunch

273

of miscellaneous items, hoping it remains unseen, then we all make my way back to the balcony.

'Did you guys see if anyone was hovering around it when Big Mummy took it away from me?' Amaka asks, trying not to sound like she's investigating.

'No, I was too distracted watching David trying to shaku.' Seni snickers. 'Why?'

'No reason.'

Dérin finally comes out of the bathroom, looking nervous and adjusting her skirt as she walks.

Alika runs up the stairs and races to the balcony.

'They've told me to come and collect you. Kayode's segment is nearly finished. Are you all ready?' she says, catching her breath. We all nod. 'Okay, good. Your cousins are downstairs and will join you all at the door. Music is cued up.'

We start walking, then Dérin abruptly stops the line. 'Hey, hey, hey. Where's my veil?'

Alika turns around, and her eyes linger on us. 'It's supposed to be up here.'

'Well, it's not. Otherwise, it would be on my head,' Dérin says, sounding more and more agitated.

Can this day get any worse? Everyone scatters: Seni looks on the balcony, Dérin searches the dressing room, Amaka and I take the corridor and Alika paces up and down the stairs checking all the other places we've walked past today.

'Who was supposed to have it?' I yell out to Dérin.

'Seni!' she yells back. I look at Seni, who turns pale.

'Hey, *do not* blame me. I gave it to Aunty Adélé before we left the house.'

'That's fine. I can call Mum and ask where she put it,' I say, making my way back to the viewing room. Phone pressed to my ear, I stand on the balcony and watch Mum sitting in the hall with the rest of the family. I see her phone ring, but it's on the table behind her so she doesn't see it. Of all times, we need her to have her phone in her hand now. I call Babs. He picks up after two rings, as he leaves his seat.

'Hello?'

'Can you pass the phone to Mummy, please? Or rather, can you ask her where Dérin's veil is?'

'You couldn't come down and ask her yourself?'

'Babs. I will beat you up with a—'

'Okay, calm down. I was joking.'

I see him roll his eyes, then make his way over to Mum, tapping her on the back. He whispers in her ear, and she screws up her face, confused. I can tell he has to repeat himself, and once he does, her eyes shoot open and her hand goes to her mouth.

'It's in the car,' Babs says, putting the phone back to his ear, an unamused look on his face. I see Mum hand him the car keys and instruct him to hurry. He jogs out of the hall My heart can finally rest.

'It's okay! It's in the car. Babs is getting it now,' I say, joining Seni, Amaka and Alika in the corridor. Dérin comes out of the dressing room, tears welling up in her eyes. 'Do not cry. We don't have time to fix your make-up again,' I say, staring steadily at her.

Babs comes up two minutes later, carrying a white box. We remove the veil carefully and hold it up to make sure there are no imperfections. Our eyes go wide as we see the big gaping holes. Everyone gasps and turns to Dérin. She looks like she's about to faint. I'm trying to think quickly, but I'm paralysed.

Dérin stares at Seni. '*What* did you do?'

'*Me?!* Did you not hear that I gave it straight to Aunty Adélé?' Seni protests.

'Why would Aunty Adélé *shred* my veil?' Dérin shrieks at her.

As far as we all know, it was intact when Seni gave it to Mum. If Seni didn't ruin it, then who? Joseph? He didn't seem happy when he left the dressing room after his private chat with Dérin. He'd have had more than enough time to shred it between then and the start of the wedding. But would he do something that petty?

Babs tries to mediate by taking Dérin aside. He talks to her quietly and we can't tell from her blank expression if she's even listening. Dérin then rushes into the dressing room and comes out a minute later with white tulle on her head.

'Is that . . .?' Amaka asks, not knowing how to fill in the rest of the question.

'The curtain? Yes,' Dérin says, powdering her under-eyes with a make-up brush. 'You're a life-saver, thank you.' She blows a kiss to Babs, who nods then takes his leave. 'Alika, tell them we'll pay them whatever they want for it.' She turns around and looks at Seni sharply; Seni's eyes avert Dérin's death stare.

Alika watches Dérin with the same confused look we all have, then snaps out of it and nods. She speaks into her headset and says, 'We're ready.'

The intro for the remixed version of 'Woju' starts booming through the speakers and it's time for us to get moving. We dance in to the beat and Davido's lyrics. Everyone claps and cheers, hundreds of phones beaming down on us as they film the spectacle. I probably look like I'm enjoying myself, but I can't relax.

I scan the hall as I try to work out who could've switched the plaques and destroyed Dérin's veil. The dance trail dies down, we take our seats and Dérin goes up centre stage next to Kayode. As the crowd starts to disperse, I spot Alika, who is signalling for me, but I ignore her. She then rushes up behind me, pausing as she realizes she shouldn't disturb the celebrations. At the front of the hall, Dérin teases Kayode with his fila, threatening to not put it on him. He laughs then brings out a wad of dollars to start spraying her as she dances.

When the music starts to get louder, Alika bends down and finally says what we all know by now: 'We have a problem.'

CHAPTER TWENTY-SEVEN

'There's been an accident on Lekki-Ikoyi bridge,' Alika says when she finally gets me out of the hall.

'Why is that a problem for us?' I ask, confused.

'It means a lot of the guests who aren't already here are struggling to make it. It also means some of the things planned for later might not happen.'

'Oh God. Dérin's going to be crushed. What happened on the bridge?' Alika brings out her phone to show me a headline about a car crash. As she does, a notification of a WhatsApp message from an unsaved number appears at the top of her screen. It says: 'Ijose, where are you?' She swipes it away quickly.

Ijose . . . Who is that?

'Uh, thank you, Alika. I'll let Dérin know.'

Dérin comes up behind me, holding a plate of puff puff. 'Tell me what? Actually, tell me upstairs, we need to change.' She rushes me and the rest of the girls up to the dressing room. 'I felt like I was going to faint; I'm so hungry.'

'What do you mean he's not coming?' I guess someone has broken the news to Aunty Zai. She rushes into the dressing room, and paces up and down, her face like thunder.

Aunty Zai puts the call on speaker and a man's voice says: 'The car accident on the bridge has blocked traffic on both sides. We left two hours ago, and we're still here. Madam, we won't make it, I'm sorry. We will transfer you back the payment.'

The call ends and Aunty Zai frowns. 'Kizz Daniel can't perform. Who's going to sing Dérin into the hall now?'

'So much has gone wrong today. *So* many bad omens,' she whispers under her breath so only I can hear: 'Maybe I should've cancelled.'

'Okay, calm down. We can work something out, surely,' Amaka says.

'You guys . . .' Seni says, looking at her phone. 'The car in the accident, I'm pretty sure—'

'That's . . . that's Dérin's car.' I'm looking at the article on my phone too. 'The Rolls-Royce that Kayode gifted her. It's a mangled mess, but that's the licence plate.' I hear a whimper from Dérin in the corner. 'Driver in critical condition,' I read. Shit. Moses. 'This update was an hour and a half ago . . . we left him just over two hours ago . . .' And if Moses is in critical condition . . . that means he crashed almost straight after we left him. That explains why Uncle Yinka keeps checking his phone – he's waiting for Moses to contact him about the car. But Moses can't do that because he's seriously injured.

279

Uncle Yinka only used him to steal the car. That's it. Moses complaining about ajẹbọ́tá meant nothing. It was just pure coincidence.

Everything's coming together. Uncle Yinka doesn't gain anything by sabotaging the wedding, especially when it's already been paid for. If anything, he would want it to run smoothly after the car theft – he would already have his dirty money, and ultimately that's all he cares about.

'Jésù ṣàánú fún wa. He was probably speeding to get away. I just thank God you girls weren't in the car.' Aunty Zai starts fanning at Dérin's eyes. 'Dérin, ma sokún mọ. Ó ti tó, look at the bright side. God dealt with that man quickly for what he did.'

How quickly will God deal with Uncle Yinka for orchestrating it?

As everyone attempts to calm Dérin down, Aunty Ireti shows up, all smiles as she pokes her head round the door. 'Dérin? What's wrong?'

Dérin's expression brightens when she sees Aunty Ireti, and she tries to sniff her tears away. 'Um, nothing. Just a surprise I had for everyone that's now fallen through . . . Is everything okay, Aunty?'

'I was just coming to see how you were. The hall is beautiful – and I'm sure it must've been a surprise for you to see me wearing gold. I told Kayode not to tell you anything,' she says, and all of us bridesmaids turn or look at Dérin because, contrary to what she told us earlier, she did *not* know that Aunty Ireti would be wearing gold. She was in

280

the dark, just like the rest of us.

She avoids our gaze, her smile dropping ever so slightly. 'No, he didn't tell me, but it was a lovely surprise. It suits you and Uncle well.'

Another knock at the door catches our attention: Uncle Yinka comes in with a platter of small chops.

'Oh, thank God,' Amaka says dramatically, probably grateful for a distraction from the awkwardness in the room, but also for the arrival of food. Kayode, Babs and Joseph follow behind him closely, grabbing for samosas. Seni smacks their hands away as Uncle Yinka puts the plate on the table.

'We should make a toast. Dérin, go and get the rest of your family,' Aunty Ireti says and Dérin follows her instruction. Uncle Tayo, Uncle Fola and Daddy come in a moment later. Aunty Ireti pours everyone a glass of champagne.

Wooziness brought on by an empty stomach makes me feel faint. As I make a beeline for the food, my eyes lock onto Uncle Yinka. He catches my gaze, staring back at me with a blank expression. He doesn't know what we know. He doesn't know that the Rolls-Royce has been wrecked and he won't be seeing a dime.

I break eye contact as everyone moves into a closer circle. Following Aunty Ireti's lead, they raise their glasses. 'Father Lord, we thank you for this day,' she starts.

Here we go, I think, as I tune out the prayer, eyes on Uncle Yinka again. He's smiling as he listens to Aunty Ireti. The smile drops when he realizes I'm staring at him again. He squirms uncomfortably.

The prayer ends and Kayode takes over. 'May we all be family. 'Til death do us part.'

'Amen!' Aunty Ireti and Aunty Zai say, and we all clink our glasses and take a sip.

Everyone starts to head back downstairs. Amaka, Uncle Yinka and I are the last ones left in the room. I'm watching his every move.

'Ah, ah, Lara. Why are you staring at me like I've slapped your papa?' Uncle Yinka finally says. I pause, thinking what to say next.

'Uncle, have you checked the news today?' He eyes me, confused. 'Something about a car crash.'

'Why is that relevant to m—' Uncle says, then his eyes widen as he realizes. He flings his agbada upwards and fumbles urgently in his pocket for his phone. He looks a mess and I don't have the energy to deal with him right now. I link arms with Amaka and pull her out into the hallway, my head held high.

'What was that about?' Amaka whispers but I ignore her. It's best we keep this in the family.

All the parents go back into the hall to mingle, while the bridal party and the groomsmen get ready to dance in again, something they need to do because of Dérin's outfit change. Alika appears out of nowhere a few minutes later. 'The DJ has mashed up a few songs for you to dance in to since Kizz Daniel can't make it. Are we all ready?'

Everyone nods. Alika turns around but Dérin's voice stops her in her tracks.

'But, Alika, come. Why am I hearing all this news from everyone *but* you? You're supposed to always be my first point of call, but I've been left in the dark every time something goes wrong. I can never find you. What is it you're doing?'

Amaka and I sneak looks at each other.

'Dérin. Honestly, it's best that I'm running around because it means you know nothing. Trust me. Your job is to be happy; my job is to stress,' Alika says, turning back with a weary smile before walking to the door of the hall and giving the DJ a thumbs up.

He cues up 'True' by Kizz Daniel. Seni and Joseph are at the front of the line and start dancing in. As I enter the hall, my eyes bulge at the number of people in here. It's like the guest list has almost doubled.

'Do you know all these people? I thought security was supposed to be tighter,' I whisper to Dérin.

She whispers back, 'This is what tighter security looks like. They're Daddy and Mummy's friends, as well as influencers and socialites.'

I frown. There are so many people here. Anyone could be doing evil right now and we wouldn't know. The crowd starts moving closer, the flash of the lights from people's phones almost blinding.

'Is it just me or does it feel like they're closing in on us?' I ask Amaka, who's dancing next to me. She shrugs, continuing to dance with her hands in the air. The crowd gets even closer, none of the faces familiar. They're influential enough that I feel like I should know them, and be grateful that they're spraying money on me, but all I feel is intense anxiety.

I try to take my mind off things by continuing to dance, but I become hypervigilant. The person terrorizing Dérin would thrive in this situation; not only is she distracted, but so am I. I try to watch everyone's faces through the gaps in the crowd. I see a couple dancing closely with each other. The man's hands are on her waist. The woman turns and smiles at him. She looks familiar. Really fam—

Oh my God.

She's the girl I DM'd about the anonymous comments. Àdúràtọlá!

I didn't know she'd be invited, but *of course* she would if Dérin and her run in the same social circles. I need this dance to hurry up and end so I can speak to her about @ajebotashamer.

The DJ seamlessly switches songs and everyone cheers, synchronizing their dance moves. Everything is great, until another song starts.

'Last Last' by Burna Boy.

The song that Dérin *explicitly* stated that she doesn't want played at the wedding. The song she feared so much she threatened to call the wedding off.

The record gets stuck, repeating the same line over and over again. It distorts as it continues to play, to the point that it sounds sinister.

'I thought Dérin didn't want this song?' Seni calls over the music. I look over at Dérin and see that she's trying not to panic. I fight my way through the crowd, holding on to my gèlè so that it doesn't fall off. I finally get through, lifting my dress to run to the DJ.

'What the hell are you doing? You were told not to play this song!' I yell over the music.

'I'm not!' he shouts back. 'I've lost control of my system. The next song I had cued up was by Asake.' He holds his hands up to show that he's not doing anything. My face scrunches as I look at his computer. I click a few buttons and nothing works. The song just keeps playing. He stares at me with a look that confirms he's already tried that.

'We just have to pull the plug,' I say, and he nods.

I run over to the live band to tell them that they need to get ready to play because I'm going to cut the speakers. They nod, putting down their plates of food, the drummer no longer fighting a piece of chicken. I run back to the DJ booth and study the wires, but everything's a tangled mess.

'Which one is connected to the speaker?' I yell, and he points to the blue cable. I yank it out and the hall goes silent. All heads turn my way. The guests look both angry and confused as the hall is plunged into total silence. I turn to the live band. The drummer begins and the rest of them follow, starting to play 'Ijo Fuji A'. I give a sheepish smile as I turn back to the crowd. They seem satisfied enough, and a few aunties in the corner of the room start dancing again.

'What the fuck is going on?' I whisper to myself.

CHAPTER TWENTY-EIGHT

Seni and Amaka manage to break away from the crowd a few minutes later, running towards me. I'm still in shock, trying to process what the hell is going on.

'You need to come now,' Seni yells to the DJ. He looks like he's just been told off, but he hops out of the booth and comes into the corridor with us. 'What happened?' she says to both of us. I shake my head in confusion.

'My screen froze. I had a playlist cued up because Kizz Daniel wasn't coming any more. Next thing you know, the song changes to "Last Last". I'm thinking, *oh I've hit something wrong*, so I quickly tried to jump to the next song I had lined up. But it wouldn't work. Kayode, Uncle Tayo and Uncle Niyi made it clear, "Last Last" isn't playing. If you could see the way my eyes bulged when it came up. Ah, módàràn. I'm finished. Do you know how scared I was? I tapped every button on my system to try and get it to stop but it just wouldn't.' He sounds defeated.

Like his ears were burning, Dad joins us. 'Didn't I tell you not to play that song?' He's shouting, and the DJ immediately falls to his knees and starts begging, hands clasped together.

'Daddy, it wasn't him. His system crashed,' I say, feeling defeated myself. 'He doesn't know how it happened either.'

'Honestly, sir, I don't know.' The DJ rubs his hands together.

'Joseph can check the computer for you.' Dad pulls up his agbada and brings out his phone. Joseph answers a few seconds later and Dad instructs him to meet us at the DJ booth. We make our way over there too.

I pull Dad quickly aside. 'I'm not sure Joseph is the best person to look at the computer.'

'Why? His job is in tech. Who else am I going to ask?' Dad questions.

'A lot of things have gone wrong today and I think he might be behind some of them. If he goes through the DJ's computer, he could easily lie about where the hack came from or make the situation worse.'

Dad looks at me like I'm speaking rubbish. 'What are you talking about? What is it you're trying to tell me? We're at a wedding, things go wrong all the time. Are you making up stories for your own pleasure, Lara? Is this what you'll be doing in that university course of yours? Making up stories?'

'When have I ever made up—' But he cuts me off.

'Joseph has been in Dérin's life since he was young, why would he now sabotage her wedding? Lara, please. We've not even finished the conversation we started a few weeks ago. That one we must come to before your A-level results day.

But for now, just let the man do his job,' he says, signalling for Joseph to join us.

Joseph seems puzzled as he walks closer, which is no surprise. I must look like a scorned woman. Dad is so unreasonable. He's clearly holding a grudge about uni, which is understandable, but is now really the time to get angry about it? Here of all places, after what just happened? If he gives Joseph access to the DJ's computer and Joseph does more harm than good, Dad'll be the one who ruins the wedding, not me. I can't even caution Joseph not to try anything dodgy because Dad immediately steps in front of me when Joseph reaches us. I'm seething as I watch Dad instruct him to look through the computer to figure out what went wrong.

'It seems the system was hacked. It still hasn't got full control back,' Joseph says.

'Can you fix it?' Dad asks.

'It'll take like, an hour,' Joseph estimates. 'Can the live band keep playing until then?'

'They have no choice.' Dad kisses his teeth. 'You guys need to go and make sure Dérin eats; she looks pale. Lara, do not get into any trouble,' Dad says before walking off. I centre myself, watching the crowd dance. It's shifted from young people to older aunties, spraying each other and the live band with money.

'Can you text me the name of the person who hacked the system as soon as you get it?' I ask the DJ, showing him my phone number. He takes a picture of it and nods.

I walk away from them, closing my eyes to think. There

are so many things I need to do before the end of the night: find the plaque with Seni's name, discover who shredded Dérin's veil, and uncover who sabotaged the music.

Before I can open my eyes, someone grabs my hand. Uncle Yinka. I try to yank myself out of his grip, but he holds firm.

'Let go of me!' I hiss, but to no avail. He's pulling me so tightly that my wrist is burning. Before I know it, we're upstairs next to the dressing room and he's slamming me against the wall. Hand still gripping my wrist.

'What do you know?' he spits.

I keep struggling. 'You're hurting me,' I grit through my teeth.

'*What do you know?*' he repeats, more aggressively.

'I knew nothing until you confirmed things just now. How *could* you? You wanted the money so bad that you stole Dérin's car? Made her fear for her life. On her *wedding day*? If you had just been responsible and managed your money instead of spending it all frivolously. You've got not one, but two kids on the way, you seriously couldn't just get a grip on your lif—'

I'm interrupted by a slap across my face. The sharp sting shocks me into silence, gasping.

'Lara, I . . . I'm sorry. I di-didn't mean it,' he stammers, letting go of my hand.

My gasps turn into laughter as I shake my head. 'Is the money really worth it?'

I slide out from where he looms over me and walk away. Tears fall down my face as I escape to the balcony. I'm not even sure what I'm crying about. The fact that Uncle Yinka slapped me *over a freaking car*? That I still don't have solid evidence about who is trying to destroy the wedding? That my own dad, who used to be my biggest cheerleader, completely shut me down, just when I thought I could open up to him about everything?

God, I hate this. I hate this so much. I hate the self-doubt I feel; I hate that this is making me second-guess my life choices. I hate that this is all down to me, and I've got to make sure things go right. I allow myself a few moments to cry, sitting on the balcony watching the celebrations go on downstairs. At the very least, Dérin still looks happy. She and Kayode look as in love as ever.

I look around the hall. Mum and Aunty Yemi are spraying Aunty Zai and Uncle Tayo with money. Amaka and Babs are dancing. Alika is walking around with her headset, until she stops and starts talking to someone behind a pillar. I try to position myself better so that I can get a glimpse of who she's talking to, but I can't. She lifts a plaque in her hand as she talks to them.

Wait, what?

H-how? The only people who knew where I hid the plaque were Seni and Amaka. I run to the corridor and rummage under the various bags and shoes. But I can't find it. I search the whole area. The plaque is gone. How did Alika know it was here? Did I not hide it well enough? Did Seni tell her it was here? When did she even come up here to—

More importantly, is that the real plaque or the fake one?

The real one is missing now, and we don't know who has the fake one. I go back to the balcony and call Amaka. I watch as she answers.

'Can you see who Alika is talking to? She's behind you by the pillars.' Amaka crooks her neck and when she's not able to see, she heads over.

'She's not talking to anyone. They must have walked away.'

My eyes scan the room. I can't see Joseph or Seni anywhere. It could have been either of them.

'Is that a plaque in her hand?' Amaka gasps. 'It's not the one from upstairs, is it?'

'It could be. It's not here any more.'

'For fuck's sake! I'll make sure she doesn't display it anywhere.'

'Thank you. I'll meet you down there.' I watch Alika walking around tables, plaque still in hand. Amaka also watches from the dancefloor. Alika continues, greeting guests, until she freezes at one table, then makes a beeline in the opposite direction. I squint at the guests on that table.

I recognize one of them: Àdúràtọlá. I need to speak to her. Maybe there's a reason why Alika avoided her table and, at the very least, Àdúràtọlá can tell me more about the awful comments she received on Instagram when she was planning her wedding. Àdúràtọlá heads to the bar. I rush downstairs, hoping that she won't have left by the time I get to her.

I step in front of her just as she picks up her drink. She looks a little startled, nearly stepping into me. 'Oh, so sorry. I didn't see you there,' she says. Her accent is really posh.

'Àdúràtọ́lá, hey. You don't know me. My name is Lara, I'm Dérin's cousin. I'm sorry to stop you like this, but I sent you a DM on Instagram three weeks ago. It was about those weird comments you received when you were planning your wedding.'

'Oh, you're Dérin's cousin? Lovely to meet you. You can call me Àdúrà. Dérin and I went to secondary school together.' She extends her free hand for me to shake. 'I don't check my DMs *because* of those evil comments. Whatever you read, it's *not* true. And I've never had plastic surgery in my life.' She sounds annoyed that I've brought this all up and she has to explain herself, to a stranger, again.

'I believe you, truly I do. But that's not the reason I reached out. Basically, the comments you received . . . Well, similar ones, all anonymous, have been sent to Dérin, throughout her whole wedding planning. I wanted to know if you could tell me more about what you went through?'

'The comments and messages started once my engagement was announced. They attacked me mercilessly, but Instagram did nothing. They bullied me for appearance; they questioned my wedding choices; they mocked my fiancé; they embarrassed my family and friends. They were just jealous and *bitter.* They made me feel like a spoilt rich bitch, and that I was undeserving of what I got. I *am* spoilt, but I'm not a bitch.'

I lightly laugh at her joke. 'The same thing is happening to Dérin. Did you ever find out who was doing this to you? Did they ever go as far as stalking you? Leaving you notes?

Did they ever make attacks on your life or do anything physically dangerous?'

'No, nothing like that. Wow, are they stalking Dérin? They could never take it that far with me, Daddy's a currency exchange dealer and worth *loads*. He'd sue the shit out of them; they knew better. They stopped as soon as my big traditional wedding was over. My white wedding had sixty guests. It was like they were angry about the big wedding. Weirdo.'

'Did they try to ruin your traditional wedding on the actual day too?'

'Oh God, no. Security was airtight because of those comments and DMs. I hired a private investigator, and they figured out it was some slimy assistant called Josie. I didn't pursue anything legally because I figured, what was the point. I almost felt sorry for her. She was obviously a sad, lonely, jealous woman without much money. I didn't want to ruin her. I clearly should've if she's continuing her same wicked antics.'

Josie . . . Why is that name familiar?

I type the name *Josie* into my phone and stare at it. The letters switch around in my mind into something more recognizable.

Ijose.

Like the name I saw earlier in the notification on Alika's phone when someone WhatsApp messaged her.

Ijose, where are you?

Josie must be a nickname for Ijose.

'Do you remember what she looks like?' I ask and Àdúrà

nods. I show a picture of Alika from her Instagram.

'That's her! A-li-ka.' Àdúrà frowns, reading the Instagram handle, then scoffs. 'She's one to talk about plastic surgery. That's not her real nose. That's also not her real first name. It was definitely Josie. And her last name was something Edo, like Omoregbe?'

That would explain why I can't find Alika anywhere on the internet before last year. She's reinvented herself.

'I can't tell you how much you've helped me today. Thank you so *so* much.'

'No problem, girl! If Dérin needs a good lawyer, tell her I'm here. Take that bitter bitch down,' she says, then walks back over to her table.

Taking her down is exactly what I'm going to do. I type Alika's real name into Google to see if what Àdúrà is saying is completely correct. Sure enough, within five minutes, I've found posts from her secondary school graduation ceremony. I've found Facebook pages tagging her in family events. I've even managed to find her old Instagram page she deleted before making her current one. It's not the burner account that was messaging Àdúrà or Dérin, but it's evidence that Alika isn't who she says she is. That she shouldn't be trusted.

I knew there was reason to be suspicious of her. I pull out my phone and call Amaka again.

'Grab Alika and bring her to the kitchen.'

'Already on it.'

CHAPTER TWENTY-NINE

I run down the stairs into the kitchen to find Amaka grabbing Alika by the arm. Alika squirms, but Amaka's grip is tight enough that some of the beading starts to fall off Alika's dress.

'Let go of me! What is wrong with you?' she shrills. I look her up and down and snatch the plaque and the clipboard she's holding. '*What* are you doing? I have to be out with Dérin in less than five minutes. We have to get ready for the final outfit change and after-party and she has the cake cutting.'

Ignoring her, I skim-read the plaque: 'We are seeking your permission, yada, yada . . .' Bile rises up my throat, the acidity making my eyes water. Dérinṣọlá. It has Dérin's name on it.

'Where did you get this?' I wave it in her face.

'From the front of the hall,' Alika says in a *duh* tone. 'Next to the gifts.'

'We *hid* this upstairs. How did you know it was there? Who told you?'

'Are you okay? Did I not speak *clearly* enough? It was. Next to. The *gifts*,' Alika snarls, finally breaking free from Amaka's grip.

'Mind how you speak to her.' Amaka points her finger at Alika. 'I've been downstairs, next to the gifts, and the first time I saw the plaque it was in your hands, while you were talking to someone. Who were you talking to and who told you where this was? Where's the fake plaque with Seni's name?'

'Seni's name? W-what are you talking about?' Alika looks genuinely taken aback. She's an amazing liar.

'I know you don't have enough brains to run this operation,' I say to her, 'so tell me who you're working with and things might turn out better for you.' When she stays silent, I slam my fist into the wall half an inch from her ear. 'I know you're behind @ajcbotashamer. How can you live with yourself? Knowing for the past seven months you've attacked Dérin for no good reason, made her a nervous wreck, stressed her out, basically destroyed her mental health, when you should've been her confidante in her most important and vulnerable ti—' I stop as I hear footsteps.

'Girls?' a familiar voice says from behind us. When I turn my head, I'm irritated to see Aunty Ireti. 'Is everything okay?' I don't want to reveal all this to Aunty Ireti. She knows nothing about the situation and she'd think I was going mad. She probably already does, with how this looks.

When we don't say anything, she continues, 'Dérin is looking for you, Alika. The cake needs to come out soon, before the after-party.' She watches all our faces, completely baffled. Alika slips away from me, walks out of the kitchen and back into the hall. For fuck's sake. If she runs, I won't be surprised.

'What did you mean by all of that?' Amaka asks. 'Is she the one behind all the notes Dérin has been getting?'

'She's not who she says she is,' I reply.

Aunty Ireti clears her throat, startling me. I thought she had slipped out with Alika.

'Guests are asking where the plaque is. After everything that's publicly happened in the run-up to the wedding, I think they're looking for more scandal, which we don't need. Shall I put that back?' She looks at the plaque in my hands.

Amaka and I both nod. She scans our faces once more, then takes the plaque from me.

'Hopefully we can salvage the rest of this event so people don't talk,' she says, then walks away.

After the adrenaline rush, I sag with tiredness. I wait until I'm sure she's gone, before speaking. Dérin would freak if she overheard us.

'Do you remember Àdúrà from the first Naija Gossip Lounge article about Dérin's wedding?' I ask Amaka.

'Yeah, they thought Rin would copy her wedding. They're in the same social circles.'

'She's here and she confirmed some suspicions I had about Alika. Alika isn't even her real name. When Àdúrà

297

was planning her wedding, she received awful comments and evil messages on Instagram, nasty rumours about her fiancé and their relationship, telling her that they should cancel their wedding. As well as the notes you know about, Dérin has been receiving similar comments and messages on Instagram for the past seven months, since she started planning her traditional wedding. I found out whoever tried to ruin Àdúrà's wedding is the same person who's been trolling Dérin on Instagram and helping make her life hell. It's Alika.'

'I'll rip her apart!' Amaka rages. I hold her back. 'What is she gaining from this, Lara? What's the fucking point? To make Dérin miserable? Destroy her wedding because she's jealous? What is it?'

'That's the thing. I don't think Alika's working alone. Àdúrà said Alika only ever sent her hateful messages, and made her seem like she didn't deserve her wedding, on Instagram. She said she never received any physical notes, and no one threatened her life, nor did they try to sabotage her wedding, in the run-up or on the day. Alika is responsible for the online trolling for sure, but I think she's working with someone else, maybe helping with the other horrible things happening to Dérin. The other person is smarter and stronger. They have a wicked vendetta and are *determined* to stop this wedding and end the marriage before it can even begin.'

'I can't believe we let Alika get away. Do you think she's working with someone we know?'

'I originally suspected Joseph.'

'*Joseph?*' Amaka whisper-shouts in shock.

'It's possible. Joseph has made it abundantly clear he wants Dérin back. I've had my suspicions about him from the moment Dérin told me about the Insta messages, the notes, and everything constantly going wrong. And now the plaque. Joseph's saving grace is that he couldn't have swapped them because he was part of the groomsmen's entrance at the start of the celebrations, so he has an alibi. Plus, I feel like Joseph is audacious enough to have changed Kayode's name to *his* rather than Dérin's to Seni's. Maybe that's a reach, but it sends the message he wants everyone to receive. I also don't think he's that switched on to have sabotaged to this level of detail.'

'Joseph is an Aries man determined to get who he calls "the love of his life" back. He's more than petty enough to do those things,' Amaka deadpans. She continues, 'Joseph is a jealous ex, and his reasons are more than capable to cause enough chaos at the wedding to get Dérin to stop it from happening at all.'

'True, but Joseph still loves Dérin; they have history. I just don't think he would hurt her *this* much to get what he wants. Everything that's gone wrong in the run-up to the wedding has directly or indirectly upset Dérin, and I've constantly questioned if Joseph was responsible for them all. I even accused him. But tonight . . . Tonight, these actions seem pettier, like they're hyper-focused on things that *only* affect Dérin, that only affect the bride, in the worst way. It's as if whoever is behind them knows the magnitude because if it were to happen to them, on their wedding day, they would react the same way, like any woman would. It's as if they're attacking her, woman-to-woman. I've suspected Seni for a long ti—'

'Woah, Seni? I don't think— What makes you think it would be her? I mean, Seni is a lot of things, but this is . . .' Amaka scrambles for words.

'Amaka, Seni is the only one who knew where we hid the plaque.'

'But . . . that doesn't mean . . . I mean, Aunty Yemi saw us take it away, anyone else could've seen when we took it upstairs,' Amaka says.

'That wouldn't explain how Alika knew the *exact place* the plaque was. I don't trust Seni as far as I can throw her. Seni was at the dinner and she knew Dérin didn't want "Last Last" to be played. Seni was also in charge of looking after Dérin's veil and then that was shredded. Seni could easily have asked Kayode what the plaque looked like and secretly got a duplicate made.

'Plus, let's not forget that Seni and Kayode are each other's *exes*. Even if Kayode is over their relationship, it's pretty clear that she isn't. Seni's call to Kayode last night proves this. What could they possibly have to talk about the night before her best friend's wedding? Plus, we *still* don't know what they were talking about in her room on the night of the bachelorette party. They sure as hell weren't making secret wedding videos for Dérin, like she claimed.

Seni's been sulking most of the trip, being bitchy, making snide comments, more than likely due to her residual feelings for Kayode, or resentment towards Dérin and the wedding. And we know Alika is also fuelled by jealousy, her Instagram trolling proves that. Maybe Dérin told Seni who her wedding planner was and Seni discovered the truth about Alika's dodgy past and paid Alika to team up with her to ruin the wedding. I know it sounds crazy and should be near-impossible, seeing as Seni lives far away in London, so how could she orchestrate all this over seven months from halfway across the world? But Amaka, all fingers point to her. We've just proved that.'

Amaka looks at me in disbelief. But then her face falls as she starts to realize what I'm saying could be true.

'Seni, Joseph and my Uncle Yinka have the strongest motives. As much as I loathe Joseph, it's clear that this is bigger than him. He doesn't have the range to pull off something like this. And Uncle Yinka is just an idiot driven by money.'

'Uncle Yinka?'

'Uh, yeah. He thinks some of the money spent on this wedding should be given to him. He says he's owed it. He . . . He was behind the carjacking this morning. He wanted to sell the car for money, so he paid his friend "Solomon", whose real name is Moses, to be the driver and steal the car so it looked like he wasn't involved. That plan was foiled when Moses got into a car crash, so now there's no car to sell and no money in Uncle Yinka's pockets.'

'Wow,' Amaka gasps. She pauses, looking up at the ceiling, and then sighs. 'This is so mad. Let's just get back to the party so that we can make sure nothing else happens. We can't forget the other plaque. We need to find it; and we need to protect Dérin now.' We start walking in the direction of the hall.

When Amaka and I get back to the table where everyone is sitting Babs stands up and puts his hand on my shoulder. 'I've not seen you eat today. Are you okay?'

'You know, you're right. I've been running up and down,' I reply, suddenly exhausted.

'Let me get you something.'

'I'm just gonna go to the bathroom first. I'll meet you back at the table.' I walk over to the downstairs toilet but when I see a queue of people, I make my way upstairs to the dressing room.

Dérin and Kayode's next outfit change is laid out on the sofa. I go into the bathroom, realizing how hungry I am as soon as I sit on the toilet. My vision is hazy, and I wait for a moment, willing my head to stop spinning so that I can just get out of here and put some food in my system.

As I stand up and flush, I hear a sudden thud from outside. I pause, wondering if the noise came from the party downstairs. But then I hear a ringtone go off in the dressing room – the sound of windchimes – before stopping abruptly.

'Babs?' I call out. 'Amaka . . .? Alika?' No one answers. The floor creaks as someone walks across it, the footsteps fading away. I hear jewellery clinking very quietly. I rush to open the bathroom door, but no one is there. I run to the hallway, but that's empty too.

I twist my lips as I walk slowly back to the dressing room. Someone was definitely in here. Neither the ringtone nor the footsteps nor that thud was a figment of my imagination. I look around the room to see if anything looks unusual or could have dropped on the floor, but the only thing out of place is Dérin's shoebox, and that was on the brink of falling off the sofa when I entered the room anyway.

My head starts pounding so I pick up a leftover sausage roll from the platter Uncle Yinka brought up earlier. I take a bite and start making my way back downstairs.

Babs meets me just as I reach the table and hands me a plate. 'Sit. Eat,' he commands, plopping me down into the chair next to his. I nod, picking up my spoon to scoop up some gizdodo. I grab a bottle of 5Alive from the table and pour it into a glass. I swallow a few scoops of food before Amaka walks up to me, putting her hand on my shoulder. 'No,' Babs says, speaking for me before I can. 'She needs to eat. You can handle it yourself.' I look up at him amazed, mouthing a thank you, then focusing back on my food.

'I'm just going to put this upstairs,' Amaka says as she holds the plaque Aunty Ireti took from us and placed back by the gifts.

'Mm,' I say through a spoonful of food. 'Oh, so that wasn't you upstairs just now?'

Amaka frowns. 'No.'

'Mm, okay . . . If anything shifty happens, if an eye so

much as darts left, I will come running.' Babs clears his throat. 'As soon as I finish my food.' He nods, then I nod at Amaka.

'I didn't realize we knew this many people,' he says, sitting down next to me.

'*We* don't. It's a hall full of nosy people, at a Nigerian socialite's wedding. At least the white wedding next week will have fewer guests, so it'll be calmer and more intimate. I just hope I'm not going to have to run around then too.'

'Lara!' Mum's voice projects across the hall. I turn my head towards her. 'Come and say hi to Aunty Kemi.' I nod, bracing myself internally then turning to Babs.

'Babs is also right here?' I yell back, face scrunched. I don't understand how he always gets away with not having to say hi to relatives.

I take a deep breath and head towards Mum. She's got that smile she gets whenever she's telling someone about my career plans. Or should I say the plans that she has for my career.

'My dear, how are you?' Aunty Kemi coos as she sees me, then gives me a hug. 'You look beautiful. Our fashion line has finally taken the US by storm, so you must visit us in New York some time.'

'Thank you, Aunty. I'll come soon, I promise. You always look gorgeous so I'm not surprised it's doing well. How's Uncle?'

'He's fine. He'll pop by later; he's stuck in the traffic on the bridge. Are you ready for results day?' She cups my chin for a moment.

Mum butts in, putting her hands on my shoulders. 'She's been working hard for the past two years, there's no doubt.'

'Oh, what degree?'

'Crimi—' I start to say, but Mum abruptly pulls me towards her, slightly tightening her grip.

'She's doing Law,' Mum says. Aunty Kemi senses the weird vibe but doesn't push, though she gives me a searching look.

'I wish you nothing but the best, Lara,' she smiles, then bends down to whisper in my ear, 'whether in Law or Criminology.' She winks. 'I'm going to find Dáre and the twins.' As soon as she's out of earshot, I turn to Mum.

'Really, Mummy?' I ask, my voice laced with anger. 'It's bad enough that Daddy has been ignoring me for weeks because I told him I want to change my university degree. And then tonight, when he finally decided to talk to me, he snapped when I tried to tell him something important. But for you, now, to still be protecting your image and lying to relatives about what I want to do for a career is another low.'

'Lara, ah, ah?' Mum questions, confusion in her voice. 'Why are you speaking to me like this? Changing what plans?'

'Oh, Mummy, please. There's no way Daddy hasn't told you. Information spreads so fast in the house. So don't go along with the act for his sake. I don't want to do Law any more! I want to study Criminology and Forensics, and the quicker you guys accept it, the easier you'll make my life.' She starts to speak but I don't give her the chance. 'But don't worry, I'll keep lying to relatives for you. Whatever I have to do to continue to make you proud of me,' I say, my voice quivering as I finish. I pull up my skirt, not wanting to trip as I storm away.

Babs has seen our exchange and follows behind me as I go upstairs to the balcony. He doesn't push or pry, he just sits with me, comforting me as I cry.

CHAPTER THIRTY

With word of the traffic on Lekki-Ikoyi bridge persisting, older guests have started to leave to avoid being stuck here until the early hours of the morning, while the younger ones stay on the dancefloor. Apparently, the crash caused such a pile-up that the traffic has only just started to ease.

It's nine-thirty p.m. and time for Dérin to change into her last outfit, signalling the after-party to start. Kayode walks with me and Amaka, hand on Dérin's waist. 'Are you having fun, Rin?' Amaka says to Dérin, pinching her cheek as we reach the top of the stairs.

'So much fun,' she sighs. 'I've been so scared about today, but it's gone . . . mostly smoothly.' I try to hold in a nervous laugh as we walk into the dressing room.

'Hey, it's our plaque,' Kayode says. 'This is my first time seeing it up close.'

My heart jumps.

'Your plaque. What's it doing here?' Amaka says, trying

to sound casual, walking faster to intercept Kayode before he reaches for it. Her tone tells me she's as uncertain as I am about which plaque this is.

'Shall I read it?' Dérin smiles widely as she walks towards Amaka. They tussle slightly and Amaka tries to play it off as if she's teasing Dérin. 'Amaka . . . let it . . . let it go!' Dérin pulls it away from her with a final grunt. 'I want to see what it looks like up close.' Amaka and I visibly hold our breath. Dérin clears her throat before reading, 'From the family of Mr and Mrs Akinlola to the family of Mr and Mrs Oyinlola. Yada, yada, yada. We are seeking your permission to formalize the love and courtship between our beloved Son, Olukayode – aww, my baby – and your precious Daughter . . . *Oluwaseni*?' Dérin finishes in a bewildered tone.

Of course this is how it ends. Of course it would be the wrong plaque.

Dérin gives a weak laugh as she stares at the plaque, as if she's the one who's read it wrong. 'Oh, this is rich. What is this?' she demands of Kayode.

He stutters, 'I-I don't know. Seriously, I have no clue. Are you sure you read it right?' He rushes over, taking the plaque from her. His eyebrows knit as he reads. 'Dérin, what the hell is this?'

She laughs again in shock. 'Oh, as if I'm supposed to know. Your family were in charge of the plaque, they brought it in. I should be asking you. Kayode, what the fuck? Have you been planning this since your secret meeting with Seni? Is this what you were really doing instead of that bullshit wedding video excuse? Because I'm yet to see a video! As if the photo of your secret rendezvous wasn't enough. Are you trying to embarrass me *even more*? Because according to this, it's not me you want to marry, it's Seni! *Has it always been Seni?*' She's full-on shouting; anyone outside the dressing room can definitely hear her.

Kayode tries to pacify Dérin, putting his hands on her shoulders, but she shrugs them away. 'Dérin. Baby, please. Please believe me when I say I have no fucking clue what this is and where it came from,' Kayode says, putting his hands together, pleading. He looks shocked and just as distressed as Dérin.

'It . . . it's true,' I stutter. 'When Amaka was reading the plaque, she realized it had Seni's name on it. She nearly read out the wrong name, but corrected herself before she could make the mistake. After she finished reading the plaque, she ran upstairs and told me. We're the only ones who know about it.' I sigh. 'Honestly, Dérin, a lot has happened today. We've tried so hard to make sure you didn't see the wrong plaque.'

'What do you mean the wrong plaque?'

'There's . . . two plaques. One with your name and one with Seni's. Both are here – Lara and I have seen them. They keep on turning up in random places. We just don't know where,' Amaka says.

Dérin laughs dryly. 'I'm sick and fucking tired of this person who's been screwing with me throughout the entire wedding. They know my schedule, what I was going to wear for the rehearsal dinner. What *my plaque* looks like. They destroyed my veil. Who is fucking with us? I thought you would've caught them by now, Lara. Who is it? Seni?' she asks furiously.

I'm going to ignore the insult about me not having found the person yet. And I don't want to give her a final answer when I still need hard evidence to prove my theory. If I go with my gut and say it's Seni, I could be showing my cards too early.

'It wouldn't be Seni, she's not that craz—' Kayode starts.

'*Don't* defend her,' Dérin interrupts, more serious than I've ever seen her. 'Because if it's not Seni, it's someone from your family and honestly, I can't tell if that would be better or worse. Just go and change! We'll do the last entrance dance, cut the cake and then we'll sort things out later. All I know is that if it is her, that witch is out *tonight*,' Dérin fumes. We're all still, and the atmosphere is tense, until Dérin starts flapping her hands around and Kayode tears out of the room.

'I . . . I . . . Dérin,' starts Amaka, 'I love you so much. But . . . he has no one and I know Lara will console you.' Dérin nods, shooing her to follow Kayode, and she disappears down the hall. Dérin takes deep breaths, the pace quickening as she breaks down. I run to her side, pulling her in for a hug.

'I'm sorry,' I whisper, rocking her back and forth. 'It'll all be over soon and then we can get to the bottom of things. We *will* get to the bottom of things.' Dérin nods, wiping the tears from her face gently. At least this time I'm actually closer to the truth.

CHAPTER THIRTY-ONE

'Here you go.' I hand Dérin the rest of her energy drink as she reaches the bottom of the stairs, dressed in her final outfit of the night. Kayode looks morose as he waits for her. She takes several gulps then hands it back to me.

Dérin's face softens as she looks at Kayode 'I'm sorry . . . about earlier. As my husband, I should've given you the benefit of the doubt.' Kayode gives her a small smile and then they hug.

I head into the hall and give the DJ a signal. When he nods and cues up the music for Dérin and Kayode to dance in to, I walk back to our table where Babs and Seni are sitting. My plate from earlier is still there. Babs slides it over to me. 'You still need to finish this,' he says.

I practically inhale the rest of my food as I watch Kayode and Dérin's final entrance dance. It feels like the first time today that I can truly relax. After their minor domestic a few moments ago, Dérin and Kayode look so happy together.

They shimmy into the hall, holding hands and smiling at one another. Everyone has their phones out, recording the final dance of the night. Dérin breaks away, moving in front of Kayode so it looks like she's dancing on him. Kayode fans himself like he can't take the heat and everyone laughs. Dérin bends her knees so that she goes lower, making Kayode do the same, almost to the point where he's going to fall. It looks like he does and everyone cheers, until Dérin starts to rise and Kayode wipes the top of his head as if he's just survived the most intense dance of his life.

As they make their way into the centre of the hall, the wedding cake is already positioned for the last event of the night: the cake cutting. Everyone leaves their seat to get the perfect view.

'Where are you going now?' Babs asks me.

'To watch them cut the cake.' I give him a pleading look. He eventually gives in and we barge our way to the front of the crowd. The cake is nothing short of spectacular, though I didn't expect anything less. It's a four-tiered, intricately decorated pillow cake. The bottom tiers are white with gold and silver fondant, designed to look like lace all around it. The top two are white, beaded with pearls, and there's a personalized cake topper designed to look exactly like Kayode and Dérin perfectly positioned in the middle. Dérin squeals, jumping up and down, as she sees it for the first time. With all the constant catastrophes, Dérin has been too preoccupied to engage with the wedding cake after Rotimi dropped out. Instead, she put her trust in Alika and, miraculously, Alika finally did *one* part of her job and found another popular wedding cake designer.

Big Mummy takes the mic from the DJ booth and gives a final speech; I get my phone camera ready. 'Okay let's get this done so the young ones can enjoy their after-party without us.' Mum and Aunty Ireti stand behind me and Babs, Aunty Zai and Uncle Tayo are standing close to Dérin. Big Mummy continues: 'Everybody knows how to spell LOVE, abi?' The crowd shouts yes and she smiles. 'When we finish spelling, Kayode and Dérin, you'll cut the cake. Okay, *L*!'

Alika appears behind Aunty Zai and whispers in her ear. Aunty Zai sneers, '*Now?*' and Alika nods. Aunty Zai kisses her teeth. She whispers in Uncle Tayo's ear and he looks equally displeased.

'*O!*'

Aunty Zai and Uncle Tayo leave their positions. A few moments later, I hear Aunty Zai's voice from behind me.

'Ireti, Adélé. Alhaji is leaving, come and say goodbye. Fola and Niyi are already outside,' Aunty Zai whisper-yells over the sounds of the crowd's excitement.

'*Now?*' Aunty Ireti questions.

'I'm filming, ah, ah,' Mum snaps. 'Must we say bye to him? That man acts like his mother gave birth to all of us.'

'*Adélé*,' Aunty Zai says through gritted teeth.

'*V!*'

I hear Mum let out an exasperated groan, then I feel the space of two fewer bodies behind me. I hope their voices haven't drifted into my video because it'll be entirely unusable.

'E!' Big Mummy finishes, and there's a massive cheer as Dérin and Kayode cut the bottom tier of the cake together. The live band erupts into music.

Kayode puts a slice of cake on a plate and uses a fork to feed Dérin a chunk. She smiles at Kayode, then closes her eyes as she chews, like she's tasting heaven. Dérin grabs the fork from Kayode to feed him, then, at the last minute, changes her mind and swipes a finger along the cake and smears icing onto Kayode's face, then turns to everyone with a mischievous grin. We laugh and then cheer. Kayode chuckles then excuses himself to go and clean up, while the cake is wheeled away. Dérin stops it and cuts another slice for herself.

The crowd starts to disperse, either heading back to their seats or onto the dancefloor as the DJ announces the official start of the after-party. Dérin dances her way to Babs and me, cake still in hand. 'This is *really* good. It's so moist,' she says between bites. 'It might even be better than Rotimi's . . . This is exactly what I needed after barely eating today.' Dérin swallows the final morsel of cake and puts her empty plate on our table.

Things might be over for today. Amaka and I thankfully prevented the worst from happening. Whoever is persecuting Dérin didn't achieve their ultimate goal. Now that the traditional wedding has happened, maybe they'll finally stop like they did with Àdúrà.

Seni and Amaka appear from the crowd. Seni says, 'Lara's dad left you a plate of food by your thrones on the head table. He said you looked pale.'

Dérin's jaw stiffens at the sight of Seni, but she continues: 'Leave it. I was kinda prepared for not eating today. There was food sent to the house, so I'll eat when I'm home. You guys need to make sure you grab a slice of cake before it finishes.'

'You really need to eat, Dérin. All you've had today is a few small chops, an energy drink and cake,' Seni persists.

'I told you to leave it. And stop telling me what to do. It's not like you care, anyway.' Dérin screws up her face. Mine and Amaka's eyes both bulge at the same time. I look at Seni out of the corner of my eye. Her expression mirrors Dérin's but is even more confused.

The live band stops playing, and the DJ takes over. He cues up 'Living Things' by 9ice and Dérin finally lets loose, ushering all the guests onto the dancefloor. Babs, Amaka and I two-step in. Seni hesitates but eventually follows.

It actually feels like freedom to enjoy ourselves. We form a circle around Dérin, celebrating her as she dances in the middle. Her eyes shine as she looks at us like she's finally found the happiness she's wanted since she started planning this wedding. 'Is Kayode still cleaning his face?' Dérin shouts over the music. I look around and realize I can't see him.

'He must be. Don't worry, I'll go look for him,' I say, turning around to make my way out of the hall. I take three steps before I hear lots of people saying Dérin's name.

I turn on my heel and head into the circle. 'Dérin?' My mouth drops open. She's panting, clawing at first her chest and then her neck like she's looking for an opening. She stretches her neck, trying to take a huge breath. Her forehead is wet with sweat. This is not the person I left twenty seconds ago. Her eyes grow wider and wider with terror. 'Dérin?' My voice and Babs' combine, both of us horrified. Babs puts two fingers on her neck.

'Her pulse is racing.' Babs panics. 'She could collapse at any minute. Dérin, if you can, try to talk to me. Try to tell me what you're feeling?'

'I—' she starts, but it comes out slurred. 'Chest,' she manages, but her eyes start to roll back into her head. Everyone in the crowd starts screaming. Dérin falls to her knees. The beads on her dress collide with the floor, scattering in all directions. The air feels heavy, and my throat is tight.

'Dérin?' I say, but I sound strangled. 'Please,' I beg. I wonder if anyone can even hear me. My voice is so small. 'We need help! Help! Please!' I yell into the crowd. Amaka and Seni join in, tears in their eyes. Dérin takes a shuddering breath and her body crumples to the floor. I feel helpless as I watch Babs feel her pulse once more. I will never forget his look of fear as he glances up at me.

Babs rips open Dérin's corset, scattering more beads across the floor, and starts pumping at her chest. 'Lara! Lara!' I hear him cry, but everything sounds muffled, and I'm starting to get double vision. 'My record for CPR is four minutes, after that I'm useless. You need to find someone who can take over from me, can you do that?' I nod rapidly. Half processing what he's saying.

Four minutes. Four minutes. I've got four minutes.

I finally manage to yell at the top of my voice, 'We need help!'

CHAPTER THIRTY-TWO

The world slows, and then speeds up again as my adrenaline kicks in.

I race through the crowd, asking different people if they know how to do CPR. No one really responds, and I have zero time to waste on them. I move on quickly, wading through people, asking everyone I see until I eventually reach the end of the hall. No one has said they can help. A sinking feeling floods me and I have to force my legs to keep moving.

I run down the corridor and up to the main entrance, but stop abruptly when I see Aunty Zai, Uncle Tayo, Uncle Yinka and Aunty Yemi walking up the steps back into the venue. Aunty Zai takes one look at my face and starts panicking. 'What is it, what's going on?'

'Dérin,' I reply simply, and her face pales. She and Uncle Tayo run into the hall, Uncle Yinka and Aunty Yemi following behind them. People are milling about outside, including the rest of our family, but I ignore them as I yell,

'Is anybody a medic? Can anyone do CPR?' The family charge past me and run into the hall as they hear my words. A man with a greying afro throws his hand up and shouts 'I am,' before running to his car and grabbing a medical bag like they do in the movies.

I send up a silent prayer as he rushes back into the hall with me. When we reach Dérin, we find Aunty Zai hysterical as she watches Babs pump Dérin's chest. Joseph is sitting next to Dérin, holding her hand and rocking back and forth. In between rescue breaths, he strokes her head.

'How long has it been?' the doctor beside me asks as we get to the middle of the massive circle now formed around Dérin.

'A-approaching three minutes.' Seni's voice breaks as she answers.

'He can only do four. Babs can only do four,' I hear myself mumbling through tears. The world feels like it's slowing down then speeding up again. My vision goes blurry, and I can't tell if it's from tears or from shock. My ears pop and every attempt to unblock them fails; voices sound muffled and then become clearer over and over again. I feel like I'm outside my body.

I was so stupid for thinking that everything would work out. That the worst wouldn't happen. And now the attacker has succeeded. They've finally destroyed Dérin.

This is my fault. This is all my fault. I should've shut things down. This. Is. My. Faul—

Amaka's voice brings me out of my head. In between sobs she says, 'All the ambulances have gone to help at the accident on Lekki-Ikoyi bridge. They're trying to get to us as fast as they can, but they don't know how long it will be.'

'Jésù,' the doctor whispers under his breath, then moves towards Babs.

I edge closer, trying to watch what's going on. Babs is sweating as he counts along with each chest pump. The doctor gets out a CPR mask from his bag and puts it over Dérin's face. He signals to Babs that he's ready to swap over and, after he counts down, they switch places. Babs pants. His hands are shaking. The doctor thumps Dérin's chest with the side of his fist, and there's a loud *crack*. Those still watching wince at the sound. Joseph holds Dérin's hand tighter and kisses it.

The doctor calls out for Babs to give him a handover and Babs shouts out a lot of medical jargon. The worry on the doctor's face deepens as he listens.

'She also has—' Aunty Zai starts to shout something out, but Uncle Tayo stops her. He whispers something in the doctor's ear. The doctor continues CPR for the longest minutes of my life. The room is still, everyone's eyes glued to Dérin until suddenly, an alarm starts blaring.

'W-what is that?' Seni screams over it, covering her ears.

'It sounds like the fire alarm,' Uncle Damola says and then the crowd around us starts to panic. More and more people grab their purses from tables, along with their gift bags, and shuffle towards the door. The lights suddenly cut out. Screams come from all around the room, then the lights switch back on a few seconds later. The backup generator has kicked in.

People stop shuffling and start running frantically. Uncle Damola and Dad try to prevent anyone from leaving, but it's no good; there are too many people in the hall, all desperate to get out. It almost turns into a stampede, but Uncle Damola reaches the main entrance in time to open both doors so that everyone can exit easily and safely.

It soon becomes apparent that the only people staying in the hall are the family and the wedding party.

'What do we do . . .? Do we stay or go . . .? How do we transport Dérin . . .? What if there *is* a fire?' Amaka shouts continuous questions over the alarm, but gets choked up on every sentence. In between covering her ears, she swipes at her falling tears. Everyone is too shocked to answer.

'Do you smell smoke? Because I don't. What if it's a false alarm?' Seni yells. 'And wouldn't the sprinklers go off if there actually was a fire?'

'Yo, where the fuck is Kayode? He should be here!' Joseph yells. And it suddenly dawns on us that none of us have any idea where Kayode is.

'Where *is* Kayode?' Aunty Ireti panics. 'Is he collapsed somewhere too?'

'He was supposed to be washing his face after Dérin smeared it with icing. But he never came back,' Amaka yells.

'Oh my God. What if he's trapped behind a fire door?' Uncle Fola shouts, removing his hands from his ears.

'There shouldn't be any fire doors that he couldn't get past,' Seni cuts in. 'Fire doors automatically close for safety, but they don't lock. He should be back by now! Somebody go and look for him. He needs to know what's happened to Dérin.'

The alarm finally stops, and we all look at each other. No one moves apart from Aunty Ireti, who sprints off to find Kayode. The rest of us watch Babs and the doctor swap places once more. I sneak a peek at the time on my phone: nearly eight minutes have passed since Dérin collapsed. Seven minutes is the median time needed for survival after CPR. I know this from school, I know this from my podcasts. Most people who are revived in seven minutes, survive. But the more time passes, the lower the chance of a good outcome. We are already exceeding the optimal time for Dérin to wake up and be okay. She *needs* to be okay.

'Joseph, let go. Let them do what they need to,' Aunty Tiwa pleads, as she tries to pull him up.

'No!' Joseph shouts. 'She needs to feel something, she needs to know who will miss her if she's not here.' He holds Dérin's hand tighter, if that's possible. Her body is still lifeless, her chest the only part of her moving after each rescue breath.

The clacking of heels draws our attention away from Dérin for a few moments. Alika appears in the hall doorway, panting. 'I'm so sorry about the alarm! One of the caterers overheated something in the kitchen. Where is— Oh my,' she says, dropping a glass on the floor as she realizes what's going on. No one else pays attention; but the sight of her fills me with so much rage. We all watch for four more minutes as Babs and the doctor switch places again.

'Where is the ambulance?' Aunty Zai shouts. It's been almost fifteen minutes since Amaka called them, but the accident Uncle Yinka caused has affected us more than we could've ever imagined. 'Please, somebody, google the nearest hospital, we need to get her there!'

'Zainab, they need to do continuous compressions or Dérin becomes more susceptible to brain damage,' Uncle Damola says calmly. 'They can't do them effectively in a car.' Aunty Zai lets out a long, loud wail. We can see the doctor growing tired, sweat starting to drip from his forehead. Babs asks if he wants to swap, but the look the doctor gives him chills me.

No . . . No. No. No. No!

As if she's reading my mind, Aunty Zainab screams, 'Don't stop! I will never forgive you if you stop!'

'Ma . . . It's been nearly twenty minutes,' he pants. 'The fact . . . that she's not responsive yet is worrying. There was no delay to the CPR and it's been continuous. Her ribs are broken . . . I'm happy to keep going, but the more I press into her chest, the more damage to her body, and the longer her recovery, if she regains consciousness . . . ' Everyone winces at his words.

'Keep going!' Aunty Zai orders, rushing towards him. Uncle Tayo has to hold her back. 'Why are you holding me? Tayo, let me go!' she cries, trying to escape from his grip. 'Let me go! If Dérin dies, I will never forgive him. I will never forgive *you*.'

Uncle Tayo sighs deeply. 'She's gone.' His words turn into a sob. 'You can stop. It's okay.' He waves his hand, directing his words to the doctor. Aunty Zainab stares at him with eyes wider than tennis balls, before she crashes down on him in a faint.

The doctor continues with the compressions as one last attempt, with less energy than before. He's about to stop when a small gasp comes out of Dérin.

Her eyes flicker slowly open.

CHAPTER THIRTY-THREE

The doors burst open and paramedics pour in. The doctor spits information at them, but I'm too stunned to pay attention. The world is moving so slowly as they do their assessments of Dérin.

'Lara, go find the man some juice. He must be tired,' Dad says, snapping me out of my trance and, suddenly, the world speeds up again. The doctor collapses to the ground next to Dérin and attempts to catch his breath. I walk to the nearest table and grab a bottle of 5Alive. My hand shakes as I pour the juice into a glass.

I walk over to the doctor, who has managed to drag himself onto one of the chairs. The paramedics have now laid out their gurney. One is prepping it while the other is taking care of Dérin.

'Here you go,' I say as I hear screams from Aunty Tiwa, urging the paramedics not to leave until Aunty Zai has woken up.

The doctor mouths *Thank you*, before taking a large gulp of 5Alive. 'I haven't done CPR in ten years,' he says once he's caught his breath. 'I'm retired.' I nod wearily. That makes sense; he was out of breath quicker than Babs was. I'm about to head back to Dérin when he says, 'Hold on, has anyone called the police?'

My heart flutters. From the corner of my eye, I can see the paramedics move Dérin onto the gurney. Aunty Tiwa screams for Aunty Zai to wake up. Mum, Dad and Uncle Tayo run after the paramedics as they start to wheel Dérin out.

'The police?' I say, my voice so dull and lifeless I don't recognize it. 'The only people we called were the ambulance. Why do you want the police?'

He takes one last sip of the juice. 'I was a cardiologist,' the doctor says, putting the glass down and getting up from his seat. He starts to walk and I just about manage to force my shaking legs to follow him. 'Twenty-two-year-olds don't have cardiac arrests. It's rare. Very rare. And in my experience, every time it's happened, they've had a pre-existing condition. Or . . .' I stare at him as he continues walking, aligning himself with the paramedics carrying Dérin. I scan his face. He's trying to send the family away, holding his hands out for them to stop. Why is he stopping them? Someone needs to go with Dérin. *They* need to go with Dérin.

'Look, I suspect foul play,' he says abruptly, walking towards the door. It takes me a moment to absorb his words. I try to follow him but my legs won't move.

Babs appears next to me. Dérin's body is no longer in sight as the paramedics wheel her out of the door. Now Uncle Damola is stopping anyone else from leaving. Why is he stopping us? Why can't we go with her?

My ears start ringing and I can just about hear the doctor shout, 'You need to shut this place down now. None of you can leave until the police have interviewed everyone.'

My legs turn numb and suddenly Babs is holding me up.

A hysterical scream fills the room. Aunty Zai is awake.

'Dérin! Dérin!' Aunty Zai shrieks, as she struggles to sit up, her voice turning hoarse. 'Why are you stopping me? Let me go with her! She needs me. She needs her mum! Dérin!' Aunty Zai tries to run out of the hall, but Uncle Damola pulls her back. She wrestles him and manages to break through, running to the entrance. Uncle Tayo follows her closely, then we all start running to see if she'll be allowed to go with Dérin. If she is, there's nothing stopping the rest of us.

The doctor watches Aunty Zai as she tries to touch Dérin. He holds her back when she's close, begging her to let the paramedics do their job.

'Zainab, I promise you. I will keep her safe,' the doctor says. Aunty Zai is still crying. She's ripped her gèlè off her head and flung it on to the ground. 'I will update you with everything. You people *can't* leave. You're the only ones who can help the police do their job. Stay here. Tell them everything you know, and then come and meet me at the hospital.'

327

'No! No! She needs one of us with her!' Auntie Zai screams, then grabs Babs. 'Babs, you are a doctor, you go! Make sure she is safe.' Babs is shocked, but does as he's told and moves towards the paramedics.

For the first time I see Uncle Tayo break down in tears. He embraces his wife as she resists every urge to touch Dérin. The scene is heartbreaking, and blurred by my tears. I can hear Uncle Damola's voice as he calls the police and then he tries to scoop us all back into the hall.

Then I hear Kayode yell, 'Dérin? Dérin! What's happening? Who is in the ambulance?'

I turn around to see Uncle Fola restraining Kayode. Uncle Fola whispers to him, trying to console his son. But Kayode isn't listening. He's watching the ambulance as it drives off with his bride, his wife. My cousin. Our favourite person, taken away without any knowledge of what her condition is.

Uncle Damola has managed to get us all into the hall. Everyone has a vacant look on their face.

'What just happened?' Kayode pants one more time, despair in his voice, and everyone's eyes turn to him.

Aunty Zai's distress turns to anger. 'And *where* have you been? While I watched my daughter lying unconscious. While I was fighting for the right to stay with her?' Aunty Zai's tone is venomous. She marches straight over to him and raises her hand as if to slap him, when another hand grabs her wrist.

'What were you just going to do?' Aunty Ireti snaps, holding Aunty Zai's hand mid-air.

Aunty Zai yanks her hand away and says to Aunty Ireti, 'My daughter lay there, having CPR done for nearly twenty minutes.' She turns to Kayode. 'So I have every right to ask, where were *you*?'

'He was locked in the bathroom upstairs,' Aunty Ireti says.

'For that long? You can't expect us to believe that,' Uncle Tayo interjects.

'I had to break down the door. It was jammed,' Aunty Ireti continues, irritation growing in her voice. Everyone looks at Kayode, who stares around at us with hurt in his eyes.

'Do you . . . Do you really think I would miss that moment on purpose? That I wouldn't want to be near Dérin when that happened?' He tears up and has to hold his hand to his mouth to prevent his cries from spilling out. 'Dérin's been wheeled off to hospital and, instead of being able to go with her, I'm stuck in a room with people who think I'd abandon her when she needs me the most.' He breaks down as Uncle Fola puts a hand on his back.

I finally find my voice, and it's full of rage. 'The doctor said the only reason Dérin would've had a cardiac arrest is if she had a heart problem . . . Or, if there was foul play.'

'With the amount of people in this room today, where do we even look for ill intent?' Dad says.

Amaka walks over to Alika and grabs her by her collar. Alika immediately looks frightened.

'Let go of her!' Aunty Ireti says.

'Ní sùúrù now!' Aunty Yemi exclaims, grasping her bump. '*What did you do?*' Amaka fumes. She shakes Alika,

329

releasing all of her anger into her, and repeats, *'What did you do?'*

'Amaka . . . Amaka, let go!' Mum tries to separate the two, but Amaka's grip is too strong. Alika's eyes are closed, and she whimpers as if she knows it's over. How fucking dare she sob, as if she has nothing to do with this. As if she's not part of the reason this has happened.

'She's not who she says she is!' I yell, and everyone turns to me. Alika's eyes fly open and we hold each other's stares as I say, 'For the past seven months Dérin has been receiving horrible comments and threats both on Instagram and in real life. From Alika. Alika has Dérin's schedule memorized and knows where she is at all times. On the days Alika's not working, she's been stalking Dérin. Leaving threatening notes for Dérin to find or delivering her malicious gifts, like the poisoned cupcakes. *She* was the one who organized for the photo of Seni and Kayode to be delivered to the house and to Naija Gossip Lounge. The reason Dérin was so hysterical that night is because it was her last straw after seven months of mental torture. Alika almost got what she wanted because all of the threats have included the same message: cancel the wedding. But at the last minute, Dérin changed her mind and decided to go through with it. That made you angrier, didn't it, Alika? All your efforts went to waste, so you promised surprises for today. Was that the surprise? Trying to kill her? All because of what? Envy? Jealousy? Spite? Resentment?'

'You're making all this up!' Alika shrills.

'You shut up!' Amaka snarls, raising her fist.

'Am I?' I spit back at Alika. 'Like I'm making up the fact that I watched you almost try on Dérin's bachelorette dress in her room? I knew something was off with you from that moment. How you were hired for this wedding is beyond me because you have no experience to your name. You were just a lousy assistant at your last wedding.'

'That can't be true. Ireti and I saw the last wedding she planned,' Aunty Zai cuts in.

'You saw *fakes*, Aunty Zai. The only thing Alika is good at is hiding under a fake name, bogus Instagram accounts and bullying brides all day long. She did it to one of Dérin's friends, but she couldn't cause as much damage on the wedding day because the security was airtight and as an assistant she had no real power. And even though Uncle Damola tripled the security tonight, it didn't matter because Alika was always going to get in because she's the *freaking* wedding planner! Does the name Àdúrà ring a bell, Alika?' I yell my last question and she tries to hide her shock, but fails.

'You have no proof of any of this!' Alika protests.

I stare at her, and my voice is calm when I say, 'I don't, Josie?' The blood drains from Alika's face.

'Who is Josie?' Mum demands.

'It's Alika's real name. Ijose Omoregbe.' I hear gasps around the room. 'You know, I looked into you . . . Before I even knew you were called Ijose, or Josie, as you liked to go by. Alika didn't exist before last year. You reinvented

331

yourself overnight, after Àdúrà discovered you were trying to sabotage her wedding. A new name, new social media profiles. Heck, even a new nose.'

'Hey—'

'The thing is, I bet you lived a pretty normal life before it all. Before you became consumed by hatred. But I know you didn't create all of tonight's, or the last seven months' chaos, by yourself. And the look on your face and the way you dropped your glass when you saw Dérin lying there on the floor, having CPR, tells me that you were actually shocked at the sight. Which also makes me think . . . you didn't know the *person* you're working with would take things this far. So, who are you working with? Let's start with the plaque, yeah? Maybe we'll get some answers there.'

'What happened to the plaque?' Aunty Tiwa asks, looking around.

'Dérin's name wasn't on the plaque I read out today. It was Seni's,' Amaka replies.

'Why would the plaque have Seni's name on it?' Aunty Zai practically shouts, her words directed at Kayode's parents. 'That was your family's contribution to the wedding. Your declaration to marry Dérin. How could you even mix up the two names?' She's seething now, rightfully.

Uncle Fola butts in now. 'Ẹ dúró, the plaque came into the building with Dérin's name on it. We only ordered one plaque so how can that make sense? It left Ireti's hands and went to yours. Something is going on at your end.'

'But how is Seni relevant to the wedding anyway?' Uncle

Yinka asks, and hearing his voice makes my blood boil because all of this started with him. The ambulance would've got here faster if they hadn't had to help people on the bridge because of the car accident.

'Seni and Kayode used to date,' Amaka says, clenching her jaw. 'She was his girlfriend before Dérin.'

'She's *that* Seni?' I hear Uncle Fola whisper to his wife. Aunty Ireti shows no emotion at this revelation. 'Me, I've never met her. How would I know?'

'I only met her once. Before Dérin and Kayode were together,' Aunty Ireti manages, putting her hands up. The bangles on her arms shake. 'Even so, I wasn't in charge of the plaque. I delegated it to Alika.'

'Let's speed things up.' I look over to Seni. 'Last night you called Kayode at eleven p.m. Why?'

She's been staring at the floor, but now her eyes dart up to mine. 'I . . . I didn't.'

Joseph lets out an exasperated sigh.

I roll my eyes as hard as I can. 'I was on your phone earlier after the car incident. The last call you made was to Kayode,' I say, my eyes landing on Kayode. His lips part like he's trying to speak, but can't. He turns to look at her then turns back to me, unsure what to say.

'Seni, you admitted to Dérin that the anger you've felt throughout this wedding is for Kayode. If that's the case, why has Dérin suffered so much torment for the past seven months? Why is Dérin the one in the ambulance? *Why* can't you admit that your feelings for Kayode are bigger than your so-called love for Dérin?'

'I don't have feelings for Kayode,' Seni says quietly.

'Your actions say otherwise, Seni,' Amaka says. 'Your bitchy comments, your constant moodiness. I didn't want to believe it myself, but the truth is you haven't been happy about this wedding from the start.'

'I'm not emotionless!' Seni bursts out. 'I have thoughts and feelings and get jealous just like the rest of you. Can I be an awful person at times? Yes! But I am not in the wrong here. Dérin is . . . for putting me in this situation; for continuing to be with Kayode even though she knew I still had feelings for him. For trying to help me get over him, only to stab me in the back by dating him, *when she still had Joseph*. This could've been my wedding and I am allowed to be hurt by that,' Seni says, breathing harder and harder through her nose. Her eyes land on Kayode as she continues. 'And Kayode is in the wrong too, for choosing her over me.'

Everyone looks dumbfounded, which pisses Seni off even more.

'Can everyone stop pretending that I don't have a right to be mad about my friend marrying my ex-boyfriend?!' Seni snaps. 'Okay, yes, I shredded that stupid veil, but Dérin has been *awful* to me.'

Gasps echo around the room. Even I didn't see that coming.

Seni continues. 'The fact that she had *me* look after the stupid thing . . . It felt like she was mocking my feelings. Before I knew it, I had a pair of scissors in my hand and there were gaping holes all over it. And I'm not going to lie, I didn't feel bad at all. I put it back in the box like nothing happened, waiting for the moment Dérin would see it and feel just an ounce of the hurt I'd been feeling. I was only remorseful when I saw how upset she was and then the realization of what I'd done hit me. It was foul and I'm sorry. I really am. But she looked at me like I was the devil. She *keeps* looking at me like I'm the devil. I'm not the villain in her story. I'm here, I'm sucking it up and being a bridesmaid like everyone has told me to. But, if she realized, just for one second, how much hurt she's caused me, maybe I wouldn't have done it. Everyone's so hell-bent on me getting over things without even recognizing what I've been through.' Seni angrily wipes tears from her face. Her hands are shaking as she talks, all the emotions spilling out of her. She takes a deep breath before she continues. 'As much as she and Kayode like to pretend the break-up meant nothing, it *meant something to me*. How it ended meant *everything* to me. She looks at Kayode: 'You're in the wrong too for what you let happen to us, *to me*.'

I clap, loud and slow. 'Great speech. Now, what was the phone call to Kayode about? How to get away with harming Dérin?'

Kayode points at me as his frustration grows. 'Lara, ever since the bachelorette party, you've been on me. I don't need to prove anything to you.' His hands ball into fists. 'You saw my reaction when Dérin was taken away in the ambulance I am not part of this shit.'

'Then admit what the phone call was about! And what was

your talk in Seni's room about, because I *know* it wasn't that bullshit excuse about making a wedding video for Dérin—' I shout, but I'm interrupted by Uncle Damola wrapping his arms around me to get me to stop.

'Lara! It's enough. We're not going to solve anything this way,' Mum shouts.

'Why did you and Kayode break up? 'Til now I don't even know the answer,' Amaka asks Seni, her tone serious. Seni doesn't say anything. She just looks at us, then at Kayode standing by Aunty Ireti.

'We weren't compatible,' she grits out, then purses her lips. 'And let's not act like there isn't another scorned lover right here in this room with us. I'm not part of this!' Seni yells and all eyes land on Joseph.

'Oh, I haven't forgotten about Joseph,' I say, walking closer to him as he quickly finishes whatever he's doing on his phone. 'I've gone back and forth, considering Joseph as Alika's partner in crime. And even though I've had to admit you aren't smart enough to do any of this, it doesn't mean you're innocent. You've preyed on Dérin's superstitions, always popping up to feed on her fears and trick your way back into her heart. What were your words again? That she'll be "happier" with you. That Kayode doesn't know "the gem" he has in front of him. You sound like a broken record, it's so embarrassing. Thank God Dérin saw sense when you two almost kissed.'

Out of nowhere, Kayode lunges for Joseph. A punch lands, as Kayode's other hand grips Joseph's shirt. Kayode raises his fist again, ready to connect to Joseph's face once more, but Uncle Tayo and Uncle Fola drag him away.

Aunty Ireti scoffs from the corner. 'This is a joke.'

'Nítorí Ọlọ́run, stop fighting. It isn't going to help us get anywhere,' Aunty Tiwa says, packing ice from a champagne bucket into a napkin so Joseph can nurse his cut lip.

Joseph lowers the bloody napkin from his mouth. 'I don't need to listen to this bullshit. And I don't care what any of you say. This prick doesn't deserve her. Of course, I'm pissed! How can she throw away nearly a decade of love just like that?'

'Because she's in love with *him*!' Amaka yells, exasperated.

Joseph looks at her like he's smelled something bad. 'I messed up with Dérin by being unserious and I will regret that for the rest of my life, because it allowed this dickhead to worm his way into her heart.' Kayode moves as if he wants to punch Joseph again, but Joseph continues, 'Hit me all you want, but listen to me when I say this: she only got with you out of spite. You are only with her because of a technicality.' He scowls at Kayode, spits blood onto the floor, then presses the iced napkin back to his mouth.

'*Kids* are not a technicality, they are a dealbreaker,' Amaka sneers at him.

I hear my phone vibrate in my clutch and scramble to take it out, hopeful that it's Babs with news from the hospital. Instead, I'm greeted with information that doesn't even surprise me. I start to chuckle and everyone goes silent, looking at me like I've finally lost it. 'So, Joseph, you said it would take you an hour to uncover who hacked the sound system. If that's the case, why did you only tell the DJ now?' I look down at the screen and display the text for everyone to see.

> **Wedding DJ**
> The hack came from Josie's MacBook.
>   22:20

'More of Alika's evil antics to wreck Dérin's wedding. How convenient for you, Joseph, to keep this information to yourself for hours. I bet you were hoping this Josie would hack the system again and cause more chaos. God, you're such a snake, it's sickening.'

Guilt floods Joseph's face. 'I . . . I didn't. It's not because . . . There are so many people at this wedding, it would've taken us ages to find who Josie was.'

'Mmm,' I say, shooting an *I told you so* look at Dad. He cowers and turns away.

'I've had enough. *Where* are the police? Why haven't they arrived yet?' Aunty Zai shrills. 'We can't wait here for ever; *I need to see Dérin.* I'm sure we can leave if they delay any longer?'

'We can't go, Zainab,' Uncle Damola says. 'They have to take all of our statements in one place otherwise we'll compromise the investigation. I called the police as soon as the paramedics left with Dérin.'

'Are you not able to take everyone's statement? You're a

detective; surely that holds weight?' Mum asks.

'I don't want to do anything that could harm the investigation. They're already so fickle and lazy with their inquiries, even when they have everything handed to them on a silver platter. I know it's hard with everything we've just heard, and you're desperate to see Dérin, but we need to wait a little longer. They must be on their way; the traffic's cleared.'

'Maybe we should talk about what caused the traffic in the first place,' I say, looking at Uncle Yinka.

CHAPTER THIRTY-FOUR

Bodies turn towards Uncle Yinka in anticipation.

'Aunty Yemisi,' I say. She looks at me with worry etched on her face. 'The driver who was in the car crash on Lekki-Ikoyi bridge was the same driver who stole the car from us this morning. It was Moses. The same Moses from the argument you and Uncle Yinka had when Uncle said he had a plan for how he would sort out his money issues.' Aunty Yemi's eyes widen as she takes in my words. 'That's why Uncle Yinka was on his phone so much this morning; he was figuring out Moses' whereabouts because Uncle Yinka paid Moses to steal the car for him so he could sell it. That's why Moses let us go so easily, because it was the car that he needed, not us. That's also why, when we arrived this morning, after the car was stolen, Uncle Yinka wasn't as concerned as the rest of you.' My eyes dart from Aunty Yemi to Uncle Yinka.

'Yinka!' Mum, Dad, Aunty Tiwa and Uncle Damola all

scream. Uncle Tayo and Aunty Zainab glare at Uncle Yinka.

'Why are you all calling my name?' He frowns and continues angrily, 'All you have is Lara's word to go on.'

Everyone turns back to me and he's right, I don't have any evidence. Just the fact that Moses basically confirmed things to me in the car and Uncle Yinka exposed his treachery to me earlier today, but no one else saw.

I try to look unfazed. 'Check his call log. And his texts. Under the name Moses or Solomon.'

Dad walks towards him with speed. He searches Uncle Yinka's agbada, rifling through everything for his phone. Uncle Yinka puts up a fight, attempting to get the phone out of his reach, but Dad is stronger than him. Dad commands him to unlock his phone and he does so reluctantly. It takes Dad a while to look through everything; so long that I start to worry that Uncle Yinka managed to delete every trace of his involvement. 'Hmph.' Dad looks unamused. 'Emails, deleted. Texts, deleted. Even call log, deleted. But you forgot to delete WhatsApp messages. Yinka, you are a fantastic fool,' Dad says, ending his sentence by slapping Uncle Yinka's head. All the adults in the room kiss their teeth and Dad holds up the phone for everyone to see the screen, then reads the messages out loud.

Moses
Why are you not answering my messages?
Dérin has called her mama in tears. I hope you
didn't touch them. Na, only the car we need.
15:17

Hello, why are you not answering? Where are you?
I hope you're not trying to cheat me. I will give your
name direct to the family if you try me. We are in
this together. The car go take care of us for life.

17:49

'Yinka! Yinka!' Aunty Yemi screeches. 'You can't even look at me as I'm calling you. Is it not enough that they've fed you, clothed you, helped you throughout the years? Every day I question if money is the only thing you care about, and you've shown it, again and again. You put your *nieces* in danger? How can I trust you with our children?' She cries, cradling her bump.

Uncle Tayo, who has been silent throughout all of this, finally laughs. A deep laugh without a drop of humour in it.

'My ẹlẹ̀ẹ̀dá will never let this happen,' he starts saying, which doesn't make any sense, then he repeats, '*My ẹlẹ̀ẹ̀dá* will never let this happen, but you better get on your knees now and pray that stupid driver dies in the accident and all of the evidence of the robbery dies with him; ogbeni . . .' Uncle claps his hands back and forth. 'Let me tell you now, and listen sharply with those big ears of yours. If something happens to Dérin because she reached the hospital too late, *if any complication arises because of this . . . because of traffic you caused,* God will not get the chance to deal with you. It will be me. Yinka, you will die.' He then turns to everyone, waving his index fingers around. 'You have heard it here first; I will kill him.'

Aunty Zainab now speaks, 'All of this for what, Yinka . . . for money? You risked my daughter's life for *money*? I'm sure it's you that sabotaged the wedding. To . . . to what? To prove to Tayo that he spent too much? To get back at us for not sending you more money?' She takes a few steps towards him. 'Alika, is he the one who paid you to do this?' I breathe a sigh of relief. She believes me. Aunty Zai's head snaps towards Alika then the door as voices clamour into the room.

The police have arrived.

CHAPTER THIRTY-FIVE

The police officers take everyone's statements separately and I repeat everything that happened throughout the night and in the lead-up to the wedding as thoroughly as I can. The officer I'm talking to seems so distracted, I could speak gibberish and he wouldn't notice. I have to prompt him to ask for details, even with all the evidence I'm giving him. Not to mention that he looks completely uninterested in taking Alika into custody for further questioning.

In between questions, I watch as the police move around, taking photos of the hall and marking sections off. It's killing me that we don't know what's happening to Dérin. When I've finished, the officer thanks me for my statement before waving me off to the side. As I sit next to Amaka, she whispers, 'Is it just me or does it seem like they don't care about our answers?' I nod in response.

It takes another ten minutes for everyone's interviews to wrap up, then the police tell us they'll be in contact again as the investigation continues. We grab our things and rush outside, desperate to finally get to Dérin. We women have all removed our gèlès and replaced our heels with the flats we brought this morning.

'We need to go to the hospital. *Now*. Can we please get a police escort?' Mum asks, holding Aunty Yemi's hand as she walks down the steps. The officer looks at her and nods, so we all start piling into cars.

'Hold on, hold on!' Aunty Zai shouts back at the officers. 'That one can't be allowed to roam freely. Take. Her. Into. Custody,' she insists, pointing to Alika standing at the top of the stairs. The head police officer nods reluctantly, and orders his two juniors to handcuff Alika. She screeches and squirms as they do. Relief washes over me as I watch one part of justice being served.

I somehow get pushed into a car with Joseph, who rests his head on the window and breathes heavily. After I click my seatbelt, all the adrenaline rushes out of my body. I feel limp, like a thousand bricks have hit me. I don't realize that I've closed my eyes until I wake up outside the hospital thirty minutes later.

One of the nurses on reception stops us as we all crowd inside. 'Hey, hey, hey!' she protests, spreading out her arms to prevent us from all rushing past her. 'Ònírànú ni okùnrin yìí,' she tells her co-worker at the desk, gesturing to the security guard who did nothing to stop us from all entering at once. 'If you are family members of the car-crash victims, please form a line and we will let you know the status of

345

your loved one. *Only* family members are permitted to see them,' she says, her voice stern, as if she's been dealing with relatives all day and no longer has the patience.

'We're here for Dérinsọlá Oyinlola. She came through less than two hours ago,' Aunty Zainab says.

'Ma, is that supposed to mean something to me?' The nurse twists her lips, her tolerance waning further. 'Let me check the system, we've had a lot of people come through here to—'

'The. Bride,' Aunty Zai sneers through her teeth. This makes the nurse look straight up at us, eyes widening slightly. My stomach drops.

'I'm so sorry, ma. She's right this way. Please, only immediate family inside.' She cranes her neck to look at all of us.

Aunty Zainab turns to us. We all nod and then step back accordingly, while Kayode and Uncle Tayo step forward.

The three of them start walking, then Aunty Zai stops and turns around to me. 'Lara, Niyi, do you want to come with us?' She looks pleadingly at the nurse. 'They're very important to Dérin.' The nurse reluctantly concedes.

The woman leads us to a private room in the ICU where Dérin has been admitted and tells us that the doctor will be around soon. When we enter, we see Babs seated on one side of Dérin's bed, praying, while the grey-haired doctor from the wedding is on the other side studying the hospital notes. He gets up at the sound of our voices, and consoles Aunty Zai and Uncle Tayo. They both thank him profusely. He gives them his number to keep him updated, then takes his leave.

Dérin is lying down, eyes closed, looking peaceful. She has an oxygen mask over her face and her chest is just about rising and falling.

We wait in silence. Uncle Tayo and Aunty Zai are pacing up and down the room, while Kayode sits by Dérin's side. He strokes the exposed parts of her face.

'Lara,' Dad whispers and motions for me to come over. I approach him, anxious that he's going to tell me off for my outbursts in the hall. He opens his mouth, but is immediately interrupted by a doctor in a white coat asking us if we're the Oyinlola family. She introduces herself as Dr Tekenah, ties her wig up with a claw clip from her coat and apologizes for not getting to us sooner.

'Dérin has substantial swelling on her brain and has been placed in a medically induced coma to minimize brain injury. We're taking precautions for the best outcome. She underwent CPR for a long time so we won't know what her true state is until she wakes up. We're going to monitor her brain activity and go from there. But we need to discuss why she has so much potassium in her blood.' Concern is growing in Dr Tekenah's voice. 'Some foods contain potassium. In small quantities it's harmless; but the amount in Dérin's blood was extremely high. Potassium triggers heart attacks. Her cousin said she'd barely eaten all day. With that amount of potassium in her blood, she is *very* lucky that CPR was started instantly.' Dr Tekenah smiles softly at Babs and continues, 'If she was alone when she collapsed, she would've died.' She pauses as we process the information. Aunty Zai sobs. 'Do you have any idea how she could've ingested so much?' she asks.

Everyone looks lost. My mind races through the events of the day until I finally see it.

'I think it was in her wedding cake,' I say, finding my voice. 'She ate two slices and collapsed immediately after. It was pretty much the only thing she ate all day. She was fine one moment, then she was really sweaty, clutching her chest, her eyes rolled back.' My own eyes start watering. Dad rubs my shoulder.

'But I had our cake too and I'm fine,' Kayode says. 'I mean, I think I was hot, but I put it down to the amount of people in the hall.'

'You didn't eat it, Kayode. Dérin wiped the icing on your face and then you left to clean yourself up before you could actually have any, remember?' I answer and Kayode pauses to think and then nods, blood drained from his face.

Dr Tekenah chimes in. 'I saw in her records that Dérin was admitted into hospital for a sickle cell crisis earlier this year where she was prescribed potassium. Are we sure she didn't overdose herself accidentally?'

'Sickle cell? Crisis?' I exclaim and everyone glances at me then turns back to the doctor. 'Dérin doesn't have sickle cell.' Everyone apart from myself and Babs looks uncomfortable, like Dr Tekenah has just revealed a secret. But that's not true; it can't be. 'Dérin wouldn't keep something as serious as that from me. That's something you have from birth? Not randomly.'

Kayode ignores me, saying, 'Dérin had a sickle cell crisis for the first time six months ago, which was induced by wedding stress. She had to be admitted to hospital and the doctors discovered that her potassium levels were low. She was kept in for a week for monitoring, and they put her on these fizzy potassium tablets after she was discharged. The hospital only took her off them a month ago, at her last appointment. She hates how they taste and was warned of side effects so she's very careful with them. She wouldn't take them without direction, let alone take more than she should,' Kayode says and my head whips around to him.

A week in hospital? Potassium tablets? *Sickle cell?* Dérin does *not* have sickle cell. Why am I the only one protesting this?

The doctor continues, 'I'm going to assume that only a select number of family members knew about Dérin's diagnosis, especially because it wasn't on the admission forms her cousin, Babs, filled out on her behalf. Dr Akanni, who accompanied Babs, advised me to treat this as a police matter upon arrival, and I think this is wise. We'll arrange for security to stay by Dérin's door. If there is anyone outside those of you who were originally privy to Dérin's diagnosis and know what medication she was taking, I would inform the police.' She turns to Aunty Zai and Uncle Tayo. 'Can I ask that you complete her forms? Some information is missing from when she first arrived.'

Aunty Zai leaves the room.

Uncle Tayo mutters to himself, running a hand over his

face. 'Potassium tablets . . . Why would anybody—?'

'Why am I the only one who's shocked? Did you know about this?' I ask Dad.

He stares back at me, hand holding his chin, then nods. 'I've known since she was a baby.'

'But Dérin doesn't . . . I mean, is it wrong to say . . . Dérin doesn't look like she has sickle cell? How can we have grown up together and I never had a clue?' I'm perplexed by everything that's happening.

'That's on purpose.' Uncle Tayo breathes heavily. 'Dérin is one of the lucky few who hasn't had any problems with her sickle cell, so there's never been any reason to share it publicly. The only people we've told are your dad and Kayode's family. We don't know who else Dérin told . . .'

Clearly not me. Dérin and I are practically sisters. I thought we shared everything. So to know that she's had this illness her whole life and not told me . . . I feel betrayed. I know that's selfish, especially when Dérin is here, in front of me, lying in a hospital bed in a coma. But that's how I feel. How could she not trust me?

'But we're family. Why would she keep such a big secret like that from me?'

'Lara, she doesn't owe you her medical history,' Dad says. 'If you knew about her sickle cell, you would've treated her differently, whether you think so or not. You babied Dérin when you thought she'd hurt her back. Imagine if you found out she had a chronic illness? You would've never had as much fun as you did growing up together. You would constantly be thinking about her and would assume she's too fragile to really live,' Dad says, and I stare around the room thinking about how I wish what he's saying wasn't true, but I know it is.

'It's nothing personal, Lara. It's like what your dad said. Dérin didn't want anyone thinking of her differently,' Kayode says, squeezing Dérin's hand.

Her back . . .

'She didn't really have a slipped disc, did she? When she said, *it's never been this bad* she was having a—'

'Another crisis.' Uncle Tayo finishes my sentence. 'But she didn't want to be admitted to hospital because of the wedding. She's been on painkillers to try to cope. It's been hell watching her fight with her body just to get through things. I'm ready for this whole wedding season to be over so she can go back to normal.'

The medications she took every day which she said were 'vitamins'. The codeine in her drawer. How did I not catch on that Dérin was ill?

Aunty Zai comes back into the room and closes the door. She sinks on to the edge of Dérin's bed; she covers her mouth to hold in her cries, but it's useless. 'How can someone do this to her?'

CHAPTER THIRTY-SIX

It's been four days since Dérin was taken to hospital. Four days of Dérin in an induced coma. Four days of everyone taking turns to sit by her bedside. The swelling on her brain hasn't gone down but she's more stable so we were able to move her to a better hospital closer to home, making it easier to visit her.

In these four days, the police haven't contacted us with any news. The last thing they told us was that they were asking guests if they'd seen anything suspicious on the day of the traditional wedding. We don't know if they've found anything substantial. Alika didn't answer any questions the entire time she was in police custody. Even when faced with the law, she still refused to come clean. I gave Uncle Damola the original notes and printed photos of the Instagram messages so that he could give them to the police. I was hopeful that his position as a detective would mean that they would listen to him, take him seriously, but he was essentially told to mind his business.

For the last four days I've been desperate to talk to someone about all of my discoveries. It's as if no one in the family wants to address them. But now that everything's out in the open, there's no reason not to. There's a knock on my bedroom door and I open it to Uncle Damola.

'What did you need help wi— Oh.' He stops when he sees my investigation board, which has become even more chaotic in the last four days, with barely legible scribbles and arrows criss-crossing everywhere.

'It's a lot, I know. I've been collecting information since before Dérin was poisoned. If I'd known it would come to this, I would've exposed people before the wedding. But if the police aren't going to solve Dérin's case, then I'll do it myself.'

'Talk me through it,' he says, taking a seat on my bed.

'The question that will – *should* – help us solve everything is, who knew that Dérin was taking potassium tablets? I mean, that's not a common murder weapon, not even a common choice of poison, right?'

'You'd be surprised the things people use as murder weapons,' Uncle Damola answers. 'But you're right, it's not common. Even if they didn't know she was taking them, it is an odd choice.'

'That means that if they knew Dérin was taking potassium tablets, they would also know about her sickle cell?'

'Not necessarily, but go through the thought process.' Uncle Damola cups his chin in his hand.

'I've been repeatedly replaying that night in my mind

353

and giving myself headaches about what Seni and Joseph said. They've been *so* vague about why they broke up with their respective exes. But what if that's because they couldn't disclose the real reasons, because they relate to Dérin's sickle cell, which she's been keeping secret?' Uncle Damola doesn't say anything, but his face shows he thinks it's possible. 'Seni did this massive speech about how Kayode shouldn't have put her in that situation, all to explain how they *weren't compatible*. The same with Joseph. He drones on and on about how *he's* the one who's right for Dérin, but then says that they only broke up because of a *technicality*.

'I've been reading up about sickle cell since the hospital visit. People with the full disease have SC or SS genotypes. People who have the trait have AC or AS genotypes, which means they carry the disease but don't actually have it. People unaffected by the disease have AA genotypes. It's a lot to take in, but basically, if two people with the full disease, or one with the full disease and one with the trait, or two people with the trait, or one with the full disease and one unaffected, have children, there is a massive chance that their children will either inherit the disease or carry it. The only way that chances are slim to none of a child having or carrying the disease is either if both parents are unaffected or if one is unaffected and the other has the trait. There are so many articles saying prevention is better than cure; that the most important thing to do before having kids is to test your genotypes to make sure they match and avoid increasing the numbers of children born with the disease.

Aunty Zai said it to me, the pastor at the blood drive did a sermon on it. It's always been there, it's just been encoded.

'If Seni and Kayode had genotypes that didn't match, they wouldn't be compatible. That would mean they'd have to put a stop to their relationship. An abrupt stop. Seni also said her sister has sickle cell. She didn't even hide that information. But she made a donation at the blood drive. Research says that people with the full disease can't donate blood because their blood isn't viable for transfusions. That means that if sickle cell runs in her family, and Seni could still donate blood, she must at least have the trait, AC or AS, and that's why she wasn't compatible with Kayode.'

'Lara.' Uncle Damola gulps, as if I'm on the right path. 'But . . . Kayode . . . If he and Seni were incompatible, that could mean he also has the disease or is a carrier. It could be both of them.'

'Maybe not. Maybe he's AA. It would explain why Joseph said that he and Dérin were only together because of a *technicality*.' I clap my hands as I recall a surge of information. 'What if the reason Dérin and Joseph broke up was also because of their incompatibility? Dérin has sickle cell, so she's SC or SS. What if Joseph has the trait? What if he's AC or AS? That's why Dérin didn't want to have kids with him – they would have sickle cell. If Kayode is AA, their kids would only have the trait.'

'We all know the horrible stigma surrounding sickle cell,' says Uncle Damola. 'People are so small-minded; they don't want to be associated with it. But these "technicalities",' he does air quotes, 'would they be enough of a motive for someone to stop the wedding, and in a harmful way? If we're on the right path now, the question is, why would they want to harm Dérin?'

I look back at my board, scanning the lists of suspects. 'There's one way we can confirm this theory. Aunty Zai and Uncle Tayo made us all test for our genotypes at the blood drive. The results should come to the house,' I look at the date on my phone then back at Uncle Damola, 'tomorrow.'

CHAPTER THIRTY-SEVEN

Another four days have passed. The results from the genotype tests have not arrived and the doctors have decided to bring Dérin out of her coma today.

Dérin's sickle cell meant she was more at risk of a stroke, so the doctors kept her in the coma for longer to ensure her brain swelling is reduced. Even though we still have a week left of our holiday, we need to stay longer to be here when Dérin wakes, whenever that is, so we've had to cancel our flights back home. Mum and Dad have both had to use emergency annual leave to stay in Nigeria longer, and Babs has written to his university explaining the extenuating circumstances. Family members are still taking turns sitting at Dérin's bedside. Aunty Zai even came round to the idea of including Seni in the rotation, as long as she's supervised. But I've not been brave enough to face Dérin since I last saw her in the hospital.

The only police update we've had is that the wedding cake

was laced with potassium. Which thankfully means they will be treating this as an attempted murder case.

Attempted murder. The words feel heavy on my tongue.

'There's something I'm missing,' I mumble as I lean against the frame of the open front door and look out at the compound.

I hear footsteps and feel someone's shirt brush past me. I know without looking that it's Babs. He's been hovering around me for the past eight days, begging me to get back to a normal routine. But I just *can't* go back to normal, until Dérin is awake. Until she knows how sorry I am that it's come to this.

'I've ordered Cold Stone to the house. If you're not going to eat food, you can at least have ice cream,' Babs says as he puts a hand on my shoulder.

'It's nine a.m. Are you sure you didn't sneak a hot dog into the order too?' I turn to face him.

'That's none of your business.' He flicks my forehead. I smile and hug him, whispering a thank you into his chest. 'Since you're glued to the door, you can answer it when the food comes.' He smiles when I jokily push him away.

Five minutes later, Temi parks the car in the driveway. He exits and hands me the Cold Stone. 'I met the delivery driver at the gate.' He starts to walk away but then pauses as if he's remembered something. 'Oh. Some mail arrived this morning.' He hands me a pile of envelopes and I feel like I could cry. 'I hope you find what you're looking for,' he says before walking away.

I rip open the letters, and start reading through them.

'Uncle Damola!' I shout as I sprint all the way to the second floor. 'Uncle Damola!' I bang repeatedly on his door. 'Uncle!' He opens it in a panic.

'What? What is it?'

'She's AS. Seni's AS.'

The doorbell rings three hours later. Seni spent the morning at the hospital watching Dérin with Aunty Zai, but she's the only one at the door now. Uncle Damola and I open it for her. 'Thank— Oh?' Her eyebrows wrinkle as she sees our stern stares.

'I need you to come with me,' I say, and her expression turns from shocked to defeated.

'It's been a long day, Lara.' She sighs, pushing past me until Uncle Damola's voice makes her stop.

'You are the only one who can help us, Seni. We need you to talk to us.' She turns to look at Uncle, lips pursed. When our expressions don't change, she realizes we're being serious.

'Are you taking over the investigation? Because I'd like a lawyer,' she says, which makes her sound even more guilty than before. Uncle Damola holds his hands up to show that he's not involved. She sighs then tells us to lead the way. We walk her into my room. She stops in her tracks when she sees my investigation board.

'What the . . .? My name is all over this. Do you guys really think I'm capable of murder? Lara, are you for real?' Seni gives me an incredulous look.

'I know that you're AS,' I say, holding up the letter detailing her genotype. 'But I've had time to think about it, to piece everything together, and I realize you didn't poison Dérin.'

Seni lets out a miserable laugh. 'My results told you that?'

'You knew that Dérin has sickle cell. That's why you knew she couldn't donate at the blood drive. Not because of her piercing, but because people with the disease aren't allowed to; their blood is essentially sick and so can't be used. I'm going to assume that you've known since uni, which is when everything started, because why would Kayode break up with you when you've only got the trait and Dérin has the full disease?'

Seni avoids eye contact, but I can see her struggling to hide her sadness.

I continue, 'While you were jealous, and ultimately hurt – and even though you've shown how you feel in the most vindictive ways – *some* of your actions were to protect Dérin. But from what, I don't know . . . And that's where you come in.'

Seni aggressively wipes tears from her eyes and sniffs. It takes her a while to compose herself and answer me. 'Lara, you need to let this go. I'm telling you. Let the police do their job. I can't help you. I'm sorry.'

I stare at Seni, dumbfounded; I can't believe what she's saying. 'You've spent the best part of the day sitting by Dérin's bedside. And now you refuse to help her? What was that this morning, then? Just playing the role of distraught friend?'

Uncle Damola adds, 'Seni. We know you know more than you're letting on. We've done the hard work for you. Just tell us what we need to know.'

Seni looks at me, eyes wild and blinking rapidly.

'*Answer me!*' I scream.

'Lara, please. Listen to me. Leave this alone. It's bigger than either of us. Trust me.'

'What the *fuck* is that supposed to mean, Seni? We're here *pleading* with you because you are literally the only person who can help us, who can help Dérin. Why won't you?'

'Whatever. I don't have to listen to this. I've said everything I have to say. In fact, I've said too much.' She strides to the door.

I jump in front of her, blocking her exit. I'm right in her face now, jabbing my finger at her chest as the words fly out of my mouth like bullets. 'You're not leaving here until you tell me everything you know. If I have to physically force you to stay, I wi—'

The door flies opens. Amaka is out there, panting.

'Dérin's awake.'

CHAPTER THIRTY-EIGHT

Not even ten minutes later, everyone is rushing out of the house. The thought of Dérin awake fills me with relief, happiness and, most of all, fear. Amaka's words left no room for interpretation. She's awake but . . . what does that mean? I shove my shoes on and run outside. Mum calls Aunty Tiwa and Joseph to tell them to meet us at the hospital.

When we reach the hospital, we only stop when we get to Dérin's door. We can hear someone sobbing inside the room. My heart tenses in preparation as Amaka opens the door.

Aunty Zainab is lying across Dérin's legs and crying. Kayode is standing by Dérin's bedside with his back to us. Uncle Tayo is nowhere to be seen. We rush into the room, preparing ourselves for the worst.

Dérin lifts her head from the pillow. 'Oh, thank God you're here!' she croaks, voice hoarse. 'She's been blubbering for ages, despite my efforts to tell her that I'm *alive*. Make it stop.' She adjusts the oxygen tubes in her nose.

There's a collective sigh of relief. Mum, Aunty Tiwá, Joseph and Dad start openly weeping, while Uncle Damola and Babs watch from a distance, as if they're scared to touch her in case she isn't real.

Amaka says through ugly sobs, 'How dare you get poisoned? Are you okay, did they say you're going to be okay? Do you need a pillow? Have you eaten? When are you allowed to eat? What do you want to eat?'

Seni stands there like a statue and repeats, 'I'm so sorry. I am *so* sorry.'

Then there's me . . . watching everything as if it's a movie playing out in front of me. As everyone crowds around Dérin, I nudge Kayode and pull him out of the room. He follows me reluctantly.

'I'm sorry for being so hard on you. I realize now that was wrong, even though you can't entirely blame me because you were acting sketch—'

'Lara!' Kayode stops me and I concede, putting my hands up.

'I am really sorry. It was unfair of me to assume you did wrong when I've not had much reason to doubt that you love Dérin,' I deflate. It takes him a while to respond, then he nods and pulls me in for a hug. I separate from him and then say, 'I just wanted to ask you a question to narrow down some things . . . and forgive me for prying. Did your parents know that Dérin had sickle cell before she went into hospital the first time?'

Kayode looks at me as if choosing his words carefully. 'Yes . . . but no.' He crosses his arms.

'I'm not following. Is it a yes or is it a no?'

Kayode pauses long enough for me to wonder if he's going to answer me. 'Dad knew when I asked Dérin to marry me. I confided in him and we sat down and discussed what it would mean. He put us in touch with a genetics counsellor and swore he'd keep it a secret, *and he did*, but Mum found out when Dérin had her first episode six months ago because of the hospital ward she was on.'

'At the wedding Seni said you and her broke up because you weren't compatible. Was that because Seni's blood type is AS, therefore she's a sickle cell carrier?'

A flash of unrecognizable emotion flickers across his face and I think I'm getting closer to the confirmation I need. 'How did you know Seni is AS?' Kayode asks.

'Did anyone else apart from you and Dérin's parents know that she was taking potassium medication?'

He thinks and then says, 'Mum and Dad came to visit Dérin with me some nights when she was in hospital, but they wouldn't have known what she was taking.'

I start to speak but a voice interrupts me. 'Lara?' Dérin calls out. I turn towards her hospital door.

'Can I have a hug? Not too tight, though, my ribs,' Dérin says and I walk over and hold her close. She smells like the chlorinated fumes of a hospital. When I let go, she grabs my hand. 'Thank you.'

'For what?' I say quietly.

'Kayode told me what happened when the paramedics took me away. How you interrogated everyone.' Her eyes widen with concern. 'I haven't missed results day, have I?' I shake my head and she squeezes my hand harder.

'What was the last thing you remember?' I ask.

'I remember eating the cake and talking to you guys. Being on the dancefloor, wondering where Kayode was. Then suddenly, the room went dim. I thought maybe it was the lights for the after-party, but then I couldn't catch my breath, my chest was tight and my throat was closing. My vision started blurring. Then I had pain in my arms. This stabbing, shooting pain. Then . . . then I woke up here.'

An hour passes by as Dérin reassures us over and over again that she feels okay and Aunty Zai finally manages to stop crying. New voices emerge as Uncle Tayo ushers Uncle Fola and Aunty Ireti into the room.

Aunty Ireti stands close to Dérin and sweeps the hair out of her face. 'How are you, my dear?' I move away from Dérin's bed to give her and Aunty Ireti some privacy.

Music starts playing from Mum's phone at the back of the room. We all look at her. 'Sorry. I'm just replaying the videos I took that night for Facebook. We all looked so happy.'

I walk over and watch them with her. Most of the videos have Mum at the centre, extending her arms to show Facebook Live the crowd in the hall. She then shows us footage she took of Dérin and Kayode dancing to the live band.

As she swipes to the next video, the camera zooms out, and Babs says, 'Look, it's me and you in the background.'

My eyes don't leave Mum's phone screen. Mum's commentary is showing the decorations in the hall. She walks from corner to corner, dancing with friends on the way. She shows Dérin and Kayode in the background, smiling at each other. Mum then walks into the kitchen and shows the caterers plating up food. Her commentary continues as she showers them with compliments.

The angle moves to a different part of the kitchen as Mum tells the waiters and waitresses that they're doing a fine job keeping everyone's belly full. Suddenly I spot something in the corner of the screen. A hand is dropping two white circles into a bottle filled with clear liquid. It looks like the same bottle I saw at the wedding when the girl in the pink apron was pouring sugar syrup over the top of the cake. The white circles start fizzing slowly. The hand moves out of frame for a second and then reappears, grabs the bottle, putting the lid on and shaking it. The fizz becomes more vigorous, white circles no longer visible. Bracelets shake with the bottle, clinking faintly as Mum continues her commentary. I concentrate on the corner of the video and the unmistakeable glistening gold handpiece around the person's hand that's now pushing the pointed nozzle of the bottle lid into the bottom tier of the cake and squeezing the sugar syrup into it.

The soft sound of windchimes floats around the hospital room at the same time as the familiar clanging of bangles pierces the atmosphere. The culprit is reaching for their phone. My head snaps round so fast. A laugh almost pours out of me.

'Oh my God. *Oh my God*,' I blurt out before I can stop myself.

Aunty Ireti answers her phone, moving away from Dérin. 'Máa pè é padà.' Then she cuts the call and looks in my direction.

I stare at her, not knowing what to say until it all comes out.

'It was you.' My stare intensifies as Aunty Ireti frowns. 'You poisoned the cake. In fact, you don't even have to answer the question. I know it was you because Mum's video confirms it.' Now I do let out a shocked laugh. 'I *knew* Alika couldn't have done it alone, I *knew* there'd have to be someone stronger and more powerful in charge and I can't believe it was *you* . . . You stood there in silence when I exposed Alika because you wanted her to be blamed for it all. Alika's guilt helped paint you as innocent. She was just your pawn in the grand scheme. A puppet to do your bidding. And when that didn't work, you took matters into your own hands.'

'Lara . . . What are you doing, who are you talking to?' Mum pulls me back with a hand on my shoulder.

'You played the doting mother-in-law, helping Dérin find a new wedding cake designer, *knowing* that would be your murder weapon. The cake . . . it's incredible.' I turn to everyone. 'Aunty Ireti is the one who poisoned Dérin because she didn't want her to marry Kayode. For the same reason she didn't want Seni and Kayode together: Seni has the sickle cell trait and Dérin has sickle cell.'

A deadly silence consumes the room. No one moves. But my eyes are locked onto Aunty Ireti.

'I never understood why *everyone* was so *cryptic*. It was driving me mad. Until the letters revealing our genotypes arrived and I pieced things together. Seni has the sickle cell trait, and I'm guessing, Seni, that Aunty Ireti discovered this, and that was the reason you and Kayode broke up.' I look at Seni, hopeful for an answer.

Seni is silent for a long moment, then finally says, 'You're right. I have the sickle cell trait. Kayode's genotype is AA, which means he isn't affected by the disease, but I'm AS. It shouldn't be a problem if we were to ever have kids. In fact, it wouldn't be, but Aunty Ireti didn't care. The minute she found out that Kayode and I were together, she demanded I do a full body blood test. She came to visit me at university two days after I got the results and told me to break up with Kayode. That her family has never had sickle cell, not even the trait, and they weren't going to start with the possibility because of me. I explained that the odds of that happening were practically zero, that it would be extremely rare for someone with the trait and someone unaffected to pass on the disease in any way, but she didn't care. She even offered me money to break up with Kayode. I told Kayode everything and *he* broke up with me. Told me we were better off as friends. But I knew the real reason was because he listened to his mother's poison.'

I shudder. 'That's why you've been so angry. Because Dérin has *full-blown sickle cell* and you just have the trait, so why do *they* get to be together?'

Everything is finally making sense. I turn to Kayode.

'You confirmed some vital details for me when we spoke an hour ago. You knew what your mum did to you and Seni, but I'm assuming you didn't see that relationship going anywhere, so it didn't faze you . . . And then you met Dérin. That relationship was different. She was the one. When Dérin told you she had sickle cell, you weren't prepared for what happened before to happen again, you didn't want to take the risk, so you only told your father about her diagnosis. But your mother found out when Dérin had her first crisis and went to hospital.' I face the rest of the family again and continue: '*That's* why Kayode's family backed out of paying for the wedding. They're not broke. It's just that *Aunty Ireti* didn't want to waste their money because she believed she would eventually get them to end things.' I glare at Aunty Ireti again. 'Kayode loves Dérin, and you hated seeing it.'

Aunty Ireti says nothing.

'You spent the entire day making Dérin miserable, pushing the limits. Only your family's side of the hall was decorated. You wore gold, even though you were told to wear silver, playing it off as the loving joining of families. The chaotic music. The *plaque*. Genius! Your best work! You thought Amaka would say the wrong name in front of everyone, and when she didn't, you had to try other things. You or Alika put the fake plaque, the one with Seni's name on it, in the dressing room knowing that Dérin would eventually see it. You kept pushing Dérin to call off the wedding, even right there in the middle of it.'

Everyone is still, anticipating mine or Aunty Ireti's next words.

'The Instagram trolling, the stalking, the notes, weren't your doing, those were Alika's. But it must've felt good, knowing you bought your way into protecting your family's image. Your bloodline.'

Aunty Ireti still says nothing.

Uncle Fola grabs her by both arms, crying, 'Speak, Ireti! Speak. They're accusing you of *attempted murder. They're accusing you of eugenics!* Say something!' He shakes her.

At last, the slightest smirk creeps onto her lips. She yanks herself out of Uncle Fola's hands then smooths her flowy pink dress.

'You really do look so much alike,' she scoffs, half smiling. 'I thought you were Dérin, heading to the dressing room, fed up with the chaos. So I thought I'd offer you a final deal: leave Kayode amicably and nothing would happen. *I would even pay for the wedding.*' She sighs, exasperated. 'For someone who's so superstitious, you really don't know how to take an out.' She looks at Dérin. 'I even gave you one before the wedding. I tried to plant doubt in your mind about whether Kayode was trustworthy because of the photo of him and Seni. And still . . . Did you want me to spell it out for you, or what?'

Her sneer makes me want to rip her eyes out.

'You were *asking* for chaos, and chaos I promised. Right before a big bang.' She looks at me with a now deranged smile and I know, in this moment, I'm dealing with someone without a conscience. 'You left me no choice, Dérin, but thankfully, I can always rely on Alika's incompetence. Somehow she managed to find a useless wedding cake designer who could only finish the cake on the day of the wedding. Simple syrup just lying around, ready for me to add the potassium tablets to poison it and squeeze it into the bottom tier – where the bride and groom usually cut the cake together. It's like it was fate . . . Surprisingly, Adélé, you helped me too – once the kitchen staff were engrossed in your camera antics, no one paid attention to what I was doing. I tried to remain out of shot, but these things happen. You can't blame me. I mean, I tried to reason with you, Dérin, give you one more chance, by talking to you in the dressing room. But when I heard Lara's voice call out, I chuckled to myself. I realized that I had stopped caring about you, noticing you, so much so that I'd mistaken *the bride* for her cousin. In that moment, I knew I was going to go through with it, with no remorse at all.'

'What about Kayode? He's your son! You could have poisoned him too! Or did you not care?' Amaka spits.

Aunty Ireti snickers. 'Please. Give me some credit. Kayode is my world. I would never risk his life. How do you think the bathroom door got "jammed"?' She has a sickening sneer plastered on her face and continues, 'Despite your surprising refusal to cancel the wedding, Dérin, you are predictable. I had *seven months* to observe you. I knew you'd finally feel relaxed by the time we reached the cake cutting. All the important events of the day had happened – just about – and the chaos, while jarring and upsetting, could be easily brushed off as unfortunate wedding mishaps, so you'd be happy enough to be playful with Kayode. I should have known you'd do something idiotic like smear the cake on his face. I really do not know what my son sees in you, he can do so much better. *And* as *soon* as he left to clean himself up, that cake was out of eyesight. Alika's proximity comes in handy, *sometimes*.'

'How did you even get Alika to agree to do any of this?' I demand. 'How much did you bribe her?'

'Bribe her?' She gives me an incredulous look. 'Alika was all for it. She just didn't know how far I would take things. When she saw Dérin on the floor of the hall, unconscious, having CPR, her shock was real.' She rolls her eyes. 'I was sitting next to Alika at Àdúrà's wedding when she handed me her business card and then showed me her "wedding planner business page" on Instagram.' She puts 'wedding planner business page' in air quotes. 'But the idiot was still logged into the account she used to troll Àdúrà. When she realized she was still logged in, she panicked, clicking on so many different options to try and log out, but I saw everything: the comments, the DMs, even the weird account name. I admit, I was surprised at what I saw. But me, ah, who am I to judge? I know what it means to do evil for the greater good.

'When Kayode told us that he and Dérin were getting

married, I knew exactly who to find. It wasn't difficult to seal the deal. Alika didn't even want much, just the funds for a nose job so she could conceal her true identity, and the promise she'd get to work on more weddings, for good or evil, who knows, that was none of my business. Of course, I paid her a hefty sum for her services, but that money came with the agreement that if I went down, so did she. When Lara accosted Alika at the wedding, I knew it was a sinking ship but at least all my t's were crossed, and my i's were dotted. I just had to carry out the final act: the wedding cake. I paid Alika to do everything else and she was more than willing.

'You are right, Lara, I am a genius. But you all must remember, Alika is a bitter, jealous girl who's done this before and I just capitalized on that. With the money, power and control I gave her, she was free to do what she wanted, take her torment to higher heights. The Instagram trolling, the stalking, the threats, the notes, the poisoned cupcakes, the shredded rehearsal-dinner dress, the photo of Kayode and Seni, the wedding day disasters – all Alika, by my hand.' She looks at Dérin and Dérin looks back at her with red eyes. 'Frankly, it was easy. As the wedding planner, Alika knew your schedule, your life. You are too trusting, Dérin, that is one of your many problems. You should have questioned why I would recommend Alika, an unknown, in the first place. Sad that she won't go far now.'

Gasps echo around the room.

'This is insane!' Seni shouts out. 'If you knew Dérin had sickle cell, why did you let the relationship go on for this long? Why didn't you stop things like you did with me?'

Aunty Ireti looks at Seni like she's not sure if she should dignify her question with an answer, but then she says, 'The same can be asked of *you*, no? You knew who I was, you knew what I'd done in the past, what I could do now, and you still kept quiet. What kind of friend does that make you? One so driven by envy she destroys her best friend's wedding veil to make herself feel better. Ah, we are cut from the same cloth, Seni. You are as bad as me.'

'Seni is *nothing* like you,' I grit out.

'Whatever. I could've stopped things, but I needed everyone, including Kayode, to know that I wasn't to be messed with on this matter.'

Aunty Ireti walks towards Dérin's bed, her heels clacking with every step she takes, as Dérin lies there, eyes wide, paralysed with shock and fear. 'I've known for longer than six months about her condition. I looked into her records the moment Kayode got serious about her. No hospital admissions, only six-monthly check-ups. I sat back and waited, not thinking the relationship would last. Then they got engaged; my eye twitched, but I left it alone. But that hospital admission confirmed to me there was no way that she was marrying *my* son. What would it do for my image if I let you two marry? How would I explain that to my friends, my *family*?'

She turns her head towards Uncle Tayo and Aunty Zai. They both cower from her death stare. 'You're irresponsible. Truthfully, it's not your fault, Dérin; it's theirs for having

374

you. For putting you through pain for their own selfish intent, and I was not going to let it continue and ruin my family's bloodline. It was better to put Dérin out of her misery for good.'

Aunty Zainab's lip quivers and a tear drips from Uncle Tayo's face.

'You're disgusting,' Amaka spits out.

Aunty Ireti turns on her heel to face Amaka. 'Disgusting, maybe. But at least I'm realistic; I've seen what sickle cell can do and that trip to the hospital proved it . . . Besides,' she turns back to the rest of the group, '*I told you*. I gave you ample opportunity to back out. I promised and performed chaos multiple times. I hope now you'll take signs more seriously.' She turns to glance at Dérin on the bed, then turns back, focusing on Uncle Tayo and Aunty Zai and continues, 'You ought to be careful about who you hire to work for you these days. Money can buy *almost* anything. How do you think I had *access* to Dérin's medication? How do you think the cupcakes that made people sick and, I heard, *bleach a tie*, came back with a clear lab report?' She winks at me. 'I mean, bleaching a tie was great, but when you have such a powerful and subtle weapon like potassium, who wouldn't utilize it?'

I frown at Babs, and he looks at me equally confused. The only people besides myself who knew about testing the cupcakes at the lab were him, Dérin and . . . Temi.

Oh God. Temi. He was involved. Right in front of our faces. And we didn't suspect a thing.

Uncle Fola grabs Aunty Ireti by her arms again, this time tighter. 'What did you do? *What did you do?*' he repeats, his voice shaking. But to no avail. Its seems her mouth is now sealed and nothing is going to get her to open up.

A sharp ringing erupts from Dérin's bed and two nurses rush into the room. 'Her heart rate is dangerously high,' warns the female nurse. 'You all need to leave right now.' Dérin can't speak, tears pouring down her face. Her body is shaking with sobs. Kayode is standing stock still, an empty look on his face. It's not until the male nurse starts physically ushering everyone towards the door that he's forced to move.

Uncle Fola is shouting now, calling his wife's name over and over. 'Ireti! Ireti, I'm talking to you. Ireti! Why now, *why*? You convinced me not to pay because of tradition. Ireti, how could you be this wicked? Ireti? Ireti!'

I watch the agonizing spectacle. I never meant to cause Dérin pain. That was the last thing I ever wanted to do. But I couldn't let her go through life without knowing the truth.

Kayode is stunned into silence as he looks at his parents with eyes full of tears. Then he turns back to Uncle Tayo and Aunty Zainab. He clasps his hands and collapses onto his knees, gasping for breath.

'Please,' he just about manages to say. That breaks even Joseph, who wipes his face with his sleeve. Kayode rubs his hands together, hunched forward, his forehead threatening to touch the hospital floor. 'Please forgive me for her sins.' Aunty Zainab's eyes are glazed over and Uncle Tayo is shaking with rage. I can't look any more.

As I turn away, Uncle Damola catches my eye. He flashes me his phone, showing a video of me confronting Aunty Ireti. 'The evidence is here. Now it's in the hands of the police. But even if Ireti never gets brought to justice. At least the family now know . . . You did good.' He pats my back then pulls me in for a tight hug. 'Remember that when you go into this career. You. Did. Good.'

CHAPTER THIRTY-NINE

Several hours have passed since the afternoon's revelation. Dérin hasn't allowed anyone into her room apart from her parents; and then Kayode, but even he had to wait a lengthy time. We've all been camping out in the hospital waiting room. The police arrived twenty minutes after we were escorted out of Dérin's room, despite Uncle Fola's desperate pleas to delay calling them, to give him just a few more moments to talk some sense into his wife. But Uncle Tayo showed no mercy.

Our last sight of Aunty Ireti is her being taken away in handcuffs by police officers, her face expressionless.

No one knows what to say. Dérin's white wedding was supposed to be yesterday. She should be getting ready to go on her honeymoon, but instead, her life has been torn apart. And for what? Truly for what?

I stare at Seni who is standing in the corner. I feel a pang of guilt, upset at myself for constantly thinking badly of her.

She's not a horrible friend; maybe she's not the best either, but she's human, with valid feelings, and loyal to a fault.

I go over and tell her, 'I'm really sorry, Seni. For judging you, for thinking you were capable of hurting Dérin. For the hard time, the accusations, the evil looks. For reducing your relationship with Kayode to a fling. For everything.'

I can't imagine the pain and resentment she must've felt towards Kayode and Dérin for all these years. When Dérin rubbed salt in the wound too by asking her to be a bridesmaid. All those times she had to pretend to be happy for her friend, but was silently thinking, this relationship, this *lavish* wedding, could've been hers if not for her genetic make-up.

She wipes her eyes gently and stays silent, almost as if she's trying to compose herself. When she does speak, her voice wavers. 'I've known Dérin has had sickle cell since first year at uni, when I told her about my sister. It's something we bonded over because I see my sister live with it, so I know what it's like to have the disease. Dérin swore me to secrecy. She doesn't talk about it because it doesn't affect her deeply. Not until now.

'When she got with Kayode, I was mad. I was *really* mad, but I thought their relationship wouldn't last. Joseph was still hanging around like a bad smell. And if Aunty Ireti had stopped my relationship with Kayode, it would only be a matter of time until she killed theirs too. Then they got engaged, and I had to accept their relationship was actually real, that it was serious. When we got here and all the wedding drama started, I had an inkling that Aunty Ireti could be responsible. She's innately evil, I know that from first-hand experience, so she's capable of anything. But I kept my thoughts to myself.

'I admit I've not been a good friend. I could have told Dérin about what Aunty Ireti did to me, I could have warned her. But instead I kept my mouth shut, I let the chaos continue, not saying anything because I thought maybe Dérin would experience a lick of the embarrassment and pain that I felt, that it was karmic. I *never* thought it would go this far, though. I promise you, Lara. I acknowledge I could've stopped this much earlier, but as soon as I realized that it wasn't too late, I *did*. The call to Kayode the night before the traditional wedding was to ask if he was sure he wanted to potentially put Dérin through what I experienced. She deserved to know what type of family she was marrying into. I wasn't trying to kill her *or* steal Kayode . . . I was trying to save her. But Kayode said his mum had found out about Dérin's sickle cell and hadn't done anything, so she was safe. And the conversation in my room was him finally apologizing for everything that happened to me.' She lets out a long breath.

'I know that now, and I'm sorry again,' I say pulling her into a hug.

After five hours of fidgeting in our hospital chairs, Uncle Tayo comes into the waiting room to send everyone home because Dérin isn't up to seeing anyone today. We all get up to leave when Kayode's voice stops me.

'Dérin wants to see you.' He stares at me, then heads back to her room. Everyone's eyes lock onto me and I look back at them wearily, not knowing what to say. Then I make my way to Dérin's room. Kayode has stopped just outside the door, looking vacant.

When I enter the room, Dérin is sitting up slightly, head turned towards the window. The oxygen tubes are still in her nose. She turns her head in my direction and watches me silently, like she's replaying everything that's happened today over and over again in her mind. I squirm, wishing she would break the tension.

'Why didn't you tell me you had sickle cell?' I say, then immediately regret it. My first words should've been *I'm sorry*. And as I say them now, I start to cry. Dérin continues to stare at me for a few moments and then extends her arms out for a hug. I run straight into them, careful not to injure her further.

'I've been conditioned to not talk about it all my life because it never affected me – and then when it did, life felt like before and after,' she explains. 'I've been so scared of being viewed as fragile, and having the stigma, that I've avoided talking about it altogether.' She sighs. 'But after my hospital admission, I couldn't keep pretending that sickle cell is not that bad just because I was one of the lucky few who hasn't suffered terribly from it. Especially when deep down I worry about it constantly. I'm worried about employers finding out and not hiring me because they think I'll be out of work too often. I worry about people in church finding out because then they'll try to pray the sickle cell away, as if that's how it works.' She does a pathetic laugh and turns to look out of the window again.

I know she's trying not to cry, and I want to speak, but I need to give her the space to let out everything she's been holding in.

She turns back to me, red-eyed. 'I worried about what I would do if I found the love of my life and we didn't have the right genotypes. About what my in-laws would say when they found out . . . I never thought it'd be this bad.' She sighs. 'It's the reason why I broke things off with Joseph. When I asked him to get his blood tested, he said the outcome would mean nothing to him so he didn't want to. I didn't ask Joseph to get tested to see if we were compatible; I only asked so that we could be prepared for our futures, whatever the outcome. But he refused, *and then* decided to tell me that he's AA on the day of the traditional wedding. That's what we were talking about in the dressing room before the wedding started. But it was too late. And it didn't matter. Because I love Kayode and I chose him. I choose him. I've seen what this disease can do and I know just because I have it easy, that doesn't mean my kids will. But I just . . . I fell in love with Kayode and I should be allowed to.' She breaks down into tears.

'Hey, I am sorry. I am so, *so* sorry. I couldn't let you go through life with someone that awful creeping around behind you, plotting against you and trying to kill you. You deserve to be here. You deserve to fall in love as many times as you want. A thousand loves. You are special and I am so glad you're here. I am so glad your parents had you and I can call you my cousin, more than a cousin. My sister.' I sniff, wiping her tears as they fall.

'I don't think *anyone* could've predicted this outcome. That someone could be so hateful they'd prefer to get rid of me rather than just sit me down and talk to me. There's nothing to apologize for, Lara. I've never been more thankful for you and your genius mind,' she says, grabbing my head with both hands and shaking it slightly. 'I'm glad this happened now rather than in two years and Aunty Ireti, God forbid, plotted to kill my children. It's vile, what she did, and it was vile the way she blamed Mummy and Daddy when all they did was exactly what I did. Fell in love. Sickle cell isn't a death sentence. I can live a full and happy life. I should be able to thrive in every space. I deserve that. I know that now.'

I hold her in my arms as she continues to cry on my shoulder. She cries and cries for the next fifteen minutes until she sniffs and wipes her tears away. She tries to smile at me but fails, lip quivering. 'Thank you again, Lara. Seriously. I know I've been sort of a bridezilla. I'm sorry for being mean.'

'*Sort of?*' I tease and she laughs lightly. 'What are you going to do about Kayode?' I sniffle. 'He looks . . . rough.'

Dérin nods. 'We're going to take some time to talk things through. I know it must have been a shock to him, hearing his mum admit how evil she is. So I don't know where that leaves us. I also need to sit Seni and Joseph down, have an honest conversation with them about everything; I owe them that much. And I'm injured, so Kayode and I can't exactly have the big white wedding we wanted . . . We'll work something out. Or if that means we have to part ways, then so be it.'

'Kayode loves you, Dérin. That's one thing that's been clear from the start, despite his mum's shortcomings. And it's clear she's the only one who thinks the way she does.'

'I love him too.' She sighs. 'But I can't continue to live life as naïvely as I did,' she says, stroking my hair as I lie on her chest.

CHAPTER FORTY

Everyone leaves so Dérin can rest, except Aunty Zainab who stays to watch over her. The car is eerily silent during the entire ride home. None of us knows what to do or say. It's late when we reach the house and all anyone wants to do is sleep.

Aunty Tiwa has offered to pack an overnight bag for Aunty Zainab, and Joseph is waiting in his car to drop her back to the hospital. I figure now is the best time to swallow my pride and speak to him. I knock on his window. He winds it down, looking at me suspiciously. 'Let me guess, the police are waiting for me outside the gate.'

I sigh softly. 'I'm sorry for suspecting you. Truly.' I tilt my head from side to side. 'But you have to admit, you didn't help yourself.' I wince playfully. He kisses his teeth and rolls his eyes; I laugh in response. 'No, seriously I am. I got a bit carried away, in the name of protecting Dérin. I should've considered your history with her and known you were sincere.'

'If she doesn't have me, I'm glad she has you,' he says, rubbing my hair with the tips of his fingers. I smack his hands away. 'Put a good word in for me with Seni, yeah, and maybe I'll invite you to our wedding.' He winks, then rolls his window back up.

I'm about to head upstairs when Uncle Tayo pulls me to the side.

'How do I thank you?' he says, drawing me in for a tight hug. 'I can't.'

I rub his back in response.

'I would do it for any of you. I'm sorry if I looked crazy, though.' I smile shyly. Uncle Tayo just folds me back into his arms. 'There's one more thing that Aunty Ireti said that connected a few dots for me . . .'

Uncle Tayo lets go and looks at me with anticipation.

'At the hospital, she said, *Be careful about who you hire to work for you these days. Money can buy* almost *anything* . . . I believe she was talking about Temi; I think he was working for her. After the bachelorette party and everything that happened with the questionable cupcakes, Babs and I took one to a lab to get it tested for any toxic substances. The results came back clear.

'Temi was the only other person, apart from Dérin, who knew that Babs and I had gone to the lab – he took us there. I think he told Aunty Ireti and she instructed him to pay the lab to give us false results. And when I think about it, there have been a few strange encounters between him and Aunty Ireti that I didn't notice at the time, but now it's clear:

the tension, the glares between them. Apart from you and Aunty Zai, the only person who could get hold of Dérin's medication was Temi; he must have given the potassium tablets to Aunty Ireti. I also think Temi was helping Aunty Ireti and Alika with the notes. He's the only other person who had close access to Dérin, so he could easily make sure they actually reached her, especially in the house. In the notes some of the letters were underlined to spell out the message *I'm sorry I have to do this*. I don't know, he always looked heavy, troubled, like he was burdened with something he didn't want to do. I think he was trying to apologize for his part in everything.'

Uncle Tayo deflates. 'Okay, thank you for telling me. I'll look into it.' He squeezes me one more time and heads up the stairs.

'Lara.' Dad's head pokes out of the living-room door, and he motions for me to come. 'I heard you snapped at your mum at the wedding because she told Aunty Kemi you want to do Law. It's my fault. I didn't tell anyone about our argument or your new plans for uni. Don't be angry at her, you know she's dramatic and I'd have to prepare for a theatre performance if I told her. But today, what you did.' Dad pauses, looking at me like he's seeing me for the first time. 'I've never been more scared for or prouder of you. What you did for Dérin, how you took the investigation into your own hands and discovered the truth, how brave and courageous you were to confront the culprit . . . You're undeniably talented and we can see that this is your passion.

I . . . We . . .' Dad waits and looks back at the living-room door, where Mum appears. 'We've discussed everything and are happy for you to change courses. If that's what you still want to do.'

My jaw drops.

'But, Lara, before you do,' Mum starts, 'are you a hundred per cent sure? Pretty much all your life we've been prepping you to be a lawyer; essay practices, buying you all those books. Talking to aunties and uncles about the career. We're scared that this change could be too much for you, that you will fall behind and end up without a grad job. That you'll be making small change when your agemates are making lots of money. That you'll finish this degree, and you'll find yourself too deep into it and not be able to change direction.'

'That's the thing,' I reply. '*You* guys have been prepping me but not giving me any opportunity to have a say. I enjoy piecing puzzles together and helping to solve a case, not helping to put someone away and *especially* not listening to people dispute things in family law. If I'd been allowed to voice my opinion before, none of this would be happening.' I realize I'm telling my parents off and it feels ridiculously good. 'I blame myself too; it's not just you guys. I spent so much of the past two years reading about being a lawyer, and how much money I could make. Feeding myself the fantasy that I'll be happy if I just take that plunge. But I won't be happy. I know that for a fact.' I suck my lip in.

'How can we support you?' Dad says, and my eyebrows shoot up in shock. 'Why do you look so surprised? I came around to the idea two days after you cried your way out of our bedroom, but you were too busy avoiding me to notice or even let me say anything.'

My eyes dart to Mum, watchful of her expression. She does that upside-down smile that parents do when they're neither amused nor disappointed. 'You've never given us any reason to doubt you. But I was looking forward to going on a cruise with your first paycheque.' She wipes away a fake tear. A smile creeps over my face and I yank them into a hug.

'I love you guys.'

When I let go, Dad asks, 'So what is the big course change?'

I look at them, hopeful for the future. 'Criminology and Forensic Investigations.'

AUGUST 9, 2025 **NAIJA GOSSIP LOUNGE** ISSUE 463

ALLEGEDLY, ALLEGEDLY, ALLEGEDLY

Even me, I'm shocked as I'm typing this.

We're back again with the latest on the alleged poisoning of Dérinsọlá Oyinlola.

Monster-in-law Ireti Akinlola, arrested on suspicion of attempted murder, has been released on bail, awaiting a trial date. Sources have told us she was kicked out of the marital home by her husband, Folarin Akinlola, and divorce papers have been served. Ireti is rumoured to be staying at one of the hotels she and her now soon-to-be-ex-husband own. Her passport has been seized by Judge Kolade, a dear friend of Dérin's family – because we know that's the only way justice can be served.

With Lagos courts typically under-resourced, we wonder when a trial date will be set. But maybe money can buy anything.

In a shock twist, we have the bride's cousin, Lara Oyinlola, to thank for solving the mystery that has been on all of our lips for the past two weeks. Lara exposed the truth after compiling evidence, which has helped the police tighten up their case.

A reliable source at the hospital where Dérin is being treated and where the revelations were made, shared with us all the sordid details. Strap in, because this is a *wild* ride.

According to reports, Ireti did not work alone. She had a helper: Alika Amenze, real name Ijose Omoregbe. Alika was initially arrested after Dérin collapsed at her traditional wedding, where the family accused her of shamelessly attacking the bride.

If Alika's name sounds familiar, that's because it is. She was Dérin's wedding planner. Maybe the devil doesn't wear Prada, she wears a headset.

Sources say that Alika tormented Dérin on social media for seven months before the wedding, leaving nasty comments on Dérin's Instagram account and sending hateful DMs. More shocking, we have learned that this isn't Alika's first time trolling a bride online. Some of you may remember how Àdúràtọlá, last year's bride of the season, experienced unwarranted backlash about her wedding. We have now been told that Alika was behind that too. Alika used social media to vent her jealous frustrations about not being born into a life of luxury, and wanted to prove all that glitters isn't gold; certainly not if she's got anything to do with it.

Some people write blogs . . . others collude in attempted murder. Different strokes.

It is believed that once Ireti discovered Alika's past, she recommended her as a wedding planner – the ever-so-loving mother-in-law – and paid Alika a reported quarterly sum of one million naira to help ruin Dérin's wedding, including sending Dérin threatening notes and causing chaos and disaster in the run-up to and on the day of her traditional wedding, as well as the social media harassment. Payment would increase to a billion naira if she carried out their heinous crime without getting caught.

When Alika's methods didn't have their desired effect – the cancellation of the wedding – Ireti took matters into her own hands: poisoning Dérin with her own potassium medication. The question that everyone at Naija Gossip Lounge HQ is asking: why would Dérin be taking potassium tablets?

And we now have an answer with Dérin's latest Instagram post: a picture of herself in a hospital bed, connected to oxygen, million-dollar smile shining bright and explaining that she has sickle cell. In the lengthy caption, she talked about how she is ready to embrace all parts of herself, even the parts people think should be hidden, and promised that she will be honest about her experiences of living with the illness. Her hope is to use her platform to educate people, destigmatize the disease and show that you can have a healthy and happy life with sickle cell . . . While also continuing to showcase her luxury lifestyle. Multitasking at its finest!

But back to the heinous crime. Our source confirmed that Ireti poisoned Dérin because she didn't want her

family 'tainted' with sickle cell.

If we thought Alika was wicked, Ireti is beyond redemption.

Aunty . . . now that you're out on bail, if you like, you can transfer the one billion naira to me.

Alika, still in custody – because, unfortunately, it pays to have money – plans to strike a deal with the Attorney General, stating that she will hand over all information about her work with Ireti and will testify at her trial for a lighter sentence.

Now, you will remember that we reported on the many tumultuous incidents surrounding Dérin and Kayode's wedding, and we want to make it clear that we did not work with either Alika or Ireti to obtain any of this information. Of course, we cannot possibly say who our trusted source is – anonymity is a must in our line of work, and we know our readers love us for it. But we like to get our hands dirty with rumours, hearsay and scandals, not *murder.*

You know gossip doesn't sleep, and neither do I.

XOXO

EPILOGUE

Four weeks after the traditional wedding

Of all the places I thought I'd be ending my holiday in Nigeria, I did not think it'd be on Lekki Beach at sunset, surrounded by my friends and family at Dérin and Kayode's makeshift white wedding. After a long sermon from the pastor about the trials and tribulations the couple have been through, not including the attempted murder – he apparently thought it best to leave out that disturbing detail – he finally says the words we've all been waiting to hear since we arrived in the country.

'You may now kiss the bride!'

After the police took Aunty Ireti into custody and watched the confession video, it became irrefutably clear that she was responsible for Dérin's poisoning, no matter how much she tried to deny everything. At one point, she attempted to pin the whole thing on Alika. But Alika had more than enough evidence of their correspondence on her phone, even messages from the night of Dérin's poisoning, to make Aunty Ireti's guilt indisputable. Alika admitted her part in everything: she was paid by Aunty Ireti to torment Dérin online and in real life and make the wedding as messy as possible. Apparently, when questioned, she didn't hide her disdain for those she felt were undeserving of their privileges – and also money, once Aunty Ireti's funds disappeared from her bank account. But she had never intended for things to escalate to attempted murder.

I was unfortunately right about Temi too. As soon as he was questioned he confessed that Aunty Ireti paid him for his involvement; he'd been using the extra money to help fund his siblings' school fees. Riddled with guilt, he planted the secret apology message without Alika and Aunty Ireti's knowledge. Uncle Tayo was conflicted, taking pity on him, but also feeling betrayed. He settled on giving Temi a small lump sum for his work, but also fired him because he could no longer trust him in his house or around his family.

Uncle Damola and I had to sit Kayode down to explain everything we'd discovered. It was a rough few days for him and Dérin; lots of tears were spilled. Kayode really struggled to grasp how his mum could be so callous, not just to Dérin, but to him too. And Dérin was afraid to see Kayode because of how much she still loved him, despite his family. It took the girls and I parent trapping both of them to even get them in a room together, after the extent of Aunty Ireti's plan was revealed.

Joseph bounced back from losing Dérin and has now focused his affections on Seni. It seems playful for now, but something tells me it could get hot and heavy soon . . . Meanwhile, Uncle Fola washed his hands of his wife before we'd even left the hospital. Kayode told Uncle Fola that he would understand if he paid her legal fees, but Uncle Fola made it clear that he wanted no part in that. Uncle Fola said he'd seen Aunty Ireti as a completely different person from the moment she had failed to deny my accusations or protest her innocence. Her nauseating smile was enough to confirm who she truly was, and he threw all her stuff out of the house that night.

Despite being the family idiot who everyone wanted to suffer the consequences of his own actions, Uncle Yinka was saved by the birth of his *adorable* twins one week after Dérin was released from hospital. So, instead of reporting him to the police for arranging the car theft, indirectly causing the accident on the bridge, endangering people's lives and essentially causing more harm to Dérin, everyone agreed to keep quiet. However, he's being punished in other ways; Aunty Yemisi now has sole access to his bank account, and all his transactions have to go through her. If she ever needs funds, everyone will be there for her, but not him. Uncle Yinka has agreed to move back to Nigeria on his own dime, which worked out because Dérin is leaving for the UK and Aunty Zai isn't ready for an empty nest, so he and Aunty Yemisi are going to move into the house and Aunty Zai can help out with the twins. He'll also be working for Uncle Fola until he pays back every penny he owes for the Rolls-Royce. We figured out it'll take twenty years. Practically a prison sentence in itself . . .

I break away from my thoughts just as Kayode plants a massive kiss on Dérin's lips, dipping her as he does. As he swings her back upright, she winces and multiple family members spring out of their seats, before she reassures them that she's fine. We all sigh with relief. Music plays from a speaker we've brought with us as they dance down the fake aisle. The only person absent from the original party is Aunty Ireti. Uncle Fola claps the loudest. The newborn twins, Tókę and Tádé, gurgle as Aunty Yemisi and Uncle Yinka hold them up to watch their cousin get married.

Dérin ushers us all onto the dancefloor (aka the beach) as the song changes to 'Romantic' by Korede Bello and Tiwa Savage. Everyone surrounds the pair, dancing with them and showering them with love.

It's not how we imagined Dérin and Kayode's white wedding would be, but from the happiness in their eyes you wouldn't be able to tell.

'I still can't believe you got three A*s!' Babs says, throwing his arm around my shoulder in a typical big-brother embrace that almost knocks me off my feet. 'I spent the whole day telling everyone I know. I'm so proud of you, Lara. For real. How do you feel?'

I smile up at him. 'I mean, I would've said great, if you hadn't decided to tell Mum and Dad that you don't want to do surgery at the same moment I revealed my A-level results.' I elbow him in the ribs.

'I needed to capitalize on their joy . . . and it worked. My announcement was minor. All Mum's Facebook posts are about you.' I give him a death stare, but I'm internally beaming.

'Thank you, again, for helping me with changing unis,' I say, but he waves me off. After he blurted out his news, he cheekily left Mum and Dad to digest the information and whisked me away to help me with the clearing process for changing my degree. I never doubted that I would do well on results day, but actually seeing the fruits of my labour left me euphoric. I mean *three A*s* is insane. Though even better was the *hefty* sum of money Uncle Tayo put in my account after hearing the news. Everyone's been calling me Miss Marple or Einstein since the results came out. I'm hoping the nicknames don't stick.

'So now that this is gonna be your life for the next three years and beyond, what are you going to solve next, you crime-obsessed weirdo?' Babs asks.

'I don't know yet. It feels like the world just became my oyster.' I smile at him then at the scene in front of me.

'Just don't start a podcast,' he says and a laugh erupts out of me.

'No promises,' I reply with a grin.

AUTHOR'S NOTE

I never set out to write a mystery. I could never have dreamed how much work it would take to intricately weave a story. To keep readers not only intrigued, but also actively guessing, without revealing any spoilers or totally giving away the truth. But, *'Til Death* took a hold of me. It screamed until I wrote it, and it was the fastest thing I had ever drafted. It combines so many things I love: the dramatics and catty arguments that come with weddings (as someone who loves gist) and the beautiful intricacies of a Nigerian traditional wedding. And I loved that every time I told someone about its basic premise they would say, 'That's so Nollywood!'

But if I was going to write *'Til Death*, I had to know the ending first. I had to know who did it.

Like Dérin, I have sickle cell. I'm extremely lucky that my sickle cell, for the most part, does not affect me day-to-day; and, because of this, I've often lived like it wasn't a part of me. It wasn't something I needed to think about, until my six-monthly doctor's appointments arrived, and we'd go through the checkboxes to ensure that I was fine, and I'd see my doctor again in another six months for our usual routine. I admittedly was quite naïve about my disease, which is a privilege many sicklers are not afforded. As I got older, I realized it *was* something I had to think about, and, in all areas of life. Especially in dating. I selfishly thought, *if I've already fallen in love with someone, do we have to test his genotype?* And, very naïvely, *my sickle cell isn't that bad, so maybe my child's won't be.*

I'm an overthinker. When exploring the subject of sickle cell in

'Til Death, I imagined the worst-case scenario, and the book was born. What if I found someone, and they were the perfect compatible genotype, but secretly his family weren't happy with his decision because of this disease I have through no fault of my own? What if, no matter how much I deserve to love and be loved, I was still judged and treated differently, negatively, because of this inherited illness? What if, because of my sickle cell, I was seen as damaged goods, unworthy of life in general? I knew that I wanted to tell mine and Dérin's stories through 'Til Death to provide a small insight into the stigma that sicklers may face.

People often make comments like, 'We need to eradicate sickle cell' and 'It is so irresponsible to bring a child with sickle cell into the world.' While some may say this is true, I am incredibly conflicted about it and never know how to react. After all, I am happy to be here and living. I explored this through Dérin, but I also know that a lot of sicklers have much more difficult stories.

In 'Til Death, I want to show that sickle cell isn't a death sentence. That people with sickle cell aren't damaged goods or less than. That they aren't undeserving of love. That, instead, they deserve unlimited love. That they deserve to live full and happy lives. That they deserve to thrive in every space. That they deserve to be here.

This book is for those who suffer with sickle cell, at any point on the spectrum of the disease. This is for the lives lost and the lives still fighting. I hope 'Til Death can help encourage ongoing conversations about the disease and hopefully bring about further insight. I hope you have loved the book enough to tell a friend about it, and I hope it spreads awareness as best as it can. If no one has told you today, I am so glad you're here.

RESOURCES

Sickle cell is a serious, lifelong and potentially fatal disease that not only impacts people physically, but mentally and emotionally too. It is caused by a gene that affects how red blood cells develop. If both parents have the gene, each of their children has a one in four chance of being born with sickle cell disease. However, it is easily preventable through ensuring people test their genotypes before they plan to start a family. The main symptoms of sickle cell disease are: painful episodes called sickle cell crises, which can be very severe and last for days or weeks; an increased risk of serious infections; and anaemia (where red blood cells cannot carry enough oxygen around the body), which can cause tiredness and shortness of breath. There is no cure for the disease, although treatment can help manage many of the symptoms. Despite affecting a significant amount of the population, particularly people with an African or Caribbean family background – approximately eight per cent of Black people have the sickle cell gene – the disease is still under-researched and under-funded. This needs to change.

If you would like to learn more about the disease here are some useful organizations.

Sickle Cell 101 – a platform dedicated to educating and supporting individuals affected by sickle cell disease, with community-driven insights and patient stories.
Email: hello@sc101.org
Website: www.sc101.org/

Sickle Cell Society – the only national charity in the UK that supports and represents people affected by a sickle cell disorder to improve their overall quality of life. They offer resources, advocacy and support groups, as well as educational materials on managing the disease.
Call: 0208 961 7795; 0208 961 8346
Email: info@sicklecellsociety.org
Website: www.sicklecellsociety.org/

Cianna's Smile – a charity that offers support and education to families impacted by sickle cell in the UK. Their goals are to decrease isolation for those living with the disease, support families, and raise awareness of sickle cell and blood donation.
Call: 0753 891 9357
Email: info@ciannassmile.co.uk
Website: www.ciannassmile.co.uk/

Let's Talk Sickle Cell – this website provides information on living with sickle cell disease, including managing symptoms, mental health support and connecting with local support groups.
Call: 0203 204 5100

NICE Clinical Knowledge Summaries – NICE provides guidelines and evidence-based information for healthcare professionals, which can also be useful for patients seeking detailed clinical knowledge.
Call: 0300 323 0140
Website: cks.nice.org.uk/topics/sickle-cell-disease/

Genotype testing for sickle cell disease in the UK is a crucial part of diagnosing and managing the condition, prevention being the only way to control the disease. Here are some facilities that offer genotype testing in London. Contact them in advance to book an appointment.

City & Hackney Sickle Cell and Thalassaemia Centre

457 Queensbridge Road
Dalston
London
E8 3AS
Call: 020 7683 4570

Croydon Sickle Cell and Thalassaemia Centre

316-320 Whitehorse Road
Croydon
CR0 2LE
Call: 020 8274 6040; 020 3859 5441
Email: cscatsg@outlook.com
Website: www.cscatsg.org/

East Ham Sickle Cell and Thalassaemia Centre

19-21 High St S
East Ham
London
E6 6EN
Call: 020 8821 0800
Email: elt-tr.sickleandthal@nhs.net
Website: www.elft.nhs.uk/scyps/our-services/
sickle-cell-and-thalassaemia

South East London Sickle Cell and Thalassaemia Centre
Mary Sheridan Centre
Wooden Spoon House
5 Dugard Way
London
SE11 4TH
Call: 020 3049 5993
Email: gst-tr.referralstosickle@nhs.net

Brent Sickle Cell and Thalassaemia Centre
Central Middlesex Hospital
Acton Lane
London
NW10 7NS
Call: 020 8453 2050; 020 8453 2052; 020 8453 2292
Website: www.lnwh.nhs.uk/brent-sickle-cell-an
d-thalassaemia-centre/

For other clinics across the UK, you can search 'sickle cell and
thalassemia centre/testing/screening in my area' on the internet.
Alternatively, you can arrange genotype testing through your GP.

ACKNOWLEDGEMENTS

I am a person who wholly believes in fate and divine timing (after I've had a little moan about how long it's taking). A lot of *'Til Death*'s journey can be accredited to divine timing. Hindsight is a truly wonderful thing.

Firstly, I would like to thank my father, who is unfortunately no longer with us. The story starts with him, nurturing a talent I don't think he imagined would lead me here. When I was younger, my dad used to take us to the library during our summer holidays. At the time, it felt like punishment, but later it became a fun thing I would look forward to every summer. We'd spend hours in the library. A music lover, he'd spend time flicking through CDs to play while he ironed and we would pick books to read. I never knew you could read competitively until my dad signed us up for summer reading competitions. We read so much I actually won a competition in my borough (I am still so sorry I picked golf lessons instead of something much cooler as a prize).

Before my dad passed, I started writing and was nurtured by my tutor, Jacqueline, who believed in my creative writing skills before I even did. She told me I had a gift and made me feel like I could write anything. At the time I didn't believe her, but I have her to also thank now that I'm here.

At first I hid my writing from everyone, apart from a few friends (because it was one of those really cheesy but very popular bad-boy romances on Wattpad). But when my dad passed, I lost my love for it. I lost my love for a lot of things. One of my regrets as *'Til Death* was coming to fruition was that I hadn't told him about my writing, as embarrassing as I thought it was . . . Funnily enough, my cousin revealed to me that my dad had known all along, and *he'd sent my stories to her.* When she told me that, I was shocked and mortified because, oh my God, *what did they read*! But I kept those feelings to myself. I don't think she knew how much her actions meant to me by revealing that (thank you, Ayo). I sat with this information, and then, of course, I cried.

My dad knew. *He knew.* He knew, all along.

I like to think that my dad is always around me, guiding me as my good luck charm. It keeps me sane. And the number of extraordinary things that have happened to me proves this theory. This book being one of them. My dad sacrificed so *so* much for me and my family. My deepest sadness comes from him not being able to experience the fruits of his labour. However, I believe that he's smiling down on us and making the most life-changing things happen. I hope I've made you proud and continue to do so. Sun re o, Baba mi.

To my wonderful family, my mother and my brothers. When I asked my brother, Tobi, if he wanted to be in the acknowledgements, he said, 'Well I didn't really do anything.' I'm sure my brother, Patrick, would share the same sentiment, that he too didn't do anything. Thank you for your pats on the back and the *well done*'s. You're both so lame and I love you dearly.

To my mother, my best friend and favourite person to fight with (I'm sure you'd say otherwise), I love you so much it hurts. It was hard for my mum to believe that *'Til Death* was a thing, until it really was a 'thing'. Writing is such a solitary activity, I'm sure she thought I was lying so that she would leave me alone half the time. Despite that, her love for and faith in me have never wavered. Just like Dad, she has sacrificed so much for me and my brothers. Life hasn't always been fair to her, but she would still give us the clothes off her back. I'm so glad that she can now reap the benefits of all of her hard work, and I hope I can make her prouder than she already is, if that's possible. Again, I love you.

Bringing it back to divine timing and fate: Zainab and Kemi.

I met Zainab in Year Eight and we bonded like all Nigerian women do, through gossip. We have been inseparable ever since. Zainab has been my biggest cheerleader, my supporter and my everything. She and our friend Hannah (who we jokingly like to call 'our youngest child' – because she's the baby in our friendship group) show me daily what sisterhood looks like. Zainab has been with me since my Wattpad days, when I forged a couple of signatures to win an award (I wouldn't recommend this . . . but we won!) and she told our teachers that I had written a book akin to Shakespeare. She has had my back from day one, even more than I deserve. She has read almost every draft of all of my works, with never a moan or a grumble. Instead it's always 'And why isn't it in my inbox????' Zainab, your unwavering support for me, *'Til Death* and every book I have yet to write means the world to me. I love you; I hope I keep you forever.

Kemi's entrance into my life was also down to fate. One day, she strolled into our university common room, saw me doing my friend's make-up and just about held back her 'that is so ugly' comment. We became fast friends, and even faster sisters. One random evening in my room, we ended up talking about that dreaded Wattpad book (maybe I have Wattpad to thank also). I eventually told her about an idea for a new story that wasn't a bad-boy romance, and she told me, 'Write it, I would read it.'

Of course, I didn't listen to her (and I can hear her saying 'she never does'), but then COVID happened, the world stopped, and my nursing course was put on pause. I had all this free time and didn't know what to do with it. Kemi's voice niggled in my head and so I listened (finally!). I wrote the book that led to me meeting my phenomenal agent. Without Kemi, there would be no *'Til Death.* I am forever indebted to you. I love you, and I also hope I keep you forever. (But I wouldn't be me if I didn't air you out and say you never read any early drafts of *'Til Death,* but it's okay, I forgive you.)

To my best friends, Hannah and Etta. They read early drafts of my books, loved them and even threatened people (semi-lovingly) to buy *'Til Death.* It takes a village and I'm so glad to have you in mine. I love you, I love you, I love you.

Gyamfia Osei, my phenomenal agent extraordinaire. I just want to put you in my pocket forever. Mine and Gyamfia's worlds collided after an author randomly saw my post about *the book* on my BookTok. One introductory email later, I was wreaking havoc in Gyamfia's life and have been ever since (for better or worse, either way it's so much fun). Gyamfia's genius mind is the reason *'Til Death* came into existence so soon. She championed it before it was even anything, and had people excited at just its basic premise; from our first call, she saw what it was and knew it was *the one*. I am constantly moved by her steadfast faith in me. Gyamfia has changed my life in so many ways. Every grumble about a different submission plan, every hefty edit, has been completely worth it. I couldn't imagine going through this world of publishing with anyone else and I wouldn't want to. A psychic once told me that Gyamfia and I would make magic together, and I think magic is an understatement. *'Til Death* is just the beginning, and I can't wait for so many more years to come. I love you.

My fabulous editor, Carla Hutchinson, who is the brightest ball of sunshine. Fate dropped Carla into my lap, and I have been grateful ever since. Knowing the special connection Carla has to my book means our partnership could not have been random. Carla understands *'Til Death* completely. She knows what Lara and Dérin would and wouldn't do; she recognizes and appreciates the important messages behind the book; she thinks about the manuscript and how to better it when she should be going home and resting. And best of all, she loves to hate Joseph as much as I do. Although editing isn't my favourite thing, Carla has never made it feel like a chore. She is always there to cheer me on, especially in her in-line comments, and as a words of affirmation girlie, I can't tell you how much that means to me. As much as she calls me a superstar, I hope she knows she is one too.

To the S&S team, in particular Lucy Pearse, Rachel Denwood and Leanne Nulty. Your excitement for *'Til Death* shocks me in the best way; your kind and supportive words fill me with so much joy. Thank you for making me feel so welcome at S&S.